HELLFIRE RISING

BEING THE FIRST PART OF

THE MIDDLETON SAGA

BY
RICHARD BROOK

Cover Photo by Grant Hyatt
Website: http://granthyatt.photography
Instagram: @grant_hyatt

Proof Reading by Peter Illidge
Twitter: @peter_illidge

Design Layout by Blueprint Creative Ltd
Website: www.blueprint-creative.co.uk

ISBN: 978-1-9997381-1-2

Revised Edition 2019

To Nick, apart from myself, you have been my greatest critic. I can't thank you enough for all your advice and support.

And To Elanor Bronwyn, you swept into my life like a whirlwind. Constantly forcing me to wait or change tack and as usual always kept me wondering. A bad day was soon dispatched by your cheeky smile and infectious laugh. I was always in awe of how selfless you were, making time for anybody that needed it. You not only left an indelible impression but also rekindled an ethos and creativity that I had somehow misplaced, to which my gratitude has no bounds. I hope that wherever you are now; you have finally found a sense of peace.

Contents

ACKNOWLEDGMENTS

Special thanks to all my family and friends, for your continual support, and for putting up with my eccentricities.

To all The Libertine and Pour House baristas for providing me with inspiration, feedback and above all some of the best coffee around. Ryan I think when you finished reading the final draft is the only time that I have actually been delighted that someone wanted to punch me.

And finally to Synergy Live Band; Glen and both Juans, you guys have been fantastic. It has always been my absolute honour and pleasure making the occasional guest appearance to play alongside you.

Prologue

Some great legends are eventually lost, like streams flowing into the rivers of time; rushing torrents, crashing over rocks like a series of thunderclaps. They eventually start to widen, slow and cease to exist as they enter the seas and are swept away by the tides of history, to finally settle into the wealth of knowledge hidden amongst the cool watery depths of the oceans. They will remain lost to all; until like the great treasures of the Caribbean are rediscovered by those, who instilled by courage, brave the treacherous deep dark fathoms to release that which they seek from their freezing tombs. Rising up quickly like the bubbles of air carrying them, they break the surface just like water from a newly struck well, and glisten in the bright sunlight. It is a dazzling sight to behold like the armour of a great host glinting in the noonday sun.

And so this great tale like so many before it arose from simple beginnings, and may well have been lost forever amongst the depths had it not been for a few who stumbled upon its secrets whilst on a voyage of discovery. They vowed to protect them at all costs from those who would seek to abuse this knowledge for their own gain.

Power tends to corrupt and absolute power corrupts absolutely.
Lord Acton

The winds of change are once again rising. Dark clouds forming on the horizon threaten to cast a dark shadow over everything. They herald the beginning of the conflict to come. The race is on to draw up plans for the coming battles, yet this is only the start. It is certain that it will continue for many years and that the outcome is far from decided. What is clear is that this conflict will shake many institutions to their very core, like the impact of a massive earthquake many will fall, crashing down to earth in clouds of dust. Only the strongest foundations will remain; a testament to how carefully they were constructed and the purity of the principals that they hold dearest.

Many lives will be written out of existence; wiped out in the blink of an eye, just as the light of a dying star, imploding on itself, vanishes leaving nothing but darkness. Great pain will be suffered, as loved ones are lost. The only hope is that out of the ashes a phoenix will arise with a bright new future. Only time will tell who will prevail on that final bloody field. A field now littered with stricken corpses of many heroic souls, heroic souls that now stare blankly into space; their last expressions etched on their faces, echoing on for eternity. Acting as a reminder that to protect what we hold closest to our hearts there is always a cost. The only question is whether there is anybody that is prepared to pay it?

HELLFIRE RISING

BEING THE FIRST PART OF

THE MIDDLETON SAGA

Chapter One: New Beginnings

The sun rose slowly, breaking over the mountaintops, igniting the clouds carried on the cool autumn winds with the colours of amber and gold. The lake in the valley below perfectly mirrored the tranquil scene above; soon to be shattered by the coming storm. As the clouds overhead began to amass and boil up over the peaks, the bright morning darkened and the first raindrops began to fall. Gradually at first, but as the storm picked up pace, water was quickly falling as if all the cofferdams of the heavens had been breached.

A number of distant rumblings signalled the arrival of the collisions of charged particles high up in the atmosphere which would become much more evident when the blackening skies became set ablaze by piercing forks of purple and white fiery streaks of lightning. The wrath of Zeus scorched the skyline and destroyed all it touched on the ground below.

James Middleton had awoken with a start moments before the skies had darkened. It was as if he had sensed the changes taking place in the ether around him. He had been dozing near to the eastern shore of the lake by a secluded copse of trees, close to where a stream flowed down the mountainside into the lake. It had been a peaceful spot listening to the babbling chatter of the running water as it traced the banks down into the lake.

James was a reasonably tall man in his early thirties; he had a distant look about him, hinting that he had once been a strong confident leader but had suffered some great loss, a loss that still seemed to haunt him.

Ten years had passed since he had visited the Brecon Beacons. He had hoped that by returning to this tranquil place he might be able to piece together the events of the previous few days that had turned his mind inside out and left him feeling hazy as if he had just awoken from a strange dream. Awoken, only to discover that he was not sure of his surroundings. Unfortunately the storm had extinguished any flicker of that hope.

Just as the first drops of rain fell he started to make a move towards the shelter of his car, parked about five minutes away on the southeast corner of the lake. Reaching into his pocket he pulled out a rather dented packet of cigarettes and a zippo, as he approached the car. He felt that he should really quit but for one reason or another it had never quite seemed like the right time and anyway he enjoyed it.

He had recently returned from Helmand Province, Afghanistan. Where he had distinguished himself in a number of encounters with insurgents but he did not really care about that kind of stuff; as far as he was concerned he was just doing his duty.

James had been involved in some of the greyer areas of operations surrounding the *War on Terror*, officially he had been a section leader of a rag-tag unit that popped up randomly from time to time alongside other regiments, none of whom knew who they were. Only that they were influential enough to advise senior officers what needed to be done, and then leave. Vanishing back into the vast emptiness of the desert, not to be seen again for some time.

In reality James himself could have pulled rank over a full colonel when required but that had never really been put to the test, mainly due to the fact that the unit hardly ever came into contact with any. Most of his time had been spent with his own men searching out any little piece of Intel that they'd deemed to be of significance, or in routing out high priority targets for one of a number of agencies, who preferred to remain hidden in the shadows concealed by smoke and mirrors. All of which was very cloak and dagger and best not to be disclosed in any real length or detail.

He was through with all of that now. It had changed him completely from the man he had once been. He had seen enough bloodshed to last for generations and had lost much more than most.

His greatest love now lay in an unnamed grave, in some sandpit in the middle of a foreign land. On the day he had lost her he had vowed never to get that close to anyone again. He did not want to feel that kind of hurt ever again, an emptiness stretching right to the pit of his stomach. His deepest fear was that his soul would become irreparably tainted if he sustained another such injury. He would certainly never talk about it to anyone for years and even then not in any detail or with any real emotion behind it.

That part of his life now seemed more like a dream than actual reality, a distant memory veiled in the mists of time. In some ways it had hardened him, from then on he would always seem to be surrounded by a wall protecting him from making any real emotional connection with anybody.

Now back in the shelter of the car his mind returned to the events of the last few days. When he had left the base for the last time, never to return. For the whole duration of his train journey from Hereford up to London he'd had the uncomfortable nagging feeling that he was being watched. On the train he had put this down to years of scrutinising everybody around him and always having to watch his back. So he pretended not to notice and put it to the back of his mind. A feeling that in fact would prove to be correct.

On his departure of the train at Paddington someone stepped off just behind him. He felt the lightest touch of finger tips in his pocket. Whoever the perpetrator had been they managed to evade his grasping reaction and disappeared into the crush of people exiting the platform. Initially he'd thought that they might have taken his wallet or phone, but after checking. He was relieved to find both still there; though they were now accompanied by a crumpled piece of paper.

Upon opening the creased note, things only became stranger. Four letters had been quickly scribbled on to it, SPQR. The same letters in fact that he and somebody, whom he had thought he would never see again, had probably unwisely had tattooed on to their right shoulders some ten years previously. The question was why the hell would somebody put that on to a piece of paper, shove it into his pocket and run off? A puzzle that still teased him as he continued his journey home.

The tube and overground ride from Paddington to Clapham Junction was uneventful compared to the chain of events at Paddington. Surprisingly even the Underground ran on time for once. The whole journey only took about half an hour and from there it had just been a short walk to his house on Frere Street.

The cream-coloured four-storey house of No. 12 Frere Street stood proudly between two redbrick houses of the terrace, accessed by a flight of ten steps that rose up from the pavement leading to a glossy royal blue front door. A large brass knocker in the shape of a lion's head with a ring clenched between its impressive teeth hung three quarters of the way up the door.

James had just intended to dump his kit down in the hall and go to bed; unfortunately the events that had started at Paddington were not quite over. He'd opened the door to find an envelope had been pushed through the letterbox, with no stamp or address, just his name, written in the same hand as the note at the station.

Tearing open the envelope he discovered that the note inside just contained the same four letters; unfortunately for the messenger, James was tired and had dismissed it all as just some elaborate practical joke designed by the boys back at the base to make him as paranoid as possible.

It seemed like a feeble attempt to change his mind and return to the unit. This however, he assured himself was not going to happen. He crumpled both notes up and upon entering his smoking room tossed them into the fireplace, instantly wiping the events from his concern. After having a cigarette and a quick glance through the rest of the post James had decided to call it a night and went to bed.

The next morning, he had woken particularly early and feeling pretty tired because the dreams, which of late had been noticeably absent, had retuned to torment his sleep once again; dreams of dark things in far off lands. Sometimes he could still hear the screams of people crying out in pain only for them to be cut short by silence, that earthly silence; the sound of death that eventually enveloped everything. He had resolved to clear his head and shake off the remaining tiredness by going for a quick jog around Battersea Park.

At that time in the morning even the ever-moving city had seemed remarkably still, few people were to be seen, apart from the odd bin man. Even the roads seemed oddly devoid of traffic.

He'd made his way quickly along Latchmere Road towards the park. He was going to enjoy this run he had thought to himself. It had been a while since he had been for a run just on a whim rather than as part of some gruelling training exercise designed just to be as tedious as possible.

Alas, he had not been given the chance to enjoy it for long; twenty minutes or so had passed and then the heavens opened and by the time he reached the cover of No.12 an hour later he was soaked to the core. Sometimes he hated this infernal country for the amount of rain it seemed to attract.

When he crossed the threshold, he noticed that while he had been out another note had been posted through his door. The note was staring up from its resting place on the mat just inside the doorway. At the time James had felt that it was starting to become a bit tedious, and had been on the verge of grabbing the envelope and tossing it out into the rain soaked street, when something caught his eye. In the very corner of the still folded note had been etched in red ink a small squirrel with a broken nut lying at its feet.

He'd slowly turned his left hand over to look at the silver signet ring on his little finger that had been engraved with a very similar design except for one small distinction; the nut was whole in the squirrel's hands.

Without a second thought he'd quickly unfolded the note. He had hoped that he would never have to see that symbol in use. It had been given out to a very select group of people, the majority of whom had been comrades in arms at one point or another over the past ten years, with the specific instruction that if they were ever in any kind of real danger they should contact either him or one of the others. He had been very clear at the time that this was only to be used in times of imminent danger and he did not want to sort out every life problem people were going through.

The resources and contacts that had been built up were not to be taken for granted. Favours did not come around very often. Having said all that, he knew all of these people and expected that if one of them had sent this it would be a matter of life or death.

The final note had read thus:

'Loyal Devoir'
*((D)) L ((D)) **X** L ((D)) **X** L*
SPQR

To anybody else this would have had very little meaning, but to James this had told him everything he needed to know. 'Loyal Devoir' his family motto, also selected as the call for aid; ((D)) L ((D)) X L ((D)) X L referred to a chronogram, '*Tecta **D**raco custos **L**eo vin**D**e**X** f**L**os **D**ecus auctor **R**e**X** pius haec servat protegit ornat a**L**it.*' (The dragon protects this building as guard, the lion protects this as avenger, the flower adorns it as decoration, the pious king, nurtures it.) This referred to the location, date and time of the covert meeting.

The location of the meeting place, Sherborne School where the chronogram was inscribed above the main door of the Old School Room (aka the OSR), the time of the meeting was calculated by adding the roman numerals together in pairs, then taking the original sequence, reversing it and doing the same process again. Surprisingly the sequence had almost palindromic qualities as both came to 1550, combining the two answers and dividing by twenty as the two **X**s were highlighted, equalled 155 which when converted into military time meant 0155. The double brackets around the Ds meant the third day in the week with only two vowels in starting with Monday, therefore Friday.

James couldn't help the small hint of a smile at the corner of his mouth as the sheer irony of the cypher dawned on him. Arguably the most notable person to have ever graced those hallowed halls of learning was Alan Turing, famous for his vital contribution in cracking the German Enigma Code during the Second World War. James wondered whether the original chronograph had inspired the great code breaker during his spell at Sherborne.

Finally SPQR referred to the person who had sent the note. The person he had got the tattoo with, Chris Flack.

He and Chris had joined up at the same time and had served in many campaigns together, mainly in the Middle East. Some five years ago Chris had left without a word, no contact number, and without any reason as to why?

Due to the nature of some of their missions James had just assumed that he had be recruited by one of the other covert agencies and to be honest had not really given it much more thought. There had been a few rumours and random stories he had heard over the next few years but he had just viewed these as idle gossip.

Now however, his mind had begun to run back through some of the snippets of information that he had heard over the years. Most of them did not really seem that plausible: drug running, secret brotherhoods and assassin's guilds to name but a few. True, they had been trained by the best in special intelligence and had on occasion taken out their fair share of strategic military targets, high ranking officials, including a few on the US Most Wanted List, which certainly made them extremely desirable in the eyes of many different types of organisation, but what they had done had all been in the name of Duty, they had taken an oath which they had felt honour bound by:

I swear by Almighty God that I will be faithful and bear true allegiance to Her Majesty Queen Elizabeth the Second, Her Heirs and Successors, and that I will, as in duty bound, honestly and faithfully defend Her Majesty, Her Heirs and Successors, in Person, Crown and Dignity against all enemies, and will observe and obey all orders of Her Majesty, Her Heirs and Successors, and of the generals and officers set over me. So help me God.

This oath had been their life for enough years to know that they would never break it.

Chris had always been a bit of an adrenaline junkie and had occasionally taken unnecessary risks to *make life more interesting* as he put it. He had once said *what's the point of living if you don't ride on the edge with death once in a while.* A statement which even James had to agree had tested his own skills of survival to almost breaking point on a handful of missions, like the time they had scuba dived up to the Al Basrah oil terminal to assess whether it needed extra protection on the very same day that suicide bombers in speedboats had tried to blow it up. The shockwaves of the first boat exploding had left both of them a little hard of hearing for the next few days. Chris had been so close to the second blast that he was lucky he hadn't been left permanently deaf.

One thing Chris was not however, was a fool. He knew where the line was and had never intentionally put himself or others directly into harm's way with his cavalier attitude towards life. He had been a true friend, the one person whom James could have done with six months ago when all had started to fall apart.

The rain outside clattered down on the roof of his car whilst his mind continued to ponder over these recent events; before he hit the roads for the three and a bit hour journey down towards his old school.

In the last few years before Chris had left, the unit had change its focus and had come up with an elaborate scheme that had involved them all going off to work at different outdoor pursuits companies. The idea was that working under the pretence of being climbers and water sports enthusiasts they could gain access to some of the more remote and secure locations in some countries without really attracting too much attention, a concept that had proven highly successful.

They would meet up from time to time, to run *overseas expeditions*, when they could get the time off, without so much as a blink of an eye from their so called employers; even when they had to take 'compassionate leave for personal reasons'.

Top brass had been so impressed at the idea; not that it was a new concept. Similar tactics had been employed during the Napoleonic War and both Great Wars. The military had used cartographers and famous explorers to gain vital information inside enemy occupied territories under their scientific guises. Nevertheless, the powers that be had been impressed by how Chris and James had modernised the operation. James, Chris and a few others had ended up running training exercises for potential new recruits.

This had suited James as it meant he could take a back seat from the front lines for a while. Chris however, missed the action, the constant long periods on the move and especially the confrontation. It had been during this period that Chris had left.

After that things had had to change; the ongoing conflict in Afghanistan, and the movement of terrorists into Northern Pakistan had meant that intelligence gathering was a priority and James along with many other trainers had been reassigned back to service on the front lines.

James then became involved with a girl at one of the bases just outside Bagram; in the end it was to be his relationship to this girl that would ultimately cause him to end his military career. But that's a tale, which James would not reveal to Chris for quite sometime.

A large frown creased his brow, a mixture of deep regret and to a certain extent shame, as the memory he had thought he had buried so deep that he wouldn't remember resurfaced for the briefest instant. James grimaced, angry in part that he had allowed himself to recall it and partly at the events themselves, before he plunged the abomination even deeper into the hidden depths of his mind than before.

At this moment in time, what was playing on James' mind, were those rumours of what Chris had gone on to do? Could it really be true that he had ended up being some sort of gun for hire?

A loud clap of thunder snapped him back to the present, he would surely know soon enough, and with that still on his mind he started the car and drove off on to the Welsh roads to wind his way down to the rolling hills of Dorset, past many of his former training grounds, back to where he had first become interested in a life of military service. It had been at Sherborne that he had come to be part of the Combined Cadet Force that had forged his desire to join up and serve his country.

Being close to 1135hrs James knew if he drove straight down to Sherborne he would arrive sometime after mid afternoon and so he decided to make a stop along the way.

There were still people who might recognise him in the town, and if the note was as important as he believed it to be then he did not want anybody to know that he had ever been there. He concluded to drive via Pensford, a small village just outside Bristol, to see his cousin who had recently moved to the village. It would be nice to have a catch up and hopefully some dinner.

He had not seen Jules for a few years and did genuinely want to know what she was up to these days. She had been living in London working for some bar doing PR but she had not really enjoyed it and so had moved back to the area where her parents had lived for many years.

James had always had a bit of a soft spot for her, she had been a great sailor on the verge of breaking into the Olympic squad but unfortunately she had not been able to cope with the pressure and had given it up. She was very attractive and had a very outgoing personality with quite a cheeky side to her that had always kept James entertained whenever they had been at the same social events.

The traffic had been far worse than he had anticipated for the time of year, and so it was almost 1400hrs by the time he pulled up on the narrow lane of Church Street where Jules' residence of Old Church Cottage was nestled, just a few doors down from the local pub called The Rising Sun. Walking up to the dark green front door set into the old stone built cottage, he knocked at the door and waited. Moments later the door opened to reveal his cousin, she had not changed much in the five years since they had last seen each other.

'James! How are you? So good to see you.' Jules exclaimed, wrapping her arms around him and kissing his cheek.

'Good, thanks. Looking as radiant as ever, I see' he replied.

'Oh! You always were a charmer. Come in I'll put the kettle on.'

'Thanks.'

He followed her through quite a narrow hallway into a spacious kitchen. Looking around he took in the light airy colours on the walls and the cream AGA centrally positioned up against the far side of the kitchen.

Beautifully carved wooden cupboards were strategically hung around the room, and in the centre was one of those island preparation tables. She had always possessed a great sense of taste, especially when it came to making the most of a space.

'This is a lovely cottage you have managed to find.' James stated.

'Well Mummy and Daddy helped me to find it.' She replied, which was code for they had helped to purchase it for her. 'Earl Grey okay? I don't seem to have anything else at the moment, unless you want coffee.'

'Earl Grey's fine.'

'Do you still just take it with a minimalistic view to milk?'

'Yeah, still a creature of habit.' He replied with a smile.

Once the tea had been made, she took him through into the sitting room; again this room was lightly decorated. It was a cosy room, but with enough space for a few armchairs, a sofa and a wall mounted television.

'So, I understand you have finally hung up the rifle.'

'I thought it was about time.'

'I'm glad, I always worried about you. Not knowing exactly where you were or what you were up to, only that wherever you were, it wasn't going to be the safest place.'

'Well now you don't have to worry. In a way I think I will miss it, especially the guys, but as you say it wasn't always the safest of career options.'

James did not mention anything about what had happened since he had left the regiment. He was very careful not to get her involved in anything that could end up getting her hurt or worse.

'Have you any idea what you will do next?'

'I have a few ideas, but I'm not going to rush into anything.'

'Will you stay the night?'

'Unfortunately, I have a really early start in Dorset so as much as I appreciate the offer. I think I'll make a move later on this evening.'

'Well you must stay for supper at least.'

'Hmm, I should really think about making a move.'

'Oh go on. We haven't seen each other for such a long time.'

'Well if you insist, as long as it's no trouble.'

'Don't be silly, it would be a pleasure.'

Having followed her Facebook page, Just Jules, he knew she had some awesome recipes and was passionate about food.

In the end it was around about midnight by the time James left

Jules and headed off towards Sherborne. He decided his timing would be perfect, as the drive would not take more than an hour. Giving him plenty of time to make a reconnoitre of the school and the surrounding town, before slipping into the school, via one of the old secret passageways built by the monks as a final escape route to exit the cloisters, during the reign of the Tudors.

Most of these passages had been blocked up or become unusable; but there were a few that still existed, although James only knew of one or two.

Chapter Two: Unexpected Meetings

His final approached to Sherborne was along the A30, having just passed through Yeovil; James decided he would park at the bottom of Digby Road. There were so many side streets around there, which he could easily duck into, and enough scope to have a few detours if he needed. He was not going to take any chances.

From the car he could make out the large silhouette of the abbey at the top of the street. Founded in 705 AD by St Aldhelm, it had a much grander feel to it than its current position in the ecclesiastical hierarchy warranted, once the Episcopal seat of the bishop of Wessex, the abbey was now just a parish church steeped in history and home to one of the finest examples of fan vaulting anywhere in the country.

James quietly exited the car and after looking around to see if anybody was around, he quickly moved off up the street towards the abbey, turning right he went down into Pageant Gardens and followed the path, which skirted the edge of the gardens. Exiting opposite a supermarket on the far side.

He turned left out of the garden and walked up South Street, carrying straight on at the second cross roads to continue up the steep incline of Cheap Street. Keeping close into all the shadows created by the shops, he walked up past The Cross Keys Inn and Bellissima lingerie shop.

Nothing seemed to be out of the ordinary so far; in fact little had changed in the sleepy Dorset town since he had left the school.

Nevertheless he was not about to drop his guard, knowing all too well not to take any chances. Weaving his way along many small side streets and alleys, doubling back every now and again to ensure nobody was following him, he finally walked back down Cheap Street before cutting up yet another narrow side street next to The Cross Keys, it was not much more than an alley really and was not well lit, he gave a slight shiver and adjusted the buttons on his black cloak as he crossed under a small stone arch high above his head.

That arch always had made him think that there was something sinister about the alley. Supposedly it had been used to hang many people during the Bloody Assizes in 1685 after the Monmouth rebellion had been put down.

The alley itself opened out at the southeast corner of the abbey, just before reaching the abbey, there was a door set into the ten foot high wall on the right that led through into the school grounds just below School House.

Unfortunately there was a code lock on the door and even James' memory was not good enough to remember what the code had been, besides it had most likely changed since his time. Luckily the wall dropped in height to no more than four foot as it merged into the abbey. He had fond memories of vaulting it many times as a boy to escape the confines of the school, long after lights-out when all the boys should have been safely tucked up in bed.

Checking to make sure that no one was around he scrambled up over the wall and dropped lightly down into the school grounds on the other side.

Sticking as close as he could to the outside wall of the Abbey to avoid the CCTV he cautiously made his way along the stone paving towards an archway between the east wall of the abbey and the OSR.

Skirting past the main entrance where the chronograph was inscribed above the doorway; he noticed a second inscription on a sign at the side of the entrance that he had forgotten about. The hint of an amused smile crossed his face as he read it. '*Hanc cigarettanis dona, sis, fibibus urnam, atria qui fumans docta, viator, adis.*' (Present this urn with your cigarette ends, if you please, visitor, you who approach these learned halls as a smoker).

He slipped through the arch under which there was a side door at that corner of the OSR, which he had used many times as a boy, to exit the house late at night when he wanted to sneak out without being caught.

He knew from experience that this door was very poorly secured, and was probably still used by boys to exit in much the same way. It was extremely convenient; it could be locked and unlocked from the outside if you knew the knack to it.

He gently eased the two bolts on the inside back and quietly opened the door into the oak panelled room just as the abbey bells sounded for a quarter to two.

Inside were many boys' names that had been carved into the oak panels over the centuries; all around the room were stain glass windows, which held the coats of arms of all the headmasters who had presided over the school.

At the end of the room was a small Portland stone statue of the school's benefactor Edward VI who had granted the school its charter. It was this end of the room that James was interested in.

When he had been a boy at the school he had discovered that one of the panels at that end of the room had a lot more to offer than it seemed. If you pushed it into the wall, it could then be slid to the side to reveal an ancient set of steps descending beneath the room.

Re-bolting the oak door behind him, he softly made his way to the panel and put his weight against it until it gave a gentle click, which echoed through the moonlit room. Waiting a few moments to make sure nobody had been disturbed by the noise he slid the panel to the side, descended a few steps, turned and replaced the panel.

The craftsmen who had made the panel had had the foresight to put handles on the reverse side of the oak panel so it could be easily removed again when one wanted to return.

The pitch darkness enveloped him as the panel locked out the last shards of moonlight from the room above; reaching into a pocket of his long cloak and fumbling around for a few seconds, he retrieved his phone and used its torch to guide him along the underground network of passages below the school and abbey.

It was a strange feeling, apart from the few times he had explored the network, these passages had never to his knowledge been walked in hundreds of years; if at all since their construction.

The main tunnel had an eerie feel to it; cobwebs were draped along the rough sandstone walls. The air smelt musty and damp, in a few places lichens had taken up residence where drops of groundwater seeped through, and trickled down the bare rock. There were many twists and turns along the route with a few side passages that led off it, passages that he had never explored fully.

He knew that the main passage would take him to just underneath the far side of the school's library in the under croft which was close enough to his final destination, a small grate in the corner of the Fifth Form Green at the far side of the building.

After a couple of minutes following the passage he arrived at the grate and lifted it as slowly as he could. The grate obviously had not been operated in a while, the rusty iron hinges screeched as he forced it open but he knew that the sound had not been loud enough for the school's security guards, known as *The Custos*, to have heard. He cautiously climbed out, angling the grate up against the Portland stone wall of the undercroft deliberately leaving it open just in case he needed to make a quick exit.

Checking his watch he knew he would not have to wait long as it was already 0153. His heart was racing; he had no fear but instead was filled with excitement and perhaps a little apprehension at the prospect of reconnecting with someone he had not seen for a very long time.

The only thing was that he had that little voice in the back of his head nagging at him that something did not feel right. It had all seemed a little too easy. But then should that not be the case? This was hardly an op in some hot arid place where insurgents could appear at any moment, and where was the danger in two friends meeting, whatever the circumstances? So he dismissed it.

Suddenly, a slender black clad figure loomed up over the large wall at the south end of the green and dropped nimbly down on to the grass. Then the little voice in his head began screaming at him.

This was definitely not his friend; the person was too slight and far shorter than his old friend. Quickly turning on his heels he was about to drop back down through the open grate and escape along the passage when he heard a lady's voice.

'Wait *Ghost*, please wait.' James stopped dead in his tracks. Only Chris had ever dared to called him that and only on a few very rare occasions when he wanted to get James to listen to what he had to say. He had always known how to push James' buttons; there had never been an explanation as to why he had started referring to James as *Ghost*. Chris just knew that James hated being likened to an apparition that had no place in this world or the next.

James turned back on his heels slowly, giving himself a few moments to recover from the shock of hearing those words. His mind was racing, a torrent of questions were cascading through his head. Who was this person? How did she know that name? How had she known to come to this place? What did she want? Was she friend or foe? Quietening his thoughts, he paused and raised his head to gaze at this newcomer.

She was standing in the moonlight, dressed in black lightweight clothing which it must be said accentuated the shape of her body, although slight she was perfectly toned and well proportioned with long dark hair flowing over her shoulders.

'If you have quite finished checking me out, I believe we have a lot to discuss. My name's Rachel.' She stated with almost the hint of a smile. 'Chris told me to show you this.' She said as she tossed a silver ring to him.

Catching hold of it, James inspected the engraving, an identical twin to the one he was wearing.

'Chris sends his apologies but unfortunately recent events have prevented him from being here in person. He asked me to be here in his place and give you a brief outline of what is going on.'

'Err… yes… what?' James replied, startled by the voice interrupting his trail of thought. 'But I feel this is not the place for such conversations. If you don't mind, I'm going to skip the pleasantries, follow me please and try to keep up…' pausing as he heard footsteps echoing down the cloisters. '…I think we have already lingered here for too long. This way, quickly.' He said gesturing towards the open grate.

He helped to lower her down into the passageway before dropping down behind her and closing the grate.

They shrank back a little further into the darkness of the passageway so as not to be seen. He felt the warmth of her body close to him as they crouched in the cool darkness of the tight passage.

His view was obscured, but there were definitely two men talking in low voices above them, it was hard to overhear what was being said. Nevertheless they were obviously annoyed that their quarry had managed to elude them. Whoever they were, they were definitely not employees of the school. An indication, that James was entering this particular game far later than he had thought.

Recalling himself from his thoughts, he heard the echoes of the men's footsteps fading away into the shadows and decided that they should be doing the same.

Grabbing his new companion roughly by the arm, which caused her to let out a sudden gasp of shock, he headed off down the passageway, ignoring the fact that she had shaken herself free from his grasp. He smiled to himself and carried on down the passageway, aware that she was following behind. *She's going to be a stubborn one* he thought. Chris always did know how to pick 'em.

Making their exit from the passage back into the OSR, and quickly replacing the panelling, they left the room the same way James had entered.

Outside it had started to rain; fat drops soon ran down both of their faces. Taking a more direct route to the car straight down Digby Road from the abbey, deciding that speed rather than stealth was the better course of action, they soon reached the car.

Leaving Sherborne they headed south-west towards Devon. The journey that he planned was not that long, but he could tell that it was going to be awkward. His mind was now so full of questions that quite some time passed before he had ordered his thoughts and spoke.

James pulled into a layby on the A3088 after passing Yeovil.

'Give me your phone.' He said bluntly as he turned to face the girl sitting next to him in the car.

'Why?' She replied defiantly staring back at him, feeling slightly put out at the sheer audacity of the man.

'Those men found us very easily. One conclusion might be that they are tracking one of us. So give me your phone.'

'Are you suggesting that I am not to be trusted? That I am not who I claim to be?'

'Quite frankly, yes. That's exactly what I am suggesting. I'm not going to take any chances; your phone, please!' He snapped holding out his hand, without breaking eye contact with her. Reluctantly she handed it over to him. He removed the battery to access the SIM card. He put the SIM in his jacket pocket and the remaining parts of the phone he dropped out of the car window. He did the same with his own before restarting the car and continuing on down through the Wessex countryside towards his intended destination.

This girl intrigued James, however she was foreign to him. She may hold her cousin's ring or so she claimed and yet how it came to have been entrusted to her was still open to intense scrutiny. Until that had been resolved he would keep his own council as much as possible.

'So are you going to tell me where we are going? Chris is expecting us by tomorrow night at the latest.' She said breaking the silence.

Ignoring her question, he began to ask some probing questions of his own.

'How is Chris, I don't think I have seen him since our last training assignment together at Sennybridge, when he got that scar on the left side of his neck.'

'He's very well, although unless it has somehow moved, I think you will find that the scar is on the right.' Rachel replied recognising that James was testing her knowledge of his old friend.

'Well good to know that he is okay. Now that I think about it, I believe it was on the right; it's been a while since I have thought about it. When did you meet him? I don't remember him ever mentioning a cousin?'

'About four years ago. My parents were both killed in a car crash and not having any other relations, Chris sort of took me under his wing. I've been living at his ever since.' She replied.

'Is he still living in Mary Tavy? I have some fond memories of that place, it's a really nice spot in Dartmoor.' James said knowing full well that Chris had never lived in Mary Tavy.

'You're probing again, I think you mean Peter Tavy. Still don't trust me, huh?'

'Well can you blame me? I've only got your word that he sent you, but so far I'm satisfied.'

'So are you going to tell me where we are going?'

'Cotehele House, I have a few things in storage at the estate that I think may come in handy at some point.' He replied trying to limit the amount of information he gave out.

It was early morning by the time they finally wound their way along the last few country lanes to Cotehele, the sun was just starting to rise above the horizon, and the birds had already been tweeting amongst themselves for some time.

Cotehele House had been part of his family's holdings for a number of generations and over the years had undergone extensive restoration work. Now restored, the great Tudor manor house stood proudly in the early morning sunlight. James pulled up in the courtyard of the great house. The gravel crunching underfoot as he exited the car.

Instead of walking straight up to the main house he walked off in the opposite direction, past the visitors car park and continued down a narrow lane towards a group of stone outbuildings that lined the roadside.

'This place is stunning!' Rachel exclaimed as she admired the Tudor architecture, before following in James' footsteps.

'Yes it is rather fine isn't it? Its just a shame that its splendour is tarnished slightly by the means used to hoard the fortunes required to maintain it.' James replied, knowing full well the history behind the house.

The fortunes amassed to construct and maintain the great house had largely been made through the draconian use of the feudal system, over-taxing peasant farmers during the Tudor period and more recently exploitation of labour in the sugar plantations of the West Indies.

It vexed him greatly that much of his family's wealth had been gained through the exploitation of what he considered to be the barbaric use of Negroes almost two centuries ago. Somehow he felt that he needed to atone for the past sins of his family at some point. Sins, that in his eyes should never have been allowed to happen and could never be fully forgiven, an indelible stain on the family's good name.

James stopped just short of the end but one garage. Taking a bunch of keys out of his pocket, and selecting the one on a green fob that matched the colour of the doors. He unlocked the padlock and slid the doors back. As the doors slid back the alarm in the building sounded, walking into the garage he located the alarm keypad on the left hand wall. Quickly typing in the code he disarmed the alarm with the alphanumeric keypad.

He used the garage as a bit of a storage area for personal equipment, which he had acquired over the years. Some of it he had used on expeditions and some was of a rather more questionable legal status.

'Jesus, it's like an assassin's toy shop in here!' Rachel cried out as she took in the sight of all the weapons, neatly arranged in large metal cabinets, spread throughout the garage. 'Are those missiles real?' She said pointing in disbelief at the open crate of FIM-92 stinger missiles.

'Yeah, I came across them in Paris a few years ago when I was on an op.'

'I knew you guys were good, but how the hell did you get them back here?'

'I smuggled them back by boat, with Chris' help. It's one of the benefits of this house's close proximity to the River Tamar. Direct access to the estuary at Plymouth and the English Channel enabled us to smuggle quite a lot of questionable equipment into the country over the years. Don't think we will need them today, might be a little OTT.'

'Just a bit.' She said with the hint of nervousness in her laugh, as she hoped there would never come a day when they were required.

A wry smile appeared at the corner of James' mouth.

'This is only scratching the surface.' He replied, as he picked up a large black canvas bag from of a row of hooks and began to fill it with ammo clips, hand guns, a few grenades, some SA 80s and a personal favourite of his, an FN P90 machine gun.

'Right I think that will do for now.'

'I don't suppose you have got any phones stashed away somewhere amongst all this stuff. Someone broke my last one!'

'Point taken. I think there's a few iPhones knocking about somewhere over there. We had some left over from an op, so they should be clean.' James replied with a vague wave in the general direction of the far right-hand corner.

After rummaging through several boxes stacked in the corner, Rachel eventually found a box containing six brand new iPhones. She took two out and taking the SIM cards James had kept, inserted them into a converter that she also found in the box to transfer the data across to the new SIMs without the potential risk of contaminating the burner phones with the old ones.

'I don't know about you but I could do with a few hours kip at some point.' He said yawning.

'Yeah I wouldn't mind catching a few hours sleep. Although this floor looks less than appealing.'

'Don't worry Princess. Sure there's some camp beds floating around somewhere.' He said as he began to rummage around in a corner of the garage. 'Ah ha found them, and some blankets; bonus.' Rachel let the Princess comment slide; she knew he only meant it in jest.

James set them up along the inside wall of the garage and they both crashed out for a few hours.

Just over two hours later James woke and walking round to the next-door garage, slid the doors back. Inside was a green Range Rover, which he swapped with the battered 406 that he had been driving. He loaded all the gear that he had selected into the back of the Range Rover before leaving the keys next to where Rachel was still fast asleep, with a note to say that she could find him down by the river when she woke.

James headed off towards the quayside below. He hadn't been down there for a while, it was one of the places he liked to go and admire the view. The tranquillity of just watching the ever constant flow of the river passing by always took his mind off the hustle and bustle of everyday life.

The sun slowly made its way over the sky; its rays split by the wavelets, shattered into thousands of pinpricks dancing on the surface. The sound of the water gently lapping at the quayside was somehow soothing. He must have been more tired than he had thought because he soon nodded off on one of the benches along the quay, listening to the stillness.

James continued to sleep on the bench absorbing the atmosphere. It was uncannily quiet, not that he really minded, sometimes tranquillity was all that he ever wished for. He had often wondered if somewhere there was a stopwatch that one could use to freeze time, just pause everything around you so that one would be able to admire the little things. For instance to see a dandelion just as it has released all of its seeds, floating away on the breeze. Or to pause the night sky just as a star is born. That one perfect moment when suddenly out of the darkness a dim light appears growing ever brighter in strength as the reaction between particles increases until it becomes self-sustaining.

A sudden cold gust snapped him back to reality. And with it the realisation that nothing would ever be the same again. The atmosphere was changing. He could feel the hairs on the back of his neck start to stand up. He shivered as though someone had just walked across his grave and in that one moment; time did almost seem to stand still.

He heard a loud roar as the V8 engine of his 4x4 burst into life, shattering the stillness, the screech of rubber on tarmac as it came to an abrupt halt next to him.

'Get in!' Rachel screamed at him as she opened the passenger door from the inside. 'For God's sake don't just sit there. Get in! We need to go. Now!'

Guessing that they had outstayed their welcome, he jumped up from the bench and swung himself through the open door into the passenger seat.

'Go, Drive!' he exclaimed, slamming the door shut.

Chapter Three: Old History

The bar consisted of one long narrow room, a few tables stretched out along one wall and some small oil paintings hung behind the bar; painted in the baroque style of the renaissance and lavishly set into gilded frames. Around the room hung some large mirrors and a couple of stags' heads, the decadence of a bygone age.

The oil lamps hanging from the walls, created flickering shadows on the darkly painted room. Shadows that danced every time the door was opened by a newcomer allowing the cool breeze from outside to blow in.

Chris Flack sat hunched in a corner of the room peering over a ream of papers that he had managed to rescue from the flames that had ravaged his family home. Unfortunately, he had not been able to save all the contents of his family's great library, much to his dismay.

The event had left a bitter taste in his mouth. Centuries of knowledge wiped out in just a few minutes of raging heat. The inferno had engulfed the house so quickly that he was not only thankful for saving a few things but also that he'd managed to get out at all. He was certainly glad that he had possessed the foresight to move the most important books to another location some time ago.

The arson had obviously been well planned and staged perfectly to look like an accident. The police and fire services had been of no help. Any evidence of an accelerant had been carefully concealed. Their conclusion had been that a spark from some old wiring had started the blaze that soon spread to the tapestries on the walls before finally engulfing the rest of the house, a conclusion that Chris ardently disagreed with, as he knew things that they did not, but could not disclose to them. Nevertheless he had still hoped that once the wreckage had cooled down he would be able to enter and check whether the contents of the safe room were still intact.

Sir Christopher Wren had designed the room in the seventeenth century and Chris was mildly optimistic that the fire would not have penetrated the great iron doors that had been placed along the passageway leading down into the maze of cellars that ran underneath the house.

Much of the cellar network had been water-logged for years, giving him hope that the fire would not have reached all the way to the room at the end of those remarkable stone works.

Wren had spent a lot of time designing the hide away, one of many dotted around the country. Originally to be used by members of the Royal family if ever the need to seek salvation arose. A number of Royalist families had commissioned such rooms during the decades after the beheading of Charles I, they had not wanted to see that ever happen again.

Once the monarchy had become firmly established back on the throne and the threat of civil war seemed unlikely to reoccur many of these rooms had been converted to hold important family documents and secrets, of which this room was no exception.

He had returned to the house several days after the fire and as luck would have it, discovered as he had hoped, that the fire had not penetrated that far along the cellar network. He had taken some time to carefully make his way along the passages.

Fallen timbers from the floor above littered the corridors and in some places where the ceiling hadn't completely fallen through, beams had precariously wedged themselves. The slightest vibration would have caused them to continue their downward collapse that could at best easily trap him within the passageway and at worst strike him down.

Weaving through the debris he had eventually made it to the room and managed to unlock the final great door; discovering all was still intact he retrieved the relevant papers. The very same papers he was now engrossed in reading by the flickering light of the oil lamps.

Chris looked up from behind the papers as the door to the bar noisily opened. He noticed that he was shaking slightly, which may have been to do with previous events although more likely was a result of the massive amounts of both caffeine, and nicotine that now coursed through his veins; he never had learnt when to stop drinking coffee on an empty stomach.

Whilst he had noticed the couple that had walked in, he had not paid them a second thought. The man had a hood up as it was raining outside and the girl's face had been obscured by one of the wall-mounted oil lamps. So Chris had returned to peering through his papers. That was until the dim light by which he had been reading was interrupted, and a ring; his ring in fact bounced noisily across the table towards him.

Looking up to see what had caused the interference he almost let out a gasp of surprise as he met the eyes of the person blocking his light, those dark set probing eyes peering down at him from under that cavernous hood.

It did not matter how dimly lit the place was he would always recognise that look; a penetrating look that bore straight through you, delving deep into your very soul to snatch your darkest secrets. Those piercing eyes had always sent a shiver down his spine. There was something unnatural about that gaze and it had been the main reason why he had originally nicknamed James, *Ghost*. He was unable to believe that anything living should possess such a look, although he had never mentioned this to his friend.

'I see she found you then?' He stated before the man towering above could address him. 'I wondered how long it would take you. I wasn't sure if you would come with her or not.' Chris added, picking up his ring and replacing it back where it belonged.

James slowly removed his hood and without dropping his gaze from his old friend, pulled up a chair and sat down.

'I will give you boys some space to catch up.' Rachel said, noticing the intensity of the eye contact.

'Well are you going to speak or are you just going to sit there staring? I am real you know, not dead, well at least not yet.' Chris said with half a smile, trying to break the ice.

'I can see that. However a ghost might be a more welcome sight at this point. You have a lot to answer for, and I'm not sure that I want to know the half of it.' James was obviously tense; Chris could hear the slight hint of anger shaking in his voice.

The knuckles of James' tightly clenched fists on the table were turning white. 'What mess have you got me involved in now? Not to mention what the hell have you been up to for the past five years? You better not have got me involved in another one of those crazy stunts. I don't do that now. I've retired.' James was shaking, the anger now more evident in his voice.

'Yes, I suppose I deserve that. Maybe I should have kept in contact but I didn't think it was wise, not until I was sure, sorry. And I am also sorry hear about the loss of your fiancé, I know I never had the opportunity to meet her but I hear that she was the picture of elegan…'

James' fist slammed on to the table, the loud crash of fist on wood echoed around the room causing a few of the regular patrons to turn their heads in surprise to see what the commotion was about.

'Don't you ever talk about her, you have no right. That ended when you left!'

'I'm sorry, nevertheless the statement still stands. Remember we were once brothers in arms. So from one brother to another I am sorry. As for the present situation, I'm afraid there was no other way. I didn't get you involved, you were part of it already, albeit unaware of the fact. Better this way than receiving two hollow points through the back of your head; to be left staring up at the sky. Blankly wondering what you had done to deserve it for the rest of eternity. All will be revealed in due course, but for now I am going to have to be brief. You are on catch up and unfortunately I don't have the time to babysit. So you are going to have to learn fast if you want to remain outside of the divine comedy.'

'You're really leading with that? Flaming Catholics and your over zealous sense of belief.' They both laughed, which seemed to ease the tension somewhat, both remembering the debates on religion they used to have. Each stubbornly refusing to see the other's point of view. They represented the two main denominations of the Christian faith in England, two faiths that had caused so much chaos in the country over the centuries; sides that would probably never find a common ground on which to base a lasting reconciliation.

'So what is so God damned important? And how am I already involved?' James finally asked.

'Well I'm going to have to give you a quick history lesson.' Chris replied.

'If that's the case, I'm going to get a proper drink. What are you having? And I suppose I should get her something too.' James stated as he gestured in the general direction of Chris' cousin.

'Scotch, no rocks, no water and she'll have a Vodka Tonic water, I think.'

James went to the bar and ordered their drinks plus a Scotch for himself. The leggy blonde, whose hair cascaded down over her shoulders, said that she would bring the drinks over.

'Right you may as well get on with it, you better be more interesting than my fifth grade history teacher! Or I will definitely start to drop off.' James said in a rather sarcastic tone as he returned to the table.

'I'll try my best. For over twelve hundred years the Royal lines have been protected, and they will continue to be. The Roman emperors of Ancient times had the Praetorian Guard to protect the emperor and his direct family. This lasted until the reign of Constantine I, who abolished the order, and as you know only two centuries later the Roman Empire fell. Then circa 768AD at the request of the dying King Pepin the Short, a handful of the most loyal families of his court became protectors of his sons and all of the descendants thereafter. Not even he could have had the foresight to see that the majority of the Royal lines in Western Europe would one day be able to trace their lineage back to his son Charlemagne, King of the Franks and Holy Roman Emperor. Or maybe he did?'

'Sorry to interrupt you, gentleman, here are your drinks.' The barmaid said as she arrived with a tray of drinks.

'Thank you.' Chris replied.

'Is there anything else I can get for you?'

'No, I think that's it for now, thanks. Oh, can you add these to my room.'

'Certainly Sir.' She replied as she left them to continue their conversation.

'Right, now where was I? Oh yes, Pepin's wish. So, for generations these great families positioned themselves close to the descendants of Pepin in order to be able to carry out his request, to serve and protect from both foe and kin alike. They worked tirelessly from the shadows to protect these great lines, sometimes at great personal cost.

'As the centuries rolled on it became less and less necessary for these families to fulfil this role. So many of these families became concerned with other matters.

'During the crusader period many went off to Jerusalem and joined Holy Orders, fighting to protect pilgrims and also to defend the Kingdom of Jerusalem from the likes of Saladin. I'm sure you are familiar with the myths surrounding the Templar Knights and the Holy Grail?'

'Well yes, I'm sure almost everybody knows some variation of the myth. But I never actually thought that it was true.'

'And you would be right, my friend. The Grail is more myth and legend than actual fact. What you are probably less familiar with is what they did discover in Jerusalem. Along with the vast amounts of treasure, they discovered a book. On the surface this does not sound very exciting, it is however, extremely important. This book is supposedly made from the Tree of Knowledge. How it came to be is still a mystery.

'Upon first inspection the pages inside it appeared to be blank and as the story goes they were about to throw it aside when one of them read the inscription on the cover of the book, for the briefest of moments the book flickered with light, before the light went out just as quickly as it had begun.

'The once blank pages were now covered in writing, some of it in their native tongue, whilst much of it was in an ancient script and runes that none of them knew how to decipher. After careful study they concluded that the book was sacred. What they could read revealed much about the world and universe, which at that time was unknown. This is in fact the main reason that it became known as the *Liber Veritatis*, or the *Book of Truth* as it translates. They believed that it contained so much knowledge that if it were lost into the wrong hands its contents could be used for all the wrong reasons and so they vowed to protect it, from all those that would seek to abuse its power.

'My own belief is that it was the information in this book that enabled the Templars to become so powerful in Europe during the following centuries. From what I know they only used it for the benefit of the Order. However, there were those amongst the Order who wanted to go further and use it for their own gain.

'During the purge of the Templar Knights in 1307 some of the knights that had escaped arrest took it upon themselves to smuggle the book and the majority of the Templars wealth out of the Order and hide it to prevent it from being abused. Some were your ancestors and I believe that your father now knows the whereabouts of this book.

'In fact he has studied its legend for many years and it is his belief that it is not a one off, but that there are several more volumes, although he is still uncertain as to the final total. He has evidence that over the centuries some have surfaced and influenced the technological development of civilisations. Most are now lost. It is his belief that this is what our foe is looking for. Your Father, himself has come very close to locating the one that your ancestors rescued all those centuries ago.'

'What about the treasure? Does he know where that is, as well?'

'I have never asked him about that and he has never told me. I only know that at this point in time the book is far more important than any amount of treasure could be.' Chris finished, took a sip of his drink and looked across the table at James. 'So what do you think?' Trying to gauge his friend's reaction.

James took a long deep swig of his Scotch before he answered. 'Well to be honest it all seems a little far fetched but I'm sure that your assessment is correct. My father always was into historical stuff; I would say that I'm surprised he never mentioned it to me before, but actually I'm really not. As you well know we're not exactly close.'

'That's an understatement. You two haven't spoken to each other in years.'

'Yeah, well we always had a knack of driving each other up the wall. I guess in the end we just stopped making the effort to see each other and just drifted apart. Nevertheless, it does explain why he always said it was really important to build up a close network of people who could be relied upon and why he kept on sending me a handful of those signet rings from time to time to give to those people that I trusted. I often wondered what the significance was of the cross behind the squirrel. However, I don't really see why I should be concerned with any of this. You seem to be in control and I'm not convinced that my involvement would be of any real benefit. Sure Dad will be dreading it.'

'Your father thought you might say something like that. He gave me this letter to give to you in the event that you were not persuaded.' Chris replied as he took a rather crumpled envelope from his jacket pocket and handed it to James.

'Ha typical, someone should really tell him that wax seals went out of fashion centuries ago.' James mused, smiling at his father's antiquated eccentricity as he tore open the envelope.

Chris sat and waited for James to finish reading the letter. Listening to James' mutterings in response to parts of the letter, he could tell just from the way James reacted to certain parts that his relationship with his father was somewhat less that harmonious.

'Well, I'm still sceptical but he has made a few good points.' James finally said as he finished reading the letter, screwing it up into a ball and tossing it into the open fire in the bar. The letter quickly caught fire and was soon consumed by the flames.

Chris never did find out what was in the letter, he considered it to be private, a letter of truce so to speak between father and son. Nevertheless, whatever had been said had certainly moved James in such a way that his attitude towards his involvement had changed.

'The question is where do we go from here? I do have an inkling of what you might suggest, but as you have kept me in suspense for this long I'm sure I can wait a little longer. Especially as our quarry seem to be half a step ahead of me. I'm obviously getting too predictable in my middle years.' James said jokingly.

'You must remember that they have been studying too. They would have expected you to become involved at some point, which is probably one of the reasons why your father had held off from involving you for such a long time. The only problem now, is that they have had longer to prepare and have anticipated your steps.

'What concerns me is how they knew about the meeting place. Very few people knew about that and I thought we had been so careful; either someone has broken my trust or they have managed to intercept our communications. They must be getting their information from somewhere. I would like to think that it is the latter. I have known most of our network for a number of years, long enough not to doubt their loyalty and the rest your father has known for decades and as such are beyond repute.

'We may have to proceed with a little more caution than I had wanted. Speed is of the essence at the moment. I fear our adversaries have become very close to locating one of the volumes. This is something that cannot be allowed to happen, as one book may lead to others.'

'Yeah caution never was your strong point.' They both laughed.

'I know you have already been to Cotehele but we are going to have to visit another one of your family's holdings, Martinstowe Estate. There are two places that are of specific interest, notably the crypt under the chapel, and also part of the library. Although the library may prove to be slightly more challenging, as you know much of the original was destroyed by fire.'

'Why so interested in the crypt? I've been down there several times and apart from the old tombs I haven't seen anything of interest.'

'That's because you didn't know what to look for. Certainly there are tombs but we are only interested in one of them, the oldest. As you may be aware the chapel was built by James Piers St Aubyn. He was also responsible for works on both the Middle Temple and the Temple Church in London. Let's just say that some artefacts that used to reside in the Temple Church were moved and now inhabit the crypt at Martinstowe, either underneath or inside the oldest of the Heywood tombs.'

'Ha, good luck moving that thing. I've seen it. It's massive. Must weigh at least half a ton.'

'We'll find a way, I'm sure. As for the library, a small room was added behind one of the bookcases. Unfortunately I don't know exactly which one or if it is still accessible so we may have to excavate a little bit. I had hoped that its exact location was recorded in the documents in the crypt. But your father has assured me that it isn't. Apparently your uncle knows the location. So I'm going to ring him in a bit. What I do know at the moment is that the secret room was fire proof and that it was not revealed or destroyed by the fire.'

'What about our foe? They do seem rather eager to engage us. Do you know who they are?'

'From what I have gathered, they refer to themselves simply as *The Glove*, a brotherhood of sorts that seem intent on reuniting all the parts of the book. The main protagonist that your father has crossed paths with on a number of occasions in the past is a man known as Lord Norwood. He hasn't given me any further details at present, but you know what your father is like. He only ever gives you the information that he thinks you need and never paints the whole picture.

'Not to worry they are not the only ones who have done some research and I think they will be well occupied at this present moment in time or at least they will be shortly. I have sent them a few uninvited guests in the form of Messrs Gambles and Hargreaves. So I expect that they will have their minds on other things for a while.'

'Ha, that won't be pretty.' A broad smile crossed James' face as he remember his two ex comrades, Ollie Gambles and Gaz Hargreaves.

They had both mastered in chemistry at Cambridge University and joined up soon after graduating. They had rather enjoyed *blowing things up*, James fondly referred to them as the *Maestros of Chemical Mixology*, especially when it came to destroying things.

Ollie was about 6'4" tall with quite a wiry frame, shortish dark brown hair and wore square, thick black-rimmed glasses that almost gave him the look of a mad scientist, just without the white coat.

Gaz on the other hand was quite athletically built. Still tall at 6'3", his short dark hair was parted at the side and he had one of those enviable tans.

Both were exceedingly well spoken and possessed the charm and charisma to be able to sell ice to Eskimos, although Ollie believed that when it came to *the ladies* he wasn't *a closer*, that was more Gaz's area of expertise. Something that he would come to realise wasn't true, as years later he would marry and settle down with the American girl of his dreams.

For some time they had been experts in demolition and guerrilla tactics, and because of their hyperactive adrenaline fuelled personalities they sometimes let their energies get away from them; becoming caught up in the moment.

Gaz and Ollie were both agreed that if you are going to blow something up it needed to be done with as much flare and panache as possible, no half measures or messing around. To them an explosion was a thing of beauty, something to be admired, so sound and colours were crucial and if you could almost taste the aftermath so much the better.

This exuberance had often led to a few unforeseen consequences, like the time that they had taken it upon themselves to remove a few bridges along the river Dobra in the former Yugoslavia and had caused such shockwaves that the Gojak Dam a few miles down river had almost been washed away by the not so small tidal wave that they had unintentionally created.

James could well imagine that the havoc, which they were no doubt about to wreak, would be a very memorable occasion and would certainly cause their foe more than one headache and would certainly keep them well out of James and Chris' hair for a while.

'I've sorted out some transport to Martinstowe. I thought boat rather than car would be best as Martinstowe is accessible via the River Tavy. We will be able to control any unwelcome attention a little more easily from the water. Ollie and Gaz have left a few surprises to help us if we do need to discourage anybody from following us.

'I've moored a 9m Zodiac RIB down by Ince Castle that should be more than up to the task. So I suggest we all catch a few hours sleep before we set off. I want an early start, leaving before sunup. I'm just going to ring your uncle to find out where we can locate the vault at Martinstowe, as I'm sure he is the only one still alive that knows its exact location. He would have liked to have met us at Martinstowe but he has estate business in Scotland and therefore can not be there.'

'Well I've certainly never heard of a secret vault before but then that doesn't really surprise me. I'm pretty sure there's quite a few skeletons that I don't know about.'

'Here's the key for your room. I took the liberty of booking a couple here, thought it would be slightly more comfortable than sleeping in the Range Rover. The manager has kindly offered that you can leave the 4x4 round the back for a couple of days. They have CCTV so it will be perfectly safe and the gates are normally locked at night.'

'Good thinking Batman. I'll go sort the car out and might grab another of that fine scotch before I crash.' And with that James walked off in the direction of his car.

It was close to midnight by the time Chris finished his conversation with James' uncle. It had been a much longer conversation than he had anticipated nevertheless he got what he wanted.

Chapter Four: Friends and Enemies

Ollie and Gaz had left Chris, in the bar shortly before James' arrival. They had been given strict instructions by Chris to cause as much mayhem as possible but under no circumstances were they to risk being discovered.

They took the decision as they neared their destination that it would be a good idea to ditch their battered Land Rover and walk the last mile or so towards Glympton Park.

Information was key at this point. Where the patrols were and how often they rotated? How many guards there were? What would be the best placement for devices to cause as much chaos as possible? Where was the best place to conceal the Land Rover? And so on.

After spending a few hours scouting the place and fighting their way through the dense undergrowth around the park, they had acquired all the info that they needed.

'Mate I think that the *Crazy Frenchman* would be a great pattern to run here.' Ollie commented after they had made their way deeper into the forest surrounding the grounds of the estate.

They had long ago become bored with the standard guerrilla tactics and so had created there own variations most of which were now named after random cocktails they had come across.

'I'm not sure I was torn between that and the *Mad Mexican*, but it's up to you chap.' Gaz replied with a wry smile.

'Ah, that's a good point. The *Mad Mexican* had completely slipped my mind. Could always do both just to be on the safe side. We wouldn't want to disappoint, now would we? I hate it when things are boring. After all we should really give them a show to remember!' They both grinned; the excitement on their faces was plainly evident.

'Right, Ol let's get the Landy up here and start setting things up. Oh, bugger!'

'What?'

'Forgot the champers out of the fridge when we stopped at yours to pick up the gear. Would have been nice to toast the occasion.'

'Come on Ol, we're not in the OTC anymore. Think those days of officer training at uni are well and truly behind us now.'

'Still would have been nice.'

'Knowing you, you'd have brought the caviar as well, I suppose. Such a dick.'

'Nah, maybe Nik Naks.'

'Dude, what the fuck? Nik Naks and champagne, are you for real? You really are a strange one.' Gaz retorted as he climbed into the Landy, still half wondering whether Ollie was being serious or not about the bizarre combination.

They drove the last mile and a half up towards the estate turning off, a little way from the entrance to the estate, down a dirt track and into the forest. Jumping out they walked round and climbed up into the canvas-covered rear of the Land Rover.

The inside was like an anarchists dream. There were so many IEDs, claymores, mines and an array of chemicals to make some of the more creative devices that the two had designed.

'Where did you put the mercury switches, Gaz old boy?'

'Who are you calling old? You're far older than me!'

'True and yet still far better looking! I think they are behind that case of phosphorous grenades. Oh and be careful there's some nitro down there, somewhere.'

'What do you think I am, an amateur?'

'Well based on previous comments the jury is still out on that one.'

Once they had finished assembling all of the *special deliveries*, they carefully stowed them in their Bergens and waited for dark. As soon as the gloom started to descend amongst the trees they picked their way furtively through the undergrowth towards the grounds of the estate.

The moonless night made their task of infiltrating the estate easier, barely casting a shadow they moved silently through the grounds, pausing every now and then to allow a patrol to move away from them. They ducked into the dense vegetation a couple of times to allow a searchlight to continue scanning ahead of them.

Stealth was a crucial part of this type of work. They moved quickly and had eventually planted forty seven devices of varying sizes and potency in a range of different places: under the top-end cars on the driveway, in flower beds, against supporting walls of the house, under the mat on the front door, near the gatehouse, and along some of the paths frequented by patrols. To the resident housefly on the wall, the sight of the two grown men's stop-start scurrying, followed by the occasional commando roll across the front lawn must have been both bizarre and rather entertaining to watch. But would nevertheless, pale in comparison to what would follow.

The plan in essence was simple, to create as much panic, confusion and disorientation as possible.

All of the devices were linked via Wi-Fi to a single iPad, and once activated, were sensitive to motion. As soon as the first device was triggered the control programme took over, it was programmed to randomly detonate a single device at sporadic intervals, during the next 2 hours. The boys hoped that this would scatter people in all directions.

'Right Gaz, I think it is time we retired to some cover and let the fun begin.' Ollie whispered.

'Sounds like a plan.'

They cautiously made their way back to the cover of the forest and found a good spot underneath a rhododendron bush from which to watch the fireworks, close enough to the Land Rover should they need to make a quick getaway.

'Would you like to do the honours, mate?' Gaz asked Ollie.

'Your too kind. On my mark three, two, one, active.' Ollie counted down and pushed the green button on the iPad. Then they waited; they did not have to wait long. Within minutes a *skull and crossbones* flashed up on the iPad indicating that one of the IEDs on a path had been triggered, the screen showed a timer counting down from 30 seconds. As the clock neared zero Ollie excitedly announced 'Bada Bing Bada Boom!'

The sound of the IED exploding ripped through the silence, trees shuddered and shook from the shockwaves, lights went on all over the grounds, guards scattered diving for cover. As the next three or four devices exploded you could make out the cries of pain as the not so fortunate expressed their feelings, whilst others were forever silenced, instantly ripped apart by the explosions.

The bright purple Lamborghini parked outside the house was sent rocketing up into the night sky, engulfed in scarlet and ochre flames. As it crashed back down to earth Gaz exclaimed 'Now that's what I call a *Flaming Lamborghini.*' They both roared with laughter. Luckily there was so much commotion around the grounds that nobody heard them.

Not wanting to linger for longer than necessary. They decided to disappear; the searchlights had already begun to scan the treeline. It would have been enjoyable to watch the finale but they both agreed it would not be worth the risk.

They knew the final device would not go off for at least another hour, so they departed still grinning from ear to ear at a job well done.

Earlier that day Lord Anthony Norwood had been sitting behind his study desk at Glympton Park listening to two of his subordinates attempting to make some feeble excuses as to why they had failed in their task.

He was growing increasingly bored and angry with them, of course he had expected that there were going to be a few set backs to his grand scheme but he had not foreseen incompetence on this scale.

It had been such a simple task that even a monkey with half a brain should have been able to carry out the task. All they should have done was to intercept the girl and Middleton, then bring them to him. However, his men had arrived late and made too much noise, which had resulted in spooking the conspirators. Not only that, they had then lost their trail.

'Enough! Both of you are totally incompetent. It was a simple task, which I expected even two half-wits such as you to carry out. Obviously I was wrong. Even Mr Leach here managed to carry out his task and succeeded in burning down Captain Flack's home, it was unfortunate that Flack survived but at least the fire will have destroyed the documents. As for you two, you are lucky that I'm feeling generous otherwise I would have Chamberlain here drag you both outside and put a bullet in both your skulls! Now get out! I do not want to be reminded of your existence!' He bellowed at them.

A nervous glance passed between the two men at the mention of Chamberlain's name, they were scared of their lord but they were absolutely terrified of the man know as 'Chamberlain'. The two men hastily made their exit from his office, eager to escape before he changed his mind.

'Leach, have you tracked them down yet?' Lord Norwood asked turning to look at one of the two men still present in his study.

'Yes sir, we located them close to Cotehele House. Unfortunately we were unable to intercept them. The girl spotted one of my guys as she was locking some garages, and they made their escape. We are nevertheless pretty sure we know where they are headed and we plan to shadow them once they have met up with Flack, Sir.'

'Good, make sure there are no more failures. I should hate to have to punish failure. Now go and make the necessary arrangements. Chamberlain ... has everything been arranged for the next phase?' He asked turning his attention to the other man as Leach left the room.

'It has My Lord. The shipment is on schedule and the security around the grounds has been stepped up. Is that all, My Lord?'

'No, make sure those two cretins are taught that failure will not be tolerated in future.'

A menacing smile appeared across Chamberlain's face as he replied.

'With pleasure, My Lord. I doubt they will make the same mistake again; not once I have educated them.' Chamberlain left with that smile still on his face. He was already starting to plan what means of education he would dish out to those two incompetent fools.

Normally Chamberlain would have gone straight after the men and cut a finger off each of them, but just at that moment he was not quite in the mood, besides he needed to go and finalise the new security plans that he was about to implement in anticipation of the shipment's arrival tomorrow. He still did not know exactly what the shipment contained, only that his master had made very clear that it was extremely important.

Outside the sky was starting to grow dark as he walked out of the front door and down to the guardhouse on the main gate. He checked that all of the guards were happy with the new rotations and then decided to go for a brisk walk around some of the grounds to make sure the patrols had taken up their new patterns. Satisfied that all was well he returned to the house with the intention of inspecting all of the house's internal sensors.

After what seemed like rather a long time, mainly due to having to replace two of the ground floor sensors he retired for the night. It was going to be a long day tomorrow and sleep was starting to take over. He would deal with the incompetent pair in the morning, by which time he would have decided upon a suitable punishment.

The next thing that Chamberlain was aware of was a tremendous explosion outside; he instinctively awoke and scrambled to get some clothes on. The first explosion was followed shortly afterwards by another.

He dressed quickly wondering what the hell was going on? Racing down the stairs towards the front door, only to be blown back across the hall floor as the door imploded. Blown apart by the shockwaves of the Lamborghini outside erupting into the night's skyline. His head crashed into the bottom step of the staircase and he passed out, not to recover for sometime.

Lord Norwood had also been awoken along with the rest of the household at Glympton by the sudden explosions. He had reached the top of the stairs moments after Chamberlain had been blown across the hall floor.

He could clearly hear the screams outside from some of the guards as chemical flames ravaged them; they were desperately throwing water upon themselves to quench the flames. Unfortunately for them water had a rather adverse affect when added to phosphorous.

Once outside Norwood took charge of the situation, he organised the remainder of his panicked mob and eventually managed to maintain some air of decorum. After he was sure that there were no more nasty devices to go off. He surveyed the scene.

Shattered bricks lay everywhere, the mangled carcases of his once stunning cars were strewn across the driveway and, the now pockmarked, croquet lawn.

His rage began to grow as he surveyed the scene of devastation. He had a pretty good idea who was responsible for this and would make sure that they would pay the ultimate price for daring to cross him.

Out of the corner of his eye he spied those two idiots from earlier that day, emerging from a pile of rubble. His rage now boiled over.

'You two, here now!' He roared at the pair. As they raced towards him, he took out a revolver from the back of his trousers.

The two men's faces dropped in surprise as he began to raise his arm; they tried to turn and reel away but it was too late. The two shots echoed around the now silent estate. The bodies of the two men slumped to the floor. It would be the last time that they would fail him. He never could suffer fools for long.

Chamberlain staggered out from the front door, he was covered in blood. There was a large gash to the side of his head that was oozing blood. He felt pretty dizzy, his ears were still ringing and he was struggling to focus, he collapsed at his master's feet.

Lord Norwood looked down upon him and half thought about putting a third bullet into his Head of Security but decided that even as angry as he was, Chamberlain could still be useful.

'You!' He shouted pointing to one of the guards. 'Get this man to the surgeon!' As the man rapidly approached Chamberlain's limp body, another guard appeared to help him carry the man's massive figure to the nearest of three garages which miraculously had survived the blasts.

They took one of the cars, that had survived the night's mayhem and after bundling Chamberlain's limp body on to the back seat they headed round to the hangars at the back of the house where the surgeon was busily patching up the injuries of those unfortunate enough to be in the vicinity of the explosions.

Lord Norwood spent much of the rest of the night organising his men to reconnect phone lines, and to generally set the estate to rights.

The bloodied corpses were tossed on to a pile in the centre of the garden at the rear of the house, doused in diesel and set alight. Luckily there was a slight easterly breeze that took the stench of burning flesh away from the house.

Daybreak was fast approaching as he finally managed to take five minutes for himself, only to be interrupted yet again. This time was the second attempt by the local constabulary to intervene in his affairs.

A police superintendent had arrived; most likely to complain about the lack of cooperation shown to his officers the first time they had tried to gain access on to the estate.

'Superintendent before you get going; as I already explained to your officers earlier, you have no jurisdiction here, and none of this is of your concern do I make myself clear.'

'Well if I might just say…' began the Supt.

'No you may not.' Producing a MoD warrant card, he continued on 'I believe this will give you a little more clarity. Now be gone Sir.' He could see the Supt. hesitate for a few seconds, Norwood's patience snapped. 'Name! Number! I shall be having words with your Commissioner regarding your behaviour.'

'No…um… no need for that Sir I can see you have everything

well in … err … hand here, Sir. We shall be on our way.' With a slightly begrudging look over Norwood's shoulder at the devastation behind, he finished making his apologies and left.

By 1100hrs the first of the shipment on huge articulated lorries had started to roll in through the main gates, they were directed around to the rear of the main house and from there they proceeded on down a gravel track for approximately 300 yards entering the two large, former World War II RAF hangars.

Lord Norwood was now in high spirits. The events of the previous night had been exceedingly tiresome and had certainly highlighted weaknesses in his security. Nevertheless the explosions had been centred around the main house so the hangars had not been damaged at all, therefore the cargo could be moved straight in.

He was sure that the explosions had just been a diversionary tactic, although at present he could not ascertain from where attention had been diverted. He had already ensured that Security had completed a sweep of the hangars before the trucks started to arrive, just to make sure that no one had left any surprises in the buildings.

Ollie and Gaz sat in their Land Rover a few miles away from Glympton parked up in a lay-by watching a monitor. Apart from carrying out the careful placement of the explosives the night before they had also placed a few wireless cameras around the grounds, and had taken a special interest in those two huge grass-covered hangars behind the house.

Being the best climber out of the two, Ollie had managed to climb up into the metal framework of each hangar to place a couple of small cameras which were well camouflaged against the steel roof. After all, a little bit of extra Intel may prove to be most useful in the future.

They had toyed with the idea of laying a few mines at the hangar entrances, unfortunately due to time constrains they had decided against this idea.

So far not much had been seen. Most of the night had been taken up with people clearing up after the two chemical experts, and they had witnessed Lord Norwood lose his temper and shoot two men in cold blood. The last half an hour had proved to be a hive of activity as the first of eight huge lorries rolled on to the estate and began to unload their covered cargo into the two hangars.

Armoured Land Rovers and wooden crates, which definitely

appeared to be of military origin, were all carefully unloaded from the lorries. The crates were then organised into different areas of the hangars and neatly stacked according to what they contained, unfortunately none were opened so Ollie and Gaz had no definitive idea as to what was inside.

The last two trucks left nothing to the imagination as to what their cargo contained. As soon as the tarpaulins covering the flatbed trailers were removed Ollie let out a loud gasp.

'Jesus, they're Comanche attack helicopters, is he planning on starting an invasion!'

'My helicopter knowledge isn't that great. What exactly are they?'

'Very similar to the Apache but these things employ stealth technology and can carry a greater payload.'

'Shit, these guys obviously mean business. Must have some serious mular behind them to get hold of all this stuff.'

'Yeah and some friends in very high places. You don't just walk off with one of those helicopters without permission let alone all the extras that go with them.' Ollie replied.

'Do you think the batteries were included or were they extra?' Gaz sarcastically asked.

'Twat! I don't think they are worried about that kind of stuff. You always have to be the one to take the joke too far.'

'Well if I didn't, I know I could count on you to do it for me.'

'Now I wish we had rigged the hangars to blow. Imagine the colours if all that went up! It would be mind-blowing man!'

'It would be cool, unfortunately we don't really have the equipment left for that. And somehow I don't think it will be so easy to get back in there again. Better ring Chris and let him know what's going on down here. I'm sure he will be very interested to find out about this, I wonder what he will make of it?'

'Hey Chris, how's thing's your end? There's been some major developments down here that we thought you should know about. This Norwood bloke has what looks like the start of a mini army down here. The truckloads of equipment just keep coming, full of stuff. And I mean serious kit. They just dropped off two Comanche helicopters, fully loaded.'

'Interesting, I thought he was planning something.'

'What do you want us to do?'

'Just keep an eye, and keep me informed if anything changes. I suspect he's planning an expedition. Oh, and boys, don't do anything stupid.' Chris said before hanging up.

'Us do something stupid, who does he think we are.' Ollie commented after Chris had hung up.

'I think he knows you better than you think. I suppose we had better nip off and get some scran fella, we may be here for quite some time and I don't know about you but I'm starving. The cameras are still working so we can monitor what goes on without actually being here for a bit. If anything happens we can return pretty quickly'

'Yeah I could eat an elephant plus I hate just sitting around doing nothing. At least you're used to it. You never do any work.'

'Speak for yourself why don't you? 'Mr I can't be arsed' I'm not the one who could make sleeping an Olympic sport!'

'Ha, you think lying on a beach in the sun tanning is a form of work.'

'I think you need to work on your banter mate.'

'Please … the extent of your banter is calling somebody gay.'

'Oh! I see, that's how it is, is it?'

'Well I thought I would just slip that one in there, felt it would be rude not too.'

'Mate I love your banter!'

With that they drove off to find a local shop, banter still in full flow.

Chapter Five: First Encounters

Chris, James and Rachel arose early at around 0400hrs. It was still dark outside so they made their way carefully down to the quayside below Ince castle. It wasn't a castle in the conventional sense of the word but a manor house with four towers, built in 1642 by Henry Killigrew.

Supposedly, according to local folklore he had kept four wives. One in each tower, each unbeknown to the others. The house had had some pretty notable owners over the centuries that followed including Mr H. R. Somerset, who's yacht had won the Fastnet race. The current owners of the manor were 1st Viscount Boyd of Merton and his wife. They had had kindly agreed for the RIB to be left at anchor below the castle a few days before.

James and Chris prepared the boat for the trip up to Martinstowe. Chris showed James *the surprises* that Ollie and Gaz had made just in case they needed them to dissuade anybody from following them. Ten clusters of three grenades, each attached to a small buoy, which would result in the grenades being suspended just below the water's surface. Perfect for taking out any vessel that tried to follow.

'We will have to be careful with these; considering we are right next door to a naval base. There won't be a lot of time once the first one goes off. I can guarantee all hell is going to break loose ashore if we do end up using these. I don't really fancy the challenge of evading the might of the Royal Navy. It was hard enough the last time.' Chris stated as he packed them away into the side locker of the RIB's centre console, referring to the last mock war games they had both been involved with where they narrowly scraped past a frigate with a two man mini-sub.

'These should be easily accessible if the need arises to use them. Right I think that is everything. Standby to cast-off.'

Turning the key in the ignition the two twin 300hp Mercury engines roared into life. Easing their way out of the harbour into the main flow of the Tamar Estuary, they made their way upstream towards the tributary that would take them to their final destination.

All seemed relatively quite, meandering their way along the Tamar. The water was very calm with no wind to speak of. Silent running was critical at this stage, which made for a rather slow journey. The horsepower was always there if required.

James was excited, but he had one of his nagging feelings so was apprehensively looking around from the bows of the boat.

The long black boat cut quite a menacing picture as it cruised through the river estuary. It was apparent from the expression on Chris' face that he was hoping to receive a little unwanted attention. Secretly he was itching to try out those cluster buoys, just to see exactly what 'the mixologists' had created this time. Unknown to him at this time he would soon get his wish a little further upstream.

Two men sent by Mr Leach sat huddled in the cockpit of their Antares 780, lying just off the China Fleet Golf Course, having noticed Flack organising his RIB below Ince Castle they had decided to intercept him and his co-conspirators up river away from Devonport Naval Yard.

On the deck sat an open crate containing two M-16 machine guns and adjacent to this lay a tactical rocket launcher to finish the job.

James spotted the Antares 780 as they passed under the Tamar Bridge. The boat had grabbed James' attention because it was the only boat on the water to have all the cabin lights on at that time, when most other people would be fast asleep. It was possible that the occupants were rising early to catch a favourable tide or needed to set out early in order to make a port by a certain time.

He decided to keep one eye on the vessel to see what would happen as they passed it. She certainly was no longer at anchor but just on tick-over holding position which again was odd, one would expect a vessel to be making way once the anchor was aboard, and there was no evidence of any fishing rods over the sides. Chris elected to give the vessel a wider berth than usual just in case.

Sure enough as the gap between the two vessels increased to around 20 cable lengths the Antares moved off from where it had been holding station, taking up the exact course as their boat.

So his Lordship has decided to engage us after all it seems. Chris thought to himself, a large smile spreading across his face.

James could see the sheer delight on Chris' face, a mischievous look, one he had seen all too often in the past. A telling look that Chris was about to wreak absolute havoc.

'Let's see how they cope with the mixologists' concoctions shall we?' Chris declared.

Chris slowed the boat right down in order to draw their pursuers in. James opened the locker and took out two of the cluster buoys.

'How long is the fuse on these things?'

'Not exactly sure to be honest, I think they said 5 seconds but you never can quite tell with those two. Just hold off for a bit, this may just turn out to be some innocent mariners and I don't want to blow up the wrong people. We will have to let them make the first move. It's likely to get a little hot under the collar if they are Norwood's men.'

The vessel behind closed to within 20 meters; a man appeared at the bow holding a machine gun and proceeded to open fire. Rachel took cover crouching behind the engines mounted on the transom. Projectiles from the blazing muzzle whizzed past the inflated tubes of the craft, one grazed James' ear.

'Son of a bitch! That's gonna leave a scar. I've had enough of this. Have some of that!' he exclaimed as he pulled the pin from one of the clusters and tossed it over the transom of the RIB.

A little over 5 seconds later the water around the buoy erupted skywards sending spray and shards of metal in all directions. Unfortunately it did not have the desired effect of taking out the pursuing boat, as it exploded a few seconds after the boat had passed the homemade mine.

'More speed! We need to increase the gap!' James shouted to Chris at the wheel.

'Hold on!' Chris replied as he opened up the throttle. He made a series of tight turns to both port and starboard, zigzagging to avoid the incoming shots, as the gap increased between the two vessels James chucked two more of the clusters over the side in quick succession, both caused the vessel following to take avoiding action and the second detonation must have damaged one of her twin screws, she started to slow.

'They appear to be breaking off, I think she's damaged. Shall we finish them off?' James shouted to Chris.

'No time, those explosions have awoken Devonport. It's time to make a hasty exit!'

Sure enough as soon as the first of the blasts had erupted all hell broke loose at the Royal Navy docks, sirens could be heard blaring out across the water, lights were flashing all across the quaysides, spotlights from the nearest frigates were starting to scan the water. Men were visibly scrabbling up ladders ducking through hatchways and scurrying up gangways to mount their gunnery positions.

This much action had not been seen on any British ship since that fateful day when HMS *Hood* accompanied by HMS *Prince of Wales* had engaged the *Bismarck* and *Prinz Eugen*, at the Battle of the Denmark Strait.

The Antares had dropped off completely now, obviously their pursuers did not have the stomach or the skill to face the Royal Navy and had slipped away into the night, which was exactly what Chris and James decided to do as well; before the Ridged Raiders, in the process of being launched, were dispatched from Devonport.

Chris slammed the throttle right down, the Mercury engines; which up until that point had just been purring let out a mighty roar, the bite of the twin turbines was so deep that the RIB lurched forwards. The bows reared out of the water like a motorbike pulling a wheelie before gradually flattening off as the boat reached the plane.

'Make for that large fog bank over there' James shouted pointing to the large misty formation just off the coast.

'It will cause havoc with the Navy's radar. Will give us a chance to disappear.'

The RIB hurtled across the water in excess of 55 knots towards the massive bank of fog and soon was consumed by it.

'It's a good thing the GPS still works otherwise I wouldn't know where the hell I'm going! Keep a look out for any anchored boats you two. How's the ear?'

'Mate at this speed and with this visibility you wouldn't have time to avoid anything. Stay mid channel or slow the fuck down. A lot better than the shoulder.' James replied as he took his hand away from his left shoulder to reveal a large bloody area on his jacket.

'Shit, Rachel, see if you can treat that. There's a first aid kit in the port side hatch of the console.'

'It's a lot worse that it looks; the bullet just nicked the top of my shoulder. Only a flesh wound; just get me a packet of that *QuikClot* field dressing. Should do the trick for now.'

They remained inside the thick fog hugging the coastline as they navigated the last mile up the Tavy tributary that would carry them the rest of the way to Martinstowe.

The dawn was beginning to break as the craft slowly glided up towards the boathouse at Martinstowe. The early morning mist rising up from the grass floated just above the meadows in front of the great house.

Chris skilfully manoeuvred the RIB into the boathouse closing the doors behind. Nobody would see the vessel from the water now.

Stepping off the boat on to the jetty, the dissipating fog swirled around their ankles creating a strange ghostly atmosphere as they walked up to the empty house. The only sound was that of the gravel path lightly crunching under foot.

Rachel shuddered slightly and moved closer to James as they approached the great Palladian house.

'With all this mist, this place gives me the creeps. It seems to have somehow taken on a dark persona.' She whispered to James.

'That's not surprising, it gives most people the creeps now that it is deserted. It has had a pretty murky past. Many curious things have happened here over the years and not all of them were that nice.' James mysteriously replied, causing Chris to burst into laughter.

'Don't pay any attention to him, he's just trying to wind you up. Middleton, leave the poor girl alone she's had quite enough excitement for one day. We wouldn't want her fainting into your arms now would we. Actually, don't answer that question. I know what you're like.' He said with a smile.

'Can't blame a chap for trying now can you?' James retorted, winking at Rachel.

She blushed a deep shade of red. 'Exactly what kind of girl do you think I am, Middleton?'

'I'm still trying to work that one out.' James said with a cheeky grin.

'Oh, please we are not on the latest dating show. There is no time for these shenanigans. We have work to do. It will only end badly for both of you. Especially you young lady, don't let him lead you astray. I know what he is like. Middleton! Focus! Which door do we need?'

'Oh yes, the one on the left down there, it's the old servants' entrance. It will be the easiest way to access the library. I just hope that we don't have to knock down too many walls to find the secret vaults.'

'Not necessary any more, having spoken at length to your uncle last night. According to him when the decision was taken to restore the library, it was felt that it would spoil the property if it were remodelled so they only replaced what was damaged. No walls to knock down, I'm afraid. Probably a good thing considering the state of your shoulder.'

'It's not that bad. Shame I was looking forward to the exercise. Ah well, I suppose we are on a rather tight schedule. It's still going to take a bit of time to actually locate what you want. Do we not need to go to the crypt first?'

'Not now that your uncle has told me roughly where the vault is located, or more precisely how to locate it. He was exceedingly helpful and has given me a good idea of which documents may be of interest to us.'

Approaching the servants entrance James pulled out a large bunch of keys from his coat pocket and after trying a few similar keys in the lock he finally found the one to fit.

The old iron key squeaked noisily as it turned in the rusty lock of the broad oak door. With a bit of encouragement from James in the form of a hefty push, the solid door finally swung back on its worn hinges to allow them access into the north wing of the great manor.

'I see they are obviously going for the authentic look then. One would have thought that they would have at least oiled the hinges a bit.' Chris said as the door swung open to reveal a smooth stone paved passageway, polished smooth by the centuries of servants' feet that had hustled and bustled along it, behind the scenes, to ensure that the household ran like clockwork.

Following the dimly lit passageway they made their way along the servants area, until they reached a door that led into the main part of the wing itself. The first room inside the wing was the billiard room that had been lovingly restored to its former glory complete with beautiful ornately gilded cornicing.

From here they entered another long passageway, in contrast to the billiard room, which had an oak floor, this corridor had a deep red patterned carpet and was richly decorated along one wall with huge tapestries that had been painstakingly woven. The other wall had large sash windows installed each with its own set of full length wooden shutters that when drawn back settled into alcoves around the edges of the windows so as to appear as if they were just part of the wall itself.

There were two doors leading off from the passageway. The first of which opened into what would have been known as the smoking room; the second was the entrance into the library.

'I thought you said that this place was deserted? It seems really clean in here for somewhere that is not used.' Rachel commented as she admired the interior of the great house.

'It may not be in use but the estate still maintains it. I think there are plans to divide it up into flats but I'm not sure whether my Uncle can bring himself to split it, so for now it is maintained and cleaned on a regular basis.' James replied.

Entering the library Chris gasped in disbelief. He had expected the library to be large but not as vast as the sight that lay before him. So many books carefully displayed on exquisitely crafted oak cases, running around three of the four sides of the room stretching the full height from floor to ceiling. Each side had its own sliding ladder in order to access the highest shelves. It was very apparent that a great deal of trouble had been taken to restore this room; huge amounts of money had clearly been spent to replace the books that had been lost in the last fire, many of which had been rare first editions.

'Christ there must be thousands of books here' Chris exclaimed as he tried to take in the room.

'God only knows how many, I tried to count them once but lost my place and gave up.' James interjected, smiling as he watched his friend digest this snippet of information. 'Although I am not sure they are all on display here, there is a special collections room somewhere on the second floor, for the rarest books and the ones that just won't fit on the shelves.'

'These must be worth an absolute fortune!' Chris replied at last.

'Don't remind me, sometimes it almost makes me cringe at the idea of how much was spent here. The mind really does boggle. Nevertheless it is a fantastic collection. Speaking of which, what exactly are we looking for? I presume this is one of those cliché moments when you pull a book from the case which triggers a secret door to be revealed.' James jokingly said.

'Not far off, according to your uncle, we need to find five books on the east wall. Behind these books are located what looks like brass pins that at first glance appear to support the shelf above, in fact these specific pins are buttons which need to be pushed in a specific order. Once that is done I am of the understanding that a section of this bookcase will open up.

'The books in the order we want are: *Oliver Twist* by Charles Dickens, *Treasure Island* by Robert Louis Stevenson, *The Iliad* by Homer, *The Two Gentlemen of Verona* by William Shakespeare and *The Golden Treasury* by Francis T. Palgrave. Obviously the designer took great care in creating a locking mechanism that minimised the risk of the room being discovered by chance. These books are scattered throughout the middle section of the case on the east wall, from the very bottom right to the penultimate shelf. They are going to take some finding; there must be over 10,000 books in this section alone. Your uncle would not be any more specific than that for understandable reasons.'

'We had best get cracking then. At least they are not scattered through the entire collection.' James said as he clapped his hands together.

'Rach, make yourself useful and drag that ladder over here; we are definitely going to need it at some point.' Chris said smiling at his cousin. Returning the smile with a frown at the insinuation that she wasn't useful, she obliged and dragged the ladder from its position close to the southern end of the bookcase across into the middle.

It took almost forty-five minutes to locate all of the pins behind the corresponding books, as the last of the pins was pushed back into the rear of the bookcase a faint click was heard emanating from behind the case itself and the central section retreated into the wall by an inch to reveal the outline of the entrance to the secret vault.

Chris put his hand against the outlined door, expecting that it would be stiff after years of disuse. He was about to put all his weight against it. However, to his great surprise the door had already started to fall back, it floated open as if it was just suspended in the air by some unseen force.

'Wow this thing is a light as a feather, such a smooth action. St Aubyn really knew his stuff.' Chris stated.

'You mean Wren, James Piers St Aubyn only built the Chapel. It was the great cathedral builder himself who was responsible for the original library, so I assume he created this marvel of engineering.' James said correcting his friend.

Moving into the dark void, which had been produced by the bookcase's departure they stepped around the edge of the case and entered the inner sanctum of the hidden vault. Rachel flicked on a flashlight so they could see what lay inside the dark sanctuary.

Scanning the flashlight around the room they discovered that the walls appeared to be lined with lead and along them were row upon row of locked boxes similar to the kind of safety deposit boxes one would usually associate with a bank. Upon each box was a small circular brass plaque with a number engraved upon it.

'So many … any ideas as to which ones we are interested in?' Rachel asked as she indicated the rows of boxes along the walls.

'Numbers twenty-seven and fifty-eight contain documents recommended to me by James' uncle. He believes they will be of significant interest.' Chris replied. 'The combinations to the locks are 33,62,54 and 7 for number twenty-seven and 8,37,64 and 17 for the other. Rachel can I borrow your iPhone? I promised that the originals would remain inside the vault so we are going to have to take photos.'

After opening the boxes Rachel handed her phone to Chris whilst James started to pull out the contents of the two safes. After copying the reams of documents to the memory of the phone, a process that took almost an hour, the documents were returned to the safety of their boxes.

Returning to the library Chris followed the instructions he had been given about how to reseal the vault. They waited for the vault door to glide back into place before heading off to the crypt.

'I hope you aren't creeped out by the dead, there are quite a few tombs down there.' James said.

Exiting the north wing James locked the door and they walked around the southern end of the house and continued on round to the east side where the chapel had been constructed. It was a small chapel, topped with a beautiful tall spire.

The south entrance to the chapel took the form of a flight of steps leading up from the small grassy bank to the chapel itself. The door leading to the crypt was built into the side of these steps.

James found the key for the door on the same set he had used to open up the main house. Due to the doorway's low height they each had to duck down through the door as they entered.

The dust lay thick on the stone steps that led down; their footprints were left behind on the steps as they descended into the sacred house of the dead. Cobwebs hung from the walls and the ceiling of the passageway.

Rachel coughed as the disturbed dust that now filled the air caught in the back of her throat as she inhaled, before brushing a stray cobweb from her eyes. The air in the crypt had taken on a musty smell.

James found the light switch on the wall at the side of the passage as he entered the rectangular room. Inside, five large stone tombs were lined up in the middle of the room. Each belonging to one or other of the earliest Barons of Martinstowe.

Along the walls were stone plaques indicating where their spouses or children had been placed to rest along with the more recent Barons.

'We are looking for the tomb of the first Baronet of Martinstowe, Sir Andrew Michael Heywood. His tomb supposedly contains a few artefacts that we may need later.' Chris said.

'Are those the one's that had been brought here from the Temple Church in London?' Asked Rachel.

'The very same.' Replied Chris.

After wiping away the dust from the encrusted tombs they found the one they were looking for, beautifully carved Carraran marble engraved with the coat of arms of the First Baronet and below it the family motto '*Sub pace, copia*'.

'What does that motto mean?' Chris asked as he read out the inscription.

'Under peace, plenty. I think.' Rachel said.

'Yes, very good. How did you know that?' James asked.

'Just remember, from doing Latin at school.'

'I'm impressed, wouldn't have had you down as a classicist.'

'I'm sure there are many things that would surprise you about myself.'

'Um, if you two have quite finished, a little help with this lid wouldn't go amiss? It hasn't been opened since the great man was laid to rest so I suspect it is going to be quite a task to shift it.' Chris said trying to get James' attention.

'Three, two, one, heave.' The lid didn't budge an inch as they strained against the hefty stone slab.

'Rach give us a hand, this is proving harder to move than anticipated. Okay, ready? On the count of one; three, two, one…' A grating sound could be heard as very slowly the stone top started to slide over the edges of the tomb.

Little by little the lid slid across, twice they had to stop and take a breather. As the stone slab slid enough to break the seal of the tomb a small hiss of air was heard escaping from the tomb. Eventually they managed to slide the lid across just enough to peer inside.

The corpse of the lord looked so peaceful even though his dignity had just been disturbed for the first time in several centuries. His arms still lay down by his sides, head resting on a silk pillow that remarkably had remained virtually intact. Along with the corpse they found three small bundles wrapped in linen. Two lay down by the right hand side of the lord and the other rested upon his chest. Not wanting to unwrap them just yet Chris carefully lifted them out of the tomb and placed them into a small blue rucksack.

'Right, now we just have to replace this lump.' Chris said pointing at the lid. It took ten minutes to finally shift it back into position. Before they left the crypt Chris insisted on them saying a short prayer, as was his custom.

Being a devout Roman Catholic he felt slightly guilty at having just desecrated a tomb. He had the feeling that they needed to once again restore an element of peace to the sacred burial ground. As they finished their moment of respect he made the sign of the cross across his chest. Making their way back up the steps they walked out into the bright sunlight outside.

'I have arranged to meet Jack and Michael here, so we are going to have to wait until they arrive. Hopefully we will not have to wait for too long.' He said to the others. 'You'll have to forgive Michael's demeanour, he is a bit of *a Mon*.'

"A Mon'? What the hell is that?' Rachel asked slightly baffled by the slightly random terminology.

'Oh that, how would I describe it. It's a Shropshire thing. Sort of means he's a bit of a lad, you know, he sometimes comes across as being a bit overly macho.'

'Oh, one of them. Great.' Rachel said trying not to roll her eyes too much as she replied. 'I presume that's where he's from is it?'

'Yeah somewhere around that area. Don't think I have ever asked him exactly where. They are a bit of a rare lot down there from my experiences.'

They found a few benches in the gardens and relaxed in the sun waiting for Chris' friends to arrive.

Chapter Six: Chamberlain

Lord Anthony Norwood slammed his fist against the desk that stood in the centre of his office, causing the whole thing to shake violently. He could not fathom how Flack and Middleton had managed to elude his men for a second time.

'Explain to me Mr Leach how you and your men are incapable it seems of being able to complete even the simplest of tasks!' His eyes bored into the face of his Chief Intelligence Officer as he openly expressed his anger.

'Well … um, My Lord they were prepared for us and …' He started to say before trailing off as his master erupted.

'Get out!' Roared Lord Norwood. 'I don't want to hear excuses, I want results! I will deal with them myself. Clearly, if you want something done correctly. One must do it oneself! Get out of my sight! And find Chamberlain, Now!' He bellowed at the weaselly man.

Mr Leach almost tripped over his own feet in his attempt to beat a hasty retreat from his master's office before something really nasty happened to him. He had seen what his master was capable of when he was in one of those moods and he didn't want to stick around to find out if it would happen to him. He valued his life far too much to risk fanning the flames of his master's rage any further.

He quickly sought out Chamberlain, who was in one of the hangars preparing for their long awaited expedition. Nervously he addressed the man.

'His Lordship requests your presence.' The man really intimidated him. He was a real savage, and extremely sadistic.

'Failed again, have we?' A cruel smile spread across Chamberlain's face as the rhetoric left his lips.

Not wanting to get embroiled in Chamberlain's favourite new game of baiting him, Mr Leach shrank away from the man. Chamberlain really put the fear of God into him, far more than his master ever could. Mr Leach wasn't even sure if he was human, the man felt little, if any pain and took great pleasure from inflicting it on others. If there ever were such a thing as a definitive psychopath then Chamberlain would be it. Mr Leach had once witnessed Chamberlain torture a man, it had not been a pretty sight. The event had haunted Leach's dreams for the next few weeks.

Chamberlain was a master of the old arts. One of his favourite torture techniques was to tightly wrap his victim in strands of wire; their soft flesh would protrude through any gaps in the wire, which he would then slice off one piece at a time. It was extremely painful and could be maintained for weeks before a victim would die. During that period his victims would tell him whatever he wanted to know.

Chamberlain would taunt them by running the edge of his blade across the wire that bound them. He would watch the fear in their eyes as the sound of the metal blade of his knife grated along the wire registered, the whites of their eyes becoming ever more petrified.

Eventually every one would break down pleading for the pain to end. Not that he ever obliged their request for mercy. He enjoyed it too much for that. Even if he knew they had no more information to give.

It was under this constant fear that Mr Leach operated, a fear that one day his mistakes would give him a direct ticket to the wrong side of Chamberlain's blade.

Chamberlain completed the task he had been doing and headed off towards his Lordship's office in the main house. He knocked once at the door and waited to hear the familiar tones of his master's stern voice. 'Enter.' He opened the door and walked through into the study.

'Ah, Chamberlain good to see you. I hope all is on schedule.' His master's voice softened slightly as he smiled greeting his right hand man.

'Sit down, we have much to discuss.'

'Thank you, My Lord' Chamberlain said as he settled himself down into one of the two red leather armchairs positioned in front of his master's walnut desk.

'Yet again Mr Leach has failed to take care of Middleton and Flack. Nevertheless he has acquired information that they are headed towards St Michael's Mount, so we will deal with them once and for all on the island. This may be to our advantage as I was already of the belief that one of the books we are searching for could well be hidden somewhere on the island. I can't be completely sure but I have read references alluding to this.

'We shall dispose of them and take possession of the book at the same time. I shall oversee this operation personally to make sure all goes to plan. You will accompany me. I want you to select a handful of men for the task. Make sure you have enough equipment to carry this out. Prepare three jeeps for the journey. Oh, and teach Mr Leach the lesson of what it means to fail. Don't kill him; he does have his uses and therefore I may yet still require his services. Is that clear?' Lord Norwood finished addressing Chamberlain and waited for a reply.

'Crystal clear, Sir. Will you require anything else?' Hoping that he would be allowed to bring some of his toys with him, ever since he had learnt of Middleton and Flack a great desire had grown inside him to torture those two. Two men who seemed to be hell bent on meddling in his master's affairs, he wanted to see the fear in their eyes before he dispatched them into the abyss.

'Yes, bring your toys, I would like to find out what Flack knows about our plans and how big his network is.' Lord Norwood added, spotting that slightly baleful look on Chamberlain's face.

Chamberlain felt a wave of pleasure spreading over his body at his master's request. The possibility that his daydreams may finally be enacted filled him with delight. He considered those men to be as skilled as himself at causing chaos.

'It shall be done, My Lord.'

'Good, be ready by tomorrow morning. I want to put an end to those two as soon as possible. You may go.' His master finished and turned his attention back to the notes he had been working on at his desk.

Chamberlain left the study. First he was going to seek out Mr Leach. He knew he was going to enjoy re-educating him; he loved seeing the little man's facial contortions whenever their paths crossed.

He caught up with the man in the gatehouse of the estate. As he entered the building Mr Leach's face dropped; he could sense that for whatever reason Chamberlain was there, it was not a good one.

'Leach, give me your hand!' A thin twisted smile appeared across Chamberlain's face as he snarled at the man.

'No please, I can do better. I won't make a mistake again. Please, I beg you.' The man replied in a shaky voice. His mind was now running through all the gruesome outcomes that could happen. His face had almost turned completely white, as the blood drained away from his face. Fear was his master now.

'Don't be a fool. You had your chances. Give me your hand before I decide to take something else.' He snapped.

'No I shan't.' Leach replied defiantly.

'You two men! Hold him!' Chamberlain exclaimed turning to the two guards in the gatehouse.

After a small scuffle with Mr Leach they managed to take hold of the little man and held out his left arm. The man was visibly shaking as dread spread over him.

Chamberlain produced a small pair of bolt cutters from his pocket, Mr Leach tried to wriggle out of the two men's grasp but they were too strong. Escape was futile. He pleaded in vain but Chamberlain ignored the man's cries. With a single movement he put the jaws of the cutters around the base of Leach's ring finger, as the blades tightened down around the finger Mr Leach let out a blood-curdling howl.

The metallic sound of the jaws scrapping, as they bit into the flesh of the man's finger was clearly audible, before they met the bone in the middle. There was an ugly piercing crack as the razor sharp blades cleaved the bone, blood spurting on to the carpet of the gatehouse.

The finger dropped to the floor with a gentle thud. Leach had passed out. His body drooping between the two guards, the bloody stump on his left hand now just oozed blood as it started to clot.

'Take him to the surgeon. He's making a mess all over the carpet.' Commanded Chamberlain.

The two men had to drag Leach's limp body out of the gatehouse and across to the surgeon's tent that had been erected on the front lawn of the estate. It had been set up to deal with the casualties from the night of the explosions. Lord Norwood had originally decided it would be useful to employ the surgeon on a temporary basis for the upcoming expedition; and it was a fortunate coincidence that he had been at the house making preparations for that expedition when all hell had broken loose.

The surgeon looked up from behind an operating table as they entered. He was just finishing off redressing a wound for one of the security staff that had taken some shrapnel in his leg, courtesy of the *Mixologists*.

'Try to keep this one clean.' The surgeon said as he turned to see the new arrivals. 'I see Chamberlain has finally been unleashed upon Mr Leach. Put him on that table over there and I'll see what can be done with him once I've finished here.' The surgeon said bluntly gesturing towards another cold steel table in the centre of the tent surrounded by two trolleys laden with small silver trays adorned by surgical instruments.

The two men nodded and rather laboriously slung Mr Leach upon the slab before leaving the tent to return to their duties.

Chapter Seven: The Mount

Jack St Aubyn and Michael Collins arrived at Martinstowe shortly after noon. They had travelled up from Jack's apartment at Fort Picklecombe after receiving Chris' text.

Jack was in his early twenties; he was about 5'10", with short dark hair and a rather bushy gingery brown beard. He had proudly been cultivating it for the last few months. Jack had toyed with the idea of getting rid of it when it was still in the itchy stages of growth, but he was glad he had put up with the slight irritation as he thought it made him look rather dashing. He was a very energetic young man full of life and bright ideas.

The one thing he lacked in comparison to the others was life experience and could sometimes come off as being quite naïve, a characteristic that both Chris and James were sometimes secretly envious of. They both wished to be able to see the world with the same rose-tinted view that Jack had.

In contrast to Jack, Michael Collins was a hardened veteran in his late forties; he had an extremely gruff exterior and wouldn't take any shit. He still held the rank of Regimental Sergeant Major, and commanded a great deal of respect from all he worked alongside. The officers respected him because he kept the lesser ranks in check and trained them hard. The squaddies respected him because he was almost one of the lads and try as they might they could never quite get one over on him. He knew every dirty trick in the book.

They met Chris, James and Rachel just outside Martinstowe House in the courtyard and after the briefest of introductions and hello's they all piled into Jack's Range Rover and drove off down towards Saint Michael's Mount.

It was not a particularly long journey down to the historic landmark, but it was long enough for Chris and James to make a start reading through the documents that they had copied from the vault. Most of the pages seemed to be part of financial ledgers, legal papers and so forth. On the surface nothing really seemed to jump out as being of any real interest.

'Wait! Go back a page. There it is, a reference to *The Glove* I've seen that in here already. What is it?' James asked.

'To be honest apart from what your father has already told me, I know very little about them. Hopefully we may be able to build up a picture of what they are if we keep reading. There must be some more information on them in here somewhere.' Working their way diligently through the papers, a picture started to be built up.

It appeared that it was an organisation that referred to itself simply as *The Glove* and had existed in some shape or form for centuries. They had been responsible for financing a number of archaeological digs, and more intriguingly had influenced regimes in a number of countries around the world. Even financing the odd coup in order to have a pocket government.

One could have almost replaced the name *The Glove* with the CIA, but unlike the CIA they did not appear to be controlled by any particular country. They had obviously played countries off against each other for their own benefit. Not much was available on their origins or for that matter what their current status was.

James found a few lines talking about their structure during the second and third crusades and a link to the Templars so he guessed that they had possibly sprung up around that period. They certainly had had ties to the Church at some point. He really hoped they didn't have too much to do with the Knights Templar, there were far too many myths surrounding the Knights.

'There isn't anything really conclusive here. It is certainly interesting and worth further investigation. They cover their tracks very well.' He said to Chris.

'Yes, your father said they are rather elusive. Whatever they are, they are certainly well connected and have vast resources, a dangerous organisation to become involved with by the looks of things. They must have been in the process of searching for something. Maybe they were looking for parts of the book, although maybe something else. Not really sure that the Antarctic would be a likely place to find part of it. Financing expeditions such as Scott's to the Antarctic and Fawcett's to the Amazon is no mean feat.'

'My father did seem to think that the book at Saint Michael's Mount was part of a set. I would hate to think what they could do if they had access to the whole set. That must be what they were searching for. We may have to be rather careful how we proceed from now on.' James replied.

'They must have had dealings with the Royal Geographic Society to fund those expeditions. That may be a good place to start.' Jack chipped in.

'You may be on to something there, Jack. I think it would be worth sending Michael off on a little fact-finding mission to London. I would very much like to know more about this elusive organisation. I suggest starting at the Royal Geographic Society and see where it takes you … Jack we've got time to take a slight detour via Truro to drop him at the train station haven't we?' Chris asked.

'Yeah no probs.'

'Anywhere else I should try?' Michael asked.

'The National Archives at Kew might be worth a visit, although I wouldn't hold your breath this organisation does seem to lurk in the shadows a bit. They have gone out of their way to minimise their profile. Begging the question of how they ended up in these papers?' Chris mused looking at James.

'Don't start down that path, I do know that the family were involved in the East India Trade Company, another rather vile organisation. So potentially they had dealings.' James bluntly stated with a slight grimace.

'Hmmm, anyway Michael while you are in London you might try to get in contact with Louis St Clair. If he is available he will definitely be able to help. I'll give you his number.' Chris said as he took out a pen and scribbled down a number on a piece of paper from a small black notebook he carried in his jacket pocket. Tearing out the sheet he handed it to Michael.

After dropping Michael off at Truro outside the station they continued on their way down to the Mount. They pulled up and parked in a car park in the small Cornish village of Marazion, situated on the mainland just across the water from the Mount. Unfortunately because the time was 1500hrs they had missed the afternoon tidal window to cross the causeway, which was only uncovered at low water, that allow pedestrian access to the tiny island.

'We may as well go and find a pub to get something to eat. Having missed the afternoon tide to cross over to the Mount we are going to have to wait for it to recede again.' Chris said. 'The next low is at 2305hrs, the causeway is accessible about 2 hours either side of low water. Jack did you remember to bring the key to get into the underground railway on the island or are we going to have to break in?'

'No, I have got it, but you do realise that the railway was never designed to take passengers. It's a crazy steep tunnel.' Jack replied.

'Yes, I wasn't planning on riding it, or using it to get into the castle. I did however think it might be a useful escape route if we need to make a hasty exit. I don't fancy having to do a swan dive off the walls into the sea to get out in a hurry if it all goes wrong.' Chris said with an amused twinkle in his eyes.

Walking through the village they found The Godolphin Arms Hotel. It was a beautiful Georgian building with a very impressive exterior of stone cornicing and a porch supported by conic pillars, the striking exterior was mirrored by the lavish decorations inside.

They found a comfortable booth in a corner of the bar, next to a roaring log fire. James went up to order some drinks as the others sat back, relaxed and flicked through the menus on the tables.

They ordered some food from the waitress, who brought their drinks over and then returned to the bar to send the order through to the kitchens.

'We may as well continue looking through those papers, we must be able to find a bit more information about *The Glove* in them. We've got about six hours to kill before we will be able to cross the causeway. Jack are there any other ways we could quickly and easily get out of the castle if the need arises?'

'Not really apart from the main gates, because it's built into the cliff the only other option would be to rappel down the cliff and into the sea. But where you would go from there would be tricky. You would have to swim round to the harbour and that would take far too long. I think the tunnel will have to do, but I'm not looking forward to using it.' Jack replied.

James and Rachel had started to get through the documents on two iPads, having moved them across from the iPhone during the drive down. The documents were much easier to study on the larger screens of the iPads. Chris continued to talk to Jack about the layout of the castle on the mount.

'We have found a few more references to *The Glove* and they definitely did have dealings with the East India Trade Company at some point.' James said looking up from the iPad. 'Should there be some mention of where the book at the Mount is located in here?'

'I guess it might be in the second set of documents we copied. Rach you've read some of them, have you found anything?' Chris asked.

'No, nothing conclusive. There is a piece of text here about the inside of the chapel, it mentions two secret passages, one leads down to a dungeon. And I'm not sure where the other one goes, the rest of the text is illegible.' She replied.

'Great more treasure hunting. Why can't they just have a big sign saying 'Secret passage' this way?'

'Then it wouldn't be a secret, would it stupid.' Chris sarcastically put in.

'I know where they are.' Jack piped up. 'They aren't really secret, just not very well known by many people.'

'Why didn't you say so earlier, my dear boy?' Chris said delighted by the news.

'You didn't ask.' Jack replied. 'One's in the chapel, just behind a statue of St Mary, and leads down into the Crypt, the other one goes from the Keep and joins up with the underground railway. If I was a betting man I would expect that it is the one in the chapel that we will need to use to find the book that you are looking for.'

'The chapel it is then. Ah food's here, I'm famished. May as well tuck in everybody, it's gonna be a long night.' James said as the waitress began to bring the food out from the kitchen.

The sun was slowly dipping below the horizon as they finalised the details of their plan to get in and out of the castle. James was a bit of a stickler for minutia and liked to plan things down to the last detail. In his experience the less that was left to chance the better; it reduced the risk of anything untoward happening.

'We should make a move back to the 4x4 quite soon and sort the gear out.' James said as they finished ironing out the last few intricacies for the evening ahead.

The sky had begun to darken as day gave way to night; the view out across the water towards the Mount had an almost magical appearance. The gentle lapping of the sea against the pebbles on the beach was the only sound to be heard along the deserted shoreline.

The full moon had already begun to gradually arch across the dark sky, shimmering silvery patterns from the moonlight danced across the wavelets below. Every now and again these dancing mirrors ceased in the blink of an eye as a cloud passed in front of the bright silver disc in the sky, the only clue as to its whereabouts was a dim ghostly silhouette around the fringes of the passing cloud.

The causeway connecting Marazion to the Mount was beginning to appear above the crests of the wavelets. To anyone who didn't know that the sea was receding from Mount Bay it would have appeared as if the seabed itself was gradually rising up out of the water as if mother earth was shifting slightly in her sleep.

Back at the car park the four companions were busy packing Bergens with climbing gear, which might be needed for the descent down into those dark tunnels of the underground railway should the need arise for a quick escape. Along with this equipment were four sets of army webbing, bulging with ammo clips and a few grenades.

'Chris, are those grenades really necessary?' Jack asked. He hated the idea that any serious damage might be caused to the historic seat of his family.

'We probably won't need them but as a last resort they may come in handy.' James said trying to put Jack's mind at ease by assuring him that the grenades would only be used as an absolute last resort. However, Jack had his doubts about that. He was well aware of what could happen in the heat of the moment and so remained sceptical.

From the guns that James had procured at Cotehele, he issued an SA 80 to each of them, the FN P90 he kept for himself. He and Chris also took a brace of Glock 22s. Finally they smeared Camo cream over their faces and any other bits of skin showing, to help break up their profile and reduce the effect of moonlight reflecting off their skin. After all they were about to break in and wanted to reduce the likelihood of being spotted. Heaving the rucksacks up on to their backs the four set off through the now deserted streets and out into the darkness towards the causeway and beyond to the Mount.

Lord Norwood and his cohort had arrived at Marazion just after 1900hrs. Not wanting to wait for the tide to drop they had found a local boatman to ferry them across to the island.

Norwood had no idea whether or not Flack and Co were already on the island but he decided to stage some sort of ambush inside the castle once he was sure they had acquired the book, having failed in his own efforts to find any further information as to where the book was hidden he had resolved to hedge his bets that Flack already knew where it was.

His intention was to steal it from Flack and kill another bird with the same stone by disposing of the meddling party at the same time. He would be able to continue to locate the rest of the books without having to worry about any further interference from Flack or his companions.

Norwood carefully positioned his men up on top of the barbican and along the surrounding battlements of the castle. The ambush now set. They waited in the deepening gloom for their quarry to appear.

The causeway was still wet underfoot as Chris, James, Rachel and Jack picked their way across the pockmarked concrete trying to avoid the deep puddles of seawater that had pooled in the uneven surface of the causeway. Every now and then the moonlight would reflect off the black gun metal of their SA 80s.

They had brought some head torches but hoping to maintain a low profile they didn't use them, the bright moonlight was enough for them to see where they were going. Had they turned the head torches on, Norwood's men would have been able to see the lights bouncing around, like tiny globes suspended on invisible strings, in the blackness; as it was the team reached the quayside undiscovered by their awaiting foe.

They worked their way stealthily creeping along the edge of the path leading up to the massive dark granite structure looming ominously above them on the hilltop. They stuck to the shadows moving like cats hunting for rats, breaking cover only when they had to dart across a moonlit patch to the safety of the next patch of darkness. They were careful not to make a sound, talking in muffled voices when Jack pointed out which part of the castle they needed to head for.

The silhouette of the outer gate that they needed to go through, in order to get into the courtyard at the heart of the castle, from which they would then be able to access the chapel, gradually emerged out of the gloom.

The architecture and skill that had been employed in creating the great fortress was remarkable, the stone masons had literally carved the castle out of the granite cliff and where this hadn't been possible they had quarried granite from other parts of the island to complete the structure.

It was probably one of the most impregnable castles in the entire country, certainly one of the most visually imposing to any besieger. The other remarkable thing about the castle was the underground tunnel connecting the castle with the port, which meant that the castle would have been self-sufficient had it ever come under siege.

It was so impressive that during the Second World War the Nazis had thought that it would have been the perfect location for Himmler and the Waffen SS to base themselves once Britain was under their control. They weren't just interested in its strategic importance but also because of its links to ley lines and druids. Himmler was obsessed by *Grail Law* and believed that St Michael's Mount may hold the key to its existence, which was why the castle had not been targeted during the bombing raids on the neighbouring town of Penzance. Fortunately for the St Aubyn family the allies had prevailed and the striking citadel had remained as the historic seat of the family.

James and Chris remained alert as they entered the main gates, they both acknowledged the need to not be complacent as the group skirted around the outside of the courtyard towards the chapel, the problem with entering a castle was that once inside you were encased by the battlements and were then at a massive tactical disadvantage, especially to those positioned high up above on the battlements. These were designed specifically for the purpose of defence; an elevated position gave a huge advantage from which to counter-attack. Any enemy would then be trapped in a small confined space, easy pickings for defenders firing down upon them from the safety of the walls. It would be virtually impossible to survive, let alone win, against those odds.

Keeping their eyes peeled for any sign of potential threat, they carried on around the courtyard. Lord Norwood had always managed to have some sort of presence thus far. So it was more than likely that he would have one here as well, particularly as this was one of the most crucial stages in the game of cat and mouse they were playing.

The book had great value to both sides and it was highly unlikely with the stakes so high that his Lordship would pass up the opportunity to get his hands on the artefact. Whatever the ultimate goal of *The Glove* was. It was becoming increasingly clear that the book was a central part of their final objective.

Jack took the keys out of his pocket to open up the chapel; turning the cast-iron key in the lock of the thick old oak door. There was a clunk as he lifted the latch and opened the door. The iron hinges creaked as he pushed the door aside.

James took a final glance around the battlements surrounding the courtyard before he followed the rest of the group inside. He thought that he caught a glimpse of a sliver of light reflecting off a shaft of metal sticking up from behind a piece of stonework on the fortifications above him, but as he looked again a cloud obscured the moon and he was no longer able to see what it might have been. Deciding it was just the moonlight glistening off some wet stonework he disappeared inside.

High up from his position on the barbican Lord Norwood smiled, watching as the small group below entered the chapel. He was amused that they had unknowingly walked straight into his hands. He was delighted, his foe had no idea that he was about to seize his long awaited prize, right out of their hands and be dispatched straight off to the depths of Tartarus shortly afterwards.

His men were in the perfect positions to annihilate Middleton and Flack along with their insignificant companions, leaving the way clear for his organisation to proceed to the next stage.

Rubbing his hands together with glee he gave out his final instructions to his men. Kill Middleton and the two younger companions. Capture Flack at all costs. He wanted to save him for Chamberlain. He was sure that Flack was the man in charge and it was vital to find out what he knew; if it came to the point that he looked like escaping then kill Flack too. He would be better off dead than to continue being a thorn in the side of the brotherhood.

Jack showed Chris the door inside the chapel that would lead the team down a stone staircase into a labyrinth of tunnels below the chapel to where the book was located. As they made their way along the stone tunnels, through the odd cobweb, passing many skulls and bones pilled in small alcoves cut into the rock on either side of the tunnels.

Taking a narrow passage off to the right of the main tunnel they entered a small circular antechamber. The chamber had several stone panels built into the surrounding stone, evidently some of the tombs of the St Aubyn family.

'Do you know if any of these tombs have crusader connections,

Jack?' James asked as he looked around all the ancient tombs.

'Well, there are actually quite a few, but I suspect that this is the one that is the most likely, as the family legend has always been that he had Templar connections, not that anybody has ever managed to prove it.' Jack replied pointing to one, which had some peculiar religious markings on it, much like those on the Shugborough Tomb.

'From the odd occasion that I have seen pictures of Templar markings in my father's notes in the past, these certainly look like crusader markings. But I never really paid too much attention to his notes. Wish I had now.' James said as he inspected the tomb.

'I'm afraid you are going to have to break this open. From what we've read the book is most likely inside; buried with the knight who had been entrusted with its safe keeping when the purge of the Knights Templar began on Friday 13th October 1307.' Rachel said.

'If you must, but try not to damage it too much.' Jack replied hoping that they wouldn't completely destroy the tomb.

Chris unslung his rifle from his shoulder and using the butt like a battering ram smashed his way through the stone panel. The panel took some punishment before the stone started to crack and inevitably gave way completely, shattering into pieces of rock and dust. James helped him to pull out the remaining lumps of stone and as the dust settled Rachel shone a torch inside. The once mighty crusader lay inside, his bones undisturbed since his burial all those centuries ago.

'I thought you were going to be careful. Forgive us for disturbing your rest.' Jack muttered under his breath.

'Sorry Jack, we don't have the luxury of being delicate. I want to be in and out of here as soon as possible.' James replied as he pulled the last of the stone out of the way.

A huge sword lay at the side of the knight's remains along with a shield across his chest; at first there was no sign of anything that resembled a book. It was only when they removed the ancient shield from the crusader's chest that they found what they were looking for.

The book, or something that looked like it may be a book, had been placed underneath delicately wrapped in a linen cloth. Carefully replacing the shield back on top of the knight's chest with as much respect as possible, they left with the book. Retracing their steps back along the tunnels up into the chapel.

'Jack, is it possible to get to the underground railway without leaving the buildings?' James asked. 'Can we use that stairway?' He added pointing to some stairs at the far end of the chapel from where they stood.

'There is a way, but it is not a very direct route, those lead up into the bell tower. There is an exit part way up leading out on to the battlements, which can be used to access the Keep. You could then descend into the kitchens, and use the other secret passage that I mentioned to get into the tunnel but it would be far quicker to go straight across the courtyard.' Jack replied.

'The courtyard it is then.' James said decisively.

Cautiously they exited the chapel out into the courtyard. Jack was in the process of locking the chapel door behind them when the silence was broken by a numbers of clicks seemingly emanating from the upper ramparts.

'I don't like the sound of that. Reminds me very much of bolts on rifles being cocked.' James whispered to his companions as he looked up at the ramparts. His gaze was met by the sight of at least a dozen men standing up on the walls pointing automatic weapons at them.

A man matching the description of Lord Norwood, provided by Ollie and Gaz was clearly visible amongst the gunmen, his menacing face staring down at them from the barbican. He addressed them in a very smug voice.

'I suggest you hand that book over to me if you know what is good for you.' His eyes were transfixed on the bundle that Rachel gripped tightly to her chest.

'If you do so now, I will let you go unharmed.' Norwood said as his lips curled into a horrible twisted smile.

'Yeah right, I've heard that before.' Chris defiantly shouted back at him. Well aware that the book was the only bargaining chip they had.

'Do you think we are stupid? You will kill us as soon as you have that book.' He added, whilst desperately searching for a way out of this situation.

'Do not trifle with me Mr Flack your position is untenable as you are no doubt aware. Give me the book! Take my offer before I lose my temper.' Norwood growled at him.

'That's Captain Flack to you! I think I've earned it! If you want this book you'll have to come and get it yourself!' Chris shouted back. Slightly turning his head to James he whispered 'Any suggestions? We're trapped like rats in a barrel down here.'

'Working on it, try and buy a little more time. We are going to have to shoot our way out'. He replied. 'Jack … try and get back towards the chapel door, we need to get up on to the battlements. We won't survive down here; they've got the advantage of higher ground. Be subtle about it … if they catch on to what you are doing we are all dead men.' James whispered nervously glancing at Jack.

'I think I can get there. I didn't manage to finish locking the door.' Jack replied through the corner of his mouth.

'Okay wait for my signal, then you and Rachel head for the door. We'll give you some covering fire. Good luck and for God's sake keep your heads down.' James whispered back.

'Chris we might get some cover from behind that pillar by the door, if we can get there.'

Norwood had disappeared from the top of the barbican; he had obviously decided to take Chris up on his suggestion of fetching the book himself. His men had remained, poised on the fortifications, the muzzles of their guns still trained on the group below.

'Now!' James bellowed at the top of his voice. Jack and Rachel dived for the door, smashing it aside. They tumbled through into the relative safety of the chapel. At the same time, Chris and James darted across to the stone pillar, that James had pointed out, followed by a hail of bullets raining down from the guns above. Chips of stone flew off the pillar as the bullets smashed into the masonry.

Now pinned down behind the pillar James and Chris tried to work out their next move whilst taking it in turn to return fire. Fragments of metal ricocheted all around them as the hail of bullets continued to rain down from above.

James carefully lined up one of the assailants in his sights and fired. His aim was true, as the shot made its mark. The man teetered on the edge of the wall for the briefest of seconds before overbalancing, falling head first down on to the cobbles of the courtyard.

The man's skull split open as it smashed into the cobbles, spattering blood on to the stones. Had the shot not already killed him, his impact with the cold hard ground certainly would have.

'They're trying to cut us off from reaching the battlements.' James shouted as he noticed men running across the far side of the walls toward the bell tower.

'Get to the chapel. I'll cover you! Then take the others up the stairs.'

James shouted at Chris. 'Ready? Move! Go! Go! Go!'

Chris broke cover, leaping through the open doorway as James laid down fire. Chris turned as he rolled across the threshold to cover James' retreat to the shelter of the chapel slamming the door shut as James made it inside.

Once inside, they raced up the winding stairs of the tower until they reached the door to access the upper levels of the fort.

As he left the tower James tossed Jack a Glock 22 along with a few extra .40 S&W mags.

'Jack, are you ready for this? I have no idea what is on the other side of this door. Remember shoot first, ask questions later.' James said to Jack before he opened the narrow oak door, immediately coming face to face with one of the gunmen.

Before the man even had a chance to raise his gun to his shoulder and get a shot off, James smashed the butt of his rifle into the face of the man. The man crumpled to the floor as the weapon made contact, caving in the side of his head.

Jack hadn't even had a chance to do anything; he just stood there in stunned silence.

'Jack, come on concentrate. You know how to handle yourself. Hold the door until we get to the other side. We'll cover you from there.' James said trying to snap him out of his moment of shock.

Chris and Rachel started out across the palisade, Chris targeting men higher up on the towers of the Keep; dodging flying bullets they steadily made their way towards the door of the Keep on the far side.

A stray bullet clipped Chris' side, as he was about half way across the palisade. He stumbled, losing his footing as the bullet ripped through his flesh. Clutching his side he pulled himself upright, and blocking out the pain forced his way across the wall to the side of the Keep. Blood trickled in between the gaps of his fingers, dripping down on to the masonry. Luckily it wasn't serious as it was not near any organs, but that didn't mean it wouldn't become serious if he couldn't do something soon to stem the bleeding.

Jack was the last to make his way across towards his fellow companions. Concentrating so hard on his goal of reaching the far side, he had no way of knowing that there was a man behind him, now lining Jack up in his sights.

Chamberlain had followed his master down from the roof of the barbican to apprehend his master's enemies. They had heard the shots as they reached the ground floor of the gatehouse.

Adrenaline coursed through Chamberlain's veins as the shots rang out around the castle; he had secretly been hoping that Flack and Middleton would put up some resistance, although he had known his master had no intention of letting them live, he much preferred the hunt rather than a straight execution.

He wanted them to suffer, experience true fear, that absolute petrified feeling of hopelessness, the same kind of feeling a fox experiences as it races in desperation through the undergrowth away from the hounds. Searching for the safety of a bolthole, as the thundering sound of horses' hooves and yelping hounds grows ever closer. Terrified beyond belief as certain death approaches. Chamberlain really hoped that he could corner one of them just like those hounds would do before tearing the fox limb from limb.

Taking the stairs up inside the chapel he followed his prey, as he reached the doorway opening out on to the parapet he caught sight of Jack making his escape across towards the Keep. Chamberlain sneered as he lined up the fleeing figure with the barrel of his gun, deliberately aiming to immobilise him rather than taking the kill shot.

Time seemed to slow down as James, Chris and Rachel watched Jack helplessly from the relative safety of the Keep. They saw Chamberlain appear from the tower.

'Look out, Jack. Get down!' James shouted in vain trying to warn Jack, but it was too late.

'Come on Jack get out of the way.' James muttered, as he stared through the sights of his gun trying to get a clear shot of the man behind Jack. But there was no angle; Jack's running form was in the way.

James almost looked away as Chamberlain took aim. Slowly Chamberlain's finger pulled back on the trigger.

The muzzle flashed as the firing pin struck the back of the shell, igniting the powder and propelling the bullet forwards along the barrel of the rifle. And then it was over. The bullet penetrated the back of Jack's right knee; it ripped through the cartilage exploding through the front, taking the cap with it. Jack fell, reeling in agony. His agonising screams made Rachel wince. She tried to run to him but Chris caught her by the arm.

'There is nothing you can do for him now. We need to go! Now! Or we will all die here. We are still desperately outnumbered and out gunned. He knew the risks, as did we all.' Nevertheless she still tried to wrestle herself free from has grasp but he refused to let her go.

Hoping that the end would come quickly now for Jack, Chris kept hold of her arm. Before James swooped her up on to his shoulder and carried her kicking body away from the brutal scene.

With a final look of sadness at his fallen comrade Chris left the edge of the parapet into the Keep, bolting the door behind him. The dull resonating sound of the metal bar slamming down across the door echoed around the inside of the Keep masked the final moments of Jack's life.

Back outside on the parapet Jack tried to crawl along the walkway dragging his body along the stone away from the approaching figure. The thought that he was about to die filled him with dread. He was in excruciating pain, pain like he had never felt before. He kicked out, with his good leg, in desperation at the huge hulk of a man towering above him.

The man just laughed at him, which made his plight even more painful to bear. The man started to reach out to grab him. Jack weakly tried to punch the man before his strength left him, but it was to no avail, the man grasped his outstretched arm and in one swift movement produced a knife from his belt; plunging it deep into Jack's bicep.

Jack screamed as this fresh searing pain erupted. It was at that moment that Jack realised he was about to take his last few breaths; tears began to role down his cooling cheeks.

The huge hulk twisted the knife in Jack's arm causing him to scream once more as another stab of fresh pain burnt through his arm before Chamberlain finally ripped it out.

Taking hold of Jack's shoulder in one of his massive arms he plunged the knife downward straight through Jack's ribcage deep into his heart. Jack's body twitched and then stillness, his eyes glazed over as the last of his life force left him.

Chamberlain let go of the now motionless corpse. The body slumped on to the cold stone surface. Satisfied that at least one of his master's enemies was no more, the man moved off in search of another victim.

Back inside the Keep, James knew that there was no time for mourning. Chris was still bleeding and they were all still in grave danger. It was heart breaking to leave their friend but now was not the time for grief.

They were not safely out of the woods just yet; they still needed to get off this god-forsaken island. The only small consolation at the moment was that they still had the book.

Rachel was obviously more shaken up than himself or Chris. After all they were both hardened veterans and although it was always hard to lose a comrade they had seen death many times before; whereas this was the first time she had ever seen somebody fall in combat, let alone somebody she was close to. At least she hadn't witnessed Jack's final few moments. That would have scarred her for life and haunted her dreams for a long time to come.

James had to break through the door leading to the underground railway, as the keys were still with Jack's lifeless corpse. He and Rachel quickly set up the ground anchors for the rope they would use to rappel down. Chris would have helped but he was still losing a lot of blood from his wound so he was attempting to stem the bleeding. Having set up the anchors Rachel was the first to descend down the rope.

'That's me.' She called up as she reached the bottom of the tunnel.

'Okay.' James replied. He had to descend with Chris attached to his harness in tandem, as by this point there was no way Chris would have been able to descend by himself.

'On Rope!' He shouted down as he clipped the two of them into the system and gradually started their descent. It was hard going; the tunnel was tight especially for two people at once. A few times they got stuck and had to free themselves from the squeeze where the unevenly carved tunnel narrowed. They eventually made it to the bottom and not before time. It was clear from the echoing voices above that they were no longer the only ones in the tunnel.

James quickly unclipped the two of them and just to make sure that their pursuers were not able to take advantage of the rope they had left; he free climbed back up the rock about twelve meters and cut the rope. Anybody that did now attempt to use it would have an unfortunate accident arriving at the bottom far quicker than they would have imagined.

They didn't wait around to find out if any of Norwood's men would come crashing down the tunnel. They needed to get Chris back to the 4x4 as soon as possible, the injury was becoming serious, the bullet had passed straight through his side, luckily it had missed any major organs but none the less it still needed to be dressed quickly to minimise the likelihood of it becoming infected and to reduce the amount of blood loss. James broke through the last door between them and the fresh air of freedom, their luck had started to turn as they found a small RIB tied up against the quayside, James quickly hotwired it and they sped back to the mainland. He ran the boat straight up on to the beach with a large crunch as the bottom of the fibreglass boat scrapped along the rocky beach.

Rachel scrambled up over the last of the rocks on the beach to get to the Range Rover whilst James helped Chris out of the boat. As soon as Rachel reached the 4x4 she jumped in and forced the engine to start up not waiting for the glow plug light on the dashboard to go out. She drove it like a maniac down on to the beach screeching to a halt just in front of James and Chris.

James opened up the rear and dropped Chris into the back, and jumped in slamming the door shut behind him.

'Go!' He shouted. Turning his attention back to his friend. Rummaging around in the medi-kit until he found some bandages and tape. He patched his friend up and gave him a shot of penicillin to prevent infection. Once he had finished the temporary fix James climbed over the seats into the front and they sped off into the night leaving the Mount far behind them.

'Damn that man!' Lord Norwood bellowed as he surveyed the aftermath of the fire-fight from the battlements. He kicked the corpse of Jack St Aubyn with his foot several times as his rage grew. Before his rage boiled over, so uncontrollable was the red mist through which he now viewed the lifeless body of Jack that he stamped his foot straight down on to the face of the young man, completely distorting the face, which had been so full of vitality and youthfulness.

He had just lost five of his best men with another two wounded, but what angered him the most was the fact that he came so close to having the book in his possession only for his men to let it slip through his grasp. Now he would have to re-group and continue to the next stage without it.

'Chamberlain!' He shouted. 'Find me that book. I don't care how you get it; just get it! I must report to the brethren before we leave for the Americas. Leave this mess for the authorities; they are too clumsy to work out what happened here. Now go!'

'Yes My Lord.' And with that, the imposing hulk slunk off into the darkness to retrieve what his master so desperately desired.

'As for the rest of you. Make sure none of our dead remain here. The authorities will be sure to arrive soon so get a move on. You have 3 minutes and counting.' Norwood, shouted out to the remnants of his small force.

'What should we do about this one?' Asked one of the gunmen, pointing to Jack's body.

'Leave him. He has no ties to us.' Norwood said casting a look full of disdain in the direction of the bloodied corpse. He was about to turn and walk away when he caught sight of a glint of silver lying next to the body. It was Jack's signet ring that had fallen from his hand at the sheer forceful ferocity of the kicks that the body had just received. Norwood peered at the nut carrying squirrel coat of arms defiantly looking directly at him, the symbol of an organisation that had been a thorn in his side for such a long time.

The mist descended once again over his eyes, he crushed the ring under his foot before kicking it from the ramparts down into the courtyard below. The tinkle of the cracked ring reverberating around the now silent courtyard, as it bounced across the solid stone works, continued to insolently remind Norwood that although he had broken this one, there were others who would pick up the mantle against him.

Norwood joined the rest of his cohort in the boat they had arrived in, and quickly left as they could already see the flashes of blue lights making their way along the coastal roads down towards the sleepy town. As he watched the silhouette of the mount disappear over the horizon he pondered how he could finally rid himself of all those who stood in his way and how long it would be before the pieces of the codex were in his hands? Not to mention, what was he going to say to the brethren to appease them, to allay their anger that he had failed to recover a part of the codex and to reassure them that their faith in him regaining the codex had not been entrusted too freely. It was going to be a testing time; nevertheless he hoped that they would at least see the positives that they now knew some of the members of *The Order* that opposed them.

Chapter Eight: Flashes of Blue

It was long past midnight by the time the phone on the bedside table began blaring like a siren, rudely rousing DI Glen Harris from his sound sleep. Begrudgingly turning over on his side he stared at the perpetrator of his discomfort for a second or two before he answered.

'Hey man, have you any idea what time it is?' He said in his well-known Anglo-American accent, currently littered with the hint of sleep.

'Very sorry for the lateness, Sir, but your presence 'as been requested at St Michael's Mount. There's been a shooting.' Replied the familiar voice of the Desk Sergeant at Penzance Station.

'Can't armed response deal with it?' Glen asked as he pictured the familiar image of the squat, corpulent, red faced Desk Sergeant with a bristling toothbrush moustache and wild curly hair, that try as the Sergeant might, always seemed to have a mind of it's own, standing behind the desk at the station. Moustache now more than likely twitching slightly at even the hint of the idea that Glen was trying to shirk his duties. Not that he had any intention of this, it was just a little banter he had with the Sergeant.

'Honestly these young'ns today, just no work in 'em. Especially these tall dark han'some types. Always wanting their beauty sleep. C'mon young Sir get yerself outta bed, no rest for law and order. Armed Response 'ave been on the scene for a while; wouldn't want to show us up now would yer? Besides those responsible had long gone by the time they arrived.'

'Point taken, old timer. Anybody hurt?'

'Yes, Sir. Armed Response found one body, yet to be formerly identified. However, they believe it to be th't o' Jack St Aubyn. We're still trying to get hold of either the family or an estate worker to make a formal identification. The team also found a large amount of spent ammunition. It looks like a war zone down there 'cording to the reports I 'ave had so far. The Chief specifically asked for you, so I suggest you get down there as fast as you can.'

'Ok man, tell him I'll be there as soon as I can. I suppose there is no rest for the wicked either. See you later, Sergeant. Oh and Sergeant there better be some coffee waiting.'

'W'en there e'er not been?'

'Cheers man, Catch you in a bit.' Glen replied before hanging up.

'Who was it?' Asked his wife, who had also been awoken by the call.

'Work, Hun. There's been a shooting at the Mount. Sorry, but I'm gonna have to go.'

'Do you really have to go? It's not long since you got to bed.'

'Yeah, sorry Hun. At least it hasn't woken the little one.' He replied, realising almost immediately, as the words left his lips that he had jinxed it. The loud wails now clearly emanating from the room next door signalled that their eight month old was now anything but peacefully asleep and that he was not going to hold back his displeasure. If he was now awake, he was going to make sure that the whole world knew about it.

'Great, just what I needed.' Glen said, pulling his socks on, knowing full well that it could take quite a while to settle the little fella back down.

'Don't worry, Flower. You go, I'll see to him.'

'Aw, thanks Hun. You're the best. I hope he isn't up for too long. I'll text you once I've got a better idea of the situation.' He said as he slipped his favourite three quarter length tweed overcoat on.

'Take care, you know I always worry about you when guns are involved.' His wife said as she kissed him goodbye.

'I will; speak to you later. Love you.' He replied with a final loving glance at her before he left the warmth and comfort of their house for the bitter cold crime scene.

The sight of his own breath as he stepped out of his front door on to the dark dreary street sent a shiver straight through him. Although he had been living in the UK for over fourteen years he had never quite got used to how cold and damp the late autumnal weather was. He had been born and spent most of his childhood in Portugal, and even though his Mother was from Newcastle upon Tyne and his Father was from Cincinnati, both of which were renowned for having cold winters, somehow the ability to deal with the cold hadn't been passed on. The Portuguese temperament and passion had sunk in and left a lasting effect.

It didn't take long to make the drive from Penzance to the Mount, and although he had a brief idea what awaited him, even the call could not have prepared him for the sight he was met with as he drove into what he had always known as a quaint little seaside town.

Marazion was awash with the glow of dozens of blue flashing lights, and the streets were packed with an assortment of police units; from armed response to dog teams not to mention the other emergency services.

The West End down to the causeway had been completely cordoned off and due to the state of the tide they had even had to call upon the local police patrol boat to ferry services across to the now water locked landmark.

After being waved through the mêlée of locals that had all turned out from the comfort of their warm beds, intrigued by the commotion outside. DI Harris parked his car as close as he could to the square and walked the last stretch up to where the Major Serious Incident (MSI) Unit had been set up.

'Ah, nice to see you at last.' DS Jones said as he spied Glen entering the MSI Unit. 'Hope we didn't disturb anything too important.' He continued in a slightly sarcastic tone.

'Hey boss, not really, apart from the little one.'

'Oh, sorry about that. How is the little lad?'

'He's great, keeps us on our toes and well, sleepless nights are par for the course, especially as he is teething at the mo.' Glen replied, with every corner of his face lighting up with that proud loving look that only a father has for a newborn son.

'Aw, bless the little lad, all have to go through that stage at some point. I remember when our first-born was at that age and the endless sleepless nights. Thank god they grow out of it pretty quickly, glad he is doing well and trust me he will eventually start sleeping right through. Right, to business, this is what we know so far. We received a report of gunshots up at the Mount around about 11:45 this evening. Armed Response were immediately deployed and arrived not long after twenty past midnight. However, by the time of their arrival on the scene the only things they found were a huge amount of spent ammunition, areas of blood spatter and an unidentified corpse. It was only when one of the local dog handlers turned up that were we able to make an initial identification that it may be Jack St Aubyn, but that has yet to be authenticated. We are still trying to reach family members; it appears that they may be away on holiday so we may have to rely on one of the estate employees for the time being to make a formal identification.'

'Do we have a motive for the killing?'

'Currently, we are feeling in the dark a bit. From the locals we have interviewed so far, the picture we are getting is that he was well liked in the area, did a great deal for the community and was very well respected. No one has really had a bad word to say about the lad. So we have ruled out a local feud. We know he was seen earlier in the day at the Godolphin Arms Hotel in the company of what appeared to be a group of friends, two men and a woman. They have yet to be located and the descriptions we have are very generic, so not of much use to us at present. There have been reported sightings of a number of strangers in the town yesterday afternoon and evening as well as a group in boats that seemed to be heading towards the Mount but given the touristic nature of both the town and the Mount it would not be uncommon. It's a right little brain teaser.'

'A robbery gone wrong?' Glen tentatively proposed as he thought about the valuables that the family must surely have collected over the centuries.

'Perhaps, it is certainly something to consider. We will know more once we have had a thorough search of the buildings and the grounds.' The DS replied.

'What would you like me to do first?'

'Get on that patrol boat and go see the area where the body was discovered; see if there is anything that *the men in white* might have missed. Oh, and Glen see if you can get any preliminary info from Hertzog. You know what that damn pathologist is like, never likes to pre-empt the autopsy. Nevertheless give him a big push, in this particular case tell him we need all the info we can get right now. If it is Jack St Aubyn you can guarantee that when his father gets back his Lordship will raise all kinds of hell, and will be looking for answers, so we need to be well up to speed by that point. I'm going to go and interview the local who raised the alarm. You know *Jones's Law*, seventy percent of the time, the one that reported it is more than likely responsible. Ugh, that's all I need now, bloody press.' The Super added as he spotted a few familiar faces from the local Star and Gazette making their way towards the unit.

'What are you still doing here? Go, out the back. I'll deal with the vermin.'

Glen didn't wait, another moment, turning on his heels he took the back stairs out of the mobile unit, with just the hint of a wry smile on his face as he heard the customary 'Superintendent, Superintendent, What can you tells us? Can you confirm….' followed by 'No comment at this time…initial stages of enquiries' and 'when we have a clearer picture… first to know.' Knowing full well that the Super hated the press, he saw all so called wordsmiths as the lowest of the low, them and defending QCs, always spinning and misrepresenting the evidence to make a few more bucks.

Chapter Nine: Jim's World

A chill wind had begun to pick up as Glen made his way along the jetty to where the police patrol boat was currently lying. The sea state had also changed since earlier that night, instead of the flat calm there was now a slight lop on the water which for someone with not a great deal of seamanship experience required a small degree of care and attention as to where was best to board the vessel; Glen chose the right moment and deftly jumped aboard. The well-trained crew quickly cast off and soon the boat was bouncing its way across the small open expanse of water towards the now isolated island.

The occasional burst of spray flew across the bow. Glen caught the odd bit of water in the face, which reminded him why he wasn't the greatest fan of the English Waters, cold and wet. He liked the sea but not this type; wet was fine, but he much preferred the warmer waters of the Med or the Algarve to these unforgiving often treacherous depths.

'Soon be there, mate.' Said one of the crew who had caught sight of the grimace spreading across Glen's face as the first bit of spray had gave him a temperate slap across the cheek.

'No worries, I can deal with it. Don't envy you guys when it really kicks off.' Glen replied as he forced a smile.

'Jump into the wheelhouse if you like. Bit dryer in there.'

'Cheers, man. But I'll be okay, a little bit of water never hurt anybody, right?' Glen didn't want to be labelled as a soft touch or even worse by that English term 'land lubber'.

'Please yerself.' The deck hand muttered before he strode off up and over the wheelhouse to the bow to make ready the mooring lines for when the boat entered and docked in the small harbour of the Mount.

Glen watched the agile man go and wondered how it was that even though the boat was rocking and rolling a bit, the guy managed to stay upright, let alone stay on the boat without needing to have a hand to something. Must have some pretty sturdy, oh what was the term… *Sea legs*, he mused before he returned to his previous train of thought about what could have brought about this tragic set of events.

The next thing he was aware of was shouts of *Steady as she bears* and *Make that line fast there, c'mon look lively,* as the lines where thrown to those manning the quayside.

'Cheers guys. See you later.' Glen shouted his farewells to the crew as he stepped off the boat back on to the more secure feeling of dry land.

'For your sake you better hope the tide is back out so you can cross the causeway, expecting the weather to turn real nasty later.' The deckhand shouted after the departing figure of the young detective. Glen hoped that too as he could see the impending storm brewing to the south-west, as dark as the night sky was, the storm clouds were darker, and clearly visible surging towards the castle from the horizon. *What a night for it.* He thought as he crossed underneath the archway of the fortress' main gate.

The memory of bright blue lights of Marazion were replaced by the sight of the dazzling white of the portable work lights being used by the forensic team. Pockets of white tents protecting specific areas of interest were scattered throughout the courtyard as well as a lone tent high up on the ramparts themselves.

Glen headed straight for a particularly large group of *the men in white*, who were busy in discussion over something he presumed they might have found.

'Hi guys, sorry to interrupt your discussions, DI Harris.' He said as he produced his warrant card. 'Where can I find Professor Hertzog?'

'Hi Glen.' Said one of the SOCOs that he had worked with before. 'You can find him up there.' Pointing to the tent up on the rampart, just as an incredibly tall lanky man stepped out, raised his arms above his head and arched his back, stretching every sinew of muscle before yawning and disappearing back inside. 'As you can tell the Prof is feeling the effects of the late night and the amount of work to do here.'

'Yeah, man. It's gonna be a rough night for all of us by the looks of things.'

'And it's gong to get a lot worse. That's what we were just discussing. We're racing against the clock here to gather as much evidence as possible. Once that storm hits, there isn't going to be much left to find.'

'How do I get up there?'

'Through that door in the chapel, then take the staircase on the right.'

'Cheers man, good to see you. We'll have to catch up for a pint at some point. I won't delay you any longer.'

'Better grab a set of those whites from the box before you go up there. The Prof will bite your head off if you go up there looking like that. Very protective of his evidence is our Prof.'

'I remember.' Glen replied with a smile as he recalled the first encounter he'd had with the Professor at a crime scene; entering without protective overalls. The Prof had hit the roof, even deliberately misquoting the Gospel of Luke. 'If you ever dare turn up like this again to one of my crime scenes, I swear there will be weeping, there will be wailing, gnashing of teeth and buckets and buckets of tears.' Glen had found it a bit over theatrical, nevertheless he got the message; in the eyes of the professor the police just used the evidence to get a conviction but the scene itself belonged to him. You either played by his rules or you went and sat in the pavilion.

Now that he matched all the other *white lemmings* at the scene, Glen took to the stairs and wound his way round and up on to the ancient stone works. Brushing the flap of the tent aside, he took a final breath of the fresh cool air before dipping his head and entered the world of forensics.

'Good Morning, Jim. How's tricks?'

'Uh, oh it's you. Morning, can't say there is anything good about it. But at least you're dressed for a long innings for once I see.' The tall figure of Professor Hertzog replied as he briefly glanced up from examining part of the corpse on the stone floor, that hadn't been completely covered, before he returned his critical eyes back on to the corpse. Peering hard through his tortoiseshell rimmed glasses to make sure he hadn't missed anything.

'Hey man, that was one time.'

'Well I like to keep you on your toes.'

'Thanks. So, what can you tell me Jim?'

'He's dead.'

'Well, yes I can see that. I meant what can you tell me about how he died?'

'In a great deal of pain, but you'll have to wait until we have moved the body and carried out the autopsy before I can give you all the gory details.'

'C'mon Jim, you must be able to give me a rough idea. If this is the body of Jack St Aubyn you know we will have to be seen to be doin' everything in our power to catch his killers.'

'Off the record?'

'Yeah, off the record.'

'You good with corpses? This one definitely isn't for those with weak stomachs.'

'Seen my fair share. I'll be okay.'

'Okay, but don't say I didn't warn you.' Jim Hertzog said as he pulled back the sheet covering the rest of the lifeless young man.

The full sight of the body caused Glen to take a sharp intake of breath and he could feel his stomach twitch ever so slightly. He had seen many dead bodies but not many as mutilated as this one. Not to mention the sheer volume of blood pooled around it.

'Told you so, you okay?'

'Yeah, just give me a sec.' Glen replied as he tried to compose himself. By looking at it not as a person but just an object. He found that as long as he removed the personal side, he could look at almost anything.

'I'd put his age at around early to mid twenties. As you can see the body has suffered a huge amount of trauma, both pre and post mortem. Lividity hasn't set yet, nevertheless I'd be confident to say that he was killed here and that the body hasn't been moved.'

'What would you set time of death at?'

'Well taking into account that the body appears to be in good health up until the events leading up to death and also factoring the recent drop in temperature, I would say sometime in the last two to three hours, again the autopsy will help to narrow this a bit. If there are any internal health issues that one can't see here, then the window could shift, but I'd be pretty certain this is more or less the zone you are looking at.'

'Sure thing, would fit into the times between shots being reported and armed response's arrival so I'd be happy with that assessment.'

'What can you tell me about cause of death?'

'Oh, well I think I can be a little more specific than just cause of death. Step outside and I'll walk you through what I think happened.'

'Great, will give me a break from this.' Glen replied with a furtive glance in the direction of the corpse.

'Not quite as comfortable with this one as you thought.'

'It's not what you think. Just such a waste of life.'

'I know what you mean. This one could have been destined for great things by all accounts. Cut down well before his time.' Jim Hertzog replied as he stepped out of the tent into the bitter cold night air. 'Right okay, so I would suggest he was making his way along the ramparts in the direction of the Keep. Most likely running due to the way the body fell and that the first injury was to the knee rather than the arm. In my opinion he was shot from behind probably by someone standing in that doorway.' He said pointing to the doorway from the stairs that Glen had used earlier. 'Further inspection of the body will confirm this but judging on the blood spatter, this is the most likely scenario.'

'Can you postulate, what type of weapon would have been used or will you have to wait for the autopsy and ballistics.'

'Considering what I have noted from the entry and exit points you will almost certainly be looking for a rifle, and from the catastrophic damage to the front of the knee I would definitely say that either a hollow point or a nastier derivative, such as the RIP shell was used. But until we have a closer look from the table and depending on whether we find any metal fragments in the wound, I can't be any clearer at present.'

'That's pretty horrific in itself.'

'Oh yes, very. This by itself would have been enough to eventually cause death. Unfortunately for our young friend here, he went through a lot more than that before the bails were knocked off.'

'Not particularly common ammunition to get hold of over here, is it?'

'Compared to our rebellious cousins over the pond it is not readily available but you know yourself that if you operate in the right circles people can get their hands on almost anything.'

'So we could be looking at something gang related?'

'Possibly, but I would suggest that whoever was responsible had a military background at some point.'

'Why would you say that?'

'Well, firstly even at this relatively close range, you would need a certain degree of skill to be this accurate in immobilising a target moving at speed. Secondly, my initial thoughts about the knife wounds to both the upper arm and chest were that they are typical of the type of wound caused by a large combat knife. Not only this but the method of twisting the knife to inflict maximum damage and pain is certainly in line with close hand-to-hand combat training. It most certainly was the knife to the chest; which was the mortal blow. And I would add that this was done with considerable force, it appears to have cleaved two ribs on the way through to the heart. In my opinion it was a very clinical blow. One single heavy blow, most likely the attacker was standing above and behind him. This adds weight to the theory that they had military training. There are no signs of this being a frenzied attack. It was methodical, quick and clean. Something you would expect from a pro not just a random gang style attack. They don't tend to be as precise as this.'

'What about the other injuries, such as the broken check bone?'

'I have a working theory that this may be post mortem, but can't be sure at the moment as lividity hasn't set, and I may not be able to give you a definitive answer even once it has. You know yourself that trauma caused very soon after death can be hard to separate from those caused before; and this applies to the other broken ribs as well.'

'So, why do you suspect that they occurred post mortem?'

'Mainly because of the lack of blood around those areas on the floor. If they had occurred before death I would expect to see more blood, a lot more blood from those areas and it's just not present. Also in my opinion they were caused by a second person, up until the point of death all the wounds are controlled, almost refrained, where as the latter are more akin to an outburst of rage, almost hate. This change in characteristic would seem to imply that it was done by another personality.'

'Thanks for that Jim. Anything else you can add?'

'As a matter of fact yes. There are a number of things that stick out. General points about the crime scene and a specific observation pertaining to the body. Firstly, I have noticed a white ring line around the left hand little finger, presumably from a signet ring. However, we have yet to find it. Possible it was taken as a trophy or it fell off during the struggle.

'Secondly, the amount of blood left in certain areas of the scene would point to at least two other fatalities, but the bodies have been removed and I would also say that there were others with serious injuries. Hopefully blood samples will generate DNA matches on the data base, this may take some time to process so you will have to be patient and wait a bit for those.'

'Sure thing man, I understand, thanks Jim. I'll leave you to it. Any idea when you plan on moving the body.'

'Hopefully in the next hour or so as long as the weather holds. Judging on the speed that front is moving I can guarantee the covers are going to have to stay on with rain stopping play. Probably going to lose a lot of evidence I'm afraid. Unfortunately we can only work with the conditions that we have been dealt.'

'Yeah, I know. Sure you will *pull out all the stops* as you Brits put it.' Glen continued. 'Anything we can do to help speed up the process?'

'Well, a couple of extra hands to help bag up the evidence wouldn't go amiss.'

'Sure thing, I'll give the Super a call and request a few bods to be sent over. Right man, I'm gonna head off, I want to look around the courtyard and see if there's anything that might have slipped through the net.'

'We're not amateurs, you know.'

'Yeah, but an extra pair of fresh eyes can't hurt.' Glen replied, making a slightly more hurried departure than normal, as he realised his last comment had struck a bit of a nerve and didn't want to linger in case the Prof became anymore excitable. He'd seen Jim when his rage erupted and knew very well that he wouldn't want to once again be on the receiving end of a full blown dressing down. Once was quite enough.

Glen made the call to the Super as he descended the stairs back down to the chapel.

'Hey boss, any chance of sending a few extra bods to help with bagging and tagging evidence?'

'Jim struggling is he?'

'Just concerned that this storm is going to wreck his crime scene before all the evidence is processed.'

'Makes a nice change, for once he won't blame us for contaminating evidence. I'll see what I can do. Sure there are a few *plodders* twiddling their thumbs, good experience for them too. Has he given any indication as to circumstances around the death?'

'Yeah, I'll fill you in later. There are a few other points of interest I haven't looked at yet. And I want to get these covered before returning to the mainland.'

'Okay, just make sure you put everything in your note book.'

'Ah, I sort of told him, his comments were off the record.'

'Oh, never mind that. He knows how this game is played, just make sure you have a note of it somewhere.'

'No worries catch you later, Boss.'

'Good work and crack on.' The Super said before hanging up.

'DI Harris?' A voice called out, reverberating around the empty space of the chapel.

'Yeah, be down in a sec.' Glen replied as he quickly descended the last few steps.

'I think you will be interested in what has been discovered in the Crypt.'

'Wasn't on my list of things to see but lead on. What's your name?' He asked the short lady in the white overalls he encountered waiting for him.

'Graham, Sir.'

'Err, I'm presuming that's your Surname? Otherwise I think your parents were either very confused or had a bizarre sense of humour.'

'Yes.' She replied giggling at his statement. 'Becky is my first name.'

'Right, then Becky. Lets get cracking, I'm kinda running out of time and there's still a whole heap of stuff to see.'

'Won't take long, it's just down here. Oh and mind your head, this passage wasn't designed with your kind of height in mind.' Becky added as she led the way down another winding stairwell descending deep below the floor of the chapel down into the heart of the hard granite core of the Mount.

Glen thought the murky dank passageway was like something straight out of a low budget cult horror movie and he was just waiting for the predictably lame zombie to appear just around the next bend.

'So where have you guys hidden the mummy?' Glen enquired attempting to lighten the unsettling atmosphere within the tunnel.

'Oh, you know us, right where you'll least expect it.' Becky replied with a cheeky grin. 'To be fair you may wish you hadn't said that when you see what's down here.' Deliberately leaving her reply as vague as possible to send Glen's mind into overdrive.

'Ha, funny. Not biting.' He replied, determined not to give her the satisfaction of knowing that there was even the slightest paranoid thought now racing through his head.

Nevertheless, his heart did start to race as his eyes met the sight of the broken tomb as the passageway widened into the main chamber of the eerily quite crypt. He could feel the hairs on the back of his neck rise ever so slightly, just enough to send a shiver down between his shoulder blades.

'Christ, it's like something out of the Night of The Living Dead.' Glen said as he forced his pulse to slow.

'Yep, told you. However, the body hasn't moved. Looks like something was removed judging by the fact that the dust around the shield has been displaced. What was taken, I'm afraid at the moment is a mystery. You may have to delve into the old family records to find out more.' She suggested.

'Think you may be right on that one. Fancy volunteering? Olde English is definitely not my forte.'

'Neither 's proper English.' She jokingly remarked, poking fun at his American Heritage.

'Hey, it ain't that bad. Any chance you guys can take some pics and I'll see what I can dig up later, no pun intended.'

'Already done, and we've dusted for prints, but guess they were wearing velvet gloves. Couldn't find any trace of a usable paw mark.'

'That's the story of this scene so far.' Glen mused. 'It's a real tough one and the weather isn't making it any easier. But knowing Jim I'm sure no stone will be left unturned and he'll find something to kick-start the hunt. Right best get back up. Must view the courtyard before this storm wreaks havoc. I hope you've got a decent rain coat?'

'No time earlier, just hoping that we get off this rock before then.'

'That's the spirit, if a little optimistic I think. Thanks for the tour, hope you manage to stay dry. I'll leave you to your search for paw prints.' Glen said just before he stepped out of the stillness of the chapel into the swirling gusts racing around the courtyard and blazing brilliance of the work lights; so dazzling were they compared to the dimness of the chapel that he had to squint and shield his eyes for a few moments before they gradually became accustomed to the unnatural brightness for that time of night.

Chapter Ten: Bracing The Storm

Glen was glad of the thick Harris Tweed overcoat, as he made his way around the outskirts of the courtyard. The biting chill of the wintery gusts of wind that whipped across his face was bad enough to make him grit his teeth. He had elected not to go straight to the tents covering the blood-spattered areas, hoping that they would remain intact during the storm, which was now almost upon them.

His gut was telling him that if he didn't cast an eye around the perimeter a vital clue would be swept away by the maelstrom.

Inquisitive feet had undoubtedly already walked this path in search of clues, nevertheless he felt sure that another look would not be in vain. He could sense the cold gaze of Jim from high up on the ramparts bearing down upon him, a gaze he knew would be questioning why Glen felt that he would find something that others had not. Glen ignored the icy look and continued to press on.

He was about three quarters of the way round the quadrangle and was on the verge of giving up. Overhead the first battalions of storm clouds had commenced their assault on the outlying fortifications of the Mount. Huge sheets of rain lashed down against the stonework, whilst wave after wave of white horses surging across the blackening sea below flung themselves towards the granite cliffs with such force that when they finally crashed into the rock the Atlantic wave riders were sent tumbling high into the air, breaching the walls; just like fearless jockeys on furlong weary mounts, colliding headlong into Becher's Brook, are catapulted across that most infamous of high hurdles. So great was the power of the onslaught that Glen could feel the floor of the courtyard shudder with vibrations as every fresh charge of Poseidon's cavalry, spurred on by his trident, smashed against the fortress.

Glen had become so distracted by the immensity of the storm's impact that he almost fell flat on his face tripping over something that had become wedged into a seam between two stabs, just proud of the flagstones. Managing to regain his balance before hitting the ground he almost ignored whatever had caused his wrong footedness, putting his near miss down to his haste to find some cover from the ragging storm. Nevertheless his natural reaction was to quickly glance back at the area in question. It was a reflex reaction more out of curiosity as to what it could have been that had caught him out and to hopefully get a small peace of mind that he hadn't just clumsily tripped over his own feet.

His figure standing tall between the area and the bright work lights cast a long solitary shadow over the cold wet stones. In the very moment that he glanced back a sudden gust of wind caused one of the work lights behind to topple over on to the ground, and as it hit the ground, its beam lit up the area. He would never have noticed the twinkle of a small metallic fragment indefinitely stuck between a joint in the time weathered paving had it not been for the domino effect of the falling lamp.

It could have just been another spent bullet casing, but he didn't give it a second thought. In his current frame of mind any fresh evidence however trivial could potentially help with the case.

He spun on his heels and strolling over to the object, he carefully eased it from its temporary prison with the aid of a biro from his inside coat pocket. To his delighted surprise the object was not as insignificant as just another piece of virtually untraceable ammunition but was in fact the remnants of what may have once been a ring. His heart leaped with joy as he recalled the conversation with Jim earlier that night. *Could it be,* he thought, *that I might have found the missing ring and a significant piece of the puzzle?*

His satisfaction was short lived, due to the amount of water pouring out of the sky he couldn't make out much of the detail. He quickly dropped his prize into an evidence bag, making a mental note of roughly where he was in the courtyard just in case it turned out to be another dead end, and hurriedly dashed off back towards the shelter of the chapel where he could examine the object more closely.

Wiping some of the water out of his hair and eyes, the junior detective, that now resembled a wet sponge, had almost reached the peacefulness of the chapel, as the storm continued to rage around him. He was on the verge of crossing the threshold when he was almost bowled over by the express train like figure of Becky running at full steam in the opposite direction. Fortunately, she had seen him at the last second and managed to apply the breaks, so that instead of a full on wreck they just bumped each other.

'Typical, gung ho attitude, do you ever look where you are going? Don't answer that. Glen you need to come and help us. We need to get these tents anchored, now!' She pleaded, pointing to the tents on the far side of the courtyard already straining at their guy ropes. 'Otherwise they are going to be swept away. We never expected this storm to be so big.'

'But I've just found something that might be really important.'

'You've bagged it, right?'

'Course.'

'Then it will still be there later; whereas the tents will not. And if they go, all the evidence they are protecting goes with them. So come on. You need to help. Now!' She snapped at him, there was no time for pleading, this was a full on command and she was not in the mood to wait for an answer.

'But…' Glen began to reply, however before he had time to finish his sentence, Becky had already grabbed him by the arm and began pulling him off towards the tents on the far side of the swamped courtyard.

At first he dragged his feet, he had the overwhelming desire to inspect what he had just found, and yet he understood the ramifications of not helping to secure the tents. He was torn between heart and head. In the end he gave into her constant pulling and allowed himself to be dragged away from the chapel.

By the time they had crossed the courtyard, most of the SOCO team on the Mount were already making vain attempts to reinforce the anchor points of one tent. Whilst others were desperately hanging on to another by the only guy rope that remained in place. Try as they might the majority of the tent was already acting more like a kite on the end of a control line than something designed to be on the ground.

The danger lay in trying to catch hold of the other guys that had broken free; they swirled and whipped about with every fresh gust, metal stakes still in the end loops. Many of those on the ground were cautious in getting too close in case they were on the receiving end of a scorpion like blow.

Glen could see them struggle, and witnessed the first few bags of evidence gradually being blown from the tables underneath the flying canvas. It was in that moment that he decided to act.

'Keep hold of that line, and when I say pull, pull like your lives depended on it!' He shouted at the SOCOs. He didn't really have a perfect plan but he knew what had to be done and it was clear that he would just have to suck it up and get the job done.

The wind continued to swirl and buffet the walls of the fortress, the wave surges were now so huge that great plumes of spray now easily cleared the height of the outer fortifications, this combined with the volume of rain that continued to pour down from the heavens meant that the feet of those in the courtyard were now swimming in water. The decorative Gargoyle heads high up on the walls, that had up until now coped quite well with dealing with the volume of water, were finally overcome. No longer was there just a constant jet like stream spouting from their mouths, now each one had spurted a white mane as the pressure of the water became so great that excess water burst around their heads.

'Now!' Glen shouted as loud as he could in order to be heard above the din pitching around him. 'Pull! For fuck's sake pull!'

As the group began to take up the strain, like a tug of war team against far superior odds grapples with the rope, he ran and launched himself towards one of the flailing guys, he kept his arms up around his face until the very last possible moment to protect the most important parts from the rogue metal stakes thrashing about in mid air. Then he snatched at the guy rope as gravity began to take hold of him once more. He caught it and held on for dear life. At first the tent tried to wriggle free, tossing and turning in the whirlwinds, trying anything to buck the additional weight dragging it down, but he held on, he felt a sharp pain in his side as one of the other barbed tendril like guys lashed out, but he clung on and as the constant gravitational pull took hold, the tent now being pulled down in two directions could no longer maintain its unauthorised inaugural flight and just like a broken parachute, collapsed back down to earth landing right on top of, from the tent's perspective, the wrecker of its newfound source of freedom.

Glen lay on the ground for a few moments, taking stock of his sudden act of recklessness. His side burned but he was too tried after wrestling with the tent to inspect what damage he had taken in his efforts to bring the tent to heel.

' Shit, Glen. You okay?' The voice of Becky called out to him from the other side of the canvas.

'Yeah, I think so.' He replied from his position under the now lifeless tent. 'Any chance of getting this thing off me?'

A few of the SOCOs lifted the canvas from him, taking great care not to allow it to catch the breeze and re-launch itself back up into the billowing airflows.

Getting to his feet, Glen's first reaction was to check his pocket for the evidence bag, which contained the ring.

'Shit! Don't tell me it's fallen out?' He cursed as it dawned on him that it may have fallen out and been blown away during his tussle with the tent.

'Fuck, that's all I need. Fucking great!'

'Lost something?' The now familiar voice of Becky asked behind him.

'Yeah, the evidence I bagged just before you dragged me off over here.'

'You mean this evidence bag?' She asked as she smugly held up and waved the small polythene bag in front of him.

'Becky, you are a legend, if I wasn't already married I could kiss you right about now. Where did you find it?'

'Whoa, slow down there tiger.' She replied with just the hint of sarcasm resonating in her voice. 'I noticed it slip out when you were half off the ground; so thought I better grab it before it was swept away with the rest of the evidence.'

'Thank you, you're a life saver.' His relief was clearly evident across his face that it hadn't been lost along with the other bags from the tent.

'You got a magnifying glass in that kit of yours?' He asked as he was about to head back to the chapel.

'Err you're not going anywhere, mister. Not before we get that wound of yours sorted.' Becky said, pointing the area on Glen's tweed coat that was now soaked in blood.

'Oh c'mon, it's just a scratch. I'll be fine.'

'Nope, this needs to be treated.'

'Seriously? Can't we do it later.'

'Seriously, no. This needs to get sorted before you do anything else.

It's not going to take long there's a medi-kit in one of the tents. Well, at least, there used to be.'

'See it might not even still be there, it can wait.'

'Glen, don't be so pig headed. We are going to dress this, one way or another, before you do anything else.'

'Fine, I can see I'm not going to win on this one.' He said conceding the point.

'Charlie.' Becky called out to one of the other SOCOs near the main evidence tent that had managed to weather the storm. 'Can you fetch the medi-kit? Got a wounded policeman that requires some attention.'

'Yeah, pretty sure it's still on the bench.' He replied as he darted into the tent to return a few seconds later with the green box.

'You're not doing it out here are you? It's pissing it down out here. By the time you've put that on it may as well come straight off again. Can we not do it in the chapel where it's dry at least.'

'Determined to look at that evidence aren't you? But, yes. I suppose you are right it would be best done undercover.' Becky reluctantly gave into his request. She admired his dedication to his work but wasn't quite so impressed by his foolhardy approach.

'Right, top off.' She said as they entered the chapel.

'What?'

'Well, I'm not going to dress it whilst you've still got that jacket and shirt on, am I? C'mon trust me I've seen enough half naked bodies in my time.'

'Thank God the wife isn't here. That's all I can say. I think the words 'less than pleased' would be a 'pc' description.'

'I'm sure, especially if she'd seen you endangering yourself in such a manner. C'mon top off.'

'Alright, if it stops your moither. Lets get it done. Honestly you are as bad as my Mother.' He replied as he begrudgingly slipped off his overcoat, pulling his shirt off over his head to reveal his tanned rippling upper body.

'Hmmm, very nice. Certainly don't get to see that everyday.'

'Enjoying yourself, are we? I swear you're just doing this to wind me up.'

'Well, not every day a girl gets to see that. So may as well make the most of it.' She joked as she pulled out a large dressing to wind around his midriff.

'So opportunistic, you know this is bordering on harassment.'

'Oh behave.' She replied as she finished wrapping the dressing around his lower abdomen fixing it in place with a couple of safety pins.

'All done, see that wasn't so bad was it?'

'For you maybe. Right I believe you promised me a magnifying glass, unlike the coffee that I was promised hours ago and as of yet has failed to materialise, I'm hoping it will actually appear.'

'Hmmm, we are a little cranky tonight, aren't we? I know I left it somewhere around here. Do you want a left or right handed one?'

'Now you are taking the piss.'

'Alright, alright. Jesus not really the banter type, are you? Anyway what are you hoping to find? It's only a ring.' Becky asked as she rummaged around in her forensic kit.

'Jim mentioned to me that the body had a ring line, so I'm hoping this may be the ring in question. With some luck it might have some latent prints on it.'

'Ah, that would be really good. Definitely short on those at the moment.'

'Yeah tell me about it.'

'There you go.' She said passing him a magnifying glass from her case. 'You take a look while I sort out some print powder. Is that ring silver?'

'Looks like it.'

'In that case, might have to nip over to the supply tent, don't think I've got quite the right one in my case to give the best results. Be back in a bit.'

'Thanks, Becky, you're a good girl really. Not true what they say about you.'

'Pardon? What was that?'

'Oh, now who can't take a bit of banter?' Glen replied with a wry smile.

'Hmmm, I'll let you have that one.' She replied as she turned on her heels, still muttering something about 'typical men' that Glen didn't quite catch.

'See you in a bit.' He called out after her departing figure.

Glen was like a little kid unwrapping a birthday present as he tore open the evidence bag and took out the small silver ring. Blowing the excess water from it, he began to inspect the worn and battered engraving on it's round bezel. Even under the bright work lights that Becky had setup in the chapel it was difficult to make out exactly what the engraving was. Partially down to the wear and tear of everyday use and also because of the large scratches that it had no doubt picked up as it had bounced across the flagstones after plummeting from the height of the upper ramparts. Nevertheless, Glen could make out what appeared to be a squirrel standing upright on a log. The squirrel was clutching something between its outstretched forepaws, although the damage to this part of the ring obscured exactly what the prize procession was. There was also what appeared to be a Maltese cross resting on the upper back of the Squirrel with its tail curling into the centre of the cross. Glen also saw that the shoulders of the ring had been engraved with the words *Veritas et Spes*, which he presumed was a family motto of some sorts. He knew that it was a tradition of so many English families with ancient lineages to wear and pass down their family's emblems.

He was still trying to work out what the squirrel had clenched between its paws when Becky returned with the fingerprint powder.

'Having any luck?'

'Well, sort of I can make out most of it. There's a squirrel and I think it's some sort of Maltese cross. The Squirrel's holding something but I can't make out what it is. And a bit of an inscription, Latin I guess but not sure as never seen the language before.'

'Sure it's not a nut?' She suggested with the hint of sarcasm.

'I was sort of thinking that but I just can't tell.' He replied, ignoring the sarcasm. 'What do you think?' He continued handing the ring and magnifying glass to her.

'Yeah, I see what you mean. It has received a fair few knocks to that part. I wouldn't like to guess either. It could be anything. I doubt if it belongs to the body, if it does prove to be Jack St Aubyn.'

'Oh, why do you say that?' He anxiously asked as he took in her latest statement that seemed to pour water on to the flicker of hope that he'd had since finding it.

'Well, because that isn't the coat of arms or emblem of the St Aubyn Family. They have some sort of black bird standing on a rock wearing a white sash. Can't remember what the motto is but it's defiantly not theirs. Sorry to be the bearer of bad news.'

'Fuck, just can't get a break on this case.'

'Look it might belong to someone else who was here or it could be something connected to the family, that I don't know about. I'm just saying it's not their coat of arms. I wouldn't give up hope just yet. What's the inscription again?'

'Err, *Veritas et Spes*. Do you know Latin or whatever this is?'

'Course, had to when I was doing my training. Hmmm let me think, *Veritas et Spes*. Well *Veritas*, means truth, *et* is obviously and …'

'Obviously.' Glen muttered under his breath, he hated it when someone knew more than him.

Becky frowned slightly at the comment but refrained from commenting and continued with her translation.

'I can't say I have seen the word '*Spes*' before, but I know that '*Spero*' means 'I hope' so I guess it might derive from that. So I would say it probably means *Truth and Hope*, or something like that, quite a nice little motto really. The only way to really be sure would be to contact the College of Arms in London. They would be able to tell you for sure and probably tell you what it is that tree rat is holding.'

'Tree rat?'

'Yeah, pretty much what a squirrel is, right. I'm sure the College would be your best bet.'

'Crazy, anything you Brits don't have a college for? Thanks Becks, I'll give them a shout, once you've dusted this thing for prints.'

'No worries, what I'm here for. Sure you still want me to dust this for latent prints?' She asked.

'Yeah, if you can.'

'Well, I'll give it a go. But I wouldn't be too hopeful if I were you. This inclement weather may well have washed any prints away.'

'Let's just hope we have a bit of luck on our side. Wishful thinking I know but gotta have some luck at some point, right?'

Becky carefully took the ring from him and laying it on a piece of paper on one of the church pews, she carefully sprinkled the black powder over the ring before inhaling deeply and blowing the excess away. Taking up the magnifying glass she carefully inspected the ring to see if any of the powder had adhered to anything to suggest that there might be a trace of a latent print.

'Hmmm there might be a partial but if it is, it's going to be really faint on the lift. That's was what I worried about, exposure to wet weather does tend to detrimentally damage prints.'

'Yeah, I see what you mean. Anything you can do to clear it up a bit?'

'Well, possibly but not here. It would have to go to the lab and run it through the scanning electron microscope. That would produce a much better image. Will take a bit of time though.'

'Let's do it. Time is something I'm just gonna have to spare, I need all the leads I can get at this point. I'll leave it with you. Just need to take a few quick pictures of the coat of arms and the motto, to follow up on.' Glen replied as he took out his phone and took a few snaps. 'Well, I think that's me done here. Thanks Becks, you've been great. Now I've just got to get off this god-forsaken rock. Guessing that the boat won't be running at the moment?'

'I doubt it, but they do operate in some pretty heavy weather so you might be lucky. If it is, I hope you've got some good sea legs. Not going to be as easy going as it was when you arrived.'

'Great, and I thought that was bad enough. Just have to show some grit and get one with it. You staying here?'

'Yes, unfortunately some of us have got to clear up and try and recover as many of the evidence bags as possible, so that 'someone' can start putting a case together.' She replied.

'Hope it doesn't get any worse for you here. Will probably see you later at the autopsy.'

'For sure, enjoy the boat.'

'Yeah right, and thanks again Becks for your help.' Glen finished saying before he gathered up his bits and pieces and headed back to the small walled harbour where he hoped the boat was waiting.

Chapter Eleven: More Questions than Answers

The dawn was fast approaching as Glen stepped off the boat back on to the reassuring feeling of solid ground. The trip back across the water from the Mount had indeed been a harrowing experience and one that he certainly didn't want to repeat anytime soon. In fact he was pretty sure that he'd left his stomach somewhere back on the boat and it took him a few minutes before the churning sensation settled back down.

The quayside was still awash with press and local spectators all eager to keep abreast of any new developments. Trying to keep a low profile he kept his head down as he wandered up the cobbles, stopping briefly to find out from one of the police constables, keeping the crowd at bay, whereabouts the Super was currently hiding.

'Think he's in the MSI Unit. Last I heard they had managed to get hold of Lord St Leven.'

'Who?'

'Ah, he's Jack St Aubyn's father, but his title is Lord St Levan.'

'What is it with this country and your bloody titles. It's a wonder anybody can keep track of anything here.'

'Yeah, does get a bit confusing if you're not used to it.' The PC chuckled at Glen's baffled look.

'Thanks.' Glen added as he left the PC to his duties and headed off back towards the MSI Unit.

'What the hell happened to you? You look like a drowned rat. I've been inundated with questions from the 'Vultures' for the last few hours.'

The superintendent stated in a rather gruff tone as Glen entered the unit.

'Sorry boss, got a little bit stuck on the rock. I know now what it feels like to be a castaway.'

'Well now that you are back from your holiday, maybe you can enlighten me as to what we know.'

Glen didn't really appreciate the Super's tone but he understood that he must be under a great deal of pressure from several different directions to get to the bottom of the recent string of events.

'Well, I can't add much to what I told you earlier apart from that we have found a piece of evidence that might help us, but I need to make a few calls before I can say for sure whether it's a lead or not. I hear you have made contact with the father.'

'Yes, he's cancelled his holiday and will be back within hours. So I suggest that whatever calls you need to make, you better get on with it because I can promise you that when he gets here, there better be something tangible to tell him. Otherwise you and I are going to be walking on some very hot coals indeed.'

'I understand.'

'Good, has Jim given any indication of when the autopsy is likely to take place?'

'Not yet, he's having to wait for the weather to settle. They can't move the body in this. Sure he'll move it as soon as he can.'

'Hmmm, yes I can see he's on a *pretty sticky wicket* as he would say. Ah well, some things are out of our control. Haven't you got some calls to make?' The Super said in a rather softer tone than his initial greeting.

'Boss, it's six in the morning. As much as I would like to, somehow I don't think the people I need to call are going to be in at this time in the morning.'

'Well I'm sure you can find something productive to do. You better get yourself a coffee or something. Oh and try to put something together that I can tell these 'flaming vipers', I swear if I see one more reporter in here; you may have to put me in handcuffs.'

'Ha yeah, no worries. I think I can do that. What did the estate worker say?'

'Oh not a lot. Just that it was his night off. His description of Jack St Aubyn matches the body, so it seems very likely that it is him. He was surprised that Jack was at the castle according to him Jack was on business in London and hadn't been expected back for sometime. Normally the household staff is made aware in advance that family members will be resident. So not a great deal of help really, you better make a start on your report, I'm intending on giving a full press briefing at nine. Hopefully that will get the vermin off our backs for a while.'

'Where is the nearest place for a decent coffee?'

'Machine's in the back, can't say it's decent but it's hot. And try to smarten yourself up a bit before nine. Can't have you looking like that. Better ring that wife of yours as well, bet she'll be having kittens by now.'

'Ah, no way. I totally forgot to ring her earlier. Will be in the doghouse now, for sure. Hopefully she'll get over it and drop off some dry clothes too.'

'Just get a squad car to pick some up. Don't think she would like to be around here, knowing her luck she'd turn up just as the body is being moved, then you really would be in the doghouse, definitely not a sight for a young lady to witness.'

'Yeah, don't think she would appreciate that.' Glen replied, as he made a move in the direction of the coffee machine.

The Super was right. The coffee was like ditch water, but Glen didn't care, anything hot was good right about now. The cold was beginning to set in as he sat shivering in his wet clothes. He hadn't really noticed it earlier but then he had been busy working, whereas now he was just sitting trying to write up his notes into something tangible that the Super could use for the press. The heater on the wall of the cabin next to him helped a bit but it wasn't the best in the world and certainly wasn't going to dry him out by nine. It wasn't long before he plucked up the courage and rang home.

'Hey Hun, how are you? Hope the little one didn't take too long to put back to bed.'

'No he was fine. You sound tired, everything okay down there?'

'Yeah, been a long night and probably going to be an even longer day, lot going on down here. But I'm fine.' Glen said with a sigh, deciding not to tell her about the injury to his side. It wasn't an outright lie because he was feeling fine, if a little cold, wet and bruised. He just didn't want her to worry and so had made his mind up that he could deal with the repercussions later. 'Any chance that you could put some clothes together for me, have got a little wet down here. Oh and a towel would be handy.'

'Oh honey, you poor thing. Sure, anything in particular. I can drop them off in a bit if you like.'

'Um, just another suit would be good, got a press conference at nine. Don't worry about dropping them off, one of the squad cars will swing by to pick them up.'

'You sure, it won't be any trouble. Will only take ten, fifteen minutes tops.'

'It's a bit busy down here, you'll struggle to park and they may be about to bring the body from the island so don't think it's really the right time to come across. No, I think I'll get the guys to pop over.'

'Anybody we know.'

'Not really, but can't talk about that right now.'

'Well whatever you prefer, as long as you are okay.'

'All good. I'll see you a bit later, Hun.'

'Okay, just promise me you'll try and get some rest at some point. You've been up for hours.'

'I'll be fine, Hun. I can sleep later. Talk to you soon. Love you.'

'Love you too. Mwah.'

Glen didn't like not telling her everything but he knew that if he had told her about the injury there would have been an endless string of questions followed by the mandatory mini lecture on how he should take more care of himself. Not to mention the line about now that he was a father he shouldn't be putting himself in harm's way quite so often. All of which he knew would happen later and with a great deal more ferocity, but it was still a conversation he preferred to have at home in person than over the phone; especially as at that precise moment he would need to concentrate on where the evidence was going to take him, let alone what details he needed to cover for the press conference.

Looking down at the scrawled notes he was trying to put into a more ordered format, Glen's frown deepened. It didn't seem like much, just a brief section on the body and the broken tomb coupled with a few lines on the rest of the scene. The specifics about the ring and the ammunition he was going to omit at this stage. These were details that didn't need to be made public at that point. It was still very thin but it was just one of those difficult cases that popped up from time to time, testing the police's abilities to gradually piece together the fragments into something more concrete. As frustrating as it was, he also found it intriguing and exciting. It wasn't very often that he was presented with a puzzle that seemed to raise more questions than it provided answers. And that seemed to be pulling him towards the upper echelons of power.

He wondered if this could end up being a career case, one of those that can make or break you. He hoped it would be the former but only time would tell which outcome he was destined for.

The significance of the ring still played heavily on his mind but he knew that he would have to wait until the College of Arms opened before he could follow that particular line of enquiry.

He'd tried to Google the Latin motto that was on the ring but unfortunately apart from confirming that its meaning was indeed what Becky had suggested, *Truth and Hope* he couldn't find any family coat of arms referenced as having that particular phrasing and there were so many family coats of arms, crests, emblems etcetera that contained squirrels that he had to stop looking otherwise he was likely to go a little bit nuts himself.

He also couldn't fathom out what Jack was doing there if he was meant to be on business in London. And why hadn't he told any of the staff that he would be resident?

'Glen, sorry to disturb you.' One of the other DIs said interrupting his train of thought. 'There's a PC here with your change of clothes and a coffee compliments of the Desk Sergeant.'

'Well better late than never I suppose.' Glen replied referring to the promised coffee from a good six hours ago. 'What time is it?'

'Half eight.'

'Ah, no way, totally lost track of time. Right okay, can you scan these and give a copy to the Super while I change.'

'Yeah sure. Anything else you need.'

'Not at the moment. Just tell him I'll give him a quick briefing before he talks to the press. Where's he planning on holding it?'

'In The Godolphin Arms. It's the only venue big enough at short notice'

'Okay, tell him I'll be over shortly.' Glen replied as he took the parcel of clothes, dashing into an empty interview room in which to quickly change.

Glen felt slightly naked as he emerged from the interview room having put on the fresh clothes; his almost trademark Harris Tweed overcoat was still too wet to wear and without it he felt incomplete. Maybe it was just because he was so used to the extra weight, and without it, he felt something was missing or maybe it was because he felt it was like an invisible shield keeping him apart from all the nastiness that he encountered on an almost daily basis. Whichever it was, at this moment in time he felt uneasy almost vulnerable. He certainly noticed the biting cold as he left the MSI Unit and made his way over to The Godolphin Arms, pushing his way past the hoard of reporters and photographers all waiting to be allowed into the building.

'You ready for this?' The Super asked as Glen entered the bar come restaurant area that had been rearranged for the press conference, a long trestle table had been set up at one end, facing row upon row of currently empty seats.

'Ready as I will ever be. Anything you want to know before you start?'

'No, your notes are clear enough. Just follow my lead. I'll deal with the questions. You just sit there and do what you do best.' The Super added before turning to a sergeant on the door. 'Okay, Sergeant. Let's get this over with. You can let them in now.'

'Ladies and Gents. You can come in now. Please take your seats. The press conference is about to begin. All questions will be answered in due course.' The Sergeant announced to the crowd now jostling to get through the doors. 'Come on, let's have a bit of order here. There's room for everybody and it's not going to start until you are ready. So there's no need to push.' The Sergeant added as they tried to surge past him into the room.

'Thought you Brits were meant to be good at queuing?' Glen whispered in the ear of the Super sitting next to him as he watched the undignified behaviour of all the reporters as they battled with each other to get the best seats.

'Ha, this lot. You've got to be joking. I've seen wild dogs with better manners.' The Super muttered back, he had half thought about saying it just loud enough for the closest members of the press to hear, but had thought better of it at the last moment. He didn't want to get off on the wrong foot. He had been through too many of these in his time to know just how careful you had to be. These people would pick up on anything, the slightest show of weakness and they could crucify you. Twisting your words so much that by the time they hit print you wouldn't be able to recall if that was or wasn't what you had said.

'Mind your step with this lot, they have their uses but just be very careful.' The Super added.

'Right Ladies and Gentleman and Mr Ladyman.' The Super jokingly opened, breaking the tension in the room, and causing laughter to spread across the crowd. He knew it was a serious occasion but he also was well aware that he needed to get them on his side from the start if he was to have any chance of controlling the flow of information afterwards.

'Are the rumours true that Jack St Aubyn is dead?' A lady's voice called out from the back.

'Geraldine, you know how this works, we will answer questions later. For now just let me tell you what we know.' The Super replied before continuing to brief the press on what they believed had happened and what they had discovered upon arriving at the Mount.

Glen's mind began to wander about halfway through the Super's briefing, he had been over this so many times by now that he didn't really need to listen and his mind was still on the ring, the coat of arms and what the College of Arms might be able to tell him.

It was only the slight kick of the Super's foot against his ankle that snapped him back into the room as the briefing was beginning to draw to a close and the flurry of questions from the floor began.

'So can you confirm the rumours of Jack St Aubyn?' Geraldine asked repeating her question from before.

'At this time we cannot confirm this. The body has yet to be formally identified. As soon as we know we shall release a statement.'

'What line of enquires are you following. And have you ruled anything out?' Another asked.

'At this time we have not ruled anything out. There is still a great deal of evidence to process and we are actively pursuing all lines of enquiry.'

'Who is leading the investigation?'

'I am in overall command of the investigation. DI Harris, here, is the lead investigator.'

'Isn't he a bit young?'

'DI Harris has a lot of experience in the field and has worked on a number of cases of this nature. I feel very confident that he is the right man for the job. He has both mine and the Force's full support.'

'Can you confirm that there was more than one fatality?'

'There is not enough evidence at this time to either confirm or deny this.'

'Was anything taken from the Castle.'

'I'll let DI Harris answer this one.' The Super replied dropping Glen right into the mix.

'From what we have seen so far, nothing was taken from the castle. There is evidence to suggest that one of the Tombs in the crypt was broken into but at this stage we do not know if anything was taken.'

'Are you saying that this could have just been an act of wanton vandalism and a case of wrong place, wrong time?'

'At this stage we cannot rule this out.' Glen replied holding back the urge to run a finger around his collar as he began to feel the stuffy heat of the room itch, he needed to keep his cool and not look under pressure.

'Was this a gang related shooting or an act of terrorism? Is there any danger to the public?'

'We do not believe so, and we would urge the public to go about everyday activities. However, we would stress that if anybody does have any information that would help with our enquires that they should come forward and not to take matters or beliefs into their own hands.' Glen replied stressing the point of contacting the police.

'I think that is enough for now. We will keep you up to date as further developments occur.' The Super jumped in brining the briefing to a close, he desperately wanted to avoid the terrorist notion. He had seen the effects of that sort of insinuation in small communities and didn't want to have to deal with rogue members of the community carrying out their own witch-hunt.

'That's it for now folks. Please let us get on with our investigation and as soon as we have a clearer picture we will let you know.' He added as he stood and began to make his way out of the room ushered by two PCs, struggling to keep the members of the press at bay as the room filled with the sound of so many fresh unanswered questions.

Glen managed to slip out of the room unnoticed, because of the rather abrupt ending of the briefing, all of the press' attention was now directed towards the Super and they totally forgot about him. He was glad that he didn't come under too much flack. It was true that he had been in enough of these briefings to be able to hold his own, but at this point in time he just wanted to follow up with his lines of enquiry and the sooner he could do this the better.

Chapter Twelve: Patchwork

The adrenaline that had been fuelling her determination to keep her emotions at bay for the last few hours had finally run out, as Rachel parked the 4x4 at Martinstowe. The realisation that Jack was no longer with them gradually began to sink in and she broke down into a stream of tears that she could hold back, no longer.

James could see that she needed something to keep her mind occupied and off the painful events of the last few hours.

'Rach, can you help me with Chris. I need to get him into the kitchen. I will have to stitch up this wound.' She did not respond straight away as the raw emotion was still in control.

'Rach! Come on give us a hand.' The urgency in his voice had the desired effect, wiping the tears from her cheeks she finally began to motivate herself to help him to manoeuvre Chris out of the Range Rover and across the gravel, before entering the mansion and carrying Chris through the corridors to the kitchen.

'Jesus, you are a heavy lump, what the hell have you been eating?' James said as he and Rachel struggled to man-handle Chris inside.

James quickly brushed all of the magazines and newspapers off the kitchen table on to the floor, creating a mess was the least of his concerns. They managed to roll Chris up on to the table.

'I need some towels, hot water, the medi-kit and a bottle of brandy.'

'Where are the towels kept?' She asked.

'On the landing, first door on the left at the top of the stairs.' He replied as he began to remove the temporary dressing. The wound had sort of begun to clot but it looked messy and definitely required cleaning up before James could stitch it.

Rachel put the kettle on to the Aga to boil before going off to find the other bits that James would need to perform the crude operation. She soon returned with the towels and other bits, by which time the kettle had reached the boil. She fetched a bowl and filled it with the steaming hot water.

'Right fella, tilt your head up a sec and drink this.' James said to Chris as he opened the bottle of brandy and tipped a large quantity straight down his throat, causing him to cough and splutter.

'No more.' Chris just about managed to say.

'Just a bit more, you're gonna need it. This is going to hurt quite a bit I'm afraid.' James replied as he poured another decent measure into Chris before turning his attention to the wound.

James dipped one of the towels into the bowl of hot water and used it to clean in and around the wound, before he took off his leather belt.

'Sorry bud, it's the only thing I've got. Bite down on this, this may well burn a lot.' He said to Chris as he placed the folded leather strap between his teeth.

'Rach, can you pass me the bottle of surgical spirit from the medi-kit?' She was in the process of handing him the bottle, but her hands were shaking so much that she dropped it. The glass cracked before shattering, sending the spirit running off all over the floor. Rachel burst into another flood of tears at the realisation of what she had just done. James realised immediately that she was suffering from shock.

'Hey don't worry about it. Not the end of the world, will just have to use the brandy instead.'

Chris bit down heavily on the leather as the brandy felt like it seared the open flesh. His groans of pain made Rachel wince but she didn't look away. She handed James a sail maker's needle and some cotton thread that had been sterilising in a small dish of brandy.

James took about 20 minutes to finish suturing up the wound. It wasn't the prettiest of suturing and certainly wouldn't win any NHS awards but it would do the job. He finished the repair off, sticking a melolin pad over his work to protect the suture from being ripped out and then after helping Chris to his feet, wrapped a bandage around his midriff. He then assisted Chris to the sitting room and on to a sofa that would act as a makeshift bed, before he could finally turn his attention to Rachel.

He found her in the smoking room and attempted to console her. But she pushed him away.

'Rach, I know you are upset but he was our friend too.'

'But you just left him there. I thought you people never left a man behind.' She shouted at him between the tears.

'I had no choice. I had to think of everybody else and the book.'

'Oh, don't play that card with me. You lot and that stupid book. Is a bit of paper really worth more than someone's life? And don't tell me it was for the greater good because even you don't really deep down believe that, do you?'

'I don't expect you to understand, but let's be clear Jack knew what he was getting into. He understood the risks; if there had been even the slightest chance of saving him you must believe I would have taken it. At the end of the day I had to make a split second decision, one I will now have to live with; a decision that I wouldn't wish upon anybody else to have to take. I'm truly sorry that the outcome could not have been different.'

'Maybe I don't understand and maybe I'm angry because I almost lost Chris as well and could not imagine a world without him, but right now I can't talk to you about it.' She said as she pushed past him; leaving the room.

James half thought about going after her, but decided that it wasn't the prudent thing to do at that moment. The pain of the event was too fresh in her mind for her to see the bigger picture. James knew from previous experiences that everybody dealt with loss in their own way and although he would always be a shoulder to cry on maybe now was not the best time. She needed her space but also required a close-eye as there was a potential her shock might manifest into something more serious.

Chapter Thirteen: Chains of Evidence

The gentle tocking tick of the clock on the wall of the MSI Unit was beginning to get to Glen. The minutes had gradually rolled into hours as he waited to hear back from the College of Arms. He had called them soon after the press conference, and spoken briefly to a receptionist. Unfortunately the receptionist had informed him that all of the Pursuivants, who dealt with family coats of arms, were currently unavailable and that he would pass on Glen's details as soon as one of them was free.

Glen hated waiting, normally he would have just got on with something else related with the case but on this occasion due to the lack of leads there wasn't a great deal he could do.

The SOCOs had finally managed to get away from the island and begun the arduous tasks of running ballistic tests on the ammunition, DNA sequencing the blood samples and attempting to match the one and only partial print they had found on the ring. As for the body, Professor Hertzog was in the last few stages of bagging it before shipping it back to the mainland. So for the moment at least all Glen could do was sit and watch as the second hand gradually swung round and round the clock face.

'Argh, I can't deal with this, I'm going to get some air.' Glen finally announced, not really addressing anybody in particular, his impatience ultimately getting the better of him.

Grabbing his Harris Tweed, that had eventually dried, he stepped out of the stuffy confines of the mobile unit into the chill of the stiff sea breeze; the remnants of the storm from the previous night. At least the rain had stopped, he thought to himself as he strolled off down the street with no particular destination in mind. He just needed something to do to kill a bit of time and maybe to organise the jumble of questions still swirling around his head.

Turning off West End, he ended up walking along the promenade that formed the boundary between man and nature. The view of the castle seemed so peaceful now, compared to that of the night before when the wrath of the gods had unleashed a natural power that he never wanted to feel again. Glen realised that he had never been in anything quite like it, and had a newfound appreciation for all those brave volunteers of the Lifeboat service who risked their lives to save those unlucky enough to become victims of the harsh weather that battered the British coastline.

He was still puzzling out why Jack had returned to the castle unannounced. *Was he forced against his will to return? Or was he complicit? Had his important business trip gone sour, leaving him short of money and required him to steal from his own family?* It was just another line of enquiry to add to a steadily growing list of potential avenues to explore—the personal financial affairs of Jack St Aubyn. The family was clearly very well off, to the point of being obscene, but it did not necessarily follow that Jack himself didn't have financial problems.

Glen suddenly realised that he had wandered quite a fair way along the curving promenade and it was probably time that he got back to the unit, especially as he now had a new line to explore. His phone began to vibrate in his pocket.

'Hey boss, just needed to step out for a bit.' Glen said as he answered the call.

'Well I need you to step back in. Jim's bringing the body across and I want you to accompany him to the autopsy.'

'Sure thing, be back in five.' Glen replied.

'Any news from the College of Arms?'

'No, not yet. I guess they are still busy.'

'Okay, well get back here as soon as you can, and if they haven't called by the time the autopsy has finished give them another nudge. His Lordship's plane has just landed so he will be back within the next couple of hours.'

'Sure thing. Oh, and boss, any chance someone can look into Jack

St Aubyn's financial situation? Just had a thought he might have been struggling for funds and had tried to steal something from the family to raise cash. Maybe he had accomplices that he then fell out with?'

'I'll get one of the other DIs to look into it. Interesting thought, good to see you exploring all possibilities.'

'See you in a bit.' Glen replied as he hung up the phone and briskly started to make his way back to the quayside where the boat transporting the body back to the mainland would dock.

Glen arrived just after the body had been loaded into the back of a private ambulance. He had to push his way through the crush of photographers, journalists and locals all jostling for a good position to see the black body pouch being loaded into the back of the blacked out private ambulance before it moved off from Marazion, accompanied by police outriders, to make the forty minute journey back to the Scientific and Technical Services Unit's (STSU) base at Truro. He managed to catch Jim just before he left for Truro.

'Hey, Jim. Any chance I can grab a lift?'

'No problem at all. Feel free to tag along.'

'How long do you expect this to take? His father will be back in the next few hours.'

'Well, we know cause of death so it shouldn't take too long, once we get it up on the table. Couple of hours max, I should think. Luckily we don't need to do Tox otherwise you could be waiting for a couple of weeks for the results. In this case it's relatively straight forward, a few photos, try and nail down the type of knife used and see if there are any useable prints, DNA traces that may have been left on the body, etcetera. Obviously you will have to wait a bit longer for those to be processed but I'd be confident to have the basics done pretty quickly.'

'That's a relief, time is definitely of the essence on this one.' Glen replied with a large yawn. Having been up for hours, tiredness was starting to get the better of him.

'Take the back seats if you like and grab a bit of shut eye, looks like you need it.' Jim suggested noticing the tell tale signs of sleeplessness, as they approached the awaiting the car. 'I can just about sleep in the front. No way I'm doing this autopsy without some. Thank God I have a driver, that's all I can say.'

'Cheers Jim, wondered when I'd be able to catch forty winks.' Glen replied as he got into the back of the pathologists car. And it was not long before sleep took hold of him.

The next thing he knew was Jim's voice calling out to him through his subconscious state.

'Glen, come on sleepy head. The night watchman is waiting. Time to hit the wicket.'

'Ugh, remind me never to take short naps again. Always feel like crap afterwards. Give me a min, need to focus… Right, okay let's go.' Glen replied in a half sleepy voice.

'Sure you up for the second innings?'

'Yeah, I'll be fine. Let's get this over with.'

'I can see you're not the forty winks kinda guy.'

'Hell no. Far better at just powering through and then paying for it later. 'Tis what I should have done in the first place.' He replied wiping the last of the sleep from his almost panda like rings.

The outside of the STSU looked as bleak and understated as Glen expected it to be as he stepped out of the car and followed Jim inside, twisting and turning down a rabbit warren like maze of corridors until Jim stopped outside a metallic silver door marked *Autopsy Room 2* with a red and white sign just below saying *Authorised Personnel Only*.

Glen could not help but feel slightly morbid and solemn as he walked inside to the outer scrub room.

'Try these on for size.' Jim said as he passed Glen a set of surgical scrubs before donning a set himself.

'Thanks, man. Sure glad I don't have to wear these every day.'

'You get used to it. Right you ready?' Jim replied as he finished washing his hands before pulling on two sets of latex gloves.

The inner room was almost as bleak and uninspiring as the outside of the building. Its white walls and metallic tables gave the room a very cold uninviting feel, not that Glen was surprised, he had been in many such rooms before. This wasn't really a room that you wanted to end up in if one could avoid it, and if one did you would hope you would be walking in rather than being carried in like a piece of meat to be poked and prodded. The mortuary techs had already laid out the body pouch containing Jack's corpse on the table in the centre of the room ready for Jim to begin the investigatory process.

Jim took out a dictaphone from a draw in one of the side tables. The lab did actually have a full recording system but he was old school and some habits die-hard.

In a slow and steady voice he began to talk into the small recording device.

'12:30pm on Monday 29th October 2012, Autopsy Case Number: Five, Seven, Three, Four. Professor Jim Herzog Chief Forensic Pathologist of the Scientific and Technical Services Unit for Devon and Cornwall, supervising. Assisting are mortuary technicians: Rebecca Graham, who will be assisting both the external and internal examinations and Robert Watkins, who will be taking photographic evidence and cataloguing evidence collected, also present, in an observational capacity is Detective Inspector Glen Harris from the Penzance Constabulary.

The body is that of a male in his mid twenties, dressed in black combat gear, with what appears to be some sort of black camouflage cream smeared over the face and neck. Robert can you take some photos, please. Make sure you get some close ups of the wounds and full frontal aspects of the face with right and left profiles. May help with identification later, I'll take a swab of the *Camo Cream* for analysis, before we clean it up.' Professor Herzog said before he began to use an ear bud type swab to collect a sample of the *Camo Cream*, inserting it into a screw top test tube and clearly labelling the sample.

'Right, Becky can clean the face now, so Robert can take some pictures of it without the camouflage. Glen, after this we'll send the body over to the radiographer to get some X-rays, it will give us and idea if there are any metal fragments left in any of the wounds and we should get some dental X-rays which could help you with ID.'

'You're leaving the clothes on for this?' Glen asked.

'We do both, with and without the clothing, just the procedure that we have to follow. We have to do it by the book, can't afford to step outside the rules, if this went to court the defence could tear us apart for straying from procedure. Got to make sure you have the best chance of catching your man.'

'How long will it take? If it's going to be long I might step out to make some calls until you are ready to do the internal examination.'

'Probably be an hour or so.' Jim replied.

'In that case I'll leave you to it. Give me a shout when you are going to start.'

'We'll let you know when play will resume. The time is 12:40, DI Glen Harris leaving the room.' Jim added into the dictaphone.

Glen left the room walking back into the scrubbing area, depositing the used medical scrubs into a bin before heading off in the direction of reception.

'Is there a free office somewhere I can use to make a few calls?' Glen asked at the desk.

'I'll just check for you. There should be one free on the next floor up.' The receptionist replied, as she picked up the phone receiver and dialled a number. 'Hi, I've got a DI down here who was wondering if they can use an office for a bit whilst they are waiting for some results. Is there any chance he can use the meeting room?'

Glen couldn't make out the response so he had to wait until the receptionist had put the phone down.

'Looks like the meeting room is available. Up the stairs to the first floor and then second room on the left, you can't miss it, big glass double doors.'

'Thanks, much appreciated.'

'You're welcome.'

'Can you give me a shout when Jim is ready to start the internal examination.'

'Certainly.'

'Great, thanks again.' Glen replied as he headed off from the desk to find the meeting room.

Taking a seat in one of the leather backed office chairs in the meeting room Glen took out his phone and called the number for the College of Arms, by any luck one of the Pursuivants would now be available.

'Hi, DI Glen Harris speaking, I called earlier today regarding a case that I'm working on.'

'Oh yes, I remember. I was actually about to call you. I have managed to speak to the Rouge Croix Pursuivant. He is most interested in your case and would be happy to help with an identification of the coat of arms you have found.'

'Ah no way, that's great, I could do with all the help I can get right now. Is he available at the moment?'

'I think so, is it okay if I put you on hold for a minute while I check?'

'Sure thing.' Glen replied, before the standard classical music began to come through the line. Glen was never one for waiting but at least he knew that there was beginning to be some light at the end of what had begun to feel like a particularly dark tunnel. Glen drummed his fingers on the table in front of him whilst he waited, not noticing that he was drumming to the rhythm of the classical tune.

'DI Harris, thank you for waiting. He is available, I'll transfer you now.'

'Fantastic, thank you.'

'I hope he can be of some help.' The receptionist replied before transferring Glen to the Pursuivant's private line.

'Good afternoon DI Harris, Leonard Petrinella speaking. I understand from the receptionist that you have a piece of evidence pertaining to a current case bearing an unusual coat of arms.'

'Yes, Sir. That is correct. It was found on the remnants of what we believe to be a signet ring. I have tried to search for it online but so far without any success. I was hoping that you may be able to help.'

'Well, I will see what I can do. The College does have extensive records, many of which you will not be able to find online, especially if the coat of arms is no longer in use or has become obscure. What does it contain?'

'It has a squirrel cracking a nut between it's paws, with what looks like a Maltese Cross behind it's back, the end of the squirrel's tail sort of curls into the centre of the cross.'

'Interesting, not one that I would know off the top of my head, but then there are so many different coats of arms and quite a lot with squirrels. Is there a motto of any kind?'

'Yes, there appears to be the words *Veritas et Spes* engraved on to the shoulders of the ring.'

'Ah, *Truth and Hope* a fine motto. That should help to narrow it down a bit. I don't suppose you would be able to send me any pictures of the item? I realise it is a piece of evidence, nevertheless it would be helpful to actually visualise it.'

'Sure thing, I have some photos on my phone that I can happily email across. I presume you can't really give me an idea of how long it will take to research?'

'Unfortunately not, it all depends how quickly we can link the clues to what we have in our records. What area of the country was it found in, we may be able to start by looking at local families and work out from there.'

'It was found near Penzance, at present I can't be more specific for obvious reasons.'

'I think I can guess, judging on what I have seen on the news this morning. Such a shame, a real tragedy, if it turns out to be Jack St Aubyn. He was a really bright spark that one.'

'You knew him?'

'Well, not very well. But yes I did have the pleasure of crossing paths a few times. The only time we really spoke at any length was when I designed his crest for his coat of arms, for which of course there had to be a meeting to discus his preferences.'

'Oh, I thought they were passed down through the family.'

'Well yes and no. The family does have a coat of arms, but then each member will have their own variation of that. And before you ask, the answer is no. What you have is not Jack's.'

'Shame, would have made this a lot simpler. What's your email? I'll send you the photos right away.'

'Ah, now that I'm afraid you will have to get off the website. Unfortunately I can never remember the bloody thing, it's like trying to remember my mobile number. Ruddy modern technology, I can use a computer and a phone but can't for the life of me keep track of all the numbers and addresses. All those bloody dot coms, dot co dot uks, dot govs, dot orgs etcetera, drives me up the wall sometimes. One day I'm sure I'll forget my own name then I really will be in trouble.' The Pursuivant said with a slight laugh.

'Yeah I have that problem too sometimes, although normally with car keys.' Glen replied jokingly. 'I'll find your address on the website and we can go from there. Thank you for your time, Sir. And I hope we will speak again soon.'

'Not at all, anytime.'

Hanging up Glen quickly looked up the Rouge Croix Pursuivant's email and typed out a brief email on his phone with some of the photos he had taken attached, and sent it. He had hoped that he would have got an answer over the phone, but understood that as there were so many coats of arms it would take the Pursuivant sometime to research it. It was irritating, although he was beginning to make some progress at last, he still felt as if the tunnel had just got ever so slightly longer and that the light that had been getting closer had just dimmed a little. For every step forward he took, it seemed that he was destined to take three back. He hoped that he would begin to make some real progress soon otherwise he feared this could become one of those cases that remained unsolved, that irksome one off that could end up bugging him for the rest of his career.

Glen's thoughts were cut short by the receptionist bursting into the room, in somewhat of a flutter.

'DI Harris, please you must come quick. We have a bit of a situation downstairs.'

'What's wrong?'

'Lord St Leven has arrived and is demanding to see his son's body. Obviously, we can't allow that at the moment as it's still in X-ray, but he won't take no for an answer. He's kicking up an awful fuss.'

'Okay, I'll be right down. Where is he at the moment?'

'Being restrained by security in the lobby.'

'Great just what I need now, an angry lord.' Glen replied as he got up and hurriedly followed the receptionist down to the lobby.

Before Glen even reached the lobby to the sight of the Lord of the Mount being fully restrained by two burly security guards he could already hear the commotion.

'…know who I am? I demand that you release me! Let me go. I'm fully within my rights to see my son. Do you lot not understand? That's my son's body in there, let me go!' The irate and grief stricken voice of Lord St Leven clearly resonating up the staircase.

'It's okay guys, let him go.' Glen said barely looking at the two guards as he descended into the lobby. The two men stared at him in disbelief and one was about to object but was cut short by Glen's repetition. 'Let him go.'

'Thank you.' The lord said straightening his jacket as the two guards reluctantly released their hold of him. 'Now can I see my son?'

'I'm afraid it ain't as simple as that.' Glen calmly replied, quickly raising his hand before the lord erupted again. 'Please, Your Lordship, can we talk first? There are things that we need to go through. I'm not saying that you can't see the body, just not right this minute. Please, I understand it is a difficult time, being a father myself I know I would want answers too if this happened to my child, but this has to be the way.'

Glen waited for the lord to reply, watching his eyes, he could see the internal struggle that the man was going through, on the one hand the raw emotion that was firmly in control and driving his passionate demands to see the body and on the other, the calm rationale of the years, making the case that maybe he needed to take a step back.

'Very well, if this is the only way. Then I will oblige, but I still expect to see my boy.'

'All in good time. Please, Your Lordship, this way.' Glen replied, gesturing for him to take the stairs that Glen had recently descended. Turning to the receptionist 'We'll use that meeting room, if that's okay. Just tell Jim that all is under control and I'll be with him as soon as I can.'

'That's fine, I'll make sure you are not disturbed.'

'Thanks. Oh, can you sort out some tea or coffee. I think his Lordship is going to need it.'

'I'll make sure some is brought up.'

'Thanks.' Glen replied as he began to walk back up the stairs with Lord St Leven. 'Just here, Your Lordship. Please, take a seat.'

'Thank you. Now what can you tell me about my son's death?'

'Well to be honest, Sir, we haven't officially identified the body as that of your son's. This is one of the reasons why we couldn't let you see the body. Did your son have any birth marks or other distinguishing features that would help us to identify him?'

'No, he didn't have any birthmarks. Can't I just look at the body?'

'Umm, well it's not a very pretty sight, not something I would encourage a parent to have to see, if we can avoid it. Did he wear any jewellery specific to him?'

'Well as a matter of fact yes, there was a signet ring that he always seemed to wear. Although not the family one, much to mine and his mother's displeasure.'

'Oh, really. What was it?'

'Had a Squirrel and a Cross on it. Bloody thing, never understood why he choose to wear that over the family one. He never did give me a proper explanation.'

'Do you know how he came to have it?'

'A gift from a friend, I think. Must have been a very dear friend indeed to choose that over the family. We had several discussions about it, but he never took it off.'

'I take it you don't know which friend.'

'No, he never said.'

'Well unfortunately we didn't find a ring on the body. Anything else that might help and injuries that left a scar?' Glen deliberately left out the fact he had found that very ring at the scene.

'He did break his leg when he was still at school which required an operation and pins. I remember he was hobbling around on crutches for months.'

'That might be enough, they are X-raying the body at the moment so if it is your son they should find the pins.'

'If it turns out to be the case that they can match the pins, can I make a request from one father to another to see him. I take on board what you are saying about the state the body is in, nevertheless I would like to see him if I could.'

'I'm not promising anything, but I will see what I can arrange. And I can assure you, we are doing everything we can to ascertain what happened at your home.'

'I understand. I can wait.'

Glen left his Lordship staring out of the first floor window of the meeting room and ventured out to find out what Jim had found from the X-rays.

Slipping on the now familiar set of medical scrubs, Glen prepared himself to enter the autopsy room for a second time.

'Ah, your back in play I see, Jim said as he stood up straight from peering over the now naked corpse. I was just about to ring you to say we were starting the internal examination. Good timing.'

'Jim, before you start, can I have a quick word? In private.' Glen added glancing at the two mortuary technicians in the room.

'Sure, give me a second guys. We shall resume presently.' Jim said to the two techs as he made a quick note in the dictaphone about pausing the autopsy and followed Glen into the scrub room.

'So what's up?'

'Did you find anything in the X-rays?'

'Not much apart from a few metal fragments in the chest and knee, which I was about to remove for analysis.' Jim replied in a tone that hinted that he was less than pleased by the interruption to the process.

'Anything else?'

'Oh yes, pins in the leg. An old injury, would have been quite a nasty break at the time by the looks.'

'I was afraid you were going to say that.'

'Oh why? His Lordship mentioned that his son had pins in his leg from a break he suffered at school.'

'Ah, oh dear. That is sad news indeed.'

'He wants to see the body.'

'Well you certainly can't show him it in this state. That's enough to give anybody nightmares. I tell you what, let us finish the autopsy, clear up etcetera, and make it as presentable as possible and then he can see it. As long as the serial numbers on the pins match up.'

'Sure, that sounds like a good idea. I'll let him know. How long do you think you will be?'

'Well, several hours yet. There's a lot more to do than I had first anticipated.'

'Okay, I'll suggest he puts himself up somewhere for the night and he can see it in the morning. Sound fair?'

'Yes, that would suit. Now I really must get on. Are you going to watch?'

'Umm no I think I've seen enough for one day. And I still have few questions about Jack's financial situation for his Lordship.'

'That's fine, I hope you find the answers you are looking for.' Jim said before returning to the autopsy room.

Glen left to the sound of Jim's voice saying 'Right people, let play resume, sorry for the unscheduled stoppage. Now lets have a look what we've got.' Glen smiled knowing that the autopsy was in good hands and left the room to return to the Lord of the Mount.

Chapter Fourteen: Remembering the Fallen

The week that followed the tragic death of Jack St Aubyn, was a bit awkward. Rachel avoided talking to James as much as she could and when they did sit down for meals together she rarely spoke. James didn't try and force the issue, he respected her space and thought that she would eventually come around; she just needed time to process the events.

Chris was well on the way to making a full recovery. The wound that he been stitched up was definitely going to leave a scar but that didn't bother Chris, just another one to add to the collection, and besides 'chicks dig scars' he would say.

The mental scar left by Jack's demise however, was going to take longer to repair. They had all felt a great sense of loss for their fallen comrade, none more so than Rachel. She was of a similar age to Jack and although she hadn't know him for as long as either Chris or James. It had really hit her hard. She struggled to understand why it had happened to someone so young and full of life. Not to mention why James had not done more to rescue him before the end came. Maybe James was right and she just didn't understand, nevertheless wasn't he meant to be one of the most highly trained former *Special Operators*, so surely he could have done more? Her mind was just a confused mess of questions, anger and deep regret. Why did James not take that shot? Why could he not retrieve the body? How could a book, however old and valuable, be more important than somebody's life?

It took her a couple of days to realise that she was not actually angry with James. At the end of the day had it not been for his actions both herself and Chris would also probably not be there. She owed him her life and maybe that was what she was angry about; that James had been forced to make a choice, a choice that had she not been there in the first place, he may not have needed to take. She had never been in the position where you just have to make a split second decision of such importance, a God-like pronouncement as to who lives and who dies. This was the root cause of her anger that she may have been the reason for Jack's death and it vexed her greatly.

James and Chris tried their best to convince her that what happened up there on the ramparts would have happened regardless of whether she had been there or not. To believe otherwise was just her fragile state of mind trying to resolve the painful feelings of loss, that realistically were unresolvable. They knew that she would end up going one of two ways, drawing a line under the tragedy and moving on, or tearing herself apart with grief.

'We need to keep her mind on other things. This state she is in now is no good. You know what can happen, we've both seen this in the field and you know the end result is not good.' Chris remarked to James from his outstretched position on the sofa, currently acting as his makeshift bed until the wound had healed enough to allow him to move around without the danger of tearing it open again.

'I know what you mean, it's going to be an uphill battle. In this sort of state the mind plays tricks and you begin to doubt yourself. You know she shouldn't have been there in the first place, she wasn't ready.'

'Like I had a choice. She would have come even if you had told her to stay. She's incredibly strong-willed and stubborn when she wants to be. Maybe she wasn't quite ready, but let's face it; there never is a perfect time for these things. There always has to be a first time for everything and you've said it yourself many a time, that baptism by fire generally produces the best.'

'Takes after someone else in that department.' James replied in a tone directed at his injured compatriot. 'She's certainly been baptised, now. Maybe doing some more research would help, hopefully it will keep her mind occupied at least.'

'Can't hurt. What else has been going on since my 'minor' surgery? Any news from the Mount? Is anyone investigating?'

'Ha investigating would be an understatement, from what I have seen on the local news this morning there's a whole army of investigators crawling all over the place. Luckily they're being hampered by the weather so there's a chance it won't come to much.'

'Better keep an eye on the situation. Nobody can afford for the police to start poking around. That would be a disaster at this stage.'

'I know. If they have found anything, they have yet to mention it. Could be your sort of poker player running the show, keeping their cards very close to their chest. Waiting for somebody to make a mistake.'

'Have you spoken to Jack's father yet?'

'No, you know I can't. He didn't know anything about what Jack was doing or our activities. Apart from sending my condolences there wouldn't be much more I could add. Plus they haven't made a formal ID yet. If I sent my condolences a lot of questions would be heading our way very quickly. I think the best course is to wait until the funeral, which I'm sure will not be long. Could also be a good opportunity to sound out if the Police have any leads.'

'We'll have to tread carefully, if we go. A foot in the wrong place and they may end up breathing down our necks.'

'We? Are you high? Think you must have taken too much codeine if you think that you are going. There's no way you are in any fit state for that. Talk about putting feet in the wrong places, if anybody noticed your wound we'd be in an interrogation faster that you could say, *Usain Bolt.*'

'Well let's see what happens. You never know it may be weeks until the funeral.'

'We'll see, but I'm not keen.'

On the morning of the funeral, James' uncle arrived at Martinstowe, he had a few matters of estate business to address and also he possessed the only key to the Special Collections room at Martinstowe where the rarest and most valuable of the books were kept.

Like most of the males in James' family he was tall and broad shouldered. Even though he was now in his early seventies he still cut an imposing figure, although those that really knew him would describe him as one of the gentlest and kindest of souls. Much of the time he liked to keep to himself, he was an avid fisherman and enjoyed the odd choice cigar.

Leaving Rachel in the company of his uncle, James and Chris travelled back down to the Mount for Jack's funeral. Rachel did not like being left at Martinstowe and was angry about the decision that she was not to attend but she did understand the reasons behind it. Not only was there a real possibility that Norwood or some of his men would be present at the funeral but also the police had issued a plea for information regarding two men and a woman, last to be seen in the company of the late Jack St Aubyn. James and Chris were both good at blending in, whereas the sight of two men and a girl might raise more suspicion and attract too much unwanted attention.

A cold nip in the air accompanied the crisp November morning; the ground, hedgerows and trees were all softly covered in a diamond like layer of glittering frost. The overcast sky seemed to intensify the sombre atmosphere of the crowd that had gathered at the quayside of the Mount awaiting the arrival of Jack's coffin.

The coffin was transported from the mainland on a long boat manned by eight sturdy oarsmen. The oarsmen were dressed in black coats over white shirts and white trousers. All the men wore black cravats around their necks, and straw boaters surrounded by a black grosgrain ribbon upon which the golden letters of the boat's name had been embroidered by hand, *Ultima*. She had been named, at least a hundred years ago, by one of the previous Lords of St Leven.

The lord had taken a great interest in Greek Mythology, and although had known full well that the name of Charon's ferryboat had never been revealed, he had liked to think it would just be called *The Last*.

The men strained at the oars as they rowed across the 300 metre stretch from the mainland, as the boat neared the quayside, the eight oars rose slowly skyward as a mark of respect before they were carefully stowed along the gunnels of the boat as she came to rest along the dockside. The oarsmen gently took up the coffin on their shoulders, before steadily making their way up towards the castle. In front of them four drummers played a slow beat. The family followed the coffin and the rest of the crowd fell in behind them to complete the procession to the castle.

Chris was amazed at the numbers of people including many lords and ladies that had turned out to pay their final respects to Jack. He supposed it was only right, after all Jack would have been the next in line to inherit the title of Lord St Levan, an honour that would now pass to his younger brother Piers when he came of age. Still at school Piers St Aubyn would not officially be named as the heir presumptive until his 21st birthday.

Jack's parents were clearly still in shock at the abrupt death of their eldest son. So far the police had been of little help, they had found little evidence in order to track down Jack's killers, or at least that was how it appeared on the surface. Their current public position was that Jack must have stumbled upon some burglars trying to break into the castle and had died trying to protect his family home before he could raise the alarm.

James wished that he could tell Jack's father what had happened. Tell him how his son fought bravely to protect the freedom, which we all enjoy. Tell him that he had fought with the same courage that his ancestors had done during the crusades. That he had upheld the family's honour. Not that this would have helped to bring some sense of closure to the family, no parent is really prepared for the loss of a child. Unfortunately James knew that he could not. He hoped that one day he would be able to.

The procession paused outside the entrance to the chapel as the coffin followed the drummers inside. The drummers walked through the nave, bowing as they reached the transept under the tower of the church. Approaching the steps up to the chancel they removed the drums and laid them to create an altar, this was in accordance with the drumhead service, a tradition for honouring the dead of the St Aubyn family. The coffin was set down just behind this underneath the tower.

James and Chris looked up at the battlements with sadness, remembering the events of that fateful night, a night that they both wished could somehow be reversed; for the clock to rewind. Had they known then what the outcome would have been, the question that was nagging away at both of them was would they have gone through with it? A question that weighed especially heavily on James' mind, mainly because deep down inside he felt the answer would still have been yes. It was this painful realisation that he felt the greater good in preventing the codex from falling into the wrong hands at any cost, was a cost worth paying, made his guilt all the more difficult to come to terms with. Not just because of the loss of Jack but also because he had recognized that the logical conclusion to this thread was that he had already decided that he too was willing to pay the ultimate price.

A sudden sharp dig in James' ribs from Chris broke his train of thought.

'Isn't that the Detective in charge of the investigation, over there?' Chris said in a low voice so as not to be overheard.

'Where?'

'That tall chap on the phone standing near to the chapel entrance.' Chris said with the subtlest of nods in the direction of the chapel entrance.

'Does look very much like the photos I've seen in the papers. We'll have tread carefully around him. I would like to try and see if I can get some info but not at the cost of peaking his interest. We just can't afford for a policeman to start poking around.'

'Yeah, I know. C'mon let's go in before we do start attracting attention for loitering.'

Glen had intended to pay attention to who was arriving to attend the funeral. Ever since the identity of the body had been confirmed and the revelation that it had been a close friend of Jack's that had given him the signet ring, Glen had hoped that there was a chance they might attend the service. The way in which the ring had been crushed had sent him down the line of thought that may be Jack's death had been the result of a friendship turning sour, and that a fight had broken out in which the result was Jack's death. It wasn't a perfect theory. It still did not explain the gun battle at the Mount but it was the best that he could come up with at the moment. However, an untimely phone call had distracted him so he did not notice James and Chris pass him by on their way into the chapel.

'Hi DI Harris speaking.'

'Good Morning Detective, it's Leonard Petrinella from the College of Arms. I hope I haven't caught you at a bad time.'

'Well I was about to attend, Jack St Aubyn's funeral.'

'Oh, I had forgotten that was today. I can call some other time. It was really just a quick call tell you about what we have discovered regarding the coat of arms and motto that you passed on to us.'

This news took Glen slightly off guard and he didn't answer right away. He was torn, on the one hand he didn't want to miss the start of the funeral and be one of those people would had to sneak in at the back after it had started, and yet he had a burning desire to know what the Pursuivant had discovered. He knew that if he asked him to call back later, the knowledge that there was a potential new lead in the case would bug him all the way through the service. So he made a quick on the spot decision.

'No, it's okay. I think we can talk now. Will be a few more minutes before the service starts. What have you found since we last spoke?'

'Well, where to begin? I must admit it has been a bit of a roller coaster ride through some of our oldest records. And if my conclusions are correct you may have stumbled upon something that as far as we were aware was only legend.'

'Oh really, how so?'

'Well the squirrel cracking the nut along with the motto, most certainly points to an obscure line of a Jersey family, called *Pipon*, although their motto has always been written in French, *Vérité et Espérance* It translates to the same thing, *Truth and Hope*.'

'What can you tell me about that family?'

'Hmm, the earliest record we have of them in Jersey is from an Assizes Roll of 1309, but they certainly originated from France much earlier than that. The name maybe derived from the French word *pipeur* meaning trickster, although it has been suggested that it may also come from the name Pepin, which has links to Frankish kings. Originally the crest was a demi-lion argent holding a *Mullet Or* between the paws.'

'Sorry, a what now?'

'Oh yes, sorry. In lay man's terms, a blue half lion holding a five-pointed golden star. Although this was changed at some point to the squirrel *sejant* cracking a nut, *sejant* just means sitting up right. As for the family themselves they have been prominent throughout the centuries and there is far too much to go into now. There is a distinct difference however between their crest and the one on the ring.'

'The Maltese cross?'

'Yes, however it isn't just a Maltese cross. We had to blow the image up quite a bit to make sense of it. There are in fact two crosses, one overlaid inside the first. The outer is definitely a Maltese cross but the second and more significant, is the one inside it. It is a Carolingian cross.'

'A Carolingian cross, what's that?'

'It is the symbol of the Carolingian Dynasty, they ruled large parts of Europe during the eighth and ninth century. The legend goes that one of the kings known as Pepin the Short created a Royal Order of knights to protect the dynasty just before he died in 768 AD.'

'Sorry to interrupt, but you said Pepin, wasn't that one of the possible links to the family's origins?'

'Yes, hence why I think it still may be something to do with that particular family, especially as there are strong historical links between the Family and Malta. Anyway as I was saying the legend regarding *The Order of Pepin* goes on to talk about the crusades and finding a very powerful holy relic. It was said that it enabled them and the Knights Templar, who they were said to be involved with, to rise to a position of great influence. But there has never been any evidence to support this. To be honest until I saw this I had almost forgotten about it. It had always just been seen as a Myth, a bedtime story to tell the children. If it is the case that they do exist and have become active again then we are all in for some very troubling times indeed.'

'Why do you say that?'

'If *The Order* exists then so does the relic. And if the rumours about the relic are true then we are most likely witnessing the repercussions of a power struggle.'

'A power struggle?'

'Yes, I can only tell you the bits that I know, and I don't know a great deal on the subject but as far as I knew *The Order of Pepin* was always rumoured to be the protectors of the relic, but there were other parties that wanted to gain control of it. Hence why the Knights Templar were purged in 1307, as other parties tried to wrest control of the relic from them. That's about as much as I can tell you.'

'Is there anyway of finding out more?'

'From what I can recall, there was a young professor who had some bizarre theory about them and what became of them but I can't recall his name, after all, this must have been the best part of forty years ago. I seem to recall there was quite a fuss at the time, he was trying to present some findings to the Royal Historical Society, but the ridicule was so great that he was laughed out of the society and was said to have become a recluse. I'm sorry I can't be of more help, but I can't for the life of me remember his name. He must be well into his seventies by now, if he is even still alive.'

'Thank you, Sir. You have been more than helpful.'

'Not at all. I would just caution you against delving into this too much. If indeed, this is what has happened, they are not the sort of organisation you can tackle head on; they are after all, almost like fanatics. And we all know what atrocities religious fanatics are capable of. By now they will be well entrenched in the seats of power with all the levers at their disposal to continue their work unchallenged.'

'Thanks, I'll bear that in mind. I must go, I think the service may be about to start. Thank you again, you have given me a great deal to look into.' Glen said as he hung up. His head was now spinning with all the information that he had just taken in. *Fanatics, Templar Myths and holy relics, this was like something out of a work of fiction than actual reality. He would need time to process this, and then the next question was where to start?* A question he was still pondering as he quietly snuck into the back of the chapel just as the service began.

The family standards that hung from the walls of the chapel were all unfurled. Beautiful flower arrangements consisting of white and yellow lilies, lilacs, ferns, snowdrops, irises and forget-me-nots were dotted around the aisle of the church, many people laid wreaths at the foot of the drum altar before taking their seats. James had brought a wreath of white lilies and red roses that he too laid at the altar before he took his seat next to Chris.

A hush fell over the congregation as the priest stood to lead the service. He opened with a poem by Robert Burns, his voice ringing out clearly through the church as he spoke.

An honest man here lies at rest, As e'er God with his image blest;
the friend of man, the friend of truth, The friend of age, and guide of youth:
Few hearts like his, with virtue warm'd, Few heads with knowledge so informed;
If there is another world, he lives in bliss; If there is none, he made the best of this.
Robert Burns, 1784.[1]

He paused briefly at the end of the reading before he invited the congregation to stand for the first hymn *There is a green hill far away.* Everybody stood as the warm tones of the organ began to resonate through the building.

Jack's cousin Louis St Clair gave a very moving eulogy, he talked about the great fun he and Jack used to have as boys. Reminiscing about some of the mischief that they used to get up to. Praising Jack for being a true friend, someone that he could always count on for support, Louis almost broke down at one point as his emotions almost got the better of him. He had been very close to Jack, yet he managed to pull himself together to finish his speech.

Jack's father also spoke briefly; he had always been a man of few words. It was obviously a very difficult time for him as he gave a final farewell to his eldest son. Tears rolling down his cheeks as he did so.

The last to speak at the lectern was Jack's younger brother Piers who read a poem by Canon Henry Scott Holland. Piers was nervous when he spoke but his voice was steady as he read the words from the order of service.

Death is nothing at all. It does not count. I have only slipped away into the next room. Nothing has happened. Everything remains exactly as it was. I am I, and you are you, and the old life that we lived so fondly together is untouched, unchanged. Whatever we were to each other, that we are still. Call me by the old familiar name. Speak of me in the easy way which you always used. Put no difference into your tone. Wear no forced air of solemnity or sorrow. Laugh as we always laughed at the little jokes that we enjoyed together. Play, smile, think of me, pray for me. Let my name be ever the household word that it always was. Let it be spoken without an effort, without the ghost of a shadow upon it. Life means all that it ever meant. It is the same as it ever was. There is absolute and unbroken continuity. What is this death but a negligible accident? Why should I be out of mind because I am out of sight? I am but waiting for you, for an interval, somewhere very near, just round the corner. All is well. Nothing is hurt; nothing is lost. One brief moment and all will be as it was before. How we shall laugh at the trouble of parting when we meet again!

Canon Henry Scott Holland, 1910.[2]

He managed to master his emotions by remembering his eldest brother's familiar grin that he had always put on whenever the two of them got together. He paused as he finished and slowly descended from the lectern, at the bottom of the chancel steps he turned and bowed in front of the altar, before rejoining his family in the front aisle.

The final hymn was *Guide me, O thou great redeemer* by William Williams, it had been a personal favourite of Jack's and seemed fitting to end the service with. During the third verse the coffin bearers took up the coffin once again and accompanied by the family and the priest, they descended down into the darkness of the crypt to place Jack with his ancestors, finally to rest in peace.

A bugler sounded the *Last Post* as the hymn finished. It was a very poignant moment; James and Chris both recalled the memories of all those men they had served with that had lost their lives. James wondered how many more of his friends would lose their lives before this conflict was resolved. He hoped that the price would not be too high.

After the service had finished they took the opportunity to talk to Louis. They wanted to find out whether he and Michael had uncovered any further information about *The Glove*. Unfortunately they had gained very little extra information about this elusive organization. However Louis had left London as soon as they had received word of Jack's death. Michael was apparently pursuing a new lead so he may now have more information.

Lord Norwood sat behind the large Mahogany desk in his study, although he had been in regular contact with Chamberlain over the week that followed. It vexed him that his head of security had not been able to track down Flack and the others.

In the end he had decided to cut his losses and had recalled his head of security. It was time to put the next stage of operations into action. No doubt he would cross paths with Flack again, the only difference would be that when they did meet he would make sure it would be for the last time.

Flicking through the papers on his desk he jotted down a few notes on to a small pad. He was ironing out the last few details of the journey he had planned to undertake. At least his other operatives had been successful in discovering where the next part of the Codex was likely to be located.

Chapter Fifteen: Secrets and Discoveries

Michael Collins stood outside St Paul's Cathedral trying to shelter from the rain whilst he waited for his mystery contact to arrive. His fact-finding mission had proved pretty fruitless so far.

He deeply regretted that he was not able to attend Jack's funeral, but a hand delivered note that had been slipped under his hotel room door the previous night had intrigued him, and so he had resolved to meet this anonymous person who claimed to have information regarding *The Glove*. He stamped his feet on the ground trying to get some heat back into his toes, which were slowly going numb as he waited in the cold.

The great bells of St Paul's rang out overhead notifying the city that it was eleven o'clock. Blowing on his hands he continued to wait. It wasn't until about ten past the hour that he was approached by a tall slim man exiting from a small door at the side of the great cathedral. The man was dressed in a long black gown with a red trim. Michael assumed that he must be a member of St Paul's clergy.

'I must apologize for the method of contact but these are dangerous times, my son. One cannot be too careful, you never know who is watching. Follow me if you would, please.' The new stranger said as he ushered Michael inside the cathedral, through the same door he had just appeared from.

Michael obliged and followed the strange priest inside the cathedral. They walked along the south aisle, past the whispering gallery and into a small antechamber. The chamber was full of shelving littered with rolled parchments, many of them made from vellum. Michael sat down in the chair that was offered to him by the priest and waited for the man to continue.

'My name is Father John.' The priest said finally introducing himself before he continued. 'I am the Keeper of Records here at the cathedral. Many of our church records were destroyed in the great fire when the old cathedral and most of the city burnt to a cinder, and yet many still survive. We have been following your exploits for some time now and we are of the opinion that we have information vital to your cause. We too have a vested interest to safeguard the books from falling into the wrong hands.'

'Excuse me Father, but if I'm not mistaken you said books? I was only aware of the one.' Michael said interrupting the priest.

'Ah, yes I will come to that in due course. But first, my informants have brought to my attention that you are seeking information pertaining to an organisation that calls itself *The Glove*. They are a particularly vile group although I believe *organization* is the wrong term to use, they are really a *brotherhood* of sorts. Their origins go back further than even our records begin, nevertheless we believe they came into existence some time around the 21st century BC. However, they only began to attract the Church's attention when they started to exert their influence in Europe after the second crusade.'

'How do you know all of this?' Michael asked, now intrigued by these new revelations.

'The Church has always had an interest in these things; especially during that period of history, the Church was far more political then, than it is today. It has taken great interest in the morality of men and in some cases the fallibility of them. Such things, which can bring about total war and cause great suffering, trouble us greatly. So long as the books remained hidden there was little danger so we chose not to interfere. Now that this seems less certain, we believe it is our duty to ensure that good will triumph over evil.'

Father John momentarily paused before he continued. 'There is nothing good about this particular brotherhood they are tainted by their lust for knowledge and power and as such are inherently evil, driven by an overwhelming need to control. They seek ultimate power. Knowledge is power and therefore as the books are the source of absolute knowledge they can act as the gateway to absolute power. In the wrong hands this could be disastrous. *The Glove* has systematically been searching for them for centuries, millennia even. They must be prevented from locating the books at all costs.

You must tread carefully on this path. The serpent is a dangerous creature and this particular viper is the most dangerous of all. You cannot just cut off its head for a new one will sprout in its place. To succeed you must also remove the heart and pierce it with the tools of God. Only then will it be vanquished. You are partially correct about the book as the legend goes, there was originally just one. It was split into seven pieces, in part due to *The Glove* many millennia ago. The pieces were entrusted to seven great civilizations that hid them. Many of these cease to exist in the modern world; and so most of the pieces remained safe because they were lost to us. Unfortunately *The Glove* has gradually been piecing together an idea as to where they are.

It is my belief that they are now very close to being in a position to lay their hands upon many if not all of them. If this is allowed to happen they will sweep across our world like a plague carried by a whirlwind, laying waste to everything and everyone in their path. I have in my possession a map of sorts upon which three of the remaining six pieces were last known to be located. Know that you will be welcomed into any church along the way and we will give aid where we can to help you in your quest; if it is in our power to do so.' The priest said handing Michael a very delicate vellum scroll.

'Why can't you undertake this yourselves if you don't mind my asking, Father?' Michael asked as he took the scroll from the man.

'That is not our path, my son. We are just the Record Keepers and the Watchers. We do not possess the power to take on *The Glove* directly.'

'And you think we do?'

'Have faith. Sometimes even the smallest fell giants. Take this as well. Only use it in your darkest hour of need. It will protect you all.' The priest added as he handed a small object wrapped in sackcloth to Michael.

'How will we know when that is?' Michael inquired.

'You will know. Now you must leave. Go with God, my son and good luck.' The priest finished. Michael left St Paul's, his head still spinning with these new revelations.

It was late in the evening when Chris, James and Louis returned to Martinstowe from the Mount. They were all tired from the long day. They headed for the smoking room and sank down into the crimson leather armchairs in front of a roaring log fire that Rachel had lit earlier that afternoon. The day had sparked many memories. They sat and reminisced about some of the better times.

James took out a pack of cigarettes and sparked one up. Chris walked over to a walnut cabinet standing in the corner of the room and took out three brandy glasses along with a very fine crystal decanter containing a particularly smooth Louis XIV brandy. He poured a good measure into each glass, handing one to James.

'All I need now is a cigar to go with this and I'll be quite content for the rest of the evening.' Chris announced.

'There's a box in the draw of the table over there. Not sure what brand but knowing my uncle they will be something special.' James said pointing to a small table along the west wall.

'They certainly are.' Chris said as he lifted the lid on the box. 'These are the same brand of Havana's that Castro smokes if I'm not very much mistaken.'

'Why am I not surprised. He always did like the best.' James commented as he warmed the side of his glass with his zippo in order to release the brandy's full potential. As the aroma filtered up to his nostrils he took a large gulp and sighed relaxing into the soft leather back of the armchair.

His phone vibrated on the side table next to him. Picking it up he flicked through the newly received message.

'Michael's coming down tomorrow. He has some news for us.' James said. 'He will fill us in when he arrives as he doesn't want to say anything on an unsecure line. We'll have to pick him up from the station by the sounds of things.'

'Hmm, that reminds me, I've been meaning to sort out some encrypted phones. Norwood seems to know our every move almost even before we do. I wonder if he's been tapping us. Well, we will have to put a stop to that.' Chris mused.

'Well it can only be the one's that you guys are using. Rachel and I picked up two encrypted phones when we went to Cotehele.'

Rachel joined them in the smoking room. She had been busy in the library reading through the last of the documents. She hadn't found any further information on *The Glove* but had gained a great insight into the expenditure of Martinstowe estate during the nineteenth century, probably enough to write quite a sizable thesis on the subject. Feeling rather frustrated she collapsed on to the large crimson leather sofa that matched the armchairs currently occupied by the boys.

'Join us in a brandy?' Chris asked recognizing the stressed look on her face.

'Thanks, just what I need right now.' She sweetly replied.

'I don't suppose I can tempt you with a choice cigar as well?' He added, knowing full well she would say no. He just wanted to see the look of horror and disgust on her face at the mere suggestion of it.

She looked down her nose at him as she replied. 'Ugh, don't be disgusting. You know those things will kill you. Beside you two seem to be doing a fine job of smoking this room out by yourselves, thank you very much. The brandy will be fine.'

'Ha, many things have tried to kill me and none have succeeded so far.'

'There's always a first time, which in this case would also be the last. Just tempting fate are we?'

'Would be difficult when I don't believe in fate.'

'Typical smart answer.' She retorted as she settled herself deeper into the cosy cushions of the sofa. 'Thanks, Cous.' She said as she took the brandy glass from Chris.

'Is there anything interesting on the box?' Rachel asked after a few moments of sitting in silence.

'Don't know, have a look if you like.' James replied, picking up the remote off the coffee table next to his chair. He tossed it over to her. It landed on her chest right between her breasts.

'Were you intending to do that?' she asked giving him a slightly huffy look.

'No, just lucky I guess.' He replied with a cheeky grin.

'Not this again!' Chris said. 'I can see you two are going to have to be separated at some point.'

'Oh, lighten up. Its just a bit of harmless banter, a bit of fun, *Mr Grumpy*.' James retorted.

'I know what your idea of fun is and I'm not sure I approve. Behave yourselves.'

Rachel ignored this part of their conversation; her cousin could be rather over protective when he wanted to be. Yet she wasn't about to start an argument with him about it, she was her own woman and quite capable of making her own decisions and mistakes.

She flicked through the channels, there wasn't a lot on of any real interest. In the end she settled for an episode of The Big Bang Theory. It was the one with Rock, Paper, Scissors, Lizard, and Spock.

The three boys continued to drain their brandy glasses and refill; apparently they were in one of those moods to get absolutely plastered. It was their tried and tested method for dealing with the loss of friends, without really having to tackle the emotional void.

Ah well boys will be boys. Rachel thought to herself. *Best to leave them to it.*

At least it would be entertaining to watch them attempt to tackle the stairs later when they finally decided to go to bed. They would attempt them using each other's shoulders for support. Guaranteed at some point to fall over each other, tumble back down the stairs and end up in a heap laughing, before getting up and trying again.

Rachel woke early the next day and after having a lovely hot shower in one of the many bathrooms of the house. She headed downstairs to the kitchen to have breakfast. She was surprised to find James already up and cooking a fry-up on the Aga.

'I didn't expect you would be up so early after last night.' She said with a smile as she entered the kitchen taking in that great smell of bacon frying.

'I'm always up early after a heavy night. Not sure why? I could really use the extra sleep, but once I'm awake I have to get up. Your cousin on the other hand, I suspect, won't be up for hours. He's not the best after a heavy night, especially after that much brandy. I'm pretty sure we polished off the entire decanter. Might have to replace that, something neither my wallet or myself are looking forward to. I think my wallet will be burning a hole through my pocket after that.' He said with his usual cheeky grin.

'Yes you were all pretty merry by the time you headed off to bed.' Laughing as she remembered the sounds of their attempts at getting up the stairs.

'Not one of our finest moments I must admit.' He replied with a slightly sheepish grin on his face.

'Right, what can I offer you for breakfast? Cereal, toast, bacon...? What do you fancy?'

'I rather fancy joining you in a full English if that's okay. The smell of that bacon has hooked me.'

'One full English coming right up, m' lady.' He said in his most charming voice. 'Morning bud, how's the head.' James said as Louis walked into the kitchen.

'Better than expected for once. You cooking breakfast?'

'Yeah, you keen?'

'Definitely, I take it Flacky isn't up yet?'

'That would be a no. Someone isn't that great with the morning after. I'd give it at least another forty minutes before there is even the hint that the beast might be about to rise.' James said trying not to laugh as he referred to Chris as a beast.

Chris appeared at about half past ten and as predicted looked rather worse for wear.

'Where's the coffee at?' He demanded as he casually sauntered into the kitchen. 'I need something to get me over this hangover, I feel like someone has left a very angry hammer wielding Thor smashing around inside my head.'

Rachel and James both laughed at him.

'Heavy night, Cous?' Rachel asked trying her best to quell her laughter.

'Ugh, too heavy. Never, never, never again. Middleton you are a bad influence on me.' He said as he collapsed into the nearest chair. 'And as for you young lady, we will be having words. How on God's earth you ever managed to convince me that flaming brandy shots were a good idea, I will never know.'

'You didn't object last night.' She replied still trying not to laugh at her cousin's hung-over state.

'Well you need to liven up. We've got to go and pick up Michael in half an hour.' James reminded him.

'Tell him to walk.' Chris replied. 'I'm not sure I can stand let alone drive anywhere.'

'Here, get this down you. I think you will feel a lot better after eating something.' Rachel said as she placed a plate of eggs and bacon accompanied by a steaming mug of coffee in front of him.

'What no sausages! What kind of service do you call this?' He said jokingly as he hungrily eyed the plate.

'Sorry, that's what you get for staying in bed for too long. If it's any consolation they were very nice sausages.' Louis replied with a smirk.

'Thanks, I'll remember that the next time I cook for you.' Chris replied with a snort.

Half an hour later, James accompanied by a rather more invigorated Chris left the estate to go and pick up Michael from the station.

Chris had certainly perked up a bit, and was currently trying to sort out some encrypted phones from one of his contacts.

They had to wait in the station car park for ages; predictably the trains were suffering delays. Michael eventually appeared from the station and jumped into the back of the green Range Rover.

'Yer 'right boys? Good t' see ya. Have I got some news for you guys!' He exclaimed as he greeted his two friends.

'We're good thanks, all things considered.' Chris replied.

'Fancy a coffee?' He asked as he felt his last hit of caffeine was beginning to wear off.

'Sounds good to me and I can fill you in, with slightly more comfortable surroundings than this heap.' Michael replied. Having been cramped on the train all morning he liked the idea of finding somewhere to stretch out for a bit.

They found a local coffee shop called The Dock and settled down in a quite corner. Chris and James listened attentively to Michael as he brought them up to speed. Telling them all about where he had been in London and his bizarre meeting with Father John of St Paul's.

'Interesting.' Chris said as Michael finished his tale.

'I'm not surprised that the Church have taken an interest. I'd very much like to take a look at that map, but this probably isn't the best place for that.

We will be able to decide what our next move should be once we've studied it a bit.' He said as he drained the last of his enormous pint-sized mug of coffee. If you could call it a mug, it was more like a bucket than a mug.

The four of them left the coffee shop and headed back to the 4x4 and on to Martinstowe. Chris was burning with eagerness to study Father John's map.

Back in the confines of the library Michael unrolled the delicate vellum scroll, carefully spreading it out over one of the reading desks. Placing a few old books around the edges like paperweights to prevent it from rolling back up again.

It was the first time that even Michael had been able to study the thing at length. Chris' first observation was that it was incomplete; there was a huge diagonal tear that made up one side of the map. At least half of the document was missing, torn off at some point.

'Well it is a start. This priest didn't happen to mention where the rest of it was did he?' Chris asked.

'Not in so many words. I got the impression that he didn't really know.' Michael replied.

'So let's see what we have got. The Americas by the looks of things and I presume that is Antarctica. These symbols here must represent cities or places of importance I guess. I'm surprised though I wouldn't have thought there were any civilizations that could survive in Antarctica, although there are people that live in some of the coldest parts of Siberia so I guess it might be possible. These symbols or markings are rather strange. I haven't seen anything like them before.' Chris slightly puzzled by the vast amount of intricate markings that covered parts of the scroll.

'I suppose this is some sort of key.' Michael suggested, pointing to some legend in the upper left-hand corner of the parchment.

'When did he say this was made?'

'He didn't, but he did say that *The Glove* were suspected of originating from somewhere inside Mesopotamia some two thousand odd years before Christ was born. That's maybe a good place to start.' Michael replied; relieved to have been able to supply a little information that might help to crack this new piece of the puzzle.

'Well there's enough books in here. One of them must contain something of use on the subject. Best get searching.' James said as he pointed to the thousands of books surrounding them.

'Any suggestions where to start.' Michael asked slightly shocked by the suggestion, as he took in the sight of so many books. It was his first time inside the library and although he had been told about the sheer quantity of books the room held. What he had pictured had not really done the room justice.

'Don't worry, I didn't mean to search every one. There's a section on Ancient History somewhere in that corner.' James said with the smallest of laughs as he caught the shocked expression on Michael's face as the Salopian took in the sight of the volume of books in the room.

Michael soon located the relevant section in the corner where the west and north cases met. There were several books on Mesopotamia and the cultures that had ruled the area over the centuries. Out of these he found three that contained very similar symbols to that found on the map. According to the books they were Sumerian in origin, unfortunately none of the books contained the exact symbols that they needed to translate the text.

'I think we may have to find an expert to translate these symbols. The best place to start is with the authors of these books, I think.' Chris said.

'Give me the names and I'll do a search online for them.'

As Michael read the names out, Chris typed them into a search engine and waited for the results.

'Well the first two are dead so I don't think that they will be much help. What's the name of the third?'

'Dr Devan Luca Valentine.' Michael said reading out the name on the spine of the last book.

'Ah, yes here we are. Dr Devan Luca Valentine, graduated from Oxford in 2004, specializes in Mesopotamian and Mesoamerican Cultures. Let's see if we can get a contact number for her.' Chris said. His hopes had risen now that he had managed to find a living scholar.

'There's no direct number, but she can apparently be contacted via Oxford University or the British Museum.'

He rang the university only to discover that she was currently at the museum taking part in a series of lectures.

'Well, I guess I'll try the museum and hopefully catch her in between lectures.' He said as he picked up the receiver of the old bakelite phone and dialling the number for the museum he waited for someone to pick up. After a few rings he got through to one of the museum's receptionists.

'Good afternoon, the British Museum. Barbara speaking. How may I help?' The bland receptionists voice said.

'Yes, Good afternoon. May I speak to Dr Valentine if at all possible, please?'

'May I ask who's calling, please?'

'My name is Christopher Flack.'

'One moment, please. I will see if she is available. Can I ask what it is regarding?'

'Absolutely, it is regarding symbols from Mesopotamia.'

'I'll just put you on hold.' The receptionist said.

The classical music played for a good few minutes before Barbara finally returned to the phone.

'Hello, Mr Flack. I'm afraid she is currently in a lecture at the moment would you like to leave a message so she can call you back as soon as she can.'

'Yes, could you ask her to call me on my mobile, let me just look it up. I never can remember the damn thing.' He said before he looked up the number and read it out to the receptionist.

'Certainly, I will pass it on to her.'

'Thank you.' With that, Chris hung up.

'All we can do now is wait, I suppose.' Looking at his watch it was already coming up to five. 'Anyone fancy a drink? I could murder a scotch right now and there is a rather fine bottle of Macallan I have had my eye on.'

'Sounds like a good idea. I don't suppose there is any Irish?' Michael asked.

'I don't think so.'

'Ah well, I suppose that stuff you try to pass off as Whiskey will have to do.'

'Don't let's get started on the Irish-Scottish debate again. You know we will never agree.' James said with a smile.

They trooped out of the library in the direction of the smoking room to indulge themselves with some more of James' uncle's spirit collection.

Around about half past six Chris received Dr Valentine's call. He knew as soon as he had finished describing the parchment that he had sparked her curiosity.

She inquired whether he would be able to send her a copy via email for her to have a look at. He agreed he would, although he had no intention of sending all of it. He jotted down her email on a small pad of paper and promised he would send it as soon as possible.

Chris took a picture of the legend in the upper left hand corner and emailed it to the address the professor had supplied. He added a quick message to say that there was a lot more to the document, but that he would like to know if she was able to decipher that part first.

Chapter Sixteen: The Professor and The Map

Two days passed before Chris received a reply from the professor. Dr Valentine had managed to partially decrypt it; she went on to say that, it was Sumerian in origin. However, there were pieces missing to fully understand what it meant. She asked whether she could examine the rest of the document.

'Well gentlemen, it seems we have a decision to make. Shall we allow the good professor to examine the full document? You realize once she has seen it, there will be a lot more questions.' Chris said as he finished reading her reply.

'I think you are going to have to if you want to know what the rest of it says. I don't really see any other option.' James replied. 'But maybe suggest that she comes here to see it rather than sending another image. That way at least we can see how trustworthy she is.'

'Seems like a reasonable suggestion.' Chris agreed. He emailed her back to say that he would be delighted for her to see it, adding that because parts of the document were rather aged it was difficult to photograph it and asked whether it would be possible for her to come to Martinstowe to view the rest of the document.

Half an hour later she replied saying that she would be delighted to, and would try to clear her schedule for the rest of the week. She would ring later to confirm what day she would be able to arrive.

An hour later she rang to say that she had managed to create some space, and would be driving down the very next day. Adding that she planned on staying for as long as was necessary to complete the translation. Potentially that could take some time as Sumerian was not a literal language and phrases often had more than one meaning depending on the context.

Dr Devan Valentine sat in her compact study going over the image that Captain Flack had sent to her. She found it very curious. She had never seen such a well-preserved piece of Sumerian text before or for that matter one that was quite so detailed.

She wondered how he had come to acquire such a document? How genuine it was? And if it was genuine, how she had not heard of its discovery? There certainly hadn't been any major finds for at least two years, and the most recent one before that she had been a part of.

Archaeological teams had made great progress in understanding the culture. This new text might help her to publish a new thesis she had been working on. One in which she speculated that they had been great travellers and had had knowledge of the Americas well before Christopher Columbus discovered them in 1592.

It was a claim that many of her colleagues had told her was preposterous and that she would be committing professional suicide; she would be risking wide spread ridicule through out the archaeological community if she published.

So far she had resisted the urge to publish mainly because she knew she lacked the evidence to support it. Nevertheless, she was convinced that she was right and was determined to publish at some point. Either way she was intrigued by the symbols she had seen, symbols that talked about a vast store of knowledge but the text was incomplete to work out any more.

She had decided well before the invitation to view it in person, she really needed to see it in the flesh so to speak, and had cleared her schedule before Captain Flack had made the invitation. She had deliberately told Captain Flack that she needed to clear her schedule first so that she didn't seem overly keen to view the parchment.

The journey down to Martinstowe for Dr Valentine had been pleasant enough, not that she really noticed the rich autumn colours of the English countryside as her mind had been firmly fixed on the text. She was buzzing with excitement, eager to see the full text and what it all meant. Would she finally be able to publish her ground breaking thesis, turning the archaeological world on its head? Only time would tell.

Turning into the driveway she took in the splendour of the great house. Immediately falling in love with the warmth of the pink Italian architecture that was nestled into the backdrop of green coniferous forests. Chris greeted her as she stepped out of her car.

'Good afternoon Dr Valentine. I hope you found us okay. I'm Chris Flack.' He said with a warm welcoming smile.

'Yes, it was very easy to find, thank you. You have a beautiful home.' She replied in the sweet dulcet tones of her voice.

'I wish I could claim to own it but unfortunately not. It is on loan for a while, but I agree it is a very captivating setting. Can I take your bags for you?' Chris asked being every bit the gracious host.

'Thank you, that's most kind.' She replied as she handed him her suitcase.

'If you would like to follow me. I'll show you around. We thought you would enjoy one of the bedrooms on the south wing. It has some of the best views overlooking the river. I hope you will find it comfortable enough.'

'It sounds perfect.' She replied with a smile.

He left her bag in the hall while he gave her a brief tour of the ground floor so that she could get her bearings, before taking her upstairs to her room. He left her to unpack and arranged to meet her downstairs in the hall when she was ready.

The room on the south wing was as he had said, one of the best rooms in the house. It had cool yellow walls; with white plaster cornicing and matching skirting boards. There was a large Chippendale dressing table with a beautifully crafted oval mirror along the right hand sidewall; next to this stood a tall double-breasted chestnut wardrobe with intricately cast brass handles. The most impressive feature of the room was the huge super-king sized double bed up against the left hand side; it looked so inviting with soft plump feather pillows and a very plush duvet.

Devan resisted the urge to fall backwards on to it, as appealing as the feeling of gradually sinking into the soft thick mattress was, she was more eager to examine the ancient parchment. So unpacking her bag quickly, and putting her clothes away in the wardrobe, rather less neatly that she would have normally done. She hurried back down stairs to join Chris in the hall.

Chris had almost had to take a double take when he had first laid eyes on Dr Valentine. She had not at all been what he had expected a professor to look like. She was stunningly beautiful. Her elegant curvaceous body with long flowing brunette locks were captivating. She had the most mesmerizing green eyes set deeply into the sleek lines of her tanned face, they sparkled like rich emeralds.

He could have lost himself in those eyes for eternity, if he had not quickly recovered before greeting her. Luckily for him she had not noticed his initial reaction. She was just as beautiful now as she descended the stairs down to the hall.

'May I take a look at the parchment? After all that is why I am here. I am excited to get started.' She said as she walked across the polished oak floor towards where he was waiting.

'Certainly, but I must first ask that you promise not to divulge your findings to anyone. I realize that this is a rather bizarre request, it is a rather sensitive subject and I would not like its existence to become common knowledge. I'm sorry that I can't be more forth coming as to exactly why, at this time. Nevertheless, these are the terms under which you may view it.'

She looked at him closely examining his facial expressions trying to work him out but he gave no clue away as to why he would make such a request.

It was certainly a strange request, although she had expected some such thing. Private collectors tended to be rather protective about their acquisitions. She knew that the only way to see the parchment was to agree and hopefully renegotiate later.

'I understand and will agree.' She replied after a momentary pause in which she tried to think of a better solution, unable to think of one, the only option open to her was to make the agreement.

He took her from the hall through the winding corridors of the house to the library.

The parchment lay unrolled on a reading desk. Dr Valentine took out a pair of thin dark rimmed spectacles from her handbag, the kind that are popular with secretaries and began to inspect the document.

After a few minutes she looked up. 'It is certainly Sumerian in origin. I can see why you said it was better to view the actual document. It is far more detailed than I had imagined it would be. I had not realized that it would form a map, or rather part of one; regrettably it appears there is a piece missing. Torn off by the looks of it. It will take quite some time to translate it all. There are some symbols I have not come across before.

Most curious, I don't think I have ever seen anything like it. Your not one of those treasure hunters are you?' She asked, hoping to gain further insight. She wanted to know what she was getting herself into.

'Ha, I doubt what I'm looking for would make me a particularly rich man. It is very important for me that what is written here can be translated. I'm afraid I can't be clearer than that. I have a few things that I need to attend to. So I hope you won't mind if I leave you to your work. If there is anything that you should need just ring the bell.' He said indicating the tasselled rope hanging in one corner of the room.

'Thank you, I am sure I will find everything I need. I must just fetch a few books from my car before I begin.' She replied, her mind was full of questions but she knew she would have to wait to find the answers. This parchment was extraordinary, almost perfectly preserved and contained far more information than she could have ever imagined.

It was strange, the continents pictured were not the ones she had expected to find on a Sumerian map, rather than being parts of Mesopotamia she was almost certain they were the Americas. *Was it a fake? Just some kind of elaborate practical joke played by some of her colleagues at the museum. The clues would be found in the symbols themselves.* It would take a long time to decipher all of it so she decided she had best get started.

Dr Valentine returned from her car, laden with a pile of books, some of which were teetering precariously, threatening to tumble to the ground at any moment. Luckily she somehow managed to get all of the books, in a slightly less graceful manner than she would have wished, into the library and deposit them on to a desk before they fell everywhere.

Setting herself up on two reading desks she started to work through the text picking out a number of symbols she already recognized as a starting point. The further she got the more complex and weirder the translation became. The problem she faced was that many of the symbols had more than one meaning and so until she put a string of them together. The overall meaning would not reveal itself.

Chris popped his head in from time to time during the course of the afternoon to see how much progress she was making. He found the symbols fascinating and could have spent hours asking her about how the Sumerian language was developed but he refrained, not wanting to take up too much of her time.

At about ten o'clock, after rubbing her eyes for the umpteenth time she decided to call it a day. The meaning of the part she had been working on was taking her round in circles. She hoped that a pair of fresh eyes in the morning would help.

She passed Chris in the hall.

'How's it going?' He asked. 'Have you had much luck?'

'No, I'm going to head outside for a bit. I feel like staring at a wall for a bit before I end it. I'm in a good mood but I am about ready to shoot somebody. This thing keeps taking me round in circles. Just as I think I have cracked it, the meaning changes.' She sighed. She was tired and feeling a bit overwhelmed.

'That bad huh. Well as long as you don't shoot me. I'm sure you will prevail in the end. It's only the first day and it took longer than that to build Rome or so they say. Mysteries are never as easy to solve, as one would like them to be. I guess that's why we call them mysteries.' He replied hoping that a bit of humour might cheer her up.

'I suppose you are right. And I wouldn't dream of shooting you.' She laughed and left to get some air feeling slightly better already.

James, Michael and Rachel had been out for the day. They had not yet met the professor. Returning to Martinstowe at about half past ten, they headed to the smoking room to relax. Chris and Dr Valentine were already there, enjoying a bottle of red wine. Chris introduced them and they spent a few hours chatting about the parchment and her background.

Glancing at her watch Devan was amazed to discover it was almost one o'clock in the morning. She excused herself and headed off to bed. It had been a long day. She was exhausted and wanted to get an early start. The others bid her goodnight. They stayed up for a while longer discussing their first impressions of their new guest.

'She's quite sultry, isn't she? Especially when she's wearing those black rimmed glasses.'

'Crushing already, there's a surprise.' James said with a knowing look at Chris.

'Well, I wouldn't say no. I noticed she's got a cheeky tattoo of the Egyptian all seeing eye on her lower back.'

'And prey tell me how you came to notice that.'

' Her blouse was riding up as she bent down to pick up some books as I walked into the library earlier this afternoon. Always did have a thing for girls with tattoos. It can be very sexy in the right place.'

'She's certainly energetic, maybe it's that exotic blood. I'm pretty sure she said that part of her family originated from Egypt, which would also explain her choice of tattoo.'

'Hey Cous', I expected better than that from you. How about less of the savage on heat and more of the gent that I used to know? Honestly sometimes I really wish we weren't related.'

'Sorry, what I meant to say was that I think she's cute and really intelligent which I think is really attractive and that she intrigues me. Just so used to putting things in terms that those lot can understand.' He replied slightly sheepishly after being semi-berated.

'I'll be happy as long as she finishes that translation. Anyway I don't know about the rest of you but I'm heading off to bed. I think there is going to be quite a lot to do in the morning.'

Devan was awoken early the next morning by a stream of sunlight flowing through a slit between the curtains. She was tired and yet was buzzing with enthusiasm to get back to the parchment in the library. Her dreams had been filled with the implications of its discovery.

She dressed and headed downstairs. She grabbed a mug of coffee from the kitchen on the way to the library. Finally after an hour or so of going over what she had been working on the previous day she clapped her hands together with joy. The first few lines finally made sense! The double meanings had parted to reveal the truth.

'A sacred journey across the great sea...'

Originally she had thought that it had been describing a method of worship 'a religious path to the God of the Sea, Nammu'. She now understood it was an actual journey rather than a metaphorical one, a great journey undertaken across a vast stretch of water.

She was pleased by her efforts, however she was left with more questions than answers. *Why was it undertaken? Where was the destination? Who travelled?* At least the puzzle was beginning to unravel.

'Morning all.' Chris announced as he entered the kitchen to find James, Michael and Rachel sitting around the kitchen table.

'Where is the good professor?'

'Busy in the library. She was up well before any of us.' James replied. 'She is dedicated. I'll give her that.'

'I think I'll pop in and see how she is getting on. Is that toast going spare?' Chris asked as his eyes hit upon a plate lying on the table with a few left over slices.

'Someone's in a good mood this morning. Crack on, Mon. We've all finished.' Michael answered in his familiar Salopian patter.

'Sweet, I'll see you guys latter.' Chris replied as he snatched up the bits of toast and headed off in the direction of the library.

'I wonder why he's in such a good mood this morning.' James said.

'I would have thought that was obvious. He has a thing for the professor.' Rachel said. 'Honestly as soon as there is a pretty face around; you lot prance around like a bunch of peacocks.'

'I see, not jealous are we?' James' attempt at a flirtatious question was met with little amusement from Rachel.

'Probably not. He is my cousin after all.'

'That wasn't exactly what I meant…' he trailed off as he realized he was about to dig himself into a hole.

'Morning Professor.' Chris said as he entered the library. 'How goes it this morning?'

'Very well, I think I have finally started to piece parts of it together. And please call me Devan.' She said beaming at him as she looked up from behind a pile of books. She was happy to be able to share her success with somebody. 'I can take you through it, if you like?'

'I would be most interested.'

'This first line here talks about a great expedition undertaken across a great expanse of water to a far off land. The expedition met with another great civilization. They were transporting something of great importance. I haven't quite managed to work out exactly what it was, yet. The text is rather vague on precisely what it was or why they transported it. It was certainly something that the Sumerians placed a tremendous amount of significance on. Hopefully in time this will become a lot clearer.' She said smiling, happy that she finally had some good news for him.

'Sounds like you have made some good progress. I'll leave you to it unless there is anything I can get you. Let me know if anything else pops up.'

'Thanks I think I have everything I need for the moment.'

'Well I'll see you a bit later.' Chris said as he left.

Chris found James indulging in a cigarette in the smoking room.

'Ah, there you are. The professor has been filling me in on her progress.'

'I bet she has.' James said with such a tiny hint of sarcasm that James almost didn't pick up on it.

'What was that?'

'Oh nothing. What has she found?'

'I will tell you later, but first I think you and I should catch up with Ollie and Gaz. We haven't really spoken to them for a while and it should be interesting to find out what Norwood has been up to.'

'That's probably a good idea. You know what those two are like if they are left alone unsupervised for too long.' James replied thinking about the revenge he was going to exact on that man for the death of Jack.

Chapter Seventeen: The Astronomer

Ollie and Gaz had spent the last couple of weeks sleeping rough in the back of their battered Land Rover. It hadn't been the most salubrious of accommodations but at least it kept the rain off their heads.

They had taken it in turns to keep an eye on the comings and goings around Glympton Park, mainly so they could monitor it around the clock, this had the added bonus of creating a bit more sleeping space in the back of the Land Rover and far more preferable than both of them squeezing into the small space.

Recently there had been an increased amount of activity at the estate; centred around the two hangars at the rear of the main house. Lord Norwood was obviously gearing up for something.

Since the duo's explosive exploits Lord Norwood had increased the number of patrols around the perimeter of the estate and it had become increasingly more testing to gain access on to the property so they had to rely heavily on the two cameras on the hangars.

Interestingly the man they had come to know, as Chamberlain had not returned to the estate with Lord Norwood after the ambush at St Michael's Mount. They both found it rather unsettling to think that he was roaming around 'off the leash' so to speak. Gaz had passed this information on to Chris who had said he would look into it.

Today seemed to be even busier than usual. A fresh set of lorries were rolling up on to the estate. They were carrying another load of containers, it wasn't clear to Gaz whether they were full or empty and so he decided to try and take a closer look.

He found a gap in the fence that ran close to the hangars; cautiously he peered through the gap. No one was around so he squeezed himself through and crawled on his belly through some long grass towards the hangars.

Gaz soon realized that these new containers were empty; some of the crates and vehicles that had been stored in the hangars were being loaded into the containers.

Norwood was moving. The question was where? Not wanting to run the risk of lingering for too long Gaz made a hasty retreat back to the safety of the Land Rover. He was relieved that his phone had been on silent; as he had been halfway through the gap in the fence when his phone began to violently vibrate. The caller, whoever it may be, would have to wait until he was back in the Landy. It turned out that it had been Chris calling to check up on what was happening, so Gaz quickly rang him back.

Chris was not happy with this new development. Norwood was clearly ahead of them, which did not bode well. Chris gave them instructions to follow the lorries when they left the estate to wherever their final destination was.

It was most likely going to be a port. He told the chaps to keep a low profile and to let him know if there were any further developments. It was crucial to at least stay abreast of what Norwood was doing, even if they could not stay ahead of him.

After speaking to Ollie and Gaz, Chris expressed his concerns to James.

'He's on the move. I wish I could keep up with his organization. They seem to be just that little bit more informed than I would like. I hope the professor can hurry up and finish that translation. Time is starting to run out.' The anxious tone of Chris' voice mirrored his feelings of concern.

'I agree. He does seem to be rather hard to predict. He must have discovered where another one of the books is.'

'Yes, I just wish I knew where it was. If the guys find out which ship the containers are loaded on to, we may be able to find out what her destination is.'

'That's if she doesn't change her course once she has put to sea. Norwood will no doubt be expecting you to trace the ship's destination or something similar and take precautions.'

'I have already thought of that. I was hoping you might be able to get in touch with one of your contacts at Naval Intelligence and ask them to track the ship.'

'I think, I know someone who might be willing, I can put in a call once I know what the ship's called. That's if it is a ship. You never know he might have a plane. Can still track it just a bit harder to arrange.'

'Well, let's hope it's not.'

Ollie nudged Gaz awake, 'Right fella time to get going. The trucks are on the move.'

Gaz had gone back to sleep after Chris' call, he had spent most of the previous night awake keeping watch on the estate and as the trucks had taken some time to be loaded up he had decided to take the opportunity to get some much needed sleep. Ollie had taken over watch.

'Hmm, did you have to wake me I was having such a pleasant dream. Me and Kate Beckinsale on a beach, Couldn't you have waited at least fifteen more minutes? Why did you wake me?' Gaz said brushing some sleep from his eyes as he started to wake up.

'More like five you mean.'

'Hey, you didn't include the two minutes for the warm up.'

'Fine six minutes, either way the trucks are going. We need to follow, remember? Come on, you and Kate will have to finish some other time.' Ollie laughed as he started up the old Land Rover.

They kept their distance between themselves and the convoy of trucks; after all it wasn't like they would lose the massive convoy, which stuck out like a sore thumb on the small country roads.

'Right, odds on where they are going? Bet you a tenner they are headed for Dover.' Ollie said as he continued to follow the convoy along the small winding roads.

'You're on, I reckon it will be Felixstowe.'

It turned out that they were both wrong as the lorries continued down the A34 at Chieveley rather than joining the M4. They were headed for Southampton.

Gaz and Ollie pulled up into a layby close to the entrance of the container terminal and watched the convoy turn into the docks and proceed to one of the staging areas. Huge cranes quickly swung into action, lifting the containers off the lorries and adding them to the massive stacks already awaiting shipment.

'We could be here for sometime. Fancy a coffee?' Gaz asked, felling the need for a warm drink.

'Yeah may as well. There's a burger van over there. Won't be anything special but at least it'll be hot.'

They sat in the Land Rover sipping their coffee as they waited to see which out of the possible seven huge ships the containers would eventually be loaded on to.

Gaz thought about going to the Shipping Office to find out, but decided that it wasn't worth arousing suspicion. The last thing they wanted was to be discovered asking questions. Sometimes doing nothing was the best policy.

'They are probably waiting to clear customs. That might take sometime.' Ollie suggested as he sipped his coffee.

'I doubt they will wait for that. The kit in those containers would raise all kinds of hell if they were properly inspected. The port would be surrounded by all manner of security forces in a matter of minutes, if anybody decided to take too much interest into their contents.' Gaz replied.

Sure enough as the customs officer arrived one of the drivers dropped down from the cab of his lorry and entered into a conversation with the officer. After a few minutes the driver handed the man a large brown envelope and walked back to his cab.

The officer proceeded to tag the containers before heading back to the office. He must have given the green light for them to be loaded as two of the huge cranes lining the docks started up again. Picking up a container each they taxied along the docks towards one of the ships.

She wasn't the largest ship on the docks but judging by her looks she had been in service for many years. She was called the *Astronomer* and according to the white lettering on her stern she was registered in Hamburg.

'I told you they wouldn't legally get through customs.' Gaz gloated. For once he was right.

'True, but that still doesn't tell us where she is bound for. She is almost fully laden so I suggest that once she slips her moorings we go and talk to the Harbour Master. They should have a registered destination for the *Astronomer*.' Ollie suggested. 'Better ring James and let him know.' He added as he drained the last of his coffee, the fourth since they had arrived at the port.

James wasn't very convinced that they would find anything useful at the Harbour Master. He was sure that the ship had not stated its true destination. So he decided now would be the best time to contact his friend at Naval Intelligence and call in a favour.

Lieutenant Commander Thomas Bradbury sat in his office at HMS *Neptune*, Faslane. He had been attending to the mountainous pile of papers in his tray. He had been tasked with reviewing the tactical operations of the Vanguard nuclear submarines.

The subs had been busy since the political situation with Iran had deteriorated, and this workload had been added to since Intel had come to light that suggested the North Koreans intended to launch a long-range test rocket to allegedly place a satellite into space on the 12th December. This alleged test didn't fool anybody, the West knew that they were really intending on testing long-range missile capabilities for a nuclear programme and the North Koreans knew that they knew.

It was just sabre rattling, a political game of cat and mouse to see how far the West would allow them to go. As a result the Vanguards had been more active of late and there was even the possibility that HMS *Astute* would have to cut her sea trials short and help out. Either way his in tray had been rather full and he was only just starting to make a dent in the stack.

It was a pleasant surprise to receive a call from his old friend. He hadn't spoken to James for quite sometime, in fact they hadn't spoken since they had worked together in the Gulf some four years previous.

'James Middleton, of all the people who could have called. I wouldn't have guessed it would be you. Good to hear from you. It's been a while. I understand you have recently taken a break from the service, not for good I hope.' The Lt Cdr said warmly.

'Retired is more the word I'd use and it's indeed been far too long. How are things up on the Clyde?' James asked.

'Busy, these North Koreans have really put the wind up the higher ups at the moment. Mustn't say too much. I'm guessing this isn't a social call.'

'As much as I would like to have a proper catch up I am afraid that I do have a favour to ask.'

'I thought you said you were retired? You know under the circumstances I can only do so much; would be different if you were active. Nevertheless, I think I know you well enough that if you are asking it must be important enough, if it is in my power to do so, I will. As long as it doesn't involve the subs they are rather busy at the moment.'

'Ha, no nothing quite that extreme. That would be more something Chris would ask for.' James laughed. 'I am interested in finding the destination of a ship, she sailed from Southampton about an hour ago, she's called the *Astronomer* and registered in Hamburg.

The Harbour Master claims that she is bound for San Francisco but I have a feeling that is not the only place she is going to stop. If she terminates there at all.'

'That name sounds familiar.'

'Yes, it should do, she has the same name as a ship that was converted to be a helicopter carrier during the Falklands and went on to become RFA *Reliant*, but she was scrapped years ago.'

'Ah yes, I remember her well, as I recall she ended up seeing quite a lot of action. She performed very well considering she wasn't originally designed as a military vessel. You know that I am not really meant to ask Intelligence Officers without good reason. Do you have any evidence of it being a security threat? Since the WMD thing we have to be rather careful about what resources are being used for what.'

'I had a feeling that you would say something along those lines. Let's just say that she is of interest at present. Remember that thing I helped you with once, consider this the repayment.'

'Why am I not surprised you would bring that up. Is it a National Security matter?'

'I'm not at liberty to discus that.'

'Come on, I do have top level clearance.'

'Sorry, I can't say more. Let's just say that it could turn into one.'

'Fine, I suppose I could call in a training exercise for one of the newer members of the team. That would circumnavigate the red tape. But I can't take up all of our satellite time following it. Is that acceptable?'

'That's perfect. I don't need to know all of her passage details just where she stops and what is off loaded. Many thanks I'll stay in touch.'

'Great, that's my career down the toilet. I have a feeling this won't be the last favour you ask for.'

'Hopefully not. Let me know when you have something. Thanks for this Tom, I realise it's a big ask.'

'I'll get over it. You know if you ever get bored of retirement, there would always be a place for a man of your talents here.'

'Ha, thanks. But I think I've done more than my fair share.' James hung up, still slightly amused by the offer that Tom had made.

Devan had spent three days hard at it. The script kept on changing its meaning the further she got. In the end she had more questions than she had answers. So far she understood that the Sumerians had made a total of six great journeys over both land and sea.

They had split something of great value, some sort of relic into seven parts to prevent it falling into the hands of some evil power. Six of the pieces had been taken to some of the great civilisations of the world at the time. Each civilisation was entrusted with a piece, the seventh and most important piece, the Sumerians had hidden themselves.

It was still unclear exactly where the pieces had been hidden but there were a few clues, which needed further investigation. She knew that her extensive knowledge of ancient civilisations would certainly help to narrow down the possibilities.

Surely they must refer to the great civilisations that have become known as the first great peoples of the earth. In Mesoamerica the Mayans, in the Aegean Sea the Minoans, the Egyptians of the Nile Valley, the Harappa in the Indus Valley, and the Shang Dynasty of the Huang Ho. She suspected that the latter might actually turn out to be the Xi rather than the Shang.

The Xi were thought to be earlier than the Shang but to date there has never been any archaeological evidence to support the Chinese records; in total that would potentially account for six of the seven civilisations, if you include the Sumerians. The question was who was the seventh? So much of the world had yet to be explored.

In reality archaeologists had only scratched the surface of what lay beneath the dust. Part of her problem was that the map itself was incomplete. She only had the Americas and what she could only assume was Antarctica, but surely there had never been any civilisations that inhabited that cold expanse of ice. It was a wasteland. Temperatures there dropped well into double figures, ferociously cold winds ripped through the solid landscape tearing at the ice covered mountains, carving strange, bizarre and often spectacular shapes into the ancient frozen water. Ice storms far worse than any sand storm could decimate huge areas on the ice caps. Surely even humans, who as a species had proven themselves to be very adaptable to environments, could not survive those harsh conditions.

She turned her attention to the Mesoamerican region on the map. There were a few Olmec type civilisations in the region. The greatest of these had been the Maya. They had certainly been the most advanced and odds on favourites to receive such an artefact. Devan just wished she knew what the artefact was. Captain Flack clearly knew a lot more than he was letting on.

In fact it was high time that she got some answers from her mysterious employer. Something told her that she didn't really want to know; unfortunately she had a Pandora like trait and could not resist the urge to peak under the lid.

Chris and the others had set themselves up in one of the studies at Martinstowe. It was time to roll the dice and hope that luck was on their side. They might not know Norwood's intended destination but they couldn't wait any longer to find out. They needed a plan of action, and to start the preparations at least for wherever they would eventually journey to.

'I think we should go to the States.' Chris was saying. 'It's on the map. We can use that as a starting point from which to then track down the next piece of the book once the professor has finished decoding the map.'

'I'm inclined to agree with you. I'm still rather concerned that Chamberlain hasn't resurfaced yet. That man is trouble and guaranteed to throw a spanner in the works just when you aren't expecting it.' James replied.

'Yes I'm sure he will rear his ugly head at some point, but he's not my major concern at the moment.'

'Innit 'bout time to recruit some more people from *The Order* to help? Wudda be better if we can avoid a repeat of what happened at the Mount.' Michael said. Ever the tactician he was always thinking about learning from previous mistakes.

'The problem is that it's hard to travel quickly with a large group. There probably will come a time when it is necessary to have a bit more help, but I don't think we have come to the point where we need to bridge that gap quite yet.' Chris replied.

'My father agrees, I have spoken to him quite recently. He has *The Order* on alert, ready to step in if it's required. He does however think that it would be best for the moment if they could keep a low profile.' James said.

'Dunna tell me, another elusive organisation. Great!' Michael said rather sceptically.

'Funny, I see your point. They are not in the same league as *The Glove*. They were created for a completely different reason and became involved in this by accident rather than by design. They understand what is at stake. Besides they have far more resources than you do.'

It was at this point that Devan entered the room. She felt that it was high time that Capt. Flack filled her in on what was going on.

'Captain Flack, I think it is about time you shone some light on what this is all about.' She said in a demandingly stern and dominating voice.

'Right Shag, think we gunna leave you to it. Good luck, Mon.' Michael said with a wink as he and James left the room not wanting to bear witness to the fireworks that would surely follow. James had seen for quite some time that there would be a rather heated conversation between those two and didn't want to get involved. Plus he knew that there was definitely some sexual tension lightly simmering below the surface that might also come to the boil at some point and definitely wanted to avoid that awkward situation.

'Devan I'm sorry but that information is privileged and only for those who need to know. I'm afraid you just don't need to know.'

'Oh, please cut the sanctimonious bullshit. Your mysterious persona is starting to wear a little thin.'

'Girl you're starting to meddle in things that don't concern you.'

'Stop treating me like a child.'

'Then stop acting like one!'

She slapped him hard across the cheek. It was one of those slaps that if you were a bystander would have made you wince. His cheek burned with heat and he almost lost his temper but he managed to control the rising anger.

'Do that again and I won't be held responsible for the consequences.'

Devan took no notice and attempted to slap him again. This time Chris was ready for the on coming assault and caught hold of her wrist. She glared at him but he held her arm in a firm grip.

They starred into each other's eyes for a few moments trying to gauge, which one would break first.

'Let go of me, you're hurting me.'

'Young lady you need to learn some manners.' Chris replied.

Devan's back was almost up against the wall, when Chris decided that there was only one good solution to this stand off. He leant into her and planted a firm kiss on her full lips. She broke away from him.

'Well of all the ner…' Devan was cut off mid sentence as he kissed her again. Secretly she had been hoping he would do something like that. Her anger and frustration almost melted away as she embraced the moment.

Devan had a very dominating personality and wasn't about to lose control of the situation. Chris may have caught her off guard but he was in for a surprise if he thought he could have it all his own way.

The temperature in the room was rising nevertheless Devan knew exactly what she was doing. She had managed to back Chris up, just in front of a low coffee table, as he tried to take another step backwards he lost his footing and tripped over the table.

'You'll have to do better than that, I'm not that much of a push over. I'll leave you to reconsider your position, Captain.' Devan said looking down upon him as she calmly rearranged her dress before leaving the room.

Chris was at a loss as to how to respond. His bewildered face watched her depart. There was clearly some chemistry between them and he wondered what affect this would have on the dynamic of the group. However, she was certainly determined to have her questions answered. The problem he faced was that she had a narcotic effect upon him and having briefly tasted euphoria he was hooked; left wondering how he would cope without another hit of that sweet nectar but at the same time a decision needed to be made about how much he could reveal about the map, the codex and *The Glove*.

Devan returned to the library, she was now more determined than ever to find the answers hidden within the cryptic symbols of the map. It was clear to her that Chris would not give her the answers that she sought until she had managed to provide him with more information.

She knew that the artefact must have travelled to Central or South America, and yet so far she had not been able to narrow it down any further. She knew that there must be something that she was missing but it was one of those frustrating things; like looking for one's car keys. You know they must be somewhere but the harder you look the more vexing the search becomes.

After a few hours of getting nowhere with the map Devan decided to take a break, her head was fried. She just couldn't understand it, there had to be some clue hidden somewhere in the text on the parchment; and yet so far she had not had any luck at all.

Hopefully a break from the infernal thing would allow her subconscious to come up with a solution. Devan left the library in search of some much-needed caffeine.

She bumped into James in the kitchen, who had taken up most of the kitchen table with what looked like a rifle, it was hard to tell as its stripped carcass was strewn all across the table.

'A new toy?' She inquired as she put the kettle on to boil.

'What? This old thing, hardly, just in need of a bit of TLC. It's hard to break the habit of a lifetime. How are the studies going?'

'Oh don't mention that. It's as if part of the script has faded away over time to the point that it has disappeared.'

'Unless it was never there to begin with.'

'I don't think so. After all a map is made to show a location. But trying to find where the clues are hiding is proving to be rather tedious.'

'Ah, I think you are missing my meaning. What I meant was maybe it won't show up in normal light. Have you thought of trying it under UV light? We sometimes used to use invisible inks to pass on messages that we didn't want read by the wrong people.'

'I don't think they had the technology back then to do that. But they would have had lemon juice. It's only visible once heated.'

'Just be careful not to heat it too much. If you burn it, Chris would never forgive you.'

'Ha, he can go suck a lemon for all I care at the moment.' Devan replied as she left the kitchen with her coffee and a glimmer of hope that she may now be able to find the missing clue.

Fetching the map she returned to the kitchen and put the scroll into the Aga's top left, which was on the lowest heat so as not to risk setting it on fire.

'How long are you going to leave it in there' James tentatively inquired, not one hundred percent sure that he was okay with the idea of cooking the map.

'Oh it probably won't need that long, couple of minutes maybe. But that's just a guess.'

Like waiting for a kettle to boil, a couple of minutes seemed to pass by at a snail's pace. After what seemed to have been more like ten minutes, Devan carefully lifted the now slightly toasted scroll out of the oven and after James made room on the kitchen table she laid it out and they both eagerly examined it to see if anything had appeared that wasn't there before.

'I wish I had taken a photo of what it looked like before. It looks exactly the same to me.' Devan said after staring at it for a while.

'I know what you mean but then I haven't studied it as much as you have. Was this tiny little mark, there before?' James asked pointing to an almost insignificant spot near to what looked like a lake on the map.

'Now that you mention it, I don't think it was.'

'That must be it. I have been looking for that for such a long time. Looks like it's in Guatemala, which would fit in with my theory of which civilisations might have received such an artefact.'

'Then that is where we will start. I'll tell Chris to start making plans.'

Having finally made the decision on where they expected to find the book, Chris decided that Michael and Louis should remain in the UK in order to continue to research where the next part may be and also to keep tabs on what *The Glove* was up to.

They had made good preparation for their expedition to the land of the Maya. Lt Cdr Bradbury rang to say that the *Astronomer* had indeed altered her schedule slightly, originally bound for San Francisco she had crossed the Atlantic but before passing through the Panama Canal, the *Astronomer* had stopped in the Port of Balboa in Panama City citing engine problems. After the so-called *repairs* she had continued on to her final destination of San Francisco.

Tom had found her maintenance issue a little too convenient. The satellite had picked up several containers being unloaded at the port whilst the supposed maintenance took place.

'It could just be coincidence, the shipping company taking advantage of an unscheduled stop. But I thought I should let you know.' Tom said over the phone to James.

'Thanks. That is very interesting, we had a suspicion it might be a Central American destination. Stay in touch.' James replied. He hung up and confirmed the Mesoamerican destination to Chris.

'Right that settles it. Now we just need to sort out some transportation.' Chris said clapping his hands together.

'I might be able to sort out some form of transportation. I have a few friends at RAF Brize Norton that might be able to help. I'm sure if a certain Bear I know can get the army to fly a shipping container to his house on that island off the coast of North Wales; I can borrow a C-17 Globemaster for a bit.' James replied with a smile.

'Is there anything that you can't get your hands on?' Rachel asked with a slight smile.

'Well… I might be able to think of a couple of things.' James retorted with a wink. 'At least not yet anyway.'

Chapter Eighteen: Yaxhá

The flight from RAF Brize Norton into Guatemala had been pretty rough. The jet streams of early December had made the flight really bumpy. At least it wasn't hurricane season anymore.

James had also managed to borrow a couple of Land Rovers to use once they were in the Jungle. The plan was that they would be air dropped into part of the rain forest to the north of the ruins and then cut their way through the jungle to the temple at Yaxhá.

The Guatemalan Military had agreed to allow their flight access on the grounds that they were an archaeological team with heavy equipment that could only be flown into the jungle surrounding the temple complex. The explanation was accepted because Devan was with them and she had done this sort of thing several times before.

'See I told you she would come in useful.' James said as he finished talking to ground control over the headset.

Devan had also arranged for a guide to meet them at the drop point and lead them into the jungle to the great temple at Yaxhá.

'I wonder if this Mayan prophecy will come true.' Ollie said. 'It's coming up to that time of year.'

'Oh please don't tell me that you buy into all of that mumbo jumbo, do you?' Gaz scoffed.

'Well it could happen.'

'Actually, there are no grounds for it. The end of the thirteenth *baktun*, which corresponds with the 21st December, is just the end of a whole cycle. For the Maya this would have been cause for a huge celebration. It was the end of a cycle and the beginning of a new one. There is no evidence to suggest they would have expected the world to end.' Devan said. 'The whole disaster myth has arisen from modern society's fears, these have been exaggerated by our love for disaster movies and our fears of an uncertain future.' She added.

'Well that's good to know. Are we not trying to prevent a disaster?' Ollie asked.

'In a sense yes, but *The Glove* is a long way from orchestrating that.' Gaz replied.

'*The Glove*, what or who are they?' Devan asked as her curiosity at this slip of information was sparked.

'I guess you hadn't told her about them yet.' Gaz said as he passed an apologetic look to Chris.

'No, I thought it was better not to for the time being. I suppose I'm going to have to explain now. Well, maybe once we are on the ground' Chris replied, ignoring the expression on Devan's face that clearly showed that she really wanted an explanation now.

Ollie tried to distract her attention by carrying on his line of questioning regarding the Mayan myth.

'So what you are really saying is that instead of this being the end. The myth could sort of be right, and that this is just the start of a cycle that is the beginning of the end.'

'I guess if you are rather pessimistic. It could just be the start of something new.' Devan replied. 'I wouldn't worry about it too much if I were you. I believe that people are far better off in the present than worrying about what might or might not happen in the future. At the moment I'm far more concerned about jumping out of this aeroplane in about ten minutes.'

'You'll love it. It's such a rush!' Gaz said with a massive grin on his face. He couldn't wait for that feeling as the air rushed past his face.

'We have a go! Everybody ready?' Chris said as he made his way along the plane towards the tail. The air rushed in as he dropped the tail.

The noise of the swirling wind was deafening. He had to shout as loud as he could to be heard, grabbing hold of some webbing straps to prevent himself being sucked out. Removing the clamps from the Land Rovers, he released the first chute.

The tiny chute shot out of the tail of the plane like a horse bolting from the stalls, as the resistance around the chute grew it pulled out another until finally there was enough drag created to cause the first of the two Land Rovers to gradually slide out of the plane. This was quickly followed by the second. As soon as the Land Rovers were away, they followed.

Rachel and Devan who were new to parachuting were paired with Ollie and Gaz, the two most experienced skydivers. To anybody watching from the ground it would have seemed as if Guatemala was under invasion as the huge white canopies drifted down through the clear blue skies towards the ground.

The vehicles floated down and landed with a jolt as they met the solid ground, followed closely by the team. The pilot circled the plane, banking sharply around to make sure they had all landed safely before heading off towards whichever air base had been arranged for him to refuel at.

They had landed in a clearing in the jungle. Devan had been clinging so tightly to the webbing straps that her fingers had cramped up. She was probably the only one who had been totally terrified on the way down and needed a bit of time to sit down and recover her nerves after she had unclipped from Gaz.

Gaz, Ollie and James set about detaching the large chutes from the Land Rovers, carefully packing them away. They were planning on using them as tents during the expedition.

Their guide met them about twenty minutes after they had landed. He was called Lomay, and was a direct descendant of the Maya. His vast knowledge of the jungle was second to none. He told them he would take them on the shortest possible route to the temple, but warned them that the going would be very arduous even with the Land Rovers.

Lomay was right, the going was hard. Picking their way through the undergrowth of the jungle they eventually found a small clearing just before dusk. They set about making camp for the night and would continue on to the ancient ruins at first light the next day.

'According to Lomay the ruins that best fit the map's description are about half a day's drive from here. Depending slightly on how much of the trail has been engulfed by the rain forest since the end of the rains.' Devan said to Chris, who was busy lighting the fire he had built to keep them warm during the night.

'You said the one that best fits the description? How accurate is that?'

'Pretty accurate it describes a temple complex that overlooks a lake. The lake has a series of islands upon which another temple has been constructed; this was a sacred burial ground. To the best of his knowledge Yaxhá and Topoxté are the sites that best fit this description. They are not as well known as El Mirador or Tikal, but then it would be unlikely that they would have hidden something of such great importance in the most prestigious cities.'

'Well professor, I have the utmost faith in you.' He said smiling at her.

Ollie and Gaz were attempting to erect the tents.

'Man, you can't put that there, we are not making tepees.' Ollie started to say.

'Oh but I thought you would need one for all your squaws.' Replied Gaz.

'What Squaws?'

'The ones that you always claim you are going to get with on these trips and always finish up as *Lone Wolf*.' Gaz retorted with a cheeky laugh.

'Well better that than being *Angry Bear*.' Replied Ollie with a slightly mischievous twinkle in his eye.

'What do you mean by that?' Gaz's question was answered by Ollie tugging on one of the ropes holding up the canopy above his head. The entire parachute dropped down on to the unsuspecting head of Gaz. Totally engulfing him. Ollie burst out in to hysterics as Gaz struggled to get out of the mass of material. Ollie's laughter just enraged him more. He really was quite tangled inside the nylon fabric.

'Just you wait until I get out of here! Then I'll show you what an *Angry Bear* looks like!' growled Gaz from underneath the parachute.

'I think I have a pretty good idea already, but let me know and I'll take a picture. Man this is the best prank I've played on you for ages.' Ollie tried to sound serious, but couldn't manage to keep a straight face. The sight of his friend blindly fumbling around in the white fabric was just too funny. That was until he caught sight of a huge snake slithering towards the canopy.

'Gaz stop moving! Stay very still. There is a snake coming towards you.'

'Yeah very funny. I'm not falling for than one'

'I'm not joking. Don't move!'

'Not funny, I'm not going to bite Ol.'

'No but I think it will!'

'Dude, I hate snakes get it away from me before I freak out!' Gaz, suddenly realising the gravity of the situation, was now very much less angry and rather more afraid of what might be about to happen.

'Get it away from me!'

'Stay very still.'

'That's easier said than done when you are about to become dinner!' Gaz said through gritted teeth.

A loud crack echoed through the trees. James had also seen the snake and had grabbed a rifle from the back of one of the Land Rovers. He hadn't wasted any time in loading it, taking aim and shooting the snake dead before it could strike.

'When you two have quite finished fooling around can we get these tents up? It's starting to get dark and I would quite like some sort of roof over my head tonight.' He said slightly irritated with the two young men.

'Oh all right it was only a bit of fun' Ollie replied.

'For you maybe, not for me. You better sleep with one eye open. I'll get my revenge at some point.' Gaz exclaimed as he finally emerged from under the mass of material.

Devan was pondering over a line in the text on the map. She knew it was the key to revealing the book the Maya had hidden. Yet it made no sense to her.

When the Heavens align the truth will become visible.'

'You seem deep in thought.' Chris said as he walked over to where she was sitting beside the fire.

'Anything I can help with?'

'This line has been bugging me. I'm not sure what it means.' She said with a deep sigh.

'Ah yes I saw that in your translation. I have an idea what it might be referring to but I won't know if I am correct until we get to the temple.' He replied in another one of his mysterious phrases.

'And I suppose you are not going to fill me in?' She flatly asked.

'Well, not yet anyway. I wouldn't want it to be an anti-climax.' He replied with an annoyingly knowing grin before walking off to help the others finish putting up the tents.

Devan thumped her hand against the log she was sitting on. That man was infuriating, always dropping hints to peak her curiosity and yet never giving away the whole picture. He was such a tease. It drove her crazy. She wished she could get inside his head just once to know what he was thinking.

Lomay stood on the edge of the clearing observing his new companions. He was keeping watch for the Pumas and Jaguars that inhabited this part of the jungle. He was certain that the big cats would have sensed the presence of something new in their playground, and would soon come to investigate the strange new smells they had caught on the air.

'It would be advisable to keep the fire burning all night and to keep watch, just in case any of the jungle predators come to investigate, Señor.'

James took Lomay's advice and paired the group up. They would take two-hour shifts at keeping watch during the night whilst the rest of the group slept.

Chris and Lomay took the first watch. The rest turned in rather early so that they would be fresh in the morning. Chris hoped to arrive at the temple before midday, which would mean starting out early.

During their watch Chris talked to Lomay about his ancestors. He wanted to understand the Maya better. He hoped that he would gain some insight into their knowledge of the stars. They were after all the closest to *Lords of Time and Space*. Thousands of years ago they had worked out exactly how long it took for the Earth to orbit around the Sun. Something that modern civilisations only achieved using sophisticated electronic devices. This sort of accomplishment fascinated him. The Maya were the first culture to use the figure Zero within their counting system. They truly were light years ahead of other civilisations of the period.

Apart from all the usual trekking equipment Chris had also brought with him the artefacts that they had retrieved from the crypt at Martinstowe. He had examined them briefly back in the privacy of one of the studies at the house. He believed that they held the key, or rather were the key to unlocking the book in the Mayan temple.

He had originally thought that they were three separate pieces but he now understood that they were in fact part of the same mechanism although try as he might he could not get them to fit together. Coming to the conclusion that there was something else required to do this, which he hoped was in the temple. He had left them wrapped up in the linen cloth and stowed them in his rucksack.

Chris hoped that it was the only set, so that even if Norwood beat them to the temple he would not be able to find the book. That was if he even knew the exact location, which more than likely he did. Chris was hedging his bets that Norwood would be delayed travelling up from Panama, arriving after they had long departed.

James tossed and turned in his sleeping bag. His dreams were worse than ever, he dreamt of thousands of tormented souls crying out as one, in great pain. Many more were dead or dying. Wiped out by an unknown force. He could feel their pain, he felt like a bystander, powerless to help.

Unlike the others, these dreams had images that he had not actually witnessed. These images were something new, something still to come, perhaps?

He woke several times during the night with cold beads of sweat rolling down his face. Maybe it was just the humidity or just the way his subconscious grieved for the loss of Jack. Either way he was definitely not going to get much more sleep tonight; in the end he just lay there staring at the roof of the makeshift tent waiting until it was his turn to take watch.

Apart from his restless sleep the night passed relatively quietly. The fire that had been kept well stoked had done its job. The wild cats never came near the camp to investigate.

Chris and the group left early. The humidity in the forest was worse than it had ever been at this time of the year. The sun beat down on the lush green vegetation; Lomay had mentioned the wet season had been one of the wettest on record hence why the humidity now was much higher than usual for the time of year.

The Land Rovers had to stop several times in order for people to get out and chop away branches and other vegetation that had begun to grow over the tracks they were following.

At one point because the ground was so soft, part of the trail fell away down the hillside almost taking one of the Land Rovers with it. Luckily for the occupants the Land Rover's abrupt sideways slide down the slope came to a halt up against the trunk of a young tree; had the Land Rover continued down the hill it would certainly have toppled and then rolled, more than likely killing all those seated inside. They had to act fast to winch the vehicle back up on to the trail.

The tree that had initially checked the sideways movement would not hold fast for long. It was not much more than a sapling so the root system was not fully established in the fertile soil and the landslide had now exposed part of what little roots it had developed.

'Jesus, that was close. Lucky this little fella's got roots. Otherwise we'd have been gonners. Gaz, take the winch cable to that tree on the far side, Chris and I will run a rope from the running board to the tree on the far side.' James said as he took charge of the situation. The setup allowed them to gradually drag the Land rover back on to the main track by pivoting on the rope.

After a few more delays to hack away more of the dense undergrowth from the trail they finally reached the ancient site just after noon.

The temple at Yaxhá rose up like a mountain from the jungle floor. The great stone pyramid was desperately fighting a losing battle with the encroaching forest. It was gradually being smothered by the jungle soon to disappear forever back beneath the unwavering advance of the forest just like the civilisation that had created it.

Many of the complex's buildings lay in ruin. The locals had robbed the stone over the years to make stonewalls to keep in livestock, so the city had lost much of its grandeur. Nevertheless the temple unlike the rest of the site had remained virtually intact. Whether this was because the locals had left it alone fearing that they would incur the wrath of the ancient gods by disturbing it, or that they just had not needed anymore stone was a mystery. Whatever the reason, it had remained more or less complete, eroded only by the passage of time.

At the entrance to the temple stood two huge Jaguar heads carved in limestone. They represented the guardians of the temple. The team passed between them and on up the temple steps towards a doorway, the entrance to Yaxhá's inner sanctum.

The darkness inside the temple enveloped them as they entered forcing them to negotiate the passages by torchlight. The light from the torches cast long shadows on the walls as they followed the ancient stone works.

Devan pointed out many friezes carved into the limestone walls. These told the story of the Maya; one in particular caught her attention. It was part of the *Popol Vuh*, the *Book of the People*. This frieze depicted part of the Mayan creation story. How the Gods had first made men from mud and wood but they lacked speech, souls and intellect and so the Gods destroyed them. It was only when men were made from corn that they were allowed to flourish.

The friezes began to change as they ventured further into the temple. The carvings began to focus on the stars, the movement of The Sun, Moon and a few of the planets. Whilst others showed Mayan numerals making up parts of the Long Count calendar. This was made up of *baktun* or cycles. Each *baktun* consisted of one hundred and forty-four thousand days. It was from one of these friezes that they Mayan myth of the end of the world had originally been generated, the end of the thirteenth *baktun*.

In this part of the temple the first twelve *baktun* had been carved on either side of a great stone panel that protruded out from the rest of the wall by about a foot or so. There were six *baktun* on each side. In the centre of the huge panel was the thirteenth; more care had been taken to construct this one as if it was more significant than the others.

Devan carefully studied the carving with the help of Lomay, who was far more versed in the language of the Maya than she was. The carving talked of a hand and a ceremony, that the end of the thirteenth *baktun* would be cause for great celebration. Much of the rest of the frieze was illegible, as it had fallen apart over time.

'Lomay, what does this section say? I can't seem to make sense of it.' Devan asked the old Mayan guide.

'Let me see. Hmm very strange, it is gibberish. The numerals are in the wrong order. This is very unlike the Maya. They were very precise about such things. It is unusual to find a mistake on a carving, something that would have been meticulously planned out before carving.' The guide said.

'Then it must be deliberate. Maybe a puzzle to solve?' Chris suggested.

'Perhaps.' 'Replied the guide nodding his head. 'This should read 12.19.19.17.19, but instead reads 19.19.17.19.12, maybe they can be moved.' He suggested.

Chris tried to slide them but the first few he tried would not budge. It was only when he came to try the number 12 that something happened. Instead of the glyph sliding across, as he touched it, it sank back into the panel.

'Ah ha! See they must be pressed.' Lomay exclaimed.

Chris completed the sequence as Lomay directed and once the last glyph sank into place a small panel slid open to reveal part of an ancient mechanism made up of many brass wheels and cogs.

'I know what this is.' Chris said. 'I have some similar parts in my rucksack from the crypt. He quickly set his sack down and rummaged around inside it for the artefacts. He carefully unwrapped them setting each one down on the ground in front of the frieze as he moved on to the next.

'They never quite seemed to fit together when I was examining them at Martinstowe. Now I know why. They needed the parts here to complete the mechanism.' Chris explained as he began to fit them on to the parts in the frieze.

'Is this your big climax?' Devan asked as she watched him try to fit the parts together. She let out a gasp as the last piece was set in place. 'I've seen one of these before in a museum in Athens. Or at least something that looks very similar. They called it the *Antikythera Mechanism*, the world's first computer of sorts. But that was Greek and if I'm not mistaken the symbols on this are Sumerian.' She said still staring at the device in disbelief.

'The Greeks were not the only ones to understand the movements of the planets. I think this should now shed some light on that passage you were struggling with, the one about the alignment of the heavens. At the moment all the planets are in different positions but if I wind this knob they start to rotate around the Sun.' Chris said as he began to turn the knob at the side of the mechanism. The tiny spheres representing the planets gradually started to revolve around the central dial.

'Yes I understand now, you need to rotate them until they all line up.' Devan replied.

'Precisely, many cultures believed that when all the planets were in alignment great things would happen.' He replied excitedly as he continued to wind the mechanism on.

The anticipation amongst the group was growing as the planets moved ever closer to completing the alignment. They were expecting something amazing to happen. There was no sound inside the temple. Everyone was holding his or her breath as the last planet slid into alignment. Silence.

After what seemed like an eternity the silence was broken by Gaz. 'That was a bit of an anti-climax. I was expecting fireworks at least.'

'I don't understand. That can't be what is supposed to happen.' Chris said slightly frustrated that his big show had lacked a dramatic ending.

'Perhaps it is broken. It has not been used for such a long time.

Part of the mechanism may simply have perished or corroded.' Devan suggested. She too had been expecting a little more than nothing.

'No, I don't think so. It was so well protected. The craftsmen obviously intended it to last. The only thing I can think of is that the alignment is wrong.' Chris said in a rather dejected voice. He could see from the glyphs on the outer dial that the combinations were almost endless.

Lomay had been quiet for sometime. He had been studying the mechanism for a long time. Its design was alien to him and yet he understood its principle.

'Señor, if I may. I think you have the wrong eclipse. If the alignment is of great significance, then I believe that the Maya would have found a solar eclipse far more important. You have currently got a lunar eclipse, if I am reading this correctly.' The guide suggested.

'Lomay you are a genius! Of course that makes perfect sense. I wish I had thought of that. Thank you.' Chris exclaimed in relief. Chris quickly realigned the small spheres.

This time as the Moon swung round to block the Sun, the temple wall began to shake violently and then part of it fell away, engulfing them in a cloud of dust. As the dust began to settle they all peered through the hole where the wall had once stood. Through the gloom they could make out a small square room with a rectangular pedestal at its centre. The pedestal was built upon four, square platforms. Upon the pedestal lay what resembled a book covered in the thick layers of Time.

'Now that's what I call fireworks.' Said Gaz. 'Can we go home now?'

'Not just yet. It may be booby-trapped.' Chris replied.

'I think that is unlikely. The Maya would have relied on the mechanism to keep it safe.' Devan said.

'Well I'm not going to take any chances.' Chris said. He cautiously made his way towards the pedestal watching the floor for any signs of loose stones that might trigger traps. There was no sign of any.

Taking several deep breaths he built up the courage to remove the book from its resting place. He had seen too many relic hunter type movies and was thinking that as he lifted the book something nasty would happen. Devan was in fact proved to be correct as he snatched the book up from the pedestal. Nothing happened, there were no traps.

Chapter Nineteen: Fight or Flight?

'Well that was all rather uneventful.' James said as they made their way out down the temple steps.

'I'll take that!' A familiar voice said piercing through the sounds of the jungle. Cutting short their moment of celebration.

'I had a feeling it was too good to be true.' Ollie muttered.

Lord Norwood emerged from the undergrowth accompanied by at least fifty men armed with automatic weapons.

'I must congratulate you. You have done my job for me. I had always wondered how I was going to get round the temple safeguards. There is no way to escape this time! Nowhere to run to! You will hand it over.' A twisted smile spread across Lord Norwood's face as he spoke.

James knew that he was right, unlike at the Mount. This time there really was nowhere to hide.

'I think you are going to have to do as he says.' James said through gritted teeth. 'We will surely be killed if we try to run. There's too many of them. He really has out flanked us this time.'

'I know, at least he doesn't seem to know about the map. I'm hoping he might try to find out what we know. It may give us a chance to escape later.' Chris whispered back before he turned to address Norwood.

'Very well, I will give you the book on the condition that you let my companions go.' He shouted across the clearing towards their nemesis.

Norwood laughed. 'You are in no position to make demands. Seize them! Make sure they are secure, we camp here tonight before moving on.'

Six men scuttled up from the trees and roughly man handled them, pushing them towards one of the stone ruins. The ruin had once been a house, but the roof had long since rotted away, and without the support of the roof, parts of the walls had caved in. The men bound their hands and feet with strong cords and threw them to the floor inside the square ruins.

Norwood removed the book from Chris' possession before his men led him away to join the others.

'What are the rest of you standing around for? Get this camp set up.' Norwood shouted at the rest of his men who were just standing around in inactivity.

The men quickly jumped into action setting up tents and cook fires, not wanting to experience the full force of Norwood's wrath, and it was not long before they had the main tent for his Lordship set up and a number of other smaller tents for the rest to sleep in when they were not on watch.

'Lomay, if we were to escape, where is the best place to head to?' Chris asked.

'Towards Lake Yaxhá, from there we could follow the river to a small settlement, Señor. These bonds are strong; I do not think we will manage to escape. I fear we will die here.' The guide replied.

'Have faith my friend. If anyone can get us out of this, James can. He has managed to get out of tighter spots than this before.' Chris replied trying to be optimistic.

'Yes, but I had a little more to work with. Plus I only had to get myself out not extricate six people. I wouldn't hold your breath. It's going to take some time to find a weakness, if indeed there is one.' James replied.

'I don't think you are going to have a shortage of that.' Chris said rather sarcastically.

Two guards had been positioned outside the ruin. A large tarpaulin had been stretched out overhead to keep the rain out. It was late in the evening before anybody came to see them. A large burly man stepped inside the make-shift cell. He carried a sub-machine gun and as he stepped inside he addressed Chris.

'You are coming with me, his Lordship wishes to speak with you.' He said pointing his gun in Chris' general direction.

'Can you tell him I'm rather tied up at the moment? Therefore I must decline his invitation.' Chris replied.

'Think you are funny do you? You will come now! And no tricks.' The guard said as he roughly man-handled Chris to his feet, whilst one of the other guards cut the cord from around Chris' legs. The guards proceeded to shove Chris outside and across the open ground towards Norwood's tent.

The wind had picked up and large grey clouds hung overhead threatening to drop a considerable amount of water down on to the camp. Gas heaters had been set up inside Norwood's tent as well as lanterns and a large aluminium table, currently littered with paper. Three aluminium chairs were positioned around the table, one currently occupied by Lord Norwood. Five guards stood around the inside of the tent.

Norwood briefly looked up as Chris was ushered inside. His escort deposited him into one of the empty chairs to sit facing his Lordship and then left to carry out their duties.

'Well Captain. We meet face to face at last. I would say that it is a pleasure and I would greatly enjoy talking to you at some length, but unfortunately I don't have the time. So you will oblige me by telling me what I need to know.'

'I very much doubt that. You will get nothing from me.' Chris defiantly replied.

'Come, come now Captain. Don't make things difficult. I can make this very painful if you do not cooperate.'

'I'm sure you can, but you will not get the answers you want.'

'Very well if you insist. Chamberlain!' Norwood's voice bellowed through the tent.

The huge hulk of a man entered through one of the side flaps, his face lighting up as he saw the bound figure of Captain Flack in the centre.

'The Captain here has decided to be less than forth coming. Find out what he knows.' He said before turning to address Chris. 'I would explain to you all that Chamberlain does, but I think he will do a better job of that.'

'I have been looking forward to this.' The huge man said menacingly across the table.

'I bet you have.' Chris replied through gritted teeth. 'I have met your sort before.'

'I very much doubt that. I find most do not take enough pride in their work. By the time I have finished with you, you won't even be able to call yourself a man. But first let me introduce you to a few of my little friends. You will come to know each other quite well in due course.' Chamberlain said as he began to unroll a set of tools spreading them out across the table.

Inside lay many hideous metal instruments used to inflict as much pain as possible: Scalpels, serrated blades, clamps, jagged toothed saws, needles, spikes and hammers along with others that Chris didn't even know the proper names for.

Chris kept his cool at the sight of these instruments of torture. He didn't want to give Chamberlain the satisfaction of seeing fear on his face. In truth he was petrified, he had seen the results of this kind of torture before. The men who had experienced it were never the same afterwards. Just empty shells wearing vacant expressions. He steeled himself for what was to follow.

Chris' blood stained body was thrown into the stone ruin an hour later. He had taken a really vicious beating from Chamberlain, but had told him nothing. Chris had a broken wrist, and a few cracked ribs and his face was almost pulp.

Chamberlain hadn't started to properly mutilate him yet. This was what he liked to call the *softening up* stage. He was saving the rest until after Chris had regained consciousness and had had a little time to think things over.

Chris' companions had heard his screams of pain and the angry voices of both Chamberlain and Norwood demanding answers, repeating them over and over. Both the girls had winced every time Chris' screams of agony carried across to them from the tent.

'This is barbaric. Surely they can't continue with this. Why doesn't he just tell them something, anything?' Devan exclaimed as she tried to wipe away some of the blood from around his face.

'They haven't even started yet. He won't crack; he's far too stubborn for his own good sometimes. He'll die before telling them anything.' James replied with a grim look on his face. He knew full well that Chris had been one of only a handful soldiers to complete the SAS interrogation simulations without divulging a single piece of information, he was what they called a *grey-man*. He also knew that it would be pointless for Norwood to try inflicting pain on one of the others in the hope that Chris would break, as painful as it would be for Chris to watch someone else suffer because of his stubbornness. He would still say nothing.

The theory that everybody eventually broke down just didn't apply to Chris; he was a bit of a freak in that respect, an anomaly in the system. It was almost as if he enjoyed the pain, feeding off it.

The only chance they had was if James found a way to escape. A task that at present, he was struggling to fulfil. Norwood seemed to have every possible scenario covered. Their lives hung in the balance. Only the gods themselves could save them now.

James was busily trying to break his bonds by rubbing them against the loose stones of the ruined hut. The cords were gradually wearing away; nevertheless it would take sometime to finally break them. Time that he was sure they didn't have. It would not be long before the guards returned for Chris.

Outside, the rainforest, which had been awash with noise had suddenly become quiet. The birds chattering in the trees had stopped. Even the noisy tree crickets had fallen silent. Something was happening beyond the camp that had startled them.

'I hope you have a plan, Señor.' Lomay said in a low whisper. 'I think we may be about to get our chance.'

'What do you mean?' James replied.

'Listen, the forest. It is silent. I think there may be Jaguars prowling outside the camp. The forest always goes quiet when there are predators around. They probably smelt your friend's blood and have come to investigate.'

Sure enough within seconds of his observations a low growl could be perceived coming from the trees, shortly followed by a yell from someone on the perimeter. The guards had seen movement in the trees.

Just as a spotlight was shone in the direction of the movement, a dark shape stealthily sprung up from the shadows of the bushes. The large cat moved like lightning and grappled the nearest guard to the floor. The man's cries, which were far more gruesome than any that Chris had made, were cut short as the cat ripped through his jugular.

'This is our chance. There will be more than one Jaguar out there. We should go, now.' Lomay said just as James finally broke the cords around his wrists. James hastily freed his own feet before he set the others loose.

Outside, there was havoc in the camp. Gunshots could be heard echoing through the forest as men tried to deal with the cat that had attacked the guard.

The guards that had been stationed outside the ruin, holding James and the others, had left, running off to the aid of the guard who had been mauled by the big cat. They were too late. The man had died almost instantaneously. He hadn't stood a chance against one of nature's greatest predators.

The two guards were so busy scanning the trees for more of the big cats that they failed to notice Lomay leading the group out of their cell, James managed to grab Chris' rucksack before he and the other's disappeared as quickly and quietly as possible into the trees on the far side of the camp, away from the big cats. In fact it was only when a second Jaguar sprang out from the undergrowth to maul another guard that anybody bothered to check on the prisoners.

Norwood was furious that his men had left their posts and allowed his captives to escape. He shot the second big cat himself before turning his rage upon his men.

His men were more scared of him than they were of the possibility that another Jaguar would attack. They quickly began to search the nearby trees for any sign of the escapees.

'Here, My Lord. There is blood on the leaves. They must have passed this way.' One of the guardsmen called out, hoping to escape the wrath of Lord Norwood.

'Take some men and find them. Don't bother to come back until you do!'

'Yes, Sir. At once My Lord.' The man replied, eager to get away from Lord Norwood's presence.

Two-dozen men and Chamberlain soon joined the man. They spread out and began to search the forest. Most of them were nervous after the Jaguar attack and moved cautiously through the bushes. Chamberlain on the other hand didn't seem to be affected by this, he took it all in his stride. Predators tended not to go near other predators unless forced to.

Although James and the others had a head start, they were not able to extend their lead. They had to move slowly because Chris was in bad shape. His body screamed out to him to stop and rest. He knew this was not an option. Even supported between James and Gaz it was clear that their pursuers would soon catch up with them.

Lomay suggested that instead of heading straight for the lake they should find somewhere to hide. He knew the forest so well that he could almost tell every tree apart. He took them to a network of caves not far from the camp. The Maya had used the caves for grain storage after the harvest.

Along the way to the caves he stopped to cover Chris' wounds with mud explaining that it would help to block out the scent of the blood and would also prevent Chris leaving a trail of blood all over the place. It wasn't the most hygienic thing to do but it would at least keep them a little safer until they reached the caves.

They had no weapons to protect themselves as the majority of their gear had been confiscated by Norwood, it was only Chris' bag that James had managed to retrieve, and so they had to rely heavily on Lomay's knowledge of the rain forest in order to survive.

Once they had reached the safety of the caves Lomay and James left the others hiding and went back out into the jungle. They planned to lead Norwood's search party away from the caves.

A few hours later they returned breathless.

'We should be safe for a while.' James said trying to catch his breath back. 'We left Norwood's men struggling with a particularly thick part of the jungle. With any luck they won't realise for quite some time that they are looking in the wrong direction.'

'At least you are safe.' Rachel said. She had been relieved to see his familiar figure re-entering the cave. She had been really worried after the first hour since Lomay and James had left that something really dreadful had happened to him. She had already lost Jack; if James had died as well she wouldn't have known how she would have coped. She was becoming rather enamoured with him although she would be the last to admit it.

'How's the patient?' James' question snapped her back from her thoughts to the present.

'Stronger than he was but he is in really bad shape. We need to get him to a doctor as soon as possible.' The expression on her face betrayed her feelings of fear.

'Don't worry. He'll be fine. He's always been a survivor.' James said trying to reassure her. He'd seen her expression and knew exactly what she was thinking.

'Gaz can you and Ollie find something to make a stretcher with?'

'No worries, there's plenty of branches and vines outside.' Gaz replied as the pair sprang up from the floor of the cave and darted out of the cave to find what they needed. James was right, they would move far quicker if Chris was off his feet.

They crouched in the dark cave, huddling together closely. Gaz and Ollie didn't take long to construct the stretcher out of what they could find in the undergrowth. They returned shortly and tried to ease Chris up on to it. Chris was being stubborn insisting that he could make it out of the jungle on his own two feet. Ollie was having none of it.

'Don't be an idiot, you can barely stand up let alone walk. Get on, before I knock you on.'

Once they had settled him on to the stretcher they made their move, away from the caves, taking the shortest possible route to the lake. They remained vigilant, as the jungle was still an extremely dangerous place. The risk of running into Pumas and Jaguars was high, let alone the possibility of Chamberlain and the rest of Norwood's men discovering they had been led astray.

By the time the small group reached the shores of Lake Yaxhá they were short of breath and had to stop, rest and check to make sure that Chris was still conscious. He was but only just; his condition was deteriorating. Chamberlain had really done a number on him.

'Lomay how much further is it to the village?' James asked worrying that his friend may not remain conscious for that much longer.

'At our current pace an hour, maybe longer, Señor. It is difficult to tell, the jungle has grown up a lot around these parts since I was last here. I could run ahead to get help. Follow the river to the east, you will come to the village.'

'I think that would be best. I'm not sure he will last too much longer.'

With that the Mayan guide left them, running off along the edge of the lake to fetch help. The rest followed in the direction Lomay had run off in. James and Rachel took over carrying the stretcher from Gaz and Ollie. The two young men had done a sterling job so far carrying the stretcher, showing little signs of tiring. They had not complained once, even so James realised that it was about time that they had a break from the heavy work. Chris was a pretty heavy guy and it couldn't be easy carrying him over the undulating terrain of the rain forest, manoeuvring the stretcher over fallen trees and through dense undergrowth.

Chris was becoming more incoherent as they made their way along the bank of the river. They were still along way off the village. James decided that they would have to stop and take a break for a bit. Mainly to try and rehydrate Chris, he had lost quite a lot of fluids.

James hoped that Lomay had reached the village by now and was on his way back with help. It had been a risk to put all their faith into the guide. Anything could happen to him along the way, but he knew the ways of the forest and he certainly had a better chance of reaching the village with time to spare.

Lomay was already on his way back. He had had no trouble in reaching the small settlement and had banged loudly on the first door he came to until he had woken up its residents.

After explaining the situation they had pointed him in the direction of the village physician, if you could call him that.

He was by no means a doctor in the same sense of the word as in Western Society. He just had knowledge of the local herbal remedies and such like. The village physician agreed to follow Lomay back up river to find his friends.

Lomay and the physician reached James and the others just in the nick of time. Chris was not far away from totally losing consciousness; he had been drifting in and out for a good ten minutes.

The physician didn't stop to greet them; instead he immediately began to examine Chris. After a few minutes of muttering to himself, the physician took a small pouch from his side and a small wooden bowl he had brought with him. He stooped down by the bank of the river to fill the bowl with some water. Before he opened up the pouch and poured a powder out into the bowl of water. He forced Chris to drink it, saying something in his native tongue to Lomay as he did so.

'He says, this will keep him alive for now but that we need to get Chris to the settlement as soon as possible. Chris has sustained internal injuries that he can't treat here.' Lomay said as he translated the physician's words.

James suspected the physician had said more than that, but wasn't about to waste time by asking what else the physician had said. The needs of his friend came first at this point.

Chapter Twenty: A Safe Haven

Chris awoke with a start. His vision was very blurry and it took a few minutes for his eyes to begin to focus on his surroundings. He knew he was lying down but he couldn't seem to move his arms or legs. It felt as if he was bound to something.

Fear gripped him, for an awful moment he thought that they must have been recaptured. He could remember making their escape but everything was hazy up until he was put on to a stretcher then everything was a blank, he must have passed out. Had all their efforts been for nothing? Was he about to be subjected to more torture? His body still ached all over. He started to panic, struggling to free himself from whatever was preventing him from moving his limbs, before he heard a familiar voice.

'It's okay. You're safe. Just lie still. You need rest.'

It was Devan. She was sitting in a chair next to him. She beamed at him before continuing. 'We made it to the settlement. You gave us all quite a scare after you passed out. It was touch and go for a while as to whether you were going to make it or not.'

'How long have I been out for?' he managed to ask in a feeble voice.

'About three days. You developed a fever soon after we arrived, if Lomay hadn't found the physician I'm not sure you would have survived.'

'What about Norwood and the book?'

'They have gone. James, Gaz and Lomay went back after we had you settled to ensure that they hadn't discovered our trail. Norwood searched quite a large area but couldn't find us and in the end gave up. He had the book after all, so I suppose he decided not to waste too much time on us. Anyway rest now. I'll come back later.' Devan said as she ran her fingers gently through his hair.

Chris had already started to feel quite tired even though he had been completely out of it for the last three days.

The calming sensation of her fingertips brushing through his hair had relaxed him to the point where he felt totally safe and he soon drifted off to sleep again, his mind drifting off into dreams of peaceful forests with flowing rivers. The scent of the forest was the same as the sweet smell of Devan's perfume. Clearly his subconscious had already fallen deeply in love with her not that he would remember any of that when he next awoke.

Devan left the stone hut where Chris was recovering and stepped out into what could only be described as a muddy track, it was the main street of the small settlement. A number of those small huts, similar to the one she had just come from, were peppered along either side of the muddy track. If one were quick enough you would have caught quick glimpses of some of the village children peering out from behind the corners of some of the huts. They had been very interested in the arrival of these strangers to their village.

At first the children had hidden and peered out from their hiding places because they were rather shy and nervous of these strange newcomers to their village. Now that Devan and the others had been in the village for a few days, and had been welcomed by the village elders the children had become much bolder. They no longer hid out of fear. It was part of their new favourite game, attempting to dart from their hiding places and tag whichever one of the group was walking past. The ultimate aim was to then run away, normally laughing in delight at their small victory.

Devan and the others were now well accustomed to this and had entered into the spirit of the game, sometimes trying to catch the children as they reeled away to make their escape back to the safe hiding places behind the huts.

Ollie had been rather taken aback the first time he had caught one of the children. The child burst into floods of tears and screamed for a long time until he let him go. At the time Ollie had been very apologetic until he had realised that the child had only been faking, running off in hysterical laughter as soon as Ollie had released him.

Since then every child in the village had become involved in this game. James and Gaz had found this game rather amusing especially when all the children had ganged up on Ollie, clinging on to him until he fell over in the mud. The game certainly lightened their mood and acted as a welcome distraction from the events of the previous few days and the question of what to do next?

Today was going to be no exception as Devan walked down the muddy track towards the hut of the village chief, she pretended not to notice the small group of children trying to hide next to one of the huts, knowing full well what was about to happen. She let them get quite close to her before spinning around on her heels; sending the children scampering off in all directions in fits of laughter. She smiled with amusement and continued on her way to the chief's hut.

She had spent a few hours each day talking to him. He was very knowledgeable about the area's history and she had learnt a lot from him about the legends and myths surrounding the disappearance of the Maya.

The chief was short and quite thin, his sun baked skin revealed every one of his many wrinkles particularly when he smiled. He was probably in his early sixties although it was hard to tell, jungle life was hard and it had certainly taken its toll on the man. He wore the same traditional Guatemalan clothing that all the men of the village were dressed in, so unless you already knew he was the chief you would not realise that he was.

Like many small settlements it was customary for the eldest man to fulfil this role mainly because the oldest tended to be the most knowledgeable about the seasons and clearly had been wise enough to endure those harsh jungle conditions. His long hair was grey almost to the point of turning white. Despite his age his eyes had not dulled at all, they were a very dark brown and glistened like two stones of obsidian set deeply into his chocolate coloured face.

The chief excitedly greeted Devan at the entrance to his hut just as he had done on the previous occasions that she had visited him, and ushered her inside his dimly lit hut.

Her senses were met by a hedonistic smell of brewing coffee and melted chocolate, as she entered. He was making one of the drinks that the Mayans had been famous for, the Mocha; this wasn't anything like the Mochas you would find on your local high street, this was the real thing, rich dark silky smooth molten chocolate that had been made from cacao beans roasted and ground earlier that day, and was now being gently heated over an open fire and next to it, a pot of water was gradually coming to the boil. The coffee beans were almost as dark as the chocolate and had been carefully selected from the Caturra plants that grew high up above the village on the mountain slopes.

Once the chocolate had fully melted and the coffee had boiled the chief took them off the fire and taking two clay mugs from a shelf he placed them on the tiled floor next to the fire. He carefully poured a decent amount of the rich dark chocolate into each clay vessel before he added the coffee. Finally he stirred the contents to ensure that the coffee fully mixed with the hot chocolate.

Devan graciously took one of the mugs from him. This was the second reason for her visit; she had been hooked ever since the first time she had sipped his hot concoction and every time since, her love of the intoxicating liquid grew. The light fruity notes of the coffee were perfectly offset by the sharp bitterness of the hot chocolate. They both sat on their cushions in the hut for a few moments, not speaking, just savouring the flavours and rich aromas of the bittersweet muddy fluid. A broad smile spread across the old man's face and he let out a long sigh as the hot thick liquid flowed down his throat.

Devan was in chocolate heaven as the liquid slipped down like an endless silk stream. She would never be able to enjoy a high street Mocha in quite the same way again without being reminded of her time spent in the chief's cosy little hut surrounded by those seductive smells. The Mayan's had truly been master chocolatiers.

She spent the next two hours chatting with the Guatemalan elder about how the seasons were changing, how the rains were becoming heavier and less predictable and the effect that this was having on both the cacao and coffee harvests.

He reminisced on how the cacao plants used to grow all the way down the hillside right up to the back of the huts but now they had to trek a fair distance into the jungle to reach the same plants.

Many of the other nearby settlements had either shrunk or been totally deserted as farmers had relocated away from the worsening jungle conditions lured by the prospect of jobs and an easier life nearer to the ever-expanding metropolises.

Not that living conditions were much better close to the cities, as fast as the cities were developing, they could not build houses fast enough for the hordes of people emerging from the jungle. Large shanty towns had sprung up on the outskirts of these modern wonders. And with these, the familiar squalour of poor hygiene and cramped conditions followed.

The chief admitted that he had been tempted once or twice to relocate the village closer to one of these fair cities but once word had reached him about the conditions, he had decided that the village would be better off staying put. At least they had clean running water and plenty of space to expand if needed.

Devan agreed with his point of view. She had seen the phenomenon of these mass exoduses and it's effects in both Mexico City and Rio de Janeiro, the strange combination of mega rich living just a stone's throw away from absolute depravity, soaring crime rates and dangerous streets. Even with all the dangers of the jungle she could not see life being any more dangerous than the new metropolis that was Guatemala City.

James, Gaz, Ollie and Lomay had left early that morning to explore the area to the east of the settlement in order to plan their route away from the village and hopefully to cross over the border into Belize. This would be the way they would travel once Chris was well enough to make the journey. James hoped that once in Belize they would be able to secure passage on a boat back to the UK.

So far they had made good progress through the thick jungle along one of the many tracks that criss-crossed the dense vegetation, cutting a winding route along that part of the Petén basin. It was in regular use by the villagers so the jungle had not really made a great impact on it. There were a few areas where the jungle had encroached on to it and they had to hack their way through with machetes, but on the whole it was clear.

The time was approaching midday when they finally emerged from the jungle on to a main road (CA78). It was still by western standards not much more than a gravel track but this was frequently travelled by cars and buses and was a well-established road, in that sense, compared with the muddy street they had set out from that morning.

After discussing with Lomay, they decided to stop by the side of the road and have a bite to eat. Although buses did not run particularly regularly along these roads, James hoped that one may pass by whilst they were there. He would then be able to find out from the driver exactly how frequently the service ran to the border.

He still had no idea exactly how long it would be before Chris would be fit to travel but at least if he knew when the buses passed by the area he could plan to catch one rather than the group trekking through the jungle only to have to camp for several days by the side of the road waiting for a bus to magically appear. This was not a prospect that filled him with joy; trading the safety of the settlement for the dangers of the jungle would not be advisable for a group with very limited resources.

In the end they waited by the roadside for several hours and were about to call it a day and return to the village before the light started to fade, when they saw some dust being kicked up further along the road. However, it was not a bus or in fact any vehicle that emerged from around the bend to the west of them, but a herd of goats being driven by two young boys. Clearly they were moving the animals either to a settlement further down the valley or to fresh pastures. Either way they obviously travelled the road on a regular basis and would no doubt know how frequently the buses ran and what their destinations were. The boys apprehensively approached the group; this area was notorious for bandits. Their apprehension was put at ease as Lomay greeted them in their native tongue and explained the group's situation.

'Good news, Señor James. They say that there is a bus that runs along here twice a week. It will take you into Belize. They are not sure exactly what days so you may have to camp for a day or two but no longer than that. I'm sure we can arrange for a few men from the village to accompany you here when Señor Chris is better.'

'That's great news, Lomay.' James replied.

The two boys continued along the road and as the bells from the herd of goats faded into the distance the group began to make their way back along the jungle track to the village, even at a brisk pace they would not arrive back at the village until after the sun dipped below the mountain's crest.

James could just make out the lights from the village fires flickering through the trees as they finally approached the village. It had been a good day, he had enjoyed trekking through the jungle and was learning a lot from Lomay about how to navigate through the dense forests, picking up and distinguishing the trails of the various fauna that had passed through the undergrowth. Lomay had been in his element. It was obvious that he was happiest when he was tracking animals.

In all, the trip had been a successful one and hopefully they would soon be able to leave the village for good and begin their return journey back to the UK. Nevertheless, it had been a long day and James was starting to look forward to a hot meal and to find out how Chris' recovery was going.

Ollie and Gaz were also glad to be back at the village. They had been getting a bit bored of the endless jungle and the humidity that accompanied it. Both of them had been planning their next prank to play on the children of the village. Their last encounter with the children had ended in both Gaz and Ollie being covered head to toe in mud. They had vowed to get their own back on the little scamps before they left the village.

The four of them headed straight for the two huts they were staying in. They hoped to find a hot meal waiting for them. Rachel and Devan had hopefully already made something in anticipation of their return.

To their surprise they found that this was not the case as they entered the huts, the fires were burning inside but the girls had not been cooking, and were nowhere to be seen. The boys dumped their sacks down and gathered back outside the huts.

'Well that's not exactly what I was expecting.' James said. 'Where do you think they have got to?'

Just as he was about to go and look for the girls he spied Rachel coming out of the chief's hut. She smiled at the sight of the group and walked over to speak to them. She hugged James.

'Nice to see you are back safely. Have you had any luck on your travels?' She asked.

'Sort of, seems we may have found a way into Belize, well at least as far as the border. Still have to work out how to cross without a passport, but we'll bridge that gap when we come to it. What happened to the cooking plan?' James replied.

'Ah, well the chief has invited us all to eat with him this evening. So when you are ready.'

'Perfect I'm starving.' Gaz announced.

'There's a surprise.' She replied with a broad grin. Knowing full well that Gaz had a veracious appetite.

The chief warmly greeted them as they entered his hut. He gestured for them to sit and make themselves comfortable inside. There was a large fire that had been built in the centre of the hut and the heat radiating from the embers kept the hut and its occupants warm.

Above the embers hung a large cooking pot full of a stew made from a recently slaughtered goat, mixed with some local herbs and spices.

This was to be accompanied by some flat bread that had been baked earlier that day.

The group formed a circle around the fire, chatting away about the route down to the main road, and discussed with the chief about the possibility of being accompanied by some of the men from the village when they finally made their departure.

The chief thought about this request for a while before giving his answer.

'It depends on exactly when, because it is the harvest season for the coffee beans; we are very busy. However, I am sure we may be able to spare a couple of men to accompany you on your journey as far as the main road. But I think it will be at least another week before your injured friend has recovered enough to be able to make the journey. We can talk about it closer to the time. Now please relax and eat.'

Gaz and Ollie didn't need to be told twice and immediately started to heap the hot stew into some clay bowls that had been provided for the meal.

'This is great!' said Gaz in between mouthfuls. 'I haven't had a lot of goat stew before but this is probably the best I've ever tasted.'

'I'm surprised you can even taste it at the rate you are shovelling it in.' Ollie retorted, laughing at the sight of Gaz trying to lick the thick gravy like sauce from his chin, with little success.

After the meal Devan excused herself and took a bowl of stew to Chris, who was probably up by now. She had taken it upon herself to make sure that he was well fed, since he had been laid up in bed.

He was glad to see her and was certainly in higher spirits than he had been on previous occasions that she had seen him. He hated being bed bound and was eager to start moving around although it was evident that he would have to remain in bed for at least a few more days, until his strength had fully returned.

James popped in a little later and kept him up to date with what was going on, what their plans were and what had become of Norwood's party. After an hour it was clear that Chris was starting to become tired so they left him to rest and returned to the chief's hut.

They found Gaz and Ollie in full flow with the chief, talking about their next prank for the children. The chief was amused by their plans; he too had found these new games between the two young men and the children highly entertaining.

The chief thought that it was good that the children were keenly taking an interest in the newcomers. They didn't get many opportunities to interact with the outside world and therefore it was good that they had formed a bond with their guests. They would certainly be sad to see them leave, but at least they would have some fond memories of the time they had spent together.

Chapter Twenty One: Glympton Park

Lord Norwood was eagerly awaiting the arrival of the first of his guests. The staff at Glympton were busily making preparations in the ballroom. Four long banquet tables had been set up in the centre of the room; with each table to seat eight. Along one side of the great room hot plates had been set up. Servants were carefully making sure that the place mats were positioned correctly, the silverware was polished to a high shine and that the wine glasses had no smears or smudges.

This was all carried out under the eagle-eyed supervision of the head butler, Mr Jacobs. He was a tall lean man in his late fifties with grey thinning hair, a man of few vices and expected nothing but precision from the servants under his direction. He had worked at Glympton for all of his working life. Starting out as a kitchen porter in his teens, he had quickly impressed his employers and by his early thirties had been promoted to the position that he now held, by Sir Edwin Norwood.

Sir Edwin Norwood was the late father of Lord Anthony Norwood, Mr Jacobs would always remember the benevolance that Sir Edwin had shown to him and felt indebted to the family for the kindness they had shown him over the years. He had found it a tremendous day of sadness when Sir Edwin had passed away, as he had held him in such high regard, unlike Sir Edwin, whom he had always considered to be a very kind and honourable man, he found Anthony Norwood to be a hard taskmaster, a harsh and somehow evil man. Nevertheless, he felt somehow honour bound to continue to serve the family regardless of his distaste for his new master.

The announcement that there was to be a banquet at Glympton had been rather sudden, normally banquets were planned weeks in advance, in contrast this one had only been announced two days ago, almost as soon as his Lordship had returned from Central America. Everybody from the chef to the serving girls had suddenly been faced with a mad rush to organise everything. Menus had to be prepared, wines had to be brought up from the great cellars. Every nook and cranny in the house had to be dusted, brasses and mirrors polished, floors swept, and carpets hoovered. *Everything in its proper place and for every place a thing.* Mr Jacobs would say as he directed the servants.

To cap it off Lord Norwood had declared that only a handful of servants were to remain for the dinner itself and once over, all apart from Mr Jacobs would be sent home for the night. They could clean up the following day. Evidently the guests were not just coming for a good time.

The Norwood family was heavily involved in politics and Mr Jacobs therefore assumed that this was some kind of summit and that the topics to be discussed were of a somewhat sensitive nature. His master was taking every precaution to prevent what was discussed from being leaked to the press. Not that this would have happened; the servants still remembered what happened the last and only time a serving girl had leaked something to the press.

It had not been a pretty sight to see Lord Norwood reduce the girl into a mess of tearful hysterics before flinging the girl out of the house on to the gravel outside. Ever since then none of the servants would have dared to even think about divulging anything to the press.

Having taken a final look around the table settings in the ballroom Mr Jacobs left the room satisfied that everything was in order and took up his place by the main entrance to greet the guests and take their coats.

The first guests began to arrive a little after seven thirty. A long sleek black Bentley pulled up outside, the chauffer hopped out and in a well-practiced manner opened the rear door for the passengers inside to disembark. Mr James Slater, the Minister for Trade, stepped out accompanied by his lovely wife Sophia.

Mr Jacobs greeted them at the door, took their coats to the cloakroom, before leading them along the long corridor to the reception room, whereby he announced their arrival to his Lordship, returning to his post by the entrance.

The next to arrive was Mr Charles Black, a prominent lawyer in the city of London. Mr Black specialised in commercial law although had on a few occasions taken on high profile deportation cases. He was followed shortly afterwards by Lord Everard Curtis, who was accompanied by his blonde rather ditzy mistress Charlie Brakewell.

Lord Everard was married, but it was well known that he had a very strained relationship with his wife Charlotte and would often attend parties with one of his many mistresses. Mr Jacobs did not judge, but thought that it must be a very hard for Lady Charlotte to put up with such public displays of infidelity. He assumed she put up with it because she knew at the end of the day Everard would always return home to her and that she would always be Lady Charlotte Curtis.

Conrad Du Bois was the next to arrive; he was a very pompous man and was almost as wide as he was tall. He was renowned for being a great socialite and philanthropist, throwing his money around like a heavyweight champion threw punches. No one knew exactly where he had made his money, some speculated it was gambling on horses others including HMRC believed it was via less legal ways; although they had yet to find any evidence to support this theory.

Mr Jacobs was kept very busy over the next twenty or so minutes by the almost constant flow of arrivals. The last but one of the thirty-two guests to arrive was Victor Negroni, an Italian businessman. Born on the island of Sicily, Victor Negroni had entered into the family business and after his father had died suddenly in a car crash a few months later, he had become the chairman of the business.

Now that almost all the guests had arrived, Mr Jacobs made his way into the reception room and supervised the servants bringing the trays of canapés from the kitchens. The guests all seemed to be happily chatting away; small groups had formed around the room as always happened at these sorts of events.

Small cliques of ladies gossiping about the latest fashions coming over from Paris and Milan, and those of their friends going through rather public and messy divorces. Men boasting about the birds they had shot at the last shoot they had been on, or busily debating about the pros and cons of certain decisions that the present coalition government had taken. Including what had possessed the PM to tackle certain issues that weren't even on the manifesto.

The topic that seemed to feature prominently in the room was the

Pope's sudden announcement that he was to resign, something that had not occurred in over 600 years.

'I suppose in these modern times it is understandable.' Lord Norwood was saying to Conrad Du Bois and Charles Black. 'I have always found it slightly bizarre that it should be a position for life. Dementia or anything could happen in these final years, you could end up with a crazy pope that decides to have a Holy War or something.

I totally understand that if you were not mentally or physically up to the role any longer that one would consider stepping aside for a newer younger pope. One hopefully to drag the Roman Catholic Church kicking and screaming into the twenty first century.'

' I heard the next pope might be black.' Conrad Du Bois said with a slight snort as he made this remark. 'Can you imagine it, a black pontiff?'

'Well there is a black president.' Charles replied.

'Yes, and look where it has got them.'

'Now come on Conrad we are not in the 18th century anymore. It was bound to happen at some point. All credit to him I say, he hasn't done a bad job so far, I wouldn't agree with all his policies nevertheless, on the whole he's been pretty sound. It's not the colour of a man's skin that you should judge him by but the actions that he takes, and the legacy that he leaves behind. I'm not saying I am in favour of a coloured pontiff but let's just see what happens. They haven't even voted yet. You never know you might end up with one of the great reformers. For our sake I hope not, as it would impede our influence'

'Well I think the whole conclave thing is a farce. We all know that there has been a great deal of corruption in the Vatican in the past, not to mention those with wandering hands.'

'Ha, a true sceptic as ever, Conrad. One day you'll lighten up.' Lord Norwood said beaming at his two friends.

'Excuse me, Sir. I have a message for you.' Mr Jacobs said leaning over his Lordship's shoulder to say in a low voice that the one remaining guest to arrive had telephoned to apologise to the fact that she was running late and that he should start dinner without her.

'Very good, Mr Jacobs. In that case I think we should start.' Turning his attention back to his guests. 'If you are ready gentlemen I believe dinner is about to be served.'

The loud clang of a dinner gong echoed through the room. As the chatter died down Mr Jacobs made his announcement.

'My Lords, Ladies and Gentlemen. Dinner is served. I cordially invite you to make your way to the ballroom.'

Gradually the guests began to filter out of the reception room and down the brightly lit corridor towards the ballroom. Several of the guests stopped briefly to admire some of the massive portraits on the walls and the two small cannons that sat poking out of two small alcoves in the walls of the corridor. They were now merely decorative, a gift to the family from the Prince Regent for their small contributions during the Napoleonic Wars.

Taking his place at the head of the top table Lord Norwood raised his arms signalling for his guests to take their seats. It was very noticeable, for the guests on the top table, that the seat to the right of Lord Norwood was vacant.

'No guest of honour this evening?' Conrad asked.

'She has been delayed, she will be with us shortly.' Replied Norwood with a slight twist of a smile appearing at the corner of his mouth. The end of his sentence coincided with the arrival of the serving girls who began to pour wine for the guests. Soon followed by waiters bringing out the first of five courses, a set of three *amuse-bouches*.

Miss Carla Adams was the last guest to arrive, she was late but as she liked to make an entrance she was not at all flustered by the fact that she had missed the first course. She just took it all in her stride.

It was clear, especially from the reaction of the male guests as she entered the ballroom, that she was inordinately beautiful. She always seemed to have the most alluring look on her face, her long flowing extremely dark brown hair almost to the point of looking black, cascaded down over her shoulders.

The sight of her blue sparkling eyes glistening against her exotically bronzed skin was captivating. Carla was wearing a stunning black Versace evening gown that almost skimmed the floor as she strode confidently across the room, its flattering shape helped to elongate her silhouette, and the thigh high slit in the left of the gown very sensually showed off her beautifully toned calf and lower thigh. The dress was beautifully pinned at the waist with a diamond encrusted link belt.

The sweet scent of Coco Chanel that every guest caught as she passed them by seductively wooed them to forgive her lateness. Gracefully taking her seat at the right hand side of Lord Norwood she lent over towards him and in a low sweet voice apologised for her lateness.

'I trust you managed to wrap things up.' He replied as that half-smile crossed his lips.

'I have. It was quite pleasurable although I fear it left him rather more breathless than he had intended.' She casually replied.

'Oh I'm sorry to hear that I had rather liked him.'

'He had reached the limit of his usefulness, I'm afraid. I expect they'll find him by the end of the week.'

'I would hate to ever cross you my dear. You would prove to be quite a dangerous opponent, I think.'

'Let's hope that never happens, My Lord' she replied with a flirtatious look upon her face before taking a sip of champagne from her glass.

The second course was a beautifully poached piece of sole on a bed of samphire, followed by roast water buffalo. It was the dessert that stole the show. A delicate citrus parfait accompanied by wild strawberries, cubes of mint jelly and apple crisps. Lastly there was a selection of cheeses and a decanter of port for every table.

Coffee was to be served back in the reception room for those that wished it. The hour was late by the time the guests returned to the reception room, curiously from the thirty odd guests that had arrived, only ten stayed in the reception room, the rest including Lord Norwood had ventured to another part of the house.

The servants, except for Mr Jacobs, had all been dismissed. Mr Jacobs remained to look after the remaining guests in the reception room whilst the others took part in whatever order of business had brought them there in the first place.

Those that were to attend the meeting had descended down into the cellars of the mansion, all had donned black robes with blood red trim and deep cavernous hoods collected from a room just next to the steps leading down into the cellars.

This was to be the first meeting of the High Council of *The Glove* for many months. The 22 members of the High Council sat around a great stone oval table upon which was carved a globe clenched in a gloved fist. A bracelet hung around the wrist upon which was inscribed *Vincit Omnia Veritas*.

Around the table were 22 high backed chairs, one of which was slightly higher than the others; this was the chair of the Grand Master. On his right hand sat Lord Norwood and on his left sat Charles Black, the others were spread out around the table.

'I welcome you all to this meeting. It brings me great pleasure to see so many of you here tonight and at a time when we are on the verge of achieving what our sacred brethren has striven to complete for almost a millennia. I must congratulate Lord Norwood on attaining the first of the seven volumes of the codex that make up the *Liber Veritatis*. All is finally beginning to fall into place.'

'Thank you Grand Master for your kind words. I am merely a loyal servant and have done the best I could to honour the position that this council saw fit to bestow upon me. There are still many hurdles to cross and I bid this council to stand vigilantly by our cause, there are those that would try to deny us our destiny.'

'You speak of Captain Flack and his order. You had your chance to eliminate them and you failed. In my opinion Grand Master, Norwood should be replaced; he has left us in a perilous situation. I do not think he has the necessary skills for what is required of him.' One of the hooded members said loudly from across the table.

'You think you could do better?' The Grand Master replied raising one eyebrow. 'I know you are eager and seek promotion. But I do not agree with you. There are several things that only *The Seven* and myself are aware of. This was one of the reasons for this meeting to be held. The rest of you I'm sure have probably been thinking much the same thing. *The Seven* are aware of everything.' The Grand Master said indicating the three hooded figures on either side of him. 'Along with one who cannot join us this evening and will remain nameless for the time being. We have amongst us a loyal servant who has for a long time been part of Captain Flack's organisation, unbeknown to the naive Captain.'

There was a great intake of breath from many of the members around the table as this piece of information was revealed. 'We did not fail to stop Captain Flack, it was by design. Even he has a role to play, however unaware of it he is. Sometimes you have to play the field in order to seize the ultimate prize. He is perhaps the most loyal of you all; for if they were ever discovered it would probably mean certain death. So before you start bandying about words of failure, Victor. You should understand the company in which you sit.'

'I apologise for my outburst, Grand Master. I did not mean to cause offence. I merely thought that it was too great a task for one man alone to accomplish. I had no idea that Captain Flack was allowed to escape.'

'Well now you know better. Nothing ever happens by accident. You of all people should know that by now.'

'Yes, Grand Master.' Victor replied knowing full well of what the Grand Master was referring to.

'Having said that, Victor I do have a task for you. You are to use you influence with the Cardinals to engineer a favourable vote in the Conclave. It will be in our interest to have a Roman Catholic Church that is operating within our sphere of influence. Miss Adams will accompany you. She is skilled in many forms of persuasion. As I am sure many of you are aware.

Everard you are to join Lord Norwood in his preparations for the next expedition. It is of vital importance that you acquire the necessary permits for the next stage.

Mr Slater has been working tirelessly behind the scenes to ensure that the current trade negotiations between the coalition and the Chinese will not be successful and that the South China Sea region is destabilised. Our endeavours in North Korea have proven to be extremely successful. Our operatives managed to poison Kim-Jun-Il without detection. His son is young and inexperienced. He will be far easier to manipulate than his father ever was.

We have already begun to plant the idea in his mind that his uncle has been plotting to overthrow him and I have it on good authority that he will soon take the necessary steps to remove him from office.

Once this has been accomplished we will have extended our influence over the young ruler and it will not be long before we can put the final stages of our plan for the region into action. Soon nothing will be able to stand in our way.'

'May I ask Grand Master, what are your plans for acquiring the next part of the *Liber Veritatis*?' Conrad Du Bois asked.

'My researchers are in the process of discovering its location. This is one of the reasons why it is so important that Victor uses his contacts to influence the Cardinal's vote; I am of the understanding that the whereabouts of the next part of the Codex is hidden somewhere in the vaults of the Vatican. Although there is one other whom I am sure already knows the location. Professor Peter Middleton, James Middleton's father, may well have already been granted access to the vaults and I feel sure that he has already discovered the location of the Codex or at the very least has a pretty good idea of where it may be.

Steps will have to be taken to encourage him to divulge what he knows. It is fortunate that his son is presently halfway around the world and therefore cannot protect his ailing father. Nevertheless, I must stress that Professor Middleton is an incredibly wily man and may prove to be rather uncooperative. So we shall have to use all of our guile to obtain the necessary information from him.'

'What if he should refuse to cooperate?' Charles Black asked.

'Then he shall be eliminated. Better that he does not pass on what he knows to his son.' The Grand Master replied in a rather callous voice.

It was close to four in the morning by the time the discussions of *The Glove* came to an end and the majority of the members began to make their departures.

Miss Carla Adams and a handful of the others had decided to take Lord Norwood up on his offer of a bed rather than journeying home.

Carla's room was in the east wing of the great house. It was one of the largest in the house, with an immensely luxurious king sized bed made up with fine pale blue silk sheets from the finest quality silk that Egypt had to offer. Closing the door behind her she effortlessly dropped her dress on to the floor around her feet. The sight of her perfectly naked body out-stripped any of the images that the male guests had pictured.

She was about to pull the covers of the bed back and gracefully slip in between the soft silk sheets when a light knock at the door halted her. A knock that she had half been expecting, shyness clearly was not in her nature, she didn't even reach for a robe before opening the door. It had been several months since she had bedded Lord Norwood and it was about time that they indulged in each other's company again.

Norwood didn't even wait for an invitation to enter as she opened the door; he strode straight in roughly taking hold of her in his strong arms as if he were storming a castle. He may have dominated the initial moments but it was clear that Carla would be the one in control of the acts that followed.

Chapter Twenty Two: New Acquaintances

The harbour in Belize was teeming with activity as the intrepid group of travellers made their way down to the quayside. They were met with the sight of hundreds of yachts, of all shapes and sizes, busily finishing the last of their preparations for their future voyages.

A few of the larger vessels lying at anchor outside of the main harbour were taking on the last of their provisions before they set out on their yearly crossing of the Atlantic for refits, before spending the summer in the Mediterranean.

After finding a comfortable spot along the quayside, James and Chris headed off towards the Harbour Master's office in the hope of finding out if any of the yachts were looking for extra crew to work the passage across, leaving the rest of the group to chill out in the blazing heat of the midday sun.

Rachel and Devan spread themselves out on the stone paving and soaked up the rays whilst Ollie and Gaz checked out some of the stunning semi-naked girls sunning themselves on the decks of the yachts in the marina.

'How are your chat up lines these days?' Gaz jokingly asked Ollie with a cheeky little smile.

'Pretty well used, why?'

'Well, I was thinking we may be able to charm our way on-board a boat if we find the right mark. You game?'

'Dude that's like asking if the pope is a catholic.' Ollie replied.

The pair sauntered off down one of the many gangways leading down to the pontoons of the marina excited by the prospects that might arise from the shenanigans they were about to get up to.

The two of them spent the next hour or so attempting to charm many of the female occupants but with little success. That was until they caught sight of a tender leaving one of the largest super yachts and heading towards the pontoons at the far side of the marina from where they were currently standing.

The tender's lovingly polished deep blue hull matched the colouring of the mother ship. On board were three of the most captivating girls, in their late twenties, that Gaz and Ollie had ever laid eyes on.

The buxom beauties were definitely dressed to impress, attracting as much attention as possible, scantily clad in tight bikinis from which their cleavages were clearly trying to burst out from the tiny triangles of material struggling to hold back the sacred flesh that lay beneath.

Ollie knew instantly that this was it, if they put on their maximum charm factor they were bound to hit the jackpot.

Michael and Louis had spent the last several days researching in various archives around London. So far they had made little progress in finding any useful information on either the *Liber Veritatis* or *The Glove*, there had been a few vague references but nothing concrete and each time they thought they were getting somewhere it would just turn out to be another dead end in the maze.

It had been weeks since they had heard anything from Chris and the others. They had expected a certain lack of communication because of the area in which the group was operating. Nevertheless, it had been weeks since their last contact.

Louis had become increasingly concerned that something may have gone terribly wrong and had therefore taken the decision to make contact with Lt Cdr Bradbury, whom Chris had left as a contact in case of emergencies.

The Lt Cdr had shared Louis' concern and decided to use some satellite time to survey the area of their last known position. After widening the search area several times he eventually pinpointed their position as they crossed the border into Belize, much to his surprise, as Chris and James had never mentioned any plans to enter Belize.

Correctly assuming that something had forced them to change their plans and that they were most likely making their way to the city of Belize he arranged for one of his assets to make contact with them and find out what was going on.

Josh Palmer had been relaxing on his small balcony overlooking one of the small streets in the city of Belize when he had received the call from Lt Cdr Bradbury regarding Chris' team. He hadn't really understood why it was so urgent but if he was asked to do something he didn't question the motives behind it he just got the job done.

Josh had a slim athletic build, with a slightly unkempt look, due to his wiry ginger beard and scraggy hair that seemed to be untameable. He was ex-infantry, now in the employ of the intelligence services.

His stint in the Prince of Wales division had proved to be an eye opener to the dangers that existed in the world today. He had displayed, that apart from being an excellent marksman he had the dynamic ability to think outside the box, far beyond the capabilities of even the most battle-hardened veterans. It was the combination of both of these abilities that had initially sparked the interest of British Intelligence and it was not long after, that they had recruited him.

Josh eventually managed to track down Chris and his companions down by the docks, but he didn't introduce himself straight away, instead he chose to observe the group's activities for at least 45 minutes before he made contact. Well at least that was his intention, but clearly his low key observational skills were not as good as he thought.

It didn't take James long to notice that there was a ginger haired man standing by one of the warehouses near the quayside who didn't quite seem to fit in with his surroundings and appeared to be taking more than just a casual interest in James and his friends, not to mention being rather clumsy about trying to be inconspicuous. James wasn't that concerned about the gentleman; James always had this uncanny knack of being able to spot a British Intelligence man anywhere. He couldn't really put his finger on why but there was just something about the way that they carried themselves, a debonair charisma that they seemed to give off that set them apart from the rest; maybe this was down to the fact that they knew they worked for the best agency in the world or it could have just been that they were all trying to be the next James Bond either way that man definitely didn't pose a threat.

James was sure that the man would make contact when he wanted to and therefore he decided to ignore him and let the stranger make the first move when he was ready. James was a little disappointed that the stranger had been quite so easy to spot, it felt like he was letting the side down but clearly he was still young and probably lacked the necessary field experience hence why he was in Belize and not in one of the more high profile countries.

Eventually Josh decided that he had been a fly on the wall for long enough and he moved away from the shade of the buildings stepping out into the bright sunlight beating down on the quayside.

Although it was late December the temperature out of the shade was still in the high thirties not to mention the humidity which made breathing a less than pleasant necessity, it had rained heavily for the past few days and now the air was heavy with the moisture that quickly evaporated under the blazing rays of the Caribbean sun.

Josh crossed the open ground between the shade of the buildings and the group, in a few minutes, casually walking along the concrete pavement as if he were just out for a pleasant stroll to take in the sea view along the edge of the harbour. He headed directly towards James, who he had already decided would be his first point of contact as the man was the closest match to the description Tom had given to him. Even though it was clear that the weeks of trekking through the jungle had taken its toll on the man, it was unmistakeably the same person that Tom had described; just not quite so well kept.

So preoccupied had Josh been with how he was going to make the initial contact that he hadn't noticed that James had stepped into his path and he very nearly crashed straight into him. Only at the very last second did he look up and stop in his tracks, narrowly avoiding a collision.

'You should really take more care with what you are doing. Someone could end up getting hurt if you are not more careful.' James said to Josh in a slightly cold and unfriendly tone.

Josh realised that James wasn't just referring to the fact that he had almost walked straight into him but that James had spotted him earlier and meant that he should make more of an effort to be less obtrusive whilst on surveillance.

'Sorry, I'll try to take more care in future in order to avoid such things from happening again.' Josh replied, 'Tom sends his regards by the way.' He added as he began to weigh up the imposing figure standing in front of him, trying to gauge James' reaction to this snippet of information. However, James wasn't going to give him the satisfaction of showing any emotional reaction towards this piece of information, regardless of how welcome the news was that Tom had sent Josh to help them out. The steely face of James looked Josh straight in the eyes and didn't even flicker an inch.

'Well he always did have a way of knowing when his help would be welcome. What's your name, I'm presuming you already know mine?'

'Josh, and from Tom's description you must be James.' The young man replied feeling rather intimidated under that penetrating gaze, Tom had mentioned what Chris called James; and now that he was in his presence he understood why. There was a really unnatural coldness to the way James' eyes seemed to cut right through him, it almost sent shivers down his spine and he had the uncomfortable feeling that his inner most thoughts were somehow being torn from the deepest parts of his mind. Shaking off the awkwardness of the situation Josh finally got to the meat of his intensions.

'I understand that you need to return to the UK as soon as possible.'

'It would certainly be handy if we could return relatively swiftly. Although a certain amount of discreetness in the method may well be required.'

'I think I have found the perfect solution to your requirements.' Josh said turning his head slightly to look at one of the massive super yachts anchored near the entrance to the inner harbour. 'The owner owes me a favour or two and I know he is on the way back to the UK, the yacht is having a major interior refit in about three weeks.' He added returning his gaze back to James.

'That sounds perfect, funny the way fate has of dropping a golden egg just when you need one.'

'Ha I don't think fate has much to do with it. I believe a man makes his own luck.'

'Well we can't all believe in the same things. Anyway I better introduce you to the rest of the group. That is if I can pry those two away from the bikini babes.' James said pointing out the two boys deep in conversation with the girls they had met from the super yacht.

'I wouldn't worry about that too much those three girls are from the boat your going to be on anyway.'

'Ha that's all I need. Those two are a hard enough to keep under control at the best of times let alone if there are beautiful women involved, they will be like kids in a sweet shop. Nothing is ever as simple as it could be.' James laughed knowing full well that it was now going to be an interesting voyage back to the UK. 'I presume you work for *Six*. I don't suppose that they are prepared to supply us with a few bits of kit as we are in need of some supplies since being relieved of most of our gear.'

'As it happens my equipment officer Barkley is in the process of putting together a few items for you. We anticipated that you may be in need of a few items that one wouldn't pick up from the local store. Furthermore I've arranged to meet the owner of the yacht at his hotel Las Terrazas on the island of Ambergris Caye later this evening so we really should make a move to get you all sorted before we leave for the island.'

'How are we getting there? Are we flying or catching the water taxi?' James asked fully aware that you could only access the tiny island by either air or water as the stretch of water between the island and the mainland was too great an expanse to bridge.

'By boat but we are not going to take the water taxi, we'll take my boat. It's much quicker than the water taxi plus you're less likely to get pick pocketed on the ride over to the island.'

'I know what you mean, two scamps tried that trick earlier. I think they learnt their lesson.' James showed a brief telling smile as he replied. He loved the realness of this city but he knew all to well that this was not a forgiving city for travellers, those colourful characters that you met on the streets could seem friendly enough but this city had a darker more menacing side that had befouled many a tourist in the past.

Two such creatures had unwisely tried to hold the group up at knifepoint earlier in the morning; they had soon learnt a valuable lesson and received life long reminders that crime didn't pay.

Once all the introductions had been made and Ollie and Gaz had finally and reluctantly parted company with the bikini babes, James had decided not to inform them that they would shortly be reunited, they all piled into a taxi and headed in the direction of Josh's lodgings away from the downtown district towards the more developed area of St George's where Josh had modest accommodations, if that was the right description for the flat.

MI6 certainly hadn't gone to much expense on acquiring the building, the paint on the walls was desperately in need of repair as the heat and humidity had taken its toll on the building. But then if you wanted to blend in with your surroundings it was perfect and therefore a good base for operations. Not that anything exciting really happened in the area.

The United Kingdom once had a full military presence in Belize up until 2011 but since then only a few special advisers remained, the main reason being that the border dispute between Belize and Guatemala remained unsettled and tensions still existed between the two nations.

As one would have expected from an equipment officer, Barkley had a slightly geeky look about him, mainly due to the long white lab coat and bizarrely shaped spectacles that were precariously perched on the end of his nose.

He was in his element when talking about anything technical and spoke with great authority and length on certain pieces of equipment, well that was until Josh cut him off in mid flow.

'Barkley I'm sure everybody here is perfectly familiar with how a mobile phone works. We are rather pushed for time.'

'Well, yes but this is no ordinary mobile.' Barkley replied feeling rather put out at having been interrupted. 'As I was saying this device not only allows you to make and receive calls but it can also force pair with other devices, much more effective than setting up wire taps and it can also be activated as an emergency locator beacon.'

'And I bet the manual is about 800 pages long.' Ollie whispered jokingly to Gaz who tried really hard not to laugh at the jibe, making a sort of awkward snorting sound as he tried to keep the laughter back.

Chris glared at the two which seemed to have the desired effect as they both took on the look of two naughty school boys waiting outside the headmaster's office having just been caught flicking powder paint all over the back of the art master's white trousers; apparently that was not the kind of emotional reaction that modern art was meant to instil.

A good three quarters of an hour later Barkley finally finished his lecture on all the bits and pieces that he had put together for them. By which point even Josh who usually loved learning about all the *toys* as he called them, was beginning to get a little restless as he was eager to get out on the water.

They bid farewell to Barkley and left the house taking the short walk down an uneven cobbled street to the waterside of the beach at St George's where Josh's pride and joy lay at anchor.

The boat was a pirogue of Caribe design and in true Caribbean style Josh stripped off his top, dove into the crystal clear waters and swam out to the boat, deftly hauling himself on board. After heaving up the anchor and stowing it neatly in a locker he slowly manoeuvred the boat to the beach to pick up the awaiting passengers.

The twin 300hp Mercury engines roar was almost deafening as the screws bit into the water and the boat shot straight out from the shore before smoothly banking to port, taking up a northerly heading towards their island destination.

The deep 'V' shape of the *Compass Rose's* hull cut easily through the calm waters leaving a white strip of confused churning wake behind her as she powered off in pursuit of the horizon leaving the ever shrinking mainland as just a distant memory.

Chapter Twenty Three: Mr Whiting

The sun was quickly disappearing behind them as the *Compass Rose* approached the island of Ambergris Caye. The lights of Las Terrazas were like hundreds of tiny fireflies dancing around the hotel, swaying in the cool breeze of the growing dusk. It was a peaceful place bathed in the orange glow of the tiny lights.

Josh carefully glided the pirogue up to one of the vacant pontoons below the imposing structure of the hotel, nimbly hopping out on to the floating wooden platform with the bowline and deftly making it fast to a metal cleat before returning amidships to catch hold of the hull before the boat drifted away from the pontoon. James threw him the stern line and as he made this fast to another cleat James and the rest of the group began to disembark.

The palms around the grounds gently rocked in the cooling breeze of the Caribbean, casting twirling patches on the neatly kept lawns of the gardens. The sound of Swing softly wafted from one of the outside bars on the terrace.

They followed one of the garden paths up from the waterfront to the hotel and headed for the reception desk to enquire where they would find Jack Whiting, the Australian billionaire and owner of the magnificent hotel.

They were warmly greeted by a beautiful concierge who informed them that Mr Whiting was currently involved in a game of poker in the Pigeon Point Bar with some of the guests and that a bell hop would escort them round to the bar.

'I hope you have brought your cheque books. These boys play for serious cash.' The young bell hop said as he guided them around to the bar.

'Well that depends on whether Mr Whiting is feeling lucky or not.' Chris replied, his voice full of confidence.

Chris had always been a keen poker player and had on occasion been known to drop into one or another of the London Casinos with virtually no money on him and proceed to clean out a few of the high rollers at the tables in a matter of hours. The only problem was that he wasn't always the best at keeping hold of his winnings and he would often spend it as quickly as he had acquired it.

For him money was something to be used, he wasn't interested in being rich. Wealth didn't interest him; something else would always come along, so he tended to enjoy life and all it had to offer rather than putting it aside for a rainy day.

'You never know what's just around the corner so why worry about it.' He had said on a number of occasions.

The Pigeon Point Bar was typical of the type of cocktail bar found in these Caribbean resorts, bamboo cane chairs, and small outdoor structures made out of sugar canes formed the bars themselves, there were several small swimming pools connected by a network of narrow channels, the sound of running water from a nearby fountain accompanied the idyllic setting; only to be shattered by the raucousness emanating from one of the larger circular tables closest to the bar on one side of the courtyard paradise.

'You have the luck of the devil, I felt sure I had you on that last hand.' One of the players said as another casually swept up the mountain of chips from the centre of the table.

'Just my night. Another hand?'

'Well, I suppose your luck has to run out at some point, Jack. And I intend to be there when it does.'

'Luck has very little to do with it, it's all down to reading your opponents; and I'm afraid you gentlemen are far too easy to read.'

Chris decided that this was his cue to join the game.

'Mind if I sit in?' He said as he walked up to the table.

'Not at all, the more the merrier Mr…?'

'Flack.'

'I don't remember seeing that name on the hotel guest list.'

'We've only just arrived with our friend, Josh Palmer.' Chris said.

'Well, welcome to my establishment. I hope you enjoy the experience.' Jack said with a knowing smile as he heard Josh's name being dropped.

'I'm sure it will be memorable. What are the stakes?'

'Big blind $200, little is $100.'

'Are you sure this is a good idea? Remember what happened the last time you got into a proper high stakes game.' James said under his breath into Chris' ear.

'As I recall I finished up from what I started with.'

'True, but it took four days and they weren't exactly on best terms with you afterwards. We are relying on this man to get us back to the UK.'

'It'll be fine. I won't rinse him completely and besides it was hardly my fault last time, they were using a stacked deck and still lost. Not my problem if they couldn't count cards properly.'

'I understand from Josh that you are in need of some transportation to the UK.' Jack Whiting said as Chris pulled up a chair at the table.

'That seems to be the general idea. I hear you are intending to make a trip over there yourself very soon.'

'Yeah, it's time to take the old girl back to the shipyard for her annual refit. Plus I think her engines are in need of a tune up, she seems to be burning more fuel than normal. Well I'll make you a deal, you beat me in this game and I'll take you all on board.'

'And if I should lose.'

'Then you'll have to do me a favour first before we ship out.'

'What kind of a favour?'

'I'll let you know when I win. It's nothing too strenuous for men of your reputation.'

'And exactly what reputation would that be?' Chris replied as he lifted the corner of the cards he had just been dealt to see his hand.

Whiting never responded he just gave Chris a knowing look.

'I'll leave you to the negotiations; I'm going to join the others at the bar.' James said before walking off to join Ollie and the others at the dimly lit bar. He ordered a Rum and Red Bull that seemed to be the new fad in the Caribbean.

Poker didn't interest him that much, he enjoyed the thrill of playing for money but was happier playing roulette or craps; something where luck had more to do with it than skill. He looked over at the table from time to time to see how Chris was doing.

Chris wasn't losing but he certainly wasn't the chip leader either. James knew Chris' game all to well, he liked the long game, gradually wearing his opponents down, waiting for that odd lapse in concentration at which point he could capitalise.

It was nearing midnight when James and the others decided to call it a day. It had been a long few weeks and they were all in need of some long awaited sleep in more comfortable surroundings than the ones they had recently experienced.

They left Chris at the poker table and headed off towards the hotel's luxury accommodation. By this time Chris had accumulated a substantial pile of chips but he wasn't even close to catching Jack Whiting, many of the other players had thrown in the towel as the stakes began to rise to levels where the game became a bit too rich for their liking.

Soon there were just four players remaining around the table Chris, Jack, George, a Texan oil tycoon and a thin looking man called Jasper. The latter seemed to be a man of few words and was very cagey about what he did for a living, not that Chris took much notice he was far too intent on clearing up to really take much interest in the man. This was a mistake that he would later come to regret.

At around three in the morning George finally called it quits. 'I almost had you there, partner. You've cleaned me out, Sir. Fellas it's been a real pleasure but my bed is calling. Time to kick these here boots off and get some shut eye.'

'If it hadn't been for the river I think you probably would have.' Chris replied knowing full well that had it not been for that last card he would certainly have lost and would now owe Jack Whiting a favour in the morning.

'I think it's about time for a break Gentlemen, shall we say half an hour before we continue. With the blinds increasing to $5,000 and $10,000?' Jack said casually watching Chris carefully as he spoke.

'If you really feel you want me to take all your money that's fine by me.' Chris replied, and Jasper nodded in agreement.

James tossed and turned as he tired to fall asleep, after living rough for the last few weeks he just couldn't seem to get comfortable in the luxury comforts of the 5 star hotel. He ended up throwing a couple of pillows off the bed and sleeping on the floor, even then it still wasn't quite the same as the jungle surroundings he had become used to. He knew it would be a while before he could sleep in a proper bed again.

Devan couldn't sleep either but not because of the luxurious surroundings; it was due to so many thoughts running through her mind. Her life had completely turned upside down since she had met Chris and James; not to mention those historical theories that she had taken to be gospel, which were now disintegrating before her. Things that were generally accepted as being fact were nowhere near to reality.

She already had enough to write at least two papers but would never be able to publish them without becoming the laughing stock of the entire historical community.

It vexed her that she would never be able to share her discoveries with the world; and it appeared there was still a long way to go before she would reach the whole truth, if she ever did.

By five in the morning the players had decided to call it quits, it was evident that Chris and Jack were evenly matched, neither man was prepared to up the ante now that the stakes had reached stupid levels and it was clear that no one was going to make that final move and go all in. They came to the conclusion that it would have to be settled by a high card draw; whichever player drew the highest card from the deck would take the spoils.

Chris being the newcomer to the table drew first. His hand almost shook as he cut the deck; there was close to million on the table, not that a third of a million would have cause a dent in his current finances; it was the sheer excitement of it all coming down to just one card.

'Queen of Diamonds.' He said as he turned the cards over. He wished it had been at least a king, but a queen wasn't too bad.

Jasper went next; sweat was visibly starting to drip down his forehead as he cut the deck. As the Nine of Spades was revealed Chris let out a small sigh of relief. *One down, one to go.* He thought as his heart began to race. This would be the biggest amount he had won for a good few months if luck was still on his side.

'Well whatever happens it's only money.' Jack said as his hand closed around part of the deck and slowly turning it over. Chris' heart dropped as the picture of the king of spades came into view.

'Sorry chaps seems like my luck has held after all.'

'I think I need a drink.' Jasper said in a shaky voice.

'Me too. You can tell me about you errand later.' Chris said as he paced off to the bar and necked a double shot of Appleton XV.

'Again.' He said to the bartender. 'In fact, just leave the bottle.' It wasn't the loss that had irritated him; it was more the way in which he had lost. Not down to the skill of the other opponent but just the luck of the draw. Still he'd learnt a lot about the man he'd lost to. Jack was as much of a student of game play as he was, and this intrigued him.

Chris wondered if perhaps Jack also enjoyed the ancient Chinese game of Go. Anyway at this point the only things on his mind were drink and then sleep; he downed the last of the rum and headed off in the direction of his bed.

Chris awoke to the sound of a loud knocking on his door. It seemed only five minutes since he had fallen asleep; his head was thumping after all those doubles the night before. He felt as if a herd of elephants had stomped their way through his head.

Dragging himself out of bed and fumbling with the lock for a few moments he eventually managed to open the door.

'See you managed to get a good night's sleep.' James said in a particularly sarcastic tone as he entered the room. Chris just grunted in response.

'So how much did you lose in the end?'

'Not much; just our services for a day or two.' Chris managed to say as his head began to clear. 'Ugh, my head is banging. I feel like shit.'

'Well it can't be as bad as you look. Exactly what do you mean by our services?'

'Not sure, we'll find out later.'

'You really do have a habit of getting me into trouble don't you.'

'Just naturally gifted I guess.'

'That's certainly one word for it. You do realise we need to get back to the UK ASAP?'

'It's not the end of the world, just means we won't get back there for a few extra days that's all. Right breakfast or something is definitely required.'

'Good luck you do realise it's one in the afternoon.'

'Oh shit, is it really that late? Well food then and coffee, lots of coffee.'

'I think a shower wouldn't go a miss before you do anything else, you stink!'

Chris sniffed one of his armpits. 'Might be a good idea. You get used to it after the first week.'

'Well now that we are back in civilisation I don't think that the tramp look is a good one for you.'

'Probably not.'

'Right well I'm going to find the others, see you in a bit. You'll find fresh clothes in the wardrobes, provided by our host.'

'No worries. Now where the fuck does one find the shower around here?' Chris asked more to himself than to James who was already halfway out of the room.

Chris found the others down on the terrace sitting around one of the large round cane tables. Everybody looked as if they were in need of the rest in the tranquil setting. They had after all been through a lot over the past month. He joined them, ordered half the menu and sat back in one of the chairs to soak up the bright December sunshine.

Jack Whiting made his way from the manager's office out on to the hotel terrace. He had decided to give his new acquaintances some time to relax and enjoy the tropical surroundings of his hotel paradise for a few hours before approaching the subject of his *little errand* that he had bet Chris for the night before.

He knew that they wouldn't enjoy it but that wasn't what concerned him, his concern was that he didn't know if he could trust them. It was a rather sensitive matter and although Josh had recommended them, he liked to know the people that he chose to employ for these sorts of things.

In general most of his wealth came from legitimate business deals but from time to time he delved into some less than legal activities. This was one of those occasions or rather the fallout from one such activity that had spiralled out of control and had been playing on his mind for quite some time.

'Sorry to interrupt you gentlemen but I was hoping to have a quiet word.' Jack said as he approached the group.

'Not at all, I was getting a bit bored of just sitting here to be honest.' Chris replied.

'Shall we go for a walk and discuss the favour I have in mind. Ladies please stay and enjoy the ambiance.'

'Ollie, Gaz. You may as well keep the girls company. Think we will be a while.'

Chris and James left the group and walked off with Jack down one of the garden paths that led to the private beach of the hotel.

'The problem I have is a rather complicated affair. When I first looked into setting up the hotel here on the island there was a lot of local resistance. A few palms had to be greased to change public opinion and let's just say that a few people had certain connections that had ways of changing people's minds. What I didn't realise was that they would then start to call in favours, as far as I was concerned they had been paid for their services and that was the end of it.'

'Exactly what kind of people?' James asked.

'Coastal smugglers, drugs and guns mainly. They have recently been applying pressure on me to use my yacht to smuggle some of those items into the European market, something that I am just not prepared to do. I tried to explain as much to them but unfortunately they did not react very well to this and have threatened that if I do not do as they ask there will be repercussions; repercussions of a rather violent and nasty nature. I was hoping that you may be able to change their minds and demonstrate that they should look elsewhere.'

'How large an organisation are we talking about?'

'They cover most of the Caribbean and I believe that they have ties to *Los Rastrojos*, the Columbian drug cartel.'

'You do realise that the Columbians do not take kindly to being told no, and you may be better off doing what they ask.'

'I thought that gentlemen of your reputation might know of ways of dealing with this sort of thing.'

'We have dealt with similar situations in the past but our resources were slightly more extensive than what we currently have at our disposal.' James replied.

'You can have as many resources as you need. That is not a problem, believe me.'

'We will have to discuss this with the others before we can make a decision, and probably do a bit of recon. I have the inkling that there might be a way of solving the problem but I'm certainly not promising anything. This could turn out to be a rather brutal affair and by no means straight forward.' Chris said as they made their way back along the beach towards the hotel.

Jack left Chris and James to discuss the situation with their friends. Ollie and Gaz were certainly up for the challenge mainly because they hoped to get to play with some explosives and create general mayhem.

The events of Glympton Park seemed such a long time ago now and they were itching for some more fun and games.

After much discussion and smoking by James they all agreed that although this was a pretty crazy thing to be getting involved with, they didn't really have another option. After all, they really needed to get back to the UK.

They spent much of the rest of the day enjoying the tranquil scenery relaxing by the side of the hotel pool and planning their next move. In the evening the men enjoyed a few hands of poker before turning in at around about eleven. Tomorrow was going to be a long day.

Chapter Twenty Four: Vatican City

Carla had departed Glympton Park just after noon, leaving Norwood where he lay asleep in her bed. It had been an enjoyable few hours of pure lust but that was all it had been. She took great pleasure in their encounters but she wasn't the type to have lasting relationships. She saw men and occasionally women as play things; and once she had had her fun she would just throw them away.

Carla's plane to Rome would leave from Oxford Airport at four. Normally she enjoyed these private flights around the globe when she was on the job but this was one she was not looking forward to; Victor Negroni was flying with her. The man could be a bit of a letch so she had decided the best policy was to ignore him, at least the flight wasn't a long one and she might just be able to resist the urge to throttle the odious little man. The man did have his uses; especially when it came to contacts within Rome and the Vatican.

She was sure it would not be long before she managed to seduce one of these contacts and use her persuasiveness to gain access to the *Archivum Secretum Apostolicum Vaticanum.*

She casually brushed her long dark hair behind her shoulders as she stepped from the car outside the airport terminal; her sleek red dress and tinted sunglasses gave her the air of a movie star as she momentarily paused, waiting for the chauffer to collect her bags from the boot of the car, before walking off in the direction of the departure lounge. He followed in her footsteps as she strutted off towards the check-in for private flights.

She had a few hours to kill before the flight was due to leave, so once her baggage had been checked in and the chauffer had left she took up a seat in one of the small café bars in the terminal and waited for Victor to turn up. It was so typical of the man not to be on time. She watched the comings and goings of other passengers as she waited for the repulsive little man to arrive.

It was about an hour and a half later before Victor Negroni appeared; he was red in the face with beads of sweat streaming down his wrinkled forehead. He had obviously been in a rush to reach the airport before the plane left, so much so that he barged his way past a group of passengers standing in one of the lines for a gate, in order to reach the bar where Carla sat. Almost wiping out a little girl as he did so.

The sheer disregard for other people angered Carla as she watched him barge his way towards the bar. She was baffled by whatever it was that made him think that he was above all those other people. He was a poor example of a human being and certainly no gentleman.

'Ready for our little trip?' He said resting an overly friendly hand on her knee as he greeted her.

'Victor, remove your hand before I remove it for you, permanently.' She replied.

'Come now my dear, we must be civil.'

'I won't ask you again.' She snapped.

'As you wish. You can't hold out on me forever.' He replied as he reluctantly removed his hand.

Carla longed for the day that the Grand Master had no more use for the man; she would take great pleasure in sending him to meet his maker. For now she would just have to put up with the irritation of his existence.

They passed through customs with ease and boarded the Gulfstream G550 jet. Carla waited for Victor to choose somewhere to sit so that she could then position herself as far away from the little man as possible. She couldn't avoid him completely but that didn't mean that she had to sit in his vicinity. She relaxed back into the plush leather covered seat, closed her eyes and fell asleep.

Just over two hours after take-off the pilot announced that they were beginning their descent into Rome. Adding that the temperature was mild for the time of year at 16 degrees centigrade but that it was very overcast and rather blustery.

The plane made a perfectly smooth landing despite a 20 knot cross wind that pushed the plane around during the last few seconds before it touched down on the tarmac, gently coming to a halt before taxiing the short distance from the main runway to join the other private jets that had either just arrived earlier that day or were waiting to depart.

The arrivals lounge had been festively decorated for the Christmas period, glittering baubles, strands of tinsel and a large assortment of fairy lights had been dotted around the concourse. All the passengers were greeted by the airport staff in the private arrivals area, who offered them a complimentary Christmas goody bag and a glass of Champagne whilst they waited for their luggage to be unloaded from their planes.

Carla and Victor did not have to wait for long before the chauffeur that had been organised by Lord Norwood had finished loading the sleek black Maybach and was ready to take them to their respective destinations in the city.

After dropping Victor at his lavish villa apartment the driver continued on through the busy streets of Rome before passing into the separate city-state of the Vatican. It was approaching nine in the evening, and the streets were already fully under the illumination of their lamps by the time that Carla finally reached the comfort of Villa Magnolia Relais on the *Via delle Fornaci* and could relax away from the wandering eye of Victor.

She was exhausted after the long night of passion followed by the day's travel so she decided not to go out that night, instead she ran herself a hot bath with some herbal soaps and bath salts.

Whilst her bath was running she slipped out of her dress and put on a black silk bathrobe, walked into the next room selected some relaxing classical music from the CD rack and went back to check on the bath. Turning the taps off she dropped the robe from her shoulders and stepped into the hot soapy water.

The water in the free standing enamel bath gently soothed her aching muscles, her mind began to drift off from the tiresome man that had vexed her so much during the day and she began to feel at peace, almost to the point of falling asleep as the sweet scent of the herbs gradually filled the room.

Carla felt refreshed after spending the best part of half an hour in the bath, having washed away the dirt from the day.

After towelling herself down and blow-drying her hair she could think of nothing better than slipping in between the silk sheets on her bed and drifting off to sleep, ensuring that she would be totally rested for tomorrow. A day that would be the start of her next task, finding a way to access the Vatican vaults, something that she thought may prove to be problematic. Nevertheless she would find a way.

The sun had only just begun to stream through her curtains when her sleep was rudely disturbed by the sound of the phone in her bedroom breaking her peaceful sleep.

'Hello, Carla speaking.'

'Good morning, Miss Adams I trust you had a peaceful sleep.' The unmistakable voice said.

'Victor, have you any idea what time it is?'

'About six thirty.'

'Exactly.' She replied and slammed the phone back down on the hook. She normally would have gone back to sleep but she knew that the annoying little man had the persistence of a Jack Russell terrier with a bone and would probably ring her back once he thought it was safe to do so. Begrudgingly she wiped the sleep from her eyes and set about making herself up for the day ahead.

True to form about half and hour later, the letch rang her back and explained that he had organised to meet up with a few junior members of the Vatican for coffee at about eleven o'clock and that it was maybe a good opportunity for her to accidentally run into them. They may be persuaded to allow her access or at least organise access to the *Archivum Secretum Apostolicum Vaticanum.*

'And you just had to ring me at six thirty in the morning to tell me that. Honestly Victor, sometimes you really have no sense of decency.' Slamming the phone back down in a show of irritation. The sooner he had outlived his usefulness the better she thought as she continued to sort through her clothes, eventually picking out something that was fit for a chance meeting and hopefully would have the desired effect.

The chance meeting turned out to be less than productive, although the men were exceptionally taken with her and keen to see her again, none of them had the authority to give her direct access to the vaults. And it was abundantly clear to her from what they described, that the administrative process to apply for access was not just rather long-winded but also extremely thorough. Something that she just didn't have the time for. She would have to find her own way to gain access even if it meant breaking into the vaults.

Carla spent the next few days watching the comings and goings of the scholars and professors that had access to the Vatican archives until she had identified a man whom she was certain she could bend to her will. She noticed that after spending a long day in the archives he like to relax in a quiet bar not far from the archives, and she decided that this would be the best place to contrive a chance encounter.

The golden shards of light softly bathed her skin as her long locks of hair cascaded over her shoulders. Her face was a picture of wisdom and passion, a look that didn't command affection, but gently beckoned as Carla casually strolled into the intimate bar.

Dillon had noticed the girl walk into the room as he nonchalantly sat at the far end of the bar sipping his Sailor Jerry's and Coke. He didn't immediately get up and walk over, that wasn't his style. He finished his drink and ordered another whilst he decided whether or not to engage the newcomer in conversation.

He was generally quite shy and if he had a pound for every opportunity missed to talk to a member of the opposite sex he would probably be verging on being a millionaire by now, not that he regretted those missed opportunities. He firmly believed that fate would one day instigate a chance meeting and that he therefore did not need to force the issue. If it was meant to be, it would just happen; if it wasn't then *c'est la vie*.

Stuck in his inner thoughts he had failed to notice that the girl had taken up the seat next to him. It was only when he glanced up that his eyes met her gaze.

Chapter Twenty Five: Fresh Trials

The Atlantic sunrise was a beautiful sight to behold. The bright light of the new day sun behind the clouds caused the fringes to glow golden yellow and orange with the faintest hint of pink on the horizon, the water below was almost as still as a mill pond with just the smallest of ripples dancing across the surface. It was going to be another perfect day in paradise.

James and Chris rose early. They wanted to make the most of the time that they had on the island, and to find out more about those smugglers that had been causing Jack Whiting so much grief.

They had not taken long to find out that the smugglers operated out of a warehouse near to the main city of San Pedro. On the surface the warehouse appeared to be for cold storage, but that was just a front.

The smuggling had grown significantly over a short space of time, and due to the proximity of the island to Mexico and the United States, it was perfectly positioned to act as a distribution centre for the Columbian cartel. To the average person the security arrangements at the warehouse were nothing out of the ordinary, but to the trained eye there was more to this building than merely storing meat and veg.

The key card points, electric fence and thermal cameras not to mention the low-key security patrols did suggest that something far more valuable than meat was being stored in the warehouse complex.

'Those roving patrols are going to cause problems with gaining access.' Chris said after surveying the complex.

'Best bet is to approach from the sea, we could get a small inflatable under those pontoons and climb up one of those ladders.' James replied. 'It's still going to be a bit tricky. Some kind of distraction may be needed to keep the patrols occupied, and I know just the two gentlemen for the job.' With the hint of a smile.

'Yeah, but I think blowing things up is not an option. The last thing we want is for the local Busies to turn up, especial as they tend to be accompanied by the military.'

'True, besides they are probably corrupt and in the employ of the smugglers. You know what these islands are like.'

'Yeah we'll have to use a bit more guile than that. Think it's time we made a move back to the hotel and have a chat with those two before they get ahead of themselves. They do get over excited without the right supervision.'

Gaz had been busy with Ollie doing a bit of prep for what they assumed would be a full on assault of the warehouse complex. They were slightly disappointed when they eventually found out from Chris and James what the plan was, when the two finally returned from their recce, although they did understand the reasoning behind it.

It was late in the evening by the time they all left the hotel and journeyed down towards San Pedro, they had left a small inflatable in a small creek inlet about three miles to the north of the industrial area. It was pitch black as they cautiously piloted the small boat around the headland towards the bright lights of the city.

The stretch of water in front of the warehouse was dark and the lights from the neighbouring installations cast large patches of shadow on the water to the north of their final destination. Nearing the warehouse they sneaked in, close to the sea defences. Anybody looking out to sea would not notice the small boat slip silently past, the height of the quay obscuring the view of anybody looking out from the shore across the water.

'All good so far, another 30 feet and we will be under the first section of the pier.' James whispered to his companion. 'Ready with the painter?'

They quickly made the boat fast to one of the legs supporting the pier and stealthily slipped into the water to swim the last few feet to the ladder bolted to the wall of the quay, originally it had been intended to be used by the maintenance crews to gain access to the underneath of the pier to carry out repairs. The two nimbly scrambled up the rungs on to the tarmac at the top.

Crouching in the darkness they waited for the moment when Gaz and Ollie would create a disturbance at the other end of the complex that should drag the guards away from their posts leaving the waterfront unattended, enabling James and Chris to break into the warehouse.

It was not long before the two, who had by this point become really intoxicated, began to make a fuss at the other end of the complex by trying to very unsubtly gain access via the main gates. James and Chris watched as the patrols moved off from their usual routes in the direction of the noise to investigate what the commotion was. Providing them with the perfect opportunity to slip into the warehouse undetected.

The key card lock on the warehouse door was new, but not that sophisticated, and it did not take Chris long to rewire the device, effectively bypassing the lock and the alarm system that was linked to it. James felt the adrenaline start to course through his body as the excitement of the situation increased.

Inside the warehouse they came across many large freezer units, like the kind you would expect to find in any cold storage facility. On a closer inspection of some of the units it became apparent that not all of them were running, they may have been in need of repair but because of the background information that they had acquired, James suspected that this was not the reason for them not to be turned on. The only way to know for sure was to take a look inside.

'Just keep an eye on the door.' Chris said as he took out his lock picks from one for his thigh pockets and began to manipulate the tumblers of the first unit's lock. After thirty or so seconds there was a soft click as the last tumbler released and the lock fell open.

Chris carefully opened the door ensuring that he moved it very slowly so that the door wouldn't squeal too much. Peering through the darkness of the unit it was difficult on first inspection to make out what was inside so he took out his phone from another pocket, swiping the screen to select the torch from the pop-up menu. The small bright light chased the darkness as he panned it around the inside of the large metallic unit.

By the light of the torch several large packing crates were revealed to be stacked up across the middle of the unit. The majority of which appeared to be labelled up ready for shipment to the USA.

Chris found a crowbar amongst a few tools leaning up against the right hand corner nearest to the door of the unit. Just like Pandora he couldn't resist the urge to peek inside one of the crates. It took a few careful placements of the crowbar before he managed to prise open the lid of the crate. As soon as he had removed the protective polystyrene sheets on the inside of the crate and saw the coffee grounds underneath, the alarm bells started ringing. He was therefore not surprised after plunging his hands deep into the legal stimulant that there were bags of cocaine hiding in the sea of coffee, this was an old smugglers trick to conceal the smell of the cocaine from the sniffer dogs.

Chris took a few photos of the Columbian Pure before meticulously closing the crate up, making sure that everything was replaced exactly where he had found it. Nothing could look out of place. One thing about drug dealers was they were all totally paranoid and would spot even the tiniest discrepancy.

After closing the unit up he continued checking a few more of the metallic units, most of which had contents of a similar nature. However, the final two units did not contain narcotics but were bursting at the seams with genuine US caffeine free military hardware, this was clearly how part of the smugglers' payments for the narcotics were being made.

Taking a few photos of the hardware, he began to form a plan that would involve a bit of blackmail to free Mr Whiting from the influence of the gang rather than doing something more dramatic like blowing up the building and its contents which would certainly send a clear message not to meddle in the affairs of the Aussie, but would more than likely have the potential to backfire with lethal retaliations from the smugglers.

'Are we good to go?' James asked, interrupting Chris' train of thought as he returned from keeping watch on the main door.

'Yes, I think it would be best if we got out of here as quickly as possible. I'm sure we would not get a warm welcome if we were found in here. I still can't believe the firepower these guys have managed to get their hands on; there's stuff in those units that are still in stages of development, which I'm pretty sure the Pentagon would be very interested in being returned.' Chris replied as he re-locked the last unit.

'Give Gaz a ring and tell him to make a bit more noise, those patrols will have returned to their posts by now.'

The two burglars waited a few minutes before venturing back outside the warehouse. They could hear that one of the Caribe security guards was involved in a heated argument with the drunken decoys.

'Hey fellas, I don't wanna hear it. We've told ya once. Don't come back again. If ya don't listen den tings r gonna get real ugly. If ya tink a hurricane is bad den u'll be in for a nasty shock. Get your limin' asses outta here.' The guard was saying in a tone that highlighted the fact that he was beginning to lose his temper with the two intoxicated youths.

It did nevertheless give Chris and James the window they needed to scurry back to the rubber dingy and quietly make their way back to the safety of the inlet. By the time the four of them had been reunited and returned to Las Terrazas, the Atlantic horizon had begun to once again take on the orange glow from the new day sun. It was going to be just another perfect day in paradise.

'I think a drink is in order after that ordeal, where is a bloody waiter when you need one.'

'Same old Chris, any excuse for a drink, sometimes I worry about you.'

'So does my liver. But unlike Mr Bond you only live once so may as well enjoy it while one can.'

The banter continued as they walked round the front of the hotel to the outside bar. There was no point in going to bed now that the sun was almost past the horizon.

Unlike previous occasions when the men had frequented the outside bar they weren't intending to get hammered, this was more of a relaxing drink after a job well done and also an opportunity for Chris and James to discuss exactly what their next steps would be.

'I thought that last security guard was going to lose his rag and batter you round the head with that police baton.' Gaz said, as Ollie brought the drinks over to the table where the others had sat down.

'He apparently didn't like the look of your face, not surprising really. Just look at the state of you.' Ollie cuttingly replied.

'Ha, have you taken a look in the mirror lately. Think you need to go and have a word with yourself before starting along this tack.'

'Don't think you should have gone there, mate. Remind me who it was that can't remember their port from starboard, and crashed a RIB into the Port Admiral's personal yacht in Southampton.'

'As I recall you were the one who was meant to be keeping watch.'

'True but I wasn't the one at the helm now was I?'

Whilst Gaz and Ollie continued their usual high-spirited jesting,

Chris and James settled down into a deep conversation regarding the best way to use the photos they had taken in the warehouse.

They were both agreed on the fact that the photos should be delivered to the warehouse, but they could not agree on the manner in which they should be delivered. Taking a large gulp of his Sazerac, Chris began to say, 'Using a courier or just the island's daily postal service would be the safest option.'

'I understand where you are coming from but would it be taken seriously? They may just think it is some kind of practical joke. Personally, I think it would be far more successful for us to deliver them. It would have the desired impact. Besides, I'm sure we can borrow a couple of Whiting's security personnel to back us up. They wouldn't have to do much, they just have to look the part.' James replied pausing to catch his thoughts 'But of course Whiting may not agree to that and the four of us probably aren't enough if it did all kick off.'

'Well it's almost eight.' Chris said as he glanced at his watch. 'Whiting should be around shortly. He may have a better suggestion; after all he has had previous with these characters, so should have some insight into the best way to get this done.'

Jack Whiting had had a sleepless night, having been well aware of what Chris and the others had been up to during the night. He had tossed and turned, as the worry that something may go terribly wrong would not let his mind switch off. Maybe he had asked too much of the former servicemen.

He finally managed to drop off after he had heard the familiar voices of the men as they returned from their exploits. Still three hours sleep was not a great deal to work with but he supposed it could have been worse.

Rising just after eight he dressed as quickly as he could. He was anxious to find out all that they had discovered. He was hoping that he could now draw a line under his dealings with the smugglers and concentrate on running a profitable venture without the constant cloud of oppression hanging over him.

'Morning Gents, hope you boys have had a bonzer night without too much drama.' The Aussie said as he approached their table.

'No trouble at all, it was surprisingly easy, all things considered.' James replied as he stood to greet their host and new friend.

'That's a relief I did have a few twitchy moments last night, I can tell you.'

'Well you may have a few more of those. We haven't quite finished yet.' Chris said. 'But don't worry it will all be sorted soon.' He continued, trying to reassure Jack, as he had seen the happy smile drop from Jack's face at the indication of more twitchy moments to come. Chris carried on to explain the circumstances, and that they hadn't managed to agree on the best course of action.

'Well that's an easy one. Instead of sending it to them, get them to come to you.' After giving the problem some careful thought Jack replied in a more positive tone, now that he understood the minor dilemma. 'They do come here from time to time to play poker and attend VIP parties and fund raisers. So the simplest thing is to invite them to a party and whilst they are at their ease, spring the trap. They won't expect that as they would be out of their comfort zone. They will be in a corner where they will have very few options but to comply.' He finished, before waving the barman over and ordering breakfast for the group.

'I like it, it's just the kind of sneakiness that appeals to me. Trust a businessman to know how to manipulate a situation to his advantage.' James said with a wry smile, knowing full well that if a party were involved Chris would be in his element not to mention Ollie and Gaz.

It did not take long for Mr Whiting to make the necessary arrangements to host a VIP fundraiser at Las Terrazas for the following evening. In fact he had sorted most of the arrangements by the time Devan and Rachel had appeared from their rooms for a late brunch.

Unlike Mr Whiting, they were used to the guys taking on difficult scenarios and although they were still apprehensive of the outcomes of these escapades, they no longer felt it necessary to worry all night about them and therefore had not rushed out of bed the moment that the intrepid explorers had returned earlier that morning.

On the evening of the party the small jetty below the hotel was a buzz with activity. The waterfront staff was kept on their toes by the almost constant stream of private tenders that arrived to drop off some of the more prominent guests. And of course they would end up working well into the night as some people loved to arrive fashionably late. Things were more relaxed in the tropics and it was quite common for many people to not even consider going out before midnight. After all, they knew that due to the midday sun's heat they could catch up on a few hours sleep the next afternoon.

In true Caribe style the party centred around the outside bar and a large canopy that had been erected in part of the waterside gardens. A DJ booth had been placed on the terrace with speakers dotted around the bar and garden areas, the chilled evening beats floated from the hotel across the water that had been set ablaze by the deep orange glow of the setting sun.

As the sun slunk away behind the horizon giving way to the night, the chilled atmosphere began to change, the DJ's set moving from smooth rhythms to heavy Caribe vibes. It was at this point that Rachel and Devan made their entrance to the party from the hotel. Chris' jaw almost dropped at the sight of the professor descending the small flight of steps down from the terrace to the bar, she appeared to glide across the floor as the hem of her stunning light blue ball-gown brushed the floor, and he was certainly not the only one to take an interest in the entrance of the two elegant ladies.

Nevertheless, it was the DJ's set climaxing in the track *Let me see you whine*, that was the real show stopper, even Gaz and Ollie who considered themselves to be experts in the female sex raised their eyebrows at the grinding and twerking skills that several stunning local girls were showing off. It was like something that one would expect at Tobago's famous Sunday School not at a VIP fundraiser at Las Terrazas.

Jack found James and Chris propping up the bar having a leisurely conversation about the last time they had been to the tropics and how something had changed dramatically, especially the amount of industrialisation on the islands, and yet the laid back approach to life still managed to endure.

'Gents, it's time. My doorman has just informed me that they have arrived.' The doorman had run down to Mr Whiting's office the moment the two large blacked out Hummers had pulled up on the tarmac at the front of the Hotel.

'Give them half an hour to settle in before we approach them.' James replied as he nodded in the direction of the so-called gangsters that were just walking on to the terrace from the main building.

'No problem, I must just go and greet them, they will be expecting me to give them the full VIP treatment. May I suggest meeting them in the boardroom when you decide the time is right.' Jack added.

'Possibly, although I would prefer somewhere less business like. A more relaxed atmosphere would be less intimidating.' Chris said before Jack left them to greet the wanna-be VIPs.

Mr Whiting really wasn't looking forward to cosying up to the new arrivals. He felt a shiver run down his spine as he approached the group. He was well aware of what they were capable of, and it was the thought of this that still played heavily on his mind. Even though after tonight he may be free from their sphere of influence he wasn't getting his hopes up. He had been burnt in the past and therefore had always learnt not to count his chickens too early.

'Hey Jack, how r ya man. Looks like it gonna be a gre't pa'ty. Hope ya not spent too much on it man, 'cos ya know ya still gotta pay us.' One of the largest men in the group said. He was known as D-Boy, Jack didn't actually know what his name really was, he was the head honcho as far as the smugglers were concerned.

'I don't think this is the time or the place for that sort of talk.' Jack coldly replied. He had hoped to avoid any talk of money today.

'Now Jack, don't be like dat man. Don't make me angry. 'Tis a lovely pa'ty. Don't wanna go spoilin' it now do ya man? 'Cos ya know wat will happen if I get a steam on.' D-Boy said as he roughly put his hand around the back of Jack's neck giving it a firm shake. To the casual observer it appeared as just a friendly gesture of affection but the pressure that D-Boy was applying to Jack's neck was far from friendly.

'As I said, not now!' Jack's defensive tone cut through the air like a knife as he shrugged off D-Boy's grasp from around his neck. Unfortunately this approach had the affect of inflaming D-Boy, it was like dropping a spark into a keg of dry gunpowder. Not wanting to lose face in front of his entourage D-Boy grabbed Jack by the throat and shoved him through an open door on the terrace into one of the small bars.

'E'rybody out now!' he shouted.

The guests in the room didn't need to be told twice. They quickly gathered up their drinks and hastily left the building not wanting to further enrage D-Boy; he was well known on the island for his short temper.

'Ya really know how to play with fiya don't ya man.' D-Boy shouted at Jack, who was by now almost cowering in the back of the chair that D-Boy had thrown him into.

Luckily for Jack, Chris and James had watched the events on the terrace unfold.

'Looks like it won't be half and hour then. Shall we give the lad a hand?' Chris said.

'Would be rude not to intervene I suppose.' James replied as the pair left the outside bar and walked up to the terrace. Approaching the open bar door, the pair were blocked by two of D-Boy's henchmen.

'Dis room is closed. Not'ing to see here.' One of the men said.

James didn't take the slightest bit of notice. Before the man knew what had hit him James had smashed the man with his right fist just below the ribs causing the man to keel over, only for his chin to make heavy contact with James' rising knee; the man fell to floor unconscious. By which time Chris had already dealt with the other one, in much the same manner.

'Sorry to interrupt but I think we can settle this.' James said as he entered the room.

'Ya ain't got no play here, man. Dis ain't the colonies ya know. I tink ya should leave before tings get ugly.'

'I think we're fine thanks.' James replied defiantly, dropping a brown envelope at D-Boy's feet.

'What's dis?' D-Boy asked. 'Paper don't scare me. You a lawyer or sometin'?'

'Let's call it insurance. And don't worry we've kept the originals.' James' stare didn't leave the man's gaze. This was the crunch moment; who would break eye contact first?

Slowly D-Boy dropped his gaze, bent down to pick up the envelope and flicked through its contents.

'Don't look familiar to me, man. Tink ya have the wrong person.'

'Don't try to play the fool, you know exactly what it is and where. I suggest you permanently sever contact with Mr Whiting or these will make their way across the border, I'm pretty sure the Pentagon or Langley will be very interested in you after that, not to mention the DEA.' James could see the cogs turning slowly in D-Boy's eyes. He was clearly trying to weigh up whether he could bluff his way out or not. It took a few moments before D-Boy responded.

'Fine 'ave it your way, but you gonna be sleepin' with one eye open from now on, Limey.'

'Don't worry, I always do. A pleasure doing business with you gentlemen.' James replied as D-Boy pushed past him out of the room, collecting his two dazed colleagues as he left.

'Well Jack, I think it's time to enjoy this party.' James said as Jack gingerly got to his feet not quite being able to take in all that had just happened.

'You heard the man!' Jack shouted across to the DJ. The music had died down as the guests had taken an interest in what had been going on inside the small bar. As the phatt beats started up again, all was soon forgotten, the guest quickly reverted back to enjoying the party atmosphere, long into the early morning.

A few days after the night of the party Jack had finished making the final arrangements for the passage across the Atlantic to the UK.

The *Aurora* quietly slipped her moorings and slowly began to cut through the crystal clear Caribbean water, gradually building up speed as she cruised out of the harbour towards the horizon.

James watched the hotel disappear into the distance. The fair weather was forecast to hold for the majority of the crossing and yet what would be waiting for them when they finally arrived back on home shores had already begun to concern him. They had been away for far too long with no clue as to what lay ahead.

Chapter Twenty Six: The Black Dragon Scroll

The streets around the Vatican had been a buzz with activity during the day but as the day slowly slipped into night the streets became awash with stillness. The glow of the street lights illuminated the sacred city, creating a magical picture, the dome of St Peter's bathed in a dim zesty glow towering above the city appeared to be keeping a watchful eye over the peacefulness.

Carla was on her way to meet Dillon whom she had been seeing for the past three weeks, gradually working her charm to ensnare him. Not that it had been much of a challenge; Dillon was no stranger to the attentions of beautiful women; mainly due to his dashingly handsome looks and quick wit, however he was also well aware of this and had become somewhat of a player in respect to the fairer sex and therefore put up little resistance to her seductive advances.

She found Dillon sprawled out along one of the leather couches of his favourite café bar; he looked as if he owned the place. His demeanour was one of being completely at ease with his surroundings without a care in the world. She knew that this was mainly down to her attentiveness. He seemed to be like a little puppy falling deeply in love with his new mistress and his devotion was growing stronger every time his eyes met her alluring gaze.

'Hi Babe.' She said as she greeted him in her usual manner. 'Have you had a good day?' she enquired as she softly kissed him on the lips. The scent of the Coco Channel gently wafting through his nostrils heightened his sense of longing for her.

'It's been okay, so much research to document. At this rate it is going to take an age.'

'You should get an assistant to help you with your work. After all, it is really important, isn't it?' Her probing question laying the foundations in his mind that an assistant would be a good idea.

'Probably, but I just don't have the time to go out and find one.'

'Maybe I could help.' She brushed a hand through his hair as she offered her help. 'It would mean we could spend more time together and I'd like to know more about what you do. I think it's fascinating stuff.'

'Really, I never though you were that interested in history.'

'Oh, quite the opposite, I think how people's actions had a direct impact on the world around us is really interesting. How they lived and the decisions that they took are really stimulating.'

'I suppose I might be able to get a pass for you. Although you will have to be interviewed by the Archivist, he is pretty strict about who is allowed access to the vaults. Nevertheless I can certainly ask him.'

Carla spent the next few hours solidifying the idea in Dillon's mind that she would be of great assistance to him. It was therefore rather late by the time they finally left the little bar and strolled arm in arm through the deserted streets of the sacred city.

She toyed with the idea of sleeping with him but decided that it was better to keep him on the hook for a little while longer, sometimes the hint of sex was a far more powerful tool than the actual erotic act itself and besides she didn't want to over play her hand at this point. It had already taken weeks to get to this position so to lose control now would be disastrous. She continued to walk by his side back to her villa on the *Via delle Fornaci.*

Dillon waited expectantly, as she fiddled with her keys before she opened the door of the villa, hoping to be invited in just like he had been on a number of occasions before, but she stopped him by laying her hand softly on his chest.

'Not tonight, Babe. You have a busy day ahead of you and I wouldn't want to be the cause of you not getting all of your research done.' She said smiling sweetly at him as she innocently starred deeply into his eyes, before she kissed him passionately and turned to walk inside.

Dillon felt like he had just been hit by a train and his loins burned for her, the faint aroma of her perfume still teasing him as he lingered on the doorstep for a moment before shaking off the exotic images running through his mind. She was after all, probably right; it was going to be a busy day especially now he needed to speak to Father Ignacio, the Archivist, about the possibility of a pass for her as his assistant.

Father Ignacio, born in the suburbs of Rome in 1955, was an orphan and had been brought up by the Church. He had showed an aptitude in translating Latin and Hebrew and had therefore spent much of his time since in the archives. He was unwavering in his faith and had joined the Cistercian order when he was old enough.

Now in his late fifties, he had no real distinguishing features and was entering the twilight of his service with the Vatican. He had held the position of Head Librarian and Keeper of the Church's Secret Vaults for the past 20 years. He hadn't been a big mover and shaker in religious terms; he had just been a committed Roman Catholic and felt that it was of great importance to protect the ancient scripts that resided in the *Archivum Secretum Apostolicum Vaticanum*.

It had taken quite a lot of persuasion to get Father Ignacio to agree to provide a pass for Carla to act as Dillon's assistant.

'This is all highly irregular.' The old man stated. 'You should know better than to spring something like this on us at the last minute, Professor Hart. You know it normally takes weeks even months to run a full background check.'

'Father we have known each other for quite some time now and I hope we are friends. I am only asking, as it would greatly speed up my research. In no way did I intend to cause you any tribulations.'

'Well I suppose it can't do too much harm. But you are fully responsible for the girl and if she causes any problems both of you will be denied access to the vaults and will never be allowed back. Do I make myself clear?'

'I understand, Father. Thank you. She will be on her best behaviour, I promise.'

'See that she is. I will be keeping a close eye on you both.'

Dillon left Father Ignacio's office and before he descended into the vaults he sent a quick text to Carla to let her know that Father Ignacio had agreed to allow her to act as his assistant and had granted her access to the archives. Dillon suggested that they should meet up later that evening so that he could get her to fill in the necessary paperwork. Then the next day they would both visit Father Ignacio's office so that the Vatican could issue her with an ID pass to access the vaults.

Having sent the text, Dillon returned to the archives. He had been searching for a document from the Empress Dowager Wang sent to the Pope in 1656, in which she expressed the wishes of the Prince of Giu, the Yongli Emperor to become Christian. But so far his efforts to locate the *Black Dragon Scroll* had not proved to be successful. Until he found it, his thesis lacked the necessary evidence and would be in danger of being ridiculed by all of his peers. He would be the laughing stock within the academic community; something that he dearly wished to avoid. It was a make or break moment in his career.

Carla smiled as she read the message from Dillon. Her plan was starting to come together and soon she would have full access to the vaults where she could begin to look for the document that would reveal the location of the next part of the *Liber Veritatis*. She decided that Dillon needed to be rewarded for his efforts; she would make it a night he wouldn't forget. Looking at her watch she realised that if she didn't make a move quite soon from the small coffee shop near the *Fontana di Trevi* she would be in danger of missing her meeting with Victor. She decided that the little man could wait a little longer; she was enjoying basking in the Italian winter sunshine, just watching the comings and goings of the thousands of tourists who made their way to admire the sculptural perfection of the fountain. She wondered if they realised that soon much of their lives would change forever.

Draining the last of her espresso she left some change on the table for the double shot and headed off in the direction of the church of *San Carlo alle Quatro Fontane*. Borromini had designed *San Carlo*, unfortunately he had committed suicide in 1667 before the church had been completed and therefore due to the circumstances of his death he had not been buried inside.

Carla's walk to the small intricate church was not that far, but due to the hustle and bustle of the ever flowing and intertwining streams of tourists that seemed to come from everywhere, her stroll along the narrow streets to the church took rather longer than she had expected. Not that it was a dull walk; she clocked a number of pick-pockets that were operating on the streets, lightly removing wallets and other valuables from unsuspecting tourists. One even came close to thinking about her as a target but she gave him a knowing look, which seemed to make him think twice about her as a potential mark.

Victor had had a productive meeting with three of the cardinals, who would prove to be the key to influencing the vote for a new pope in the conclave that was due to take place at some point in the next few weeks.

The three cardinals were all eager to increase their influence within the Vatican and saw this as an opportunity for them to vote in a weak pope, one whom they could manipulate to their own benefit. Recent popes had curbed the power of the cardinals and purged many who had abused their positions; something that had made many of the remaining cardinals sit a little less comfortably than they had been accustomed to.

The cardinals had long since left by the time Carla arrived at *San Carlino*. Victor had been passing the time before her arrival by studying the architecture of the interior of the small church.

'Lovely to see you as always, my dear.' The fat little man said as he spied Carla entering through the main doors of the church.

'Victor.' She replied curtly.

'The cardinals all seem to be on board. How is the professor?' He asked in a slightly scornful tone.

'Coming along quite nicely. I should have the documents by the week's end.'

'There is a reception at the Vatican on Friday evening that we have been invited to. I think this may be a chance for you to mingle with some of the more influential families in Rome and make a few new contacts. You should bring your toy-boy; I'm sure he will impress.'

'I'll think about it. I don't believe it will really interest him but we shall see, speaking of which I must make a move. I'm meeting him later.'

'Well if you must. I was rather hoping we could have dinner together this evening.'

'That is something I can assure you will never happen, not tonight or any other night, Victor.'

'Never say never, my dear. You don't know what may happen in the future.'

'Oh, I'm very certain on this point.' Carla said ignoring the slight shiver she felt at the very idea of spending an evening in close company with the creepy little man.

Carla left the church of *San Carlino* before Victor had a chance to come up with a response to her blunt reply. As much as the thought of having to spend an evening in his company vexed her, she knew that the reception at the Vatican was an event that she could not miss. At least if she brought Dillon with her, the evening would not be a total bore. In fact she was already thinking about committing amorous sins within the walls of the Vatican.

Those thoughts would have to wait for now as she realised that for such a special occasion she would need a breath-taking dress, one that would shock the clergy. It amused her to cause even the most devout and pious men to question their vows.

Carla hailed a passing taxi just outside the little church and told the driver to take her back to her villa on the *Via delle Fornaci*. She had walked enough for one day and besides she wanted to save her energy for what might prove to be a highly exhilarating night. She would just have enough time to take a shower and prepare herself before she met Dillon.

Once back at the villa she spent quite some time choosing which lingerie to wear before finally deciding that she wasn't going to wear any; just a very seductive low cut black dress by Gucci. She loved the feel of silk next to her bare skin.

After applying the final touches to her hair and makeup Carla left the villa and strolled down the *Via delle Fornaci* to the *Ristorante Perdincibacco*, Dillon was already waiting for her at the small bar on the far side of the intimate restaurant.

'Hi babe, have you had a good day?' She enquired as she lent forwards wrapping her arms around his neck and kissing him softly. The Coco Channel wafting up his nostrils was beginning to ensnare him once more.

'Hmmm good and bad. Good in so much that Father Ignacio has agreed to allow you to assist me, but I'm still no closer to locating the scroll. Sometimes I wish the Vatican had a better cataloguing system. It's almost as if it is one of those documents that they don't want anybody to find. I really can't understand why? As far as I'm aware it only reveals that the Prince of Gui wanted to convert to Catholicism and that as a gesture of good faith he was prepared to gift a sacred text to the Vatican if they accepted him into the fold.'

This last comment about a sacred text had caught Carla's attention. 'Interesting, does it say what the text was?'

'I don't know, that's one of the frustrating things until I find the 'Black Dragon Scroll' I am in the dark so to speak.'

'And does that mean this text is now in the possession of the

Vatican?' Carla asked, hoping that this would be the case and that the text would turn out to be the next part of the *Liber Veritatis*. It would make her life far easier if the text was in Rome and she would be rewarded beyond measure if she found the next piece and delivered it safely into the hands of *The Glove*.

'I don't think so, as far as I'm aware the Prince of Gui was captured and executed before the Vatican had responded to his mother's request.' Dillon said, not realising he had just dashed her hopes of getting her hands on the next piece of the codex. 'But who knows, at this point without the scroll I'm only speculating.'

'Well in that case we will have to find it for you, my darling.' She said as she ran her fingers gently through his hair. At this moment a waiter interrupted them.

'*Signorina* and *Signore*, if you would kindly follow me, your table is ready.'

The waiter seated them at a table along one of the open brickwork walls. Dillon ordered a bottle of the 2005 *Bollinger La Grande Année* from the wine menu and then returned his attention to Carla.

Secretly he could spend a considerable amount of time admiring her, to him she was like one of those rare illustrated volumes that he had spent hours studying; beautiful to look at and each time one would find something else captivating. This was what peaked his fascination with her. She was a true wonder hidden amongst nature's creations.

His desire for her was growing with every moment that he spent with her and this evening it was amplified by the way every now and again Carla would slowly rub her foot up the inside of his calf muscle; by the time they had finished dining there was definitely no doubt that there was only one thing on his mind.

Apart from the briefest of moments when Carla had to unlock the door to the villa they couldn't keep their hands off each other. As soon as they crossed the threshold of the door she took full control of him. Breaking away from his lips she firmly put her hand on his chest and backed him up into the main living area until his calves hit the edge of a leather armchair.

Giving him a shove that caused him to fall into the chair, she lifted her leg and firmly planted her foot against his chest. He softly caressed her lower leg between his hands, smoothly running his hands up her leg and then digging his fingers into her delicate flesh and dragging them back down towards her ankle. She moved her foot higher and pushed it up against his throat causing him to catch his breath for a second; before she slowly began to move, turning she laid her body over his allowing him to run his hands over her firm breasts whilst she rhythmically moved her body over his groin. He loved the feel of the skin-tight silk dress against his hands allowing him to feel even the slightest of her curves as his hands moved over her.

Standing up from around the front of the armchair and gently running a hand over his chest she glided round to the far side of the chair. Now directly behind him, she began to kiss the back of his neck, whilst continuing to run her hands down his chest, he certainly wasn't expecting the slightly more than affectionate nibble on the right of his neck which to be fair was slightly more painful than he was accustomed to. She ripped his shirt open causing buttons to burst off in every direction, before digging her fingernails deep into his muscular chest. The feeling of her nails grating his chest caused him to flinch slightly, this was a new sensation for him nevertheless, he was starting to become accustomed to these higher levels of pain that gradually began to increase the pleasure he was having, becoming entrapped in the moment.

He felt the soft silk of a scarf that Carla had produced against his shoulder. Before she tied it across his eyes. Although he could no longer see anything all his other senses were now heightened and this just fuelled his growing anticipation. He felt her hand take his and he rose from the chair, blindly following as she led him to her room.

'What are you going to do to me?' He whispered with the slightest hint of anxiety in his voice.

'Don't worry babe, just let it happen.' She softly whispered into his ear. Even the gentle breeze from her breath against his ear made his whole body tingle.

He allowed her to take his hands high above his head and felt light bands being tied around his wrists. The warp bit into his skin but it didn't cause any burning sensation. It was as if she was all around him now, gentle kisses around his midriff teased him and sent small pleasurable shivers up his spine.

Dillon found it slightly frustrating that he no longer had the full use of his hands as he had the burning desire to run his hands all over her body, every time he tried to bring his hands down around her she pushed them straight back up over his head again.

Carla had produced some ice from somewhere, the sharp coolness between her lips running down over his abdomen caused him to arch his back in sheer pleasure especially when he felt the coldness of the ice fragment tracing the rim of his belly button.

The rest of Dillon's night became blurred into one as each moment he spent with Carla swept him up like a whirlwind and by the time he finally collapsed on to her bed for the last time that night he was so utterly rocked to his core after being buffeted by so many new experiences that his mind could no longer focus on any one individual memory from the past hours of passion. He had hit the point of overload. Just like any hedonistic drug Carla's form of ambrosia had taken him to new heights of ecstasy and back so many times that his thoughts were now scrambled; the only thing he now slightly dreaded was that the dizzying heights he had reached meant that the inevitable fall back down to earth was going to be unbearable.

Chapter Twenty Seven: Light Fingers

Dillon wiped the sleep from his eyes as he tried to concentrate on the parchment he was currently examining on the table in front of him in the Vatican archives; he had had very little sleep the night before and his night of passion was now beginning to take it's toll.

Much of his body now ached; in fact he seemed to have aches in places that he didn't think could ache. Carla had taken him to a place of sheer bliss; in fact she had totally broken him both mentally and physically.

This morning it was made even worse by the fact that every time he looked up and caught sight of her, she always seemed to be in some kind of alluring pose; causing him to flash back to moments of lust from the night before.

He was hoping that the parchment he was examining would give him a better idea of where the *Black Dragon Scroll* now resided within the extensive collections in the Vatican archives.

Alas, after several minutes of careful study, this again turned out to be a dead end. Just a reference to where it had been stored about 20 years previous and since then the archives had undergone an extensive refurbishment resulting in a re-categorising and re-distribution of the collections; it literally was like looking for a needle in not one but hundreds of hay-stacks. Letting out a large sigh of disgruntled resignation, he decided to go and seek the help of Father Ignacio, if anybody knew where the document was or when it had last been seen it would be the Head Curator.

Father Ignacio was busily restoring a German bible from the 16th century when Dillon entered his study.

'Ah Professor Hart, how is your research progressing? I trust you have everything that you require?' The Padre said whilst continuing to restore some of the gold leaf on the cover of the bible.

'Well I was hoping you may be able to help me, Father. There is one document that try as I might I just can't seem to locate, the *Black Dragon Scroll*. I was hoping that you might know where it has been stored or when it was last seen?'

The mention of the scroll had clearly sparked something in Father Ignacio's mind as no sooner than the name of it was mentioned Father Ignacio raised one bushy eyebrow and his normally friendly demeanour seemed to close down slightly.

'Are you sure that this is the document you are looking for?'

'Yes, it is a crucial piece of evidence for my paper.'

'Interesting, very interesting. It seems to be very popular of late. Only a few weeks ago a gentleman, who has often visited our archives requested to see the very same document. In which case it may be that it has not been replaced and could still be in conservation. We normally take recently viewed documents into the conservation labs after they have been used just to ensure their condition. I will phone the lab and ask if it is still there. If it is I will find out whether it would be possible for it to be brought up for you.

'That would be very kind of you. Now I wish I had asked you earlier, I've been searching the archives high and low for days without any luck.'

'Sometimes fortune favours those who seek help.' The Padre said with a smile.

Father Ignacio telephoned down to the lab and was told that the scroll was indeed still in the lab, and that it could be brought up to the main archives within the hour for Professor Hart to study.

'Thank you, Father. You have been a great help.'

'You are very welcome, my son. I am always here to help. I do beg that when you do publish I hope you will treat our humble institution with respect.'

'I don't think you need worry Father my paper isn't going to bring the church down. I'm not planning on being the next Professor Langdon' Dillon replied trying to hide his amusement at his little quip, before leaving the study of the ageing padre and making his way back through security and into the archives.

'Have you had any success, babe?' Carla asked as Dillon returned to the desk, piled high with books and scrolls that he had been using as his base of study.

'Yes, indeed I have. Father Ignacio has located the scroll so now my studies can continue and hopefully result in something ground breaking.'

'Good I'm so glad for you, babe.' She said beaming at him. Her open display of happiness wasn't totally because he had found what he had been looking for, but also it meant that she too was closer to her end-game.

It only took about 20 minutes for the scroll to arrive from the conservationists but to Dillon it seemed like the longest twenty minutes in the world. Time always seemed to pass at its own rate when one wanted it to fly by.

The scroll was far longer and more ornate than Dillon was expecting. Gold and black dragons had been painstakingly painted on to the parchment and the emperor's Black Dragon Seal was clearly visible at the bottom of the document. All the characters had been hand painted which made the document that much more impressive.

Dillon's ancient Mandarin was a little rusty so it was going to take a few sessions of study to fully understand all of its meanings. At least he now had it for study.

'Don't forget we are guests at the Vatican's Annual Christmas Party this evening so don't get too absorbed in your study, babe.'

'I won't, just give me some time to make a start on it. Can you find out if the last person to view it has left a copy of their notes? Sometimes people do so that others can have the benefit of their observations and opinions.'

'Sure babe, what was their name?'

'Professor Peter Middleton, from what Father Ignacio was saying.'

Carla had a double take at the mention of the name but managed to hide her surprise well.

'Are you sure that he said Middleton?'

'Yes, pretty sure. Why? Do you know him?'

Trying to cover her slip she replied saying. 'No, not personally but I recognise the name. Doesn't he specialise in the study of the Knights of the Temple?'

'Actually I'm not sure exactly what his specialty is but I think he has dedicated some time to the Templars. I believe he was always a bit outspoken on certain things and became a recluse years ago. So I must admit I was a little surprised when Father Ignacio mentioned his name. It will be interesting to see what his notes say, if he has left a copy.'

This new development was of some concern for Carla, she had been aware that the old man had caused *The Glove* some problems in the past and he was by far the most informed person with regards to the *Liber Veritatis*. It was vexing that he had managed to make the link between the Codex and the *Black Dragon Scroll* before *The Glove*.

By the time they left the archives Dillon had translated about a quarter of the scroll, most of which had been made up of all the titles of the Pope and the Emperor; a very longwinded greeting which was typical of the style used during the period.

Carla returned with what she had managed to find of Professor Middleton's notes but they weren't that straightforward to read as the wily old man had encrypted them with some sort of cypher, which could take some time to break.

'I've only managed to find these two pages of his notes, if you can call them that.' She said waving the two A5 pieces of paper in front of Dillon.

'I see what you mean. That isn't any kind of shorthand that I have seen before. Looks like he uses his own notation system, which means that they are almost useless unless one knows what all the symbols stand for. Shame I should have liked to have had his insight into the scroll.'

Carla sneaked some photos of the notes whilst Dillon wasn't looking. He may not be able to understand them but she would send them to Victor. He had a contact that had spent quite some time, as a code breaker for the Italian secret services, so no doubt, given time would be able to decipher the notes.

The evening was unexpectedly mild for the time of year, especially as one would have anticipated the temperature to drop sharply due to the absence of clouds in the night sky. Carla and Dillon re-joined each other just a few streets down from St Paul's square and walked arm in arm down towards the side entrance of the Vatican, which was being used as the guest entrance for the Christmas party.

After passing through the security check carried out by the Swiss

Guard, they were escorted through the long passages ornately decorated with brightly coloured frescos and murals. Huge paintings by some of the most famous painters like, Raphael and Bernini hung in gilded frames along the walls in between the magnificent frescos.

Dillon would have like to have paused to take some time to appreciate the artwork but then he would have lost the escort and would never have been able to find his way through the vast complex to where the party was being held.

Taking a few twists and turns off from the main passageway they entered one of the most ornately decorated parts of the Vatican; the room was vast with ceilings that seemed to stretch on forever, like much of the rest of the sacred building it was decorated to such a degree that one could only stand and marvel at the scene and attempt to appreciate the enormity of the projects, and time that must have been spent in its creation.

Victor was already somewhere in the room but luckily he had not spotted the couple enter. Something for which Carla was extremely glad of as she didn't want to have her evening spoilt right from the off.

The room was full of dignitaries, celebrities and the elite families of Rome not to mention all the senior members of the clergy, dressed in all their finery. A number of refreshment tables had been set up throughout the room, although most of the guests were just taking drinks from the wandering waiters. The chatter and laughter of the guests reverberated around the room.

It was at about a quarter to eight the guests were invited to briefly move out of the room to the terraced courtyard from which they could watch the fireworks display that was about to start, which would also coincide with the arrival of the Pope, himself.

The brilliant colourful flashes of the fireworks igniting high above St Peter's Basilica set the clear winter's night sky ablaze, passion pinks, bright ruby reds and emerald greens were just some of the colours of the scintillating display that could be seen far above the ancient architecture. It was a captivating evening of both light and sound. The high pitched whines, snap, crackle and pops of some of the more entertaining rockets filled the air; it was almost like listening to a batch of popcorn on steroids bursting inside a microwave.

The temperature had clearly begun to drop as a number of the female guests returned back inside before the display had finished. Their evening dresses where not suitable for standing out in the cold night air for too long and they had not had the foresight to collect their warm jackets and furs before they had left the warmth of the party. Even Carla was beginning to feel the chill, but she just nestled herself deeper into Dillon's side to keep warm.

The final flurry of rockets bursting into the gloomy canvas of the dark night's sky heralded the Pope's arrival, as his eminences bulletproof glass covered cavalcade slowed to a halt the Swiss Guard smartly sprung into action and lined a walkway from the car to the terrace. They almost looked like tin soldiers in their pristine yellow and blue-stripped uniforms and shiny halberds.

The ageing Pope would not stay for long at the event, his deteriorating health would not permit. This would also be one of his last public appearances as pope. He was due to step aside within the next few weeks.

Normally a pope was elected for life but it had become increasingly clear that his health was limiting his ability to carry out his duties and he had therefore taken the decision that for the greater good and benefit of the Church that he loved so dearly, a new younger man should take his place; something that had not happened for many centuries.

Returning to the warmth of the party it was not long before Dillon ended up in deep conversation with a cardinal from Seville.

Carla had left Dillon in deep conversation with the cardinal, and headed off to one of the refreshment tables. She didn't know the man standing in front of her but she had taken an instant dislike to him, already making up her mind that he wasn't very pleasant and had nick-named him, *the obnoxious bottle of champagne*. He clocked her as he walked off to take the champagne and glasses over to his fellow guests before returning almost immediately and rudely saying to the barman.

'That smoked whiskey you do, same as last time, oh and whatever she is having.' Indicating Carla, whom he had almost barged past in his haste to place the order.

'Don't waste his money, he can't afford me.' Carla bluntly said to the barman. The barman sniggered slightly before he replied.

'*Scusami Ragazza*, but it is a free bar tonight.'

'I know. I just can't stand arrogance.' She replied as she took the two glasses of red wine that she had ordered and deliberately ignoring *the obnoxious bottle of champagne's* lame attempt at a retort proudly strode off to re-join Dillon and the Cardinal.

'The problem I see Cardinal, is that in today's world, because of the speed of communication and that everybody's lives are now so full, the Christian message just doesn't seem to have the same impact in developed countries that it once did.' Dillon said as Carla re-joined their conversation. 'Thanks, Hun.' He added as he took the glass of wine from her.

'In part I agree with you. Certainly the church has not adapted as quickly as it needs to for the speed at which society has changed over the last 50 years, but I disagree that its message isn't having an impact or that it has lost relevance, if anything it is more important than ever. The instability in the world today and the gap between rich and poor is now so vast that I think the church has a vital role to play in reminding people of moral values and ensuring those in need are not forgotten. If we do not I fear we are in danger of losing touch with our humanity.'

'I didn't intend to cause any offence and I hope that you are right.'

'None taken, my son. It is refreshing to be able to have an intellectual conversation, with somebody who clearly recognises the challenges of the modern age that faces the church, away from all the politics.'

The wandering touch of a hand against Carla's waist drew her attention momentarily away from the conversation. Had she not been in public she would have snapped all of Victor's sausage like fingers before he would have realised what was happening, but she managed to resist the urge.

'Victor, how good to see you.' She said in such a way that if one weren't listening very carefully you would have missed the briefest hint of distain in her voice. 'Allow me to introduce his Excellency the Cardinal of Seville and Professor Dillon Hart.'

'An absolute pleasure to meet you both. Especially you Professor Hart, I hear you have had quite the affect on our Miss Adams here. You will have to tell me your secret one day.' Victor added in his oiliest fashion. 'If I may beg your indulgence for a little while gentlemen, I must just steal the lovely lady away from you for a brief moment or two.'

'As long as you promise to bring her back, she is by far the most interesting person here.' Replied the Cardinal, who was well known for appreciating the beauty of the flesh slightly more than one in his position probably should.

'Please excuse me your Excellency. I'm sure this will not take long.' Carla said as she stepped away from the group and accompanied Victor to a quieter part of the room.

'Victor what are you doing? You know full well we should not be seen together unless absolutely necessary.'

'I bring word from his Lordship. Since your discovery that Professor Middleton has already viewed the *Black Dragon Scroll* he has requested that you make all haste to recover the artefact from the Vatican by any means.'

'I had a feeling he would and I have already taken steps to gain access to the vaults, tonight seemed like the perfect opportunity as the guards will all be occupied with the guests and protecting the Pope that they probably won't be that attentive to their other duties.' Carla said flicking her long hair back from her shoulders.

'Well you will have to act fast in that case my dear, I don't think that his Holiness will be staying for much more than an hour.'

'Keep Dillon entertained for a while. It shouldn't be too hard even for you.' Carla said before she quietly left the room and began to wind her way through the maze of corridors towards the entrance that led down into the vaults. Just as she had expected the corridors were devoid of guards.

Using a small compact mirror from her evening purse to look around the final corner to see where the two guards were positioned at the entrance to the vaults. She knew she would have to use all of her guile and seductive charm to talk them into allowing her access at such a late stage in the evening. She took out a small vaporiser, which contained some very powerful pheromones and lightly sprayed both sides of her neck, before casually walking round the corner to engage the two men.

The two guards, who had been on duty for a few hours, stiffened as they saw Carla's familiar sultry figure approaching. They had seen her a few times before with Dillon so they were not taken too much by surprise at the sight of her.

'*Buona sera, Signorina.*' One of the two guards said warmly. 'You know it is a little late for access to the vaults now.'

'*Buona sera, Signore* I realise it is late but I have a small problem that I hoped you lovely gentlemen may be able to help me with. I have realised that I left my phone on a bookshelf in the vault and I was hoping that you might allow me access to retrieve it?'

'I really shouldn't, the Vatican has quite a strict policy on when people are allowed into the vaults.'

'Not even just for me, just this once. I promise, it will be our secret.'

She replied smiling at him sweetly.

'I will have to check with Father Ignacio, he will have to okay it.'

'I shouldn't bother him, if I was you, when I left him he seemed to be deep in conversation with one of the Brazilian Cardinals. I don't think he would appreciate the interruption. You can escort me if you like.' She added as she lightly ran a hand down the sleeve of his uniform. 'I'm sure the three of us could work something out. I expect it gets very lonely just standing here for hours.'

The guards passed a knowing look between each other as they took her implication on board.

'It is possible, maybe, but you will have to be quick.'

And with that they swiped her into the vaults. Once inside she did not take long to locate the *Black Dragon Scroll* where she had left it earlier that day. She removed what looked like one of those E-Cig vaporisers from her purse, in fact although it did work; the main cylindrical battery compartment was empty. It was designed to be able to take rolled documents through customs without being discovered and would be perfect for removing both the scroll and the two pages of Professor Middleton's notes without the guards suspecting. She removed the scroll from the short piece of bamboo it was rolled around and after rolling up the notes, stuffed them all up into the cylinder.

'Have you found your phone, *Signorina* ?' The guard asked just as she placed the E-Cig back into her purse.

'Yes thank you, here it is. Honestly I'm so forgetful sometimes.' She replied lifting her phone up from the shelf that she had deliberately left it on. 'Now about your reward…'

Dillon noticed Carla re-entering the reception room, as he was just about to leave Victor to go and look for her. She had been absent long enough that he had started to become concerned that she might have grown bored of the party and left without him.

'For a moment I thought you might have left.'

'Don't be silly babe, I wouldn't leave without you.' She replied softly brushing her lips against his neck. 'I just bumped into someone outside that I hadn't seen for a very long time and we just got chatting. Speaking of leaving, do you feel like finding a more intimate locale?' Dillon didn't need to be asked twice. Leaving the party they strolled off arm in arm into the night.

The continuous blaring of his phone on the nightstand was the first thing that Dillon was vaguely aware of when he awoke the next day. His head felt heavy as if he had drunk an entire case of vodka the night before. Strange because he didn't remember drinking that much at the party or afterwards once he had left and gone back with Carla.

Turning over in the bed he realised that he was alone in the bed. He assumed that Carla must have risen earlier and didn't want to wake him. The phone rang off before he could answer it. He was shocked when he picked it up and saw that it was almost 12 o'clock, surely he couldn't have been that tired, he thought to himself. He had over a half a dozen missed calls from Father Ignacio. Wiping the sleep from his eyes he tried to compose himself, his mouth was as dry as the desert and his head was pounding.

Whatever Father Ignacio wanted it must be of some importance so once he was a bit more alert he rang the Padre back.

'Good afternoon Father, I see you have been trying to get hold of me. Sorry I have only just seen your missed calls.'

'Good is not the term I would use Professor Hart. The Vatican has been robbed. The *Black Dragon Scroll* is missing. We would very much appreciate it if both you and Miss Adams would come into the Vatican, as you were the last people to view the scroll.'

'I hope you are not suggesting that we had anything to do with it, Father.'

'At this stage it is just routine, but we cannot rule out the possibility.'

'Well we will certainly give you as much assistance as possible. We will be there as soon as we can.' Dillon hung up; his mind was now a mess of thoughts. 'Carla!' He shouted from the bedroom. There was no reply.

Dillon quickly dressed and hurried downstairs to see where she was. He searched the whole villa but couldn't find her. She had vanished along with all of her things. 'Oh Carla, what have you done?' He thought as it dawned on him that she may have taken it and left him floundering in the bathwater.

It was several hours later that Dillon was finally allowed to leave the Head of Security's office at the Vatican. He felt absolutely drained; they had questioned him until his head felt numb.

There was really very little information that he could give them about the girl that he had employed as his assistant and they took a great deal of convincing that he had not known what she was up to. He felt utterly dejected, his clearance to the *Archivum Secretum Apostolicum Vaticanum* had been revoked and he was very unlikely to ever get it back, which meant that his thesis now lay in tatters. He was a broken man.

Chapter Twenty Eight: Noirmont

Carla's journey back from Rome had been uneventful; she had drugged Dillon to ensure he would not wake until long after she had departed, and was now returning triumphantly to Glympton Park with everything that she had been asked to retrieve and also with the knowledge that Victor's contact was very close to breaking Professor Middleton's coded notes.

Lord Norwood was in high spirits; everything was beginning to fall into place. Although Flack and his compatriots had managed to escape into the jungle without a trace, they had not resurfaced and he now not only possessed one of the fabled volumes of the *Liber Veritatis*, but also had the clue to finding the next one. He had spent the last few weeks since his return to Glympton studying the volume in his possession. A light knock on his study door momentarily broke his concentration.

'Enter.'

Carla pushed the door aside and strode through into the dimly lit room. 'My Lord, I hope I'm not disturbing you?'

'Not at all my dear. I trust you are well rested after your journey?'

'Very well, thank you. Have you come any closer to understanding how the book works?'

'Unfortunately, unlike those Templars centuries ago, the book has yet to reveal its secrets to me. From what I can ascertain the truth will only be revealed when the book is in the right place. The legend of the Templar's copy describes that it was in part of the Temple of Jerusalem when it revealed its text, so my conclusion is that it has to be in a house of God in order for it to be read. I have yet to test this theory. Has Victor's man deciphered Professor Middleton's notes yet?'

'I believe he has. He sent me a text to say that he was in the process of emailing it, but that the contents may not be what you expected. He wouldn't say more.'

'Knowing Professor Middleton as I do, that doesn't surprise me. He is a very crafty man, one who always speaks in riddles. So it may well be that it doesn't make sense straight away. Only time will tell.' Lord Norwood replied as he moved over to his computer to check if the email had been received. 'Ah yes here it is. Let's see what the good Professor has been up to.'

As Lord Norwood began to scroll through the text, the email clearly did not make for pretty reading. Carla could tell by the way his facial expression changed that Professor Middleton's notes had displeased him greatly.

'Damn that man; damn him to hell! This is the last time he interferes in our business.' He shouted before storming out of the room; leaving Carla alone in the study. His sudden outburst had taken her by surprise and peaked her curiosity. She could not resist reading what had sparked his rage. As soon as she began she immediately understood why his Lordship had had such an adverse reaction to it. The email read thus:

My Lord,

I have managed to decode the notes that Miss Adams sent to me; unfortunately I must report that the news is not good. In fact it looks like whoever wrote this expected it to be found and although it was written in code, it was not hard to crack; if anything that was the intention. I would go as far as to suggest that this note was specifically designed for your attention.

My Lord,

So sorry to have missed you, but I couldn't wait any longer. Don't worry I have made sure the 'Black Dragon Scroll' has been moved to a safe place, well out of your reach. Hope my version makes for entertaining reading. Must dash.

Sincerely,

Peter Middleton.

The rest of the notes are pretty much gibberish. Seems like he wrote them just to waste your time. I'm sorry that I could not give you better news.

Sergio.

Carla could not help but admire the sheer audacity of the professor. He was certainly bold, if not slightly foolish. She had seen what his Lordship could do when provoked, something this certainly had achieved.

Lord Norwood found Chamberlain in the security hut sorting out the weekly guard rota.

'Ah, Chamberlain there you are. Do your agents know the current whereabouts of Professor Middleton?'

'Yes My Lord. He was tracked to Jersey. I believe he has a residence there.'

'Good. That man has been allowed to meddle in my affairs for far too long. It's time to put an end to his tiresome interruptions. I want you to put together a team; we are going to pay him a visit. His son cannot help him now. We leave tonight.'

'Very good, My Lord.' Chamberlain replied as that malevolent smile gradually spread across his face.

The waters of the Bay of Biscay were like a heaving writhing mass of foaming white water and deep dark troughs; the wind whistled and howled across the tempestuous seascape. The *Aurora*, as massive as she was, struggled to keep her heading, continuously buffeted by the huge gusts from the worst storm to rage through for over a century. Unrelenting waves crashed across her bows, almost stopping her dead in her tracks, the ship's superstructure shuddered with each fresh blow. Even though the crew had spent quite some time, before the full force of the storm engulfed her, ensuring that everything on deck was lashed down securely. The best fittings available were no match for the pure awesome power of nature.

They watched in disbelief as one of the life rafts was ripped clean off the stern of the ship by a wave so large that it made the ship look like an infinitesimally small speck of flotsam feebly trying to stay together as it was tossed and turned; utterly helpless, isolated and at the mercy of the vast expanse of the deep blue.

The strength of the wind was so intense that whole sheets of spray were whipped up off the wave crests. There was nothing the ship could do but head deeper into the maelstrom, better the waves crashing over the bow than over the stern, swamping her and causing her to flounder let alone attempt to turn around; if a wave hit her side on she and all her crew would be lost.

The Captain had every confidence in her and knew that as long as they didn't get too close to land they would be fine. They would just have to battle through and bide their time until they could make landfall.

Ollie and Gaz were in their element; they loved the rough rollercoaster like ride on the storm-ridden seas.

'Here comes another one.' Ollie shouted to Gaz as another powerful wave crashed over the boat.

'This is epic. Bet you would get some real air off one of those.'

'Yeah, but you wouldn't be able to land it. You ain't no *Dr Spock.*' Ollie replied, referring to one of their windsurfing mates who had been nicknamed *Dr Spock* after becoming the first person on the island of Minorca to master the freestyle move known as a Spock.

'Like you could do better, *Professor Catapult.*'

'Well at least I know I would get some air.'

'Not really sure that is quite the same thing.'

Unlike the two young adrenaline junkies Rachel and Devan were both embracing a totally different set of feelings, they had not found their sea legs, with every lurch of the boat their queasiness deepened. Experience had taught them that the sea state was far too rough to run outside and hurl over the side.

The one and only time they had tried this they had been caught by a freak wave that had left them with that horrible feeling of saltwater streaming out of their nostrils and a distinct salty taste of the sea in their mouths which if anything made them feel even worse. So they had to make sure that they were in dashing distance of one of the heads. Even Chris who had done a fair bit of sailing had to admit that the storm was testing his limits of sea worthiness.

The Captain announced over the intercom that the ship was about to round the Brittany Peninsular, and he expected the waters should become slightly calmer once they rounded it and got to the lee side and that he expected the storm to dissipate within the next few hours.

To Rachel and Devan a few hours seemed like weeks. They felt thoroughly drained by the time the wind abated, although even then it brought them little comfort as the sea state was still a topsy-turvy mess and would take a few more hours for it to settle down.

'How are you girls holding up?' Chris enquired as he appeared from the galley with a steaming bowl of soup.

Rachel was about to answer but the wafting smell of food immediately made her feel sick and she lurched past him, hand clapped firmly over her mouth. Alas, she didn't quite make it to the head and she struggled desperately to hold back the vomit, which inevitably sprayed out between her tightly clenched fingers.

She felt there was nothing worse than that feeling of warm watery sick running between ones fingers, causing you to tear up, let alone that acidic aftertaste which always seemed to leave a burning sensation in ones mouth and nose.

The dusk was fast closing in as the ship finally came into the waters around Jersey. Not that the *Aurora* was that noticeable from the shore, a dense mist had begun to settle around the port and so her many onboard lights combined into a ghostly whitish glow through the gloom.

Although the lop on the water had reduced, the port was far too full of vessels that had sought refuge from the storm to enable the *Aurora* to dock, she therefore had to hold station to the west of Elisabeth Castle until the captain could find a suitable place to anchor.

'Sorry folks, but this is as close as the captain can go at the moment. We will have to drop a tender over the stern and ferry you across. I'm afraid you may get a touch wet.' Jack said to his newfound companions.

'Not to worry, you have done us proud, Jack. We are so grateful; without you we would still be stuck in Belize.' James replied.

'My pleasure, you have done more than enough for me. Getting those vultures off my back is very much appreciated. I wish you well for the rest of your quest. If you ever need anything you know how to get in touch.'

'Thanks, Jack' Chris said shaking him warmly by the hand. 'It's been a pleasure, if a little more eventful than we had anticipated.'

'Jack, can I ask a favour? Instead of landing us at the harbour, could your tender could run us straight up on to the beach below Noirmont? It's well positioned in the lee of the headland so should be easy and may save a bit of time. We may get wet feet but think we will be pretty wet already by the time we get there.' James asked as he gave his final farewell to their host.

'That makes a lot of sense, also means we don't have to hang around here for too long. I'll let the helm know. He's not that familiar with the island so you may have to point him in the right direction.'

'No problem, I grew up here, so could find it blindfolded, but it's really difficult to miss.' James said pointing at the glow of lights on the peninsular to the west of the *Aurora*.

'Sounds like the launch is ready.'

Boarding the launch from the bathing platform at the stern of the ship they were soon blasting their way across the small bay to the beach below the great house of Noirmont.

The gently shelving sandy beach was perfect to allow the RIB to run her bows straight up on to the sand. Once all had disembarked, Gaz and Ollie helped to push her out into deep enough water for the helm to reverse out, and shoot back across the bay to the mother ship.

They stayed on the shore for a while and watched the *Aurora* gradually disappear into the gloom, a final long blast from her foghorn signalled her farewell before the thick mist engulfed her from view.

'I suspect dad was expecting us to make our way from the harbour so maybe a bit of a surprise for him to see us coming up from the beach.' James said as they began to wander up from the beach. 'Ah, this is new.' He added as he spied the code lock on the beach gate.

'I'm presuming you don't know the code in that case.' Rachel said through chattering teeth, as the cold wind swirled around her.

'No, but knowing my father I reckon I can probably guess. Reckon it will be 1309.'

'Why's that?'

'It's the earliest record of the family on the island from the roll of assizes.'

'Yeah that sounds about right for your father.' Chris added with just the hint of sarcasm.

James' guess turned out to be correct and after locking the wooden gate behind them they continued up the beach road to the manor house.

They were warmly greeted by Peter Middleton, who realising they were all rather wet and cold ushered them into the old kitchen where there was a roaring wood burning stove on the go, plying them with hot cocoa and crumpets oozing with butter.

'Glad to see you made it in one piece. I was beginning to wonder whether you would arrive today, such has been the ferocity of the recent storm.'

'Well it was a little touch and go for a while. Any news from Michael and Louis?'

'They should arrive tomorrow, obviously the ferries have been postponed for the last few days. I take it from your method of arrival that things did not quite go to plan in Central America?'

'Norwood intercepted us and took the book.'

'Ah that is unfortunate but not unforeseen. At least you are all okay. He won't be able to use it yet and I'm sure he will be fretting over something else by now.'

'What have you done, father?'

'Oh, I just removed a scroll from the Vatican for safe keeping which he needed in order to find the next volume. Don't worry I left him a note to say it was safe.'

'Was that wise? He and his organisation have a habit of dishing out retributions upon those who meddle too much.'

'Ha, they don't scare me. Moreover they would have to find me first and I was very careful to leave the mainland quietly.'

'I wouldn't get too cocky, father. We thought we were careful and were duly punished for underestimating them.'

'Oh tosh, Norwood is a fool.'

'He may be, but a dangerous one nonetheless.'

'I would have to agree with your son's assessment. Norwood is not somebody to be taken lightly. He and his organisation have a lot of resources at their disposal.' Chris interjected knowing full well that James seldom agreed with his father and could see that if he didn't step in it would turn into a full-blown argument. 'How about you take the professor off to have a look at your research, I'm sure you two will have a lot to talk about.' Chris added trying to diffuse the situation.

'Yes I would very much like that, and I can show you the map.' Devan said, she had been eager to have the opportunity to pick the learned man's brains. She had hoped he would be able to help her make sense of the remainder of the map.

'Sounds like a plan; it will give the rest of us time to sort out some supplies. Is my gear still in the same place?'

'Well unless you've moved it, I can't see why it shouldn't be. You wouldn't believe the amount of times he can't find things and blames me for moving them and it always turns up right where he last left them. So disorganised it's a wonder he finds anything.' Professor Middleton retorted.

'Like your study is any better.'

Peter Middleton chose not to answer this final jibe and took Devan off to his study to discuss archaeological things that would have sent James to sleep.

The others headed off with James to sort out some kit, before turning into bed later on that night.

Chapter Twenty Nine: Trust and Betrayal

Lord Norwood was accompanied by Chamberlain and four burly men to deal with Professor Middleton, they had packed as if they were going on a winter's fishing expedition around Jersey, although their tackle boxes had far more dangerous tools than a few hooks and lures concealed within. They sat huddled together in a small booth in the cafeteria of the ferry discussing how they would get into Noirmont and what they would do with Professor Middleton. As much as Lord Norwood had liked the idea of killing the man, the Grand Master had over-ruled him, pointing out that Professor Middleton had a great deal of information that they could use to their advantage not only about the *Liber Veritatis* but also about *The Order of Pepin* whom they had been locked in bloody conflict with for centuries over the possession of the codex. Although they knew of the existence of *The Order* they had never until recently managed to infiltrate it and still didn't know much about their overall structure, it seemed as though they might be made up of individual cells operating in complete autonomy from one another. The Grand Master knew the history surrounding *The Order's* disappearance during the purge of the Templars. And that a family called *Pipon* seemed to be at the heart of it, the name *Pipon* came from the French *pipeur* meaning trickster. He said they had done this in jest of having managed to evade the King of France. 'The greatest trick the devil ever pulled was to make people believe that he didn't exist. It took us centuries to realise that they had managed to evade us.' He had said.

Begrudgingly Norwood had agreed to capture and interrogate Professor Middleton instead of killing him. Looking out from the booth Lord Norwood's interest was peaked by two men in deep conversation. He overheard one of them mention Flack by name.

'Those men are with Flack. We should make a move back to our vehicle. Quietly now, we don't want to draw attention.' He said in a low voice to the other men around the table.

'The ferry should be docking in about 20 minutes.' Norwood overheard Louis saying to Michael as he ducked past them. 'We should get these coffees and head back to the Landy.'

'Tidy, shudd arrive at Noirmont by about nine.' Michael replied glancing at his watch.

'Just in time for supper.'

Chamberlain followed the Land Rover off the ferry and down the narrow Jersey lanes making sure he didn't get too close to the car in front as they wound their way around the wiggly coastal lanes towards Noirmont. He watched the 4x4 turn off down the lane to the manor house but instead of following, he drove straight on past and pulled off on to the grassy verge about 500 metres further up the road, switching off the headlights as he parked the vehicle.

Louis and Michael pulled in through the gates at Noirmont and parked the Land Rover to the side of the main house.

'It's good to see you again, sir.' Louis said as Peter Middleton answered their knock at the door. 'May I introduce Michael Collins?'

'Nice to meet you at last Michael. Hope you had a good journey down, despite the weather holding up the ferry. Come in, come in. No need to stand on ceremony here. Louis you've been here before, you'll find the others in the drawing room. Let me just hang your coats up.' The friendly old professor said as he disappeared off to the boot room with their jackets. As much as he coveted his privacy, the professor really enjoyed entertaining the odd guest once in a while.

'See where James gets his mannerisms from now.' Michael said as they made their way down the corridor to the drawing room.

There was a great deal of hugs and embraces as the two entered the room, after all this was the first time they had all been reunited for over six weeks and so much had happened since they had all been together that it was quite some time before James got round to offering them a drink after their long disjointed journey.

Their celebrations however were soon cut short by the sound of the doorbell ringing.

'Are we expecting company?' James asked his father.

'Not that I'm aware of. But the old dear next door does pop in from time to time in the evening.'

'I don't buy it. Dad, do you still keep the gun cabinet unlocked?'

'Of course, if I had to keep unlocking it every time I saw a blasted squirrel trying to steal the nuts from the bird feeder, the bloody things would be long gone by the time I had a chance to have a pop at them. Bloody pesky little vermin, keep stripping all the bark off my pine trees as well.'

'Where are the cartridges?'

'Box in the cabinet, but they should already be loaded.'

'Really? Lucky the firearms officer hasn't done an inspection then.' James replied, raising an eyebrow as if to say 'are you for real'?

'Oh that man doesn't know what he's talking about. Cabinet's always locked when I'm not here.'

'Not sure that's really the point, is it? No time for this discussion now. Chris you know where the cabinet is. Take Ollie and get the shotguns, might be a revolver or two in there as well. Dad, stay here. I'll get the door.' James added.

'Ah, so nice of you to pay us a visit Your Lordship.' James said in an overly loud voice to ensure that Chris heard; buying his friend a little more time to prepare for what was likely to ensue.

'You two in there and take this.' Chris said handing the two girls a revolver and hurriedly pushing them into the small reading room attached to the drawing room. 'Don't open the door, no matter what happens.' He added, as he continued to keep an ear on James' attempt at banterish small talk with their nemesis.

'If you had telephoned in advance we could have laid places for you.' James was saying to Norwood.

'We weren't planning on staying that long and I doubt you will be around for any great period either. But, enough of your humour.' Lord Norwood replied concealing his frustration at the reappearance of James. 'I assume Captain Flack and Co are all here as well. In a way, as much as this is a surprise, it is actually rather nice to have you all together again. Inside.' Lord Norwood said waving the revolver he held. 'Come out Captain, slowly I know you and your colleagues are here somewhere.' He continued as he strode into the Manor behind James and followed him into the drawing room.

Chris, Louis and Michael stood in the centre of the room holding pump action 12 bores. Whilst Ollie and Gaz had used James' delaying tactics to sneak down the back stairs and come up behind Norwood's men.

'Looks like we have a stalemate, My Lord.'

'Oh, I don't think so.' Norwood replied with a sinister smile.

'He's right Chris put the gun down.' Michael said as he turned and pointed his gun at Chris' temple.

'Michael, what are you doing?'

'Summin I shudda done a long time ago. Drop you guns.' Michael said to Ollie and Gaz as he continued to keep his shotgun trained on Chris. 'I swear if you dunna, I'll drill his head so fulla holes you can use it as a sieve.'

'Do as he says, boys.' Chris said. 'Now I understand where they have been getting their information from.'

'Yeah, binna entertaining time watching all of yer futile scheming and plotting. I had always hoped to be here at your end. I wan'ed to have a badgers at the looks on your faces when you realised who had royally screwed you.'

'You're a dead man.' James defiantly said looking Michael straight in the eyes.

'Inna the way it looks to me, Mon, it's you who's gonna die, James. You always thought you were so clever. Tinna what you were expecting, is it Mon? On your knees! No, not you Professor Middleton, we have other plans for you, you can watch your son meet his maker.'

'No, it isn't. But I swear to God, you're fucking dead, Mon.' James said, deliberately throwing the colloquialism back at the Salopian to emphasise his point.

'You're making a mistake Norwood; kill them and you will never get the book.' Professor Middleton interjected.

'Ah yes the book. Where is it? I presume it is here and the map. I understand there is a map. Chamberlain, find it.' James pursed his lips at the mention of the map; he had hoped that Michael would have forgotten to tell them about the map.

'The map is on his study desk.' Michael said. 'I heard him talking about it earlier.'

'Very good, Michael. You have done well.'

'I've found the book, My Lord. It was hidden, and not very well I might add, in his bookcase.' Chamberlain said as he reappeared from the study after a few minutes of tossing the room.

'Father!' James exclaimed.

'What? They always say it's best to hide things in plain view.'

'Really, of all the things to do. How could you be so simplistic? Sometimes you really are beyond belief.'

'Well it seemed like a good idea at the time.'

Rachel had been listening through the reading room door. Luckily Michael had overlooked her and Devan so far; as James began to argue with his father she judged that Norwood and his men would be distracted by the family spat and choosing her moment carefully, when the argument became particularly heated, she burst through the door and ploughed her full force straight into Michael knocking him to the ground, James drove up from his kneeling position on the floor into the massive figure of Chamberlain. He knew that he couldn't match him for brute force but he caught the man off guard and they both tumbled to the ground.

Ollie and Gaz had already engaged themselves with two of the others. Lord Norwood had turned on his heels as the skirmish broke out and was halfway to the front door by the time Chris caught up with him.

Chris dodged his first backwards shot and flung himself at the man. But Norwood was ready for him and turned his flying body into the side of a wardrobe, reducing it to a pile of splintered shards as it collapsed under full force of Chris' diving body. Chris caught hold of Norwood's foot as he attempted to kick him in the head and flicked him over on to his back, causing Norwood to loose the revolver and send it spinning across the polished wooden hallway.

A number of gun shots from the drawing room signalled that some of the men had managed to get to the loose weapons on the floor, but Chris couldn't tell which side had them. There was a sound of shattering glass as one of Norwood's men took the option of escape by diving straight through a pane of glass, as James and Gaz began to gain the upper hand in the skirmish in the drawing room. The shots Chris had heard were from James gunning down two of their assailants.

Chamberlain and Michael had followed their comrade out of the broken window. Norwood having dropped his revolver, managed to plant a firm kick to Chris' head as he landed on his back, before wriggling free of Chris' grasping hand to escape through the front door.

There was no point in following after them as they could have gone off in any number of directions.

'Is everybody okay?' James asked as he surveyed the chaotic scene that had been the drawing room.

'I think so.' Replied Rachel.

'I thought I told you to stay in that room and not to come out no matter what.' James said staring at her.

'I'm perfectly capable of looking after myself. And besides you looked like you needed some help.' She replied stubbornly. 'Where is your father?'

'I think I saw him heading to the study as the fight broke out.'

'Dad, dad, it's okay they've gone. It's safe to come out now.' James called out, before going to find his father.

The scene that James took in as he entered the study was like something out of his worst nightmares. His father was slumped over his desk, there was a growing pool of deep red blood covering part of the desk and dripping on to the floor.

'Dad! Dad!' James cried out as he tried to shake the man back into consciousness. 'Rachel, call an ambulance. Dad's been shot. He must have been caught by a stray bullet.' James exclaimed as he felt for a pulse. 'He's still alive. Looks like it caught him in the shoulder. Get me some towels. Ollie put pressure here.' James instructed as his mind raced through all of his battlefield medical training.

Having managed to stem the bleeding with whatever they could find in the house, they had an agonisingly long wait until the ambulance arrived, accompanied by the police.

James accompanied his father in the ambulance to the hospital. The others stayed behind at the manor, as the police had insisted that they needed to remain behind to give statements as to what had happened.

They had all agreed prior to the police's arrival that the story should be that it was an attempted armed robbery gone wrong. Professor Middleton had a very valuable collection of silverware in the house and obviously the thieves had not expected for him to have guests.

James returned to Noirmont two days later, he was a shadow of the man that Rachel had first met, suffering from sleep derivation having stayed awake by his father's bedside since the shooting. He hadn't wanted to leave but it was clear to all that if he did not get some rest soon, he

284

was in danger of making himself ill. At first he had resisted them and it was only when Gaz volunteered to remain at the hospital that James caved to their concerned demands and returned to Noirmont. Professor Middleton had undergone emergency surgery for the gunshot as soon as he had arrived at the hospital and now lay in an induced coma in the ICU. There had been complications during the surgery, he had developed a blood clot on the brain and suffered a stroke. It was now a waiting game to see if he would recover or not.

The rage that James felt was almost overwhelming to the extent that he could not even maintain a conversation for more than a few minutes, not that anybody really tried to engage him. The people around him knew that conversation was the last thing to attempt to take his mind off recent events. James had never felt so utterly helpless in all his life. Whatever had possessed Michael to commit such an act of betrayal James could not fathom at the present moment, and he would need some time for the events of that night to fully sink in. He knew that the next time he saw Michael would be the last. There would be no hesitations, no second chances. He wouldn't even ask for an explanation. Michael would die a very painful death at his hands. Nevertheless at this precise moment what he felt like doing was to find the nearest tree, wall or inanimate object that he could take his rage out on. In times past an inanimate object would have been replaced by picking a fight with a complete random stranger in a bar. But considering all the training he had received and the severity of the betrayal that now fuelled his anger this was not an option. James knew that in his current frame of mind, he would not be able to hold back and once he started punching he wouldn't be able to stop until he no longer had the strength to lift his arms, by which time the unfortunate stranger would have long departed this world. Making up his mind James stood up from the brown leather armchair he had been slumped in and walked off into his father's study at Noirmont.

Chris had mentioned that Professor Middleton had obviously realised that he had been potentially mortally wounded and had been in the process of writing something down on a scrap of paper on the desk. Knowing his father, it was more than likely to be a clue leading to the next part of the codex. The sight of the study made him shudder as he entered; the leather on the desk still bore the fresh stain of his father's blood.

He turned on the reading lamp on the desk and looked at the blood-spattered note covered with his father's familiar scrawl.

May you be as the mountains and the hills, as the greater and the lesser heights, as the streams which flow in all directions, having the constancy of the moon, like the rising sun, with the longevity of the southern mountain and the green luxuriance of the fir and the cypress. Amongst tiger paws, sunflower seeds and weeping willows you will find that which you seek.

In typical fashion, his father had left him with a riddle. The situation he now found himself in appeared to be as bleak and unforgiving as that of the view from the study window out across the rolling breakers of the wind swept bay. James watched as one of the largest crashed into a rocky outcrop from the cliffs below erupting into a brilliant burst of white, he wondered what it had all been for?

The Glove now possessed both books and the map. And to add insult to injury, his father lying on death's door, had left him with nothing but yet another cryptic message. Where would it all end? James' rage flared again, scrunching up the paper in his fist he threw it against the opposite wall with such force that it ricocheted back, and landed spinning on the desk. 'Of all the irony.' He thought. But his mind was now made up and without saying a word to his friends he left the house and walked off to one of the outbuildings.

The building was seldom used; apart from to store his father's most prized possession, an AC Cobra 427. One of only 44 produced for the British market. He had fond memories of helping his father to restore it during his childhood, probably the only time when he and his father had actually got on and spent quality time together.

Almost all of the inside of the building was covered in thick layers of cobwebs and dust that had built up over the passage of time, the only thing that showed signs of cleanliness was a large dark blue canvas tarp draped over the car. James threw back the tarp to reveal the sleek lines of the deep metallic blue car before walking over to a padlocked small rusty grey cabinet mounted on the wall at the far side of the building. He had long since lost the key for the lock; not that this was going to deter him. He picked up an iron bar lying close to the cabinet and wrenched the lock from the front. Plucking the car keys from it, he turned and jumped into the driver's seat.

The loud roar of the V8 engine shattered the stillness of the night as the car burst into life and before anybody in the house could react to the snarling engine baying for vengeance, James tore off down the lanes towards the ferry port.

Chapter Thirty: Unfinished Business

DI Harris sat at his desk, as he had been for the last two months, still pouring through the reams of historical documents that the College of Arms had sent over containing even the smallest of references to *The Order of Pepin*, the *Pipon* family and the mysterious holy relic that seemed to be at the heart of his new line of enquiry. He was becoming increasingly concerned that the case was in danger of going cold. The DNA evidence that had been gathered from the Mount had drawn a blank on the national database. The historical documents he had managed to read so far had provided some fresh leads to living descendants of the *Pipon* family, but after further investigation none of them could have been involved in the shootings. His normally up-beat attitude was wearing thin. Even his wife had commented that he might just have to let this one go or he was in danger of running himself into the ground. He would leave home for work in the same exhausted manner that he would return, a recipe that in her opinion was not at all healthy. But she knew what he was like and that once he had the bit between his teeth he would stop at nothing in his quest for truth and justice.

Rubbing his tired strained eyes he was in the process of reaching for the next folio from the Rogue Croix Pursuivant, when the phone on his desk rang.

'Hello DI Harris speaking.'

'Glen, do you ever answer your mobile, or read emails come to that.' Asked the now familiar voice of Becky.

'Ah, I must have forgotten to charge it last night, and I haven't checked the emails yet today. Why? What's happened?'

'I've been trying to get hold of you all morning. There's been a development which I think you will be interested in.'

'To do with my case?'

'Yes, the National Ballistic Intelligence Service, have had a ballistics' match between one of the bullets found at the Mount and one used in a recent armed robbery in Jersey.'

'That's fantastic news, I had started to think that NABIS had forgotten about me. When did this happen?'

'Three days ago, but obviously it has taken them a few days to finish the tests. From what I understand it was a botched armed robbery.'

'Whereabouts in Jersey? I have tenuous links between my case and Jersey.'

'A place called Noirmont.'

'Noirmont, that name sounds familiar. I'm sure I have come across that name mentioned in some of the documents I've been reading. Fuck, I just can't remember which one. I have so many folders here.'

'Glen, chill out. It's only a ballistics' match, that gun could have been re-circulated a dozen times since the shooting at the Mount.'

'Yeah, but the odds on it being used at another location with which there are links to this case is highly improbable, if not part of the same case. Tell them I'm coming out there ASAP.'

'Okay I'll let them know, but don't get your hopes up.' Becky replied before hanging up.

Glen felt reinvigorated with the news of the potential break in the case; his adrenaline was running so quickly that he almost forgot to inform the Super of the good news as his mind raced to work out the quickest way to get to Jersey.

'Boss, NABIS have a ballistics match to my case, in Jersey.'

'So what are you still doing here? Go! Go! Get a flight from Exeter. I'll get my secretary to make the arrangements. You'll be on the next flight out. Come on boy get going; God knows how long you've been waiting for this.'

Glen didn't need to be told twice, he dashed out of the building and hit the road to Exeter like a man possessed.

The next seven hours of travelling seemed to pass by in a blur before Glen's flight finally touched down on the small runway at Jersey

Airport. Upon departing the plane he headed straight for the Hertz depot at the airport to organise some form of transport. He knew that Jersey police would have been more than happy to drive him around but he not only wanted to maintain some independence but to also keep a low profile whilst he carried out his investigations on the island.

It was late in the evening by the time that Glen had sorted out a car and checked into a B&B in St Helier. As much as he wanted to start his enquiries straight away he conceded that it was far too late in the day to do anything productive.

The ballistics report wasn't going anywhere so Noirmont could wait until the morning. Wherever the hell that was hidden on this tiny tax haven.

After arranging to have breakfast at 7am with the proprietor, he crashed for the night. Tomorrow was going to be the first of several long days and as hungry as he was; sleep had finally caught up with him, no sooner had his head hit the soft feather pillow, he drifted off into the land of slumber.

Glen awoke early the following morning feeling refreshed. It had been the first proper night's sleep he'd had for a long time. In fact he hadn't had as good a night since before this case had crossed his desk. Maybe it was down to the comfort of the quaint little B&B or more likely due to the fact that his stress levels had receded considerably after the news had reached him of the ballistics match, the first real step forward in the case for some time. Either way he felt much more like his former self.

Having breakfasted, his first port of call was to the States of Jersey Police HQ, just a short drive from where he was staying.

Parking his car, Glen made his way to reception. A desk sergeant that ironically resembled the one back in Penzance greeted him; Glen couldn't resist a small smile as he noticed the similarity.

'Good Morning, my names DI Glen Harris from Penzance. Could I please speak to the inspector in charge of the shooting that occurred at Noirmont?'

'Ah, yes. We've been expecting you. Can I just ask to see your warrant card?'

'Sure, suppose one can't be too careful these days.'

'Yeah, got to hate the formality of procedure sometimes. Thanks everything looks in order. Just bear with me a moment I'll just ring DCI Carline, who's been overseeing the investigation. Would you like a coffee while you wait?'

'Coffee would be great, milk and two for me. Cheers man.'

The desk sergeant rang through to DCI Carline to inform him of Glen's arrival and then disappeared into a back room to make the coffee.

Glen didn't have long to wait for DCI Carline to make his way over from his office down to reception.

'DI Harris pleased to meet you. I hope you had a good trip over.' The DCI said as they shook hands.

'Same, yeah trip was okay, if a little cramped. Those small planes aren't really designed for my height.'

'Ha, yes they are a little on the intimate side of things. Come into my office and I'll give you an overview of our case. Not sure how much help it will be. This one looks to be pretty cut and dried.'

'Really? I understood there were two fatalities and one seriously injured during the attempted raid.'

'Well yes, but it is quite clear from the evidence that this was an attempted robbery gone awry. It was the proprietor who was seriously injured and is still in an induced coma at Jersey General. The evidence clearly supports the witness statements that there was a struggle between the guests and the armed robbers, and that during the confusion guns went of resulting in two armed assailants dead and Professor Middleton fighting for his life.

Of course there will have to be an inquest but I'm sure the findings will rule in favour of lawful killings due to self-defence. To be honest it was very lucky for the professor that he had company that evening, otherwise I think the outcome would have been a much different story. We have seen this sort of thing before, mainland gangs targeting the rich on Jersey, after all we are a tax haven and do attract that type of resident.

I would have thought that this would tally quite nicely from what I know of your own case. Armed gang targeting a historically wealthy family.'

'Maybe, there are a few avenues that are still open. These events may help to focus our direction a bit. I don't suppose you have managed to track down the rest of the perps yet?'

'Unfortunately not, that's the only part of the case which is still on-going. Most likely they have already departed the island by now. We had pretty tight security around the ferries and the aircraft leaving for the mainland for the last 48 hours and will continue to do so for a few more days yet, but there are other ways off the island if one really wants to leave.

'I suppose there may be the possibility that they are hiding out on the island, waiting until the heat dies down, but I think this is highly unlikely. Jersey is a very small close island community and outsiders tend to stick out like a dildo in a sock draw. Forgive my rather crude analogy, but you get the point. Any gang with the moxie to pull this off or even attempt it would know that they would want to get off the island as soon as possible, the longer they are here the more likely it would become that they would be caught.'

'Yeah, I see what you mean. Any chance I can have a list of the guests that were present at Noirmont? I should like to have a chat with them if that's possible?'

'Sure, I believe they are all still at the house helping out whilst Professor Middleton recovers in hospital, if he ever does. Would you like us to ask them to come down to the station?'

'No, an informal chat would be better I think. How do I get to Noirmont from here?'

'Oh it's easy enough from here, just take the A1 to St Aubin, and then get on to the A13, take a left after about a mile on to the B57, the manor is just off on the left before you get to Battery Lothringen in St Brélande. Shouldn't take more than about 20 minutes from here. Let me just get you the list. Oh, and if you find anything related to our case you will pass it on, won't you?'

'Yeah, no worries. You scratch my back, I'll scratch yours right.'

Now furnished with the list of all the guests, Glen left the States of Jersey Police and began his short journey out to the rocky peninsular of Noirmont Point.

Glen almost followed the directions to the letter, nevertheless when the road abruptly ended in front of a giant concrete structure erupting out of the cliffs towering above the open expanse of the deep blue he realised that he had missed the turning to Noirmont Manor and had ended up at the Battery. Before he turned around he took a moment to take in the immense architecture of the fortifications; the Nazis had built them to prevent the British from recapturing the Island. They certainly were impressive if a dark reminder of a period when the British had forsaken the islanders. Ironically the Nazi forces on the island were the last soldiers to surrender, a whole three weeks after the official German surrender, evidently someone had forgotten to tell them the War was over.

Not intending to forget why he was on the island Glen spun the car around and retraced his last few tracks, keeping a close eye out for the turning that would now be on the right. No wonder he missed it, the DCI hadn't said it was a crossroads, he took the right turn on to *Le Chemin de Belcroute* leading down to the manor hidden amongst the dense woodland.

The great black arched gates were an imposing sight for Glen as he drove off the main road, down the drive to the ancient house. The significance of the armorial crest atop the centre of the arch was not lost on Glen. He knew he must be on the right track as he noticed the nut-wielding squirrel standing proudly over the entrance.

He was beginning to feel that the tricky little mammal was almost taunting him, getting his hopes up that he was almost at the end of his puzzle only to have his hopes dashed yet again. Maybe this was just another dead-end within the maze? He would find out soon enough.

Chris heard the car pull up on the gravel outside just before Glen's knock at the door.

'We are popular at the moment, aren't we?' He said to Gaz.

'Yeah, but a little too popular for my liking, well better go see what they want.' Gaz replied as he got up from a chair in the kitchen and went to answer the door.

'Good morning.' Gaz warmly said as he greeted this newcomer 'How can I help you?'

'Morning, I'm DI Harris from Penzance. I was hoping to speak to James Middleton.' Glen replied, having seen the name on the list provided by DCI Carline, and making the connection that he must be a relative of the currently comatose Peter Middleton.

'I'm afraid he isn't here at the moment.'

'Oh, when is he likely to return? Mr ... Sorry I didn't catch your name.'

'Gareth. Unfortunately you have just missed him.' Gaz replied attempting to avoid the question of James' whereabouts.

'That wouldn't be Gareth Hargreaves by any chance would it?'

'Yes, as a matter of fact. I would ask how you knew but I think I already know the answer to that. Anything I can help with in James' absence?'

'I was hoping to speak to people present at the attempted robbery a few night's ago.'

'Apart from James, and his father obviously, we are all here. But isn't this a little out of your jurisdiction, being from Penzance, if you don't mind me saying? I thought the State of Jersey Police were investigating the incident?'

'Well, yes they are. I'm here because of a related case in Cornwall.'

'Interesting, well you had best come in then.'

Chris had been eavesdropping on the conversation going on at the front door; he quickly made his way to join Devan, Rachel and Ollie in the drawing room just before Gaz invited this new detective inside.

'DI Harris, this is Chris, Rachel, Devan and Ollie. The detective here is from Penzance, apparently there is a link between what occurred here and something that happened in Penzance.' Chris didn't require this extra piece of info, as soon as DI Harris had walked in he had immediately recognised the detective, whom he had seen in newspaper articles and at the funeral of Jack St Aubyn. Chris knew exactly which case it was linked to but didn't show any sign of recognition as the tall dark detective had entered the room.

'Nice to meet you detective, long way from home.' Chris said taking the lead in the conversation.

'Yeah is a fair step to be sure.'

'How can we assist you? And would you like a drink.'

'Coffee would be great, thanks man. I was hoping I could run through the events of what happened here at the manor.'

'No problem at all, but I'm not sure if we can add anything to what we have already told the Police here. I presume you have seen our statements prior to your arrival.'

'Sure, but I always think it's best to get these things first hand if possible, you never know what piece of info that may seem trivial. A beat cop here might not pick up on.'

'You have an interesting accent, if you don't mind me saying. Your not originally from the UK are you?'

'Nah, born in Portugal, dad was from The States.'

'How did you end up in the UK?'

'Mum was from the UK, Newcastle in fact. Always wanted to settle down here.'

'Personally I think I would have stayed in Portugal.'

'Yeah, can get a bit nostalgic sometimes 'specially when it's cold. So pretty much all the time.' Glen jokingly added. ' But on the whole I like the life here. So what brought you guys here?'

'Was a bit of a reunion of sorts, and a get away from work. Professor Middleton kindly invited us to stay. We are all long standing family friends.'

'What do you do for work?'

'Well, Devan here is an archaeologist and the rest of us are consultants.'

'I see nice and you didn't recognise any of the assailants?'

'No, to be honest it all happened so quickly; one minute we were about to sit down for dinner and the next armed men were forcing entry into the house, so we didn't really get the chance. I remember one of them was massive, that is to say he was built like a brick. Apart from him I can't really give you a great description of any of them.'

'No worries, was a bit of a long shot anyway.'

'If you don't mind me asking what is the link between the two cases?'

'Similar MO and a ballistics match, obviously I can't give you the details of my case.'

'Interesting, so you think that it may be the same people responsible for both crimes?'

'It's a possibility. What do you know of the *Pipon* family?' Glen asked, trying to drop the hammer and gauge the reaction to the name.

'Never heard of them.'

'Really? Isn't it their crest on the gates here?'

'To be honest I don't know much about the history of this place. James' father bought it in the late sixties, I think. But I couldn't tell you anything about who owned it before that. What's the connection?'

'Oh it's not of any importance, I have a personal curiosity with Jersey history. Just wondered if you knew anything about them. Where is James Middleton by the way?'

'I couldn't tell you, he didn't say where he was going only that he had some urgent unfinished business on the mainland that couldn't wait, even in these circumstances life must go on.'

'Yeah I know what you mean. Have you ever been to Penzance?'

'No, spent time in Polzeath and Truro as a boy but never had the opportunity to go to Penzance. Why do you ask?'

'Oh, you just seem familiar that's all. I wondered if I'd passed you in the street at some point.'

'Ha, must just have one of those faces.'

'Do you have a contact number for James, I would like to speak to him at some point.'

'I do as it happens but it appears that in his haste to resolve his business he left his phone behind, so not sure it will be of much use to you.'

'That's too bad, would have been good to have his input.' Glen replied, thinking to himself that Chris was going to run him round and round in circles. He could tell there was more going on than Chris was letting on and certain answers just didn't add up, and really who leaves their phone behind when they have urgent business to conduct whilst your father is in a coma? ' Well thanks for the coffee and the info; it's been enlightening to talk to you; I may be in touch again and if you do think of anything else here's my number.' Glen said handing Chris his card.

'Certainly, and feel free to drop by unannounced at anytime.'

'Oh what does James do by the way?'

'He's recently retired.'

'From what?'

'You'll have to ask him that, I never really did understand his work.'

'Well thanks anyway. Sorry for disturbing you at this time.'

'Don't mention it, anytime.'

'And if you do manage to contact James, please let him know I'm after him.'

'Sure, will do. Thank you again detective. Hope you have a safe journey back to Penzance. It's been a real pleasure.' Chris replied, knowing full well what implications the stressed emphasis DI Harris had just used on the words 'after him' meant.

'I don't like him. He was very clever in the way he probed. Think he may cause us some trouble in the future.' Chris said after Glen had left.

'You mean he reminds you of yourself. Do you think he knows about *The Order* and the Codex? He did mention the *Pipon* family by name.' Gaz asked.

'Possibly, I really hope not. That will be a big problem if he does. I think he's just trying to rattle cages and see what falls out.'

'You'd better warn James. I hope he's alright and not gone to do something rash.' Rachel said in a worried tone of voice.

'I think we all know deep down what he has gone to do. All we can hope for is that he covers his tracks well. Otherwise that DI will have a field day. I'll contact him later. That DI might be monitoring the phones,

I will have to send James a Facebook message, they've got end-to-end encryption. Harder for people like that DI to intercept.' Chris replied. 'And we better make a start on working out the meaning of that bloody riddle of Peter's. Shame we can't just ask him, bloody man never makes things easy does he?'

'Not to mention how we get the books and map back from Norwood.' Gaz dejectedly pointed out.

The winter rain poured down through the dark night's sky, falling heavily on to the old cobbled streets. The water formed mini rivers as it meandered through the gaps in between the cobbles. The old Victorian style street lamps, although now electrified, bathed the streets of the old town with a soft orange glow.

Most people had retreated inside since the downpour had started either returning to the comfort of their own homes or to the salubrious confines of one of the many bars that were dotted around the old town. Only the hardiest of the smokers intermittently braved the wetness for that much needed hit of nicotine.

If it wasn't for the occasional cherry like glow on the end of his cigarette and the wispy trail of smoke that followed, most people would not have noticed the tall man half concealed in the entrance to the narrow alleyway just off the main high street.

Clearly he had been standing there for quite some time as his normally light brown hair looked almost black due to the amount of water that had soaked it. Adjusting the collar of the long black overcoat, he dropped the butt on to the floor and snuck out of the shadows from where he had been observing the comings and goings of the locals. He had seen enough for one night; it was time for a drink. Almost twelve hours had gone by since any alcohol had passed his lips. He wouldn't consider that he had become an alcoholic since the events at Noirmont, but he knew he was certainly walking a very fine line. A line that every now and again became slightly blurred depending on how deeply the dark dreams that often plagued his periods of sleep tormented him. Dreams not only of that sight of his father bleeding out on to the desk but also of past deeds and memories that would continue to haunt him for much of his life. Consciously he could shut these out but once asleep they would relentlessly prevent him from completely forgetting his past. It was as if karma was punishing him, not only for previous actions but also for the darkness that still resided inside him. A darkness that he often struggled to control, he had always known that at some point it would re-emerge and that when it did he would be powerless to stop the devastation that would follow. Chaos that may only be resorted to order upon his death; what bothered him wasn't that he would only find total peace as he took his last breaths but that many people would suffer in the meantime.

Brushing the excess water from his eyes he strode off from his viewpoint to the nearest watering hole, the first of many that he would visit that night. He would eventually catch up with his prey; just not tonight.

A sense of relaxation rose up through him as that first mouthful of the sweet amber nectar flowed down his throat and it would not be long before his demeanour changed from one of passive obscurity to that of boisterous confidence.

It wasn't until he had probably been into at least half a dozen establishments and probably had twice as much as that to drink when he received the message from Chris. James had indeed deliberately left his original phone at Noirmont, nevertheless he had always believed in keeping a back channel open just in case the others needed to contact him. In this particular case he had elected to keep a Facebook account open, under the name of Samuel Pepys, Facebook was ideal as it used end-to-end encryption within its messenger service so only the intended parties could read the flow of information. Chris' message was as usual short, brief and to the point.

Penzance detective been here. He's coming for you, watch your back.

James was so drunk by this point that he really didn't care. Let him come if he dares he thought to himself. Knowing full well that he would be long gone by the time the detective arrived, if the detective even managed to work out where James' current location was.

James necked the remainder of his pint draining it completely of the bitter amber fluid. The message from Chris had at least had the positive effect of reminding him that he had some unfinished business to take care of, business that could wait no longer. He left the watering hole he was in and made his way to the only drinking house in town where he would find the information he needed to track down Michael … The Bricklayers Arms.

The Brick as it was referred to locally was on the outskirts of town, a bit of a ram-shackled looking building that was ironically in desperate need of a builder to repoint the brickwork. James visited this pub specifically because it was frequented by the squaddies from the local barracks who would most certainly know where Michael's old haunts were and where he might hold himself up when he needed to keep a low profile.

'Yes, sir what are you having.'

'Pint of Banks', thanks Mon.' James replied slipping in to the local dialect to blend in a bit more into his surroundings. Past experiences had taught him that locals were a lot more forthcoming if they thought you were from around the area, regardless if you had never been seen in the place before.

'Dunna think I've seen you in 'ere before.'

'Dunna get into town much, live up in the sticks. Just fancied a bit of a change.' James replied. 'Got much on this evening?'

'Nah, not 'lot. You know what it's like this time of year. Regulars just want a good fire and a fresh pint.'

'Aye, canna do better than that this time of year. What do you know?' James asked, deliberately using a colloquial term for 'any gossip?'

'Not a lot, to be fair. Business is okay, never gunna be much after the New Year. Apparently there's been a bit of a fuss up at the barracks. Some RSM, came back off leave, packed a bag and walked out. AWOL, so I believe.'

'Local was he?'

'Ironbridge, I think. He use' come in now and then. Mick something or other I think his name was. Guess he just cunna hack it.'

'Hard life, not for everyone.'

'Ah, 'tis that. You forces?'

'Was once, long time ago. Occasionally miss it, but on the whole think it was right time to go. Ten years was enough.'

'Aye, that's a fair stretch. 'Nother pint?'

'No ta, think that's me done for the night. Nice to meet you, may pop in again some time. Cheers bud.'

'Anytime Mon, more than welcome.'

James left the dingy little pub and headed back to the hotel where he was staying. The info that he'd picked up had sparked a couple of long lost memories, one that the squaddies always used to refer to him as Mick and secondly that he had mentioned when he first met James that he had a small holding or cottage nestled in the forest on the far side of the river. Revenge was going to be sweet, but for now James needed to crash. A clear head would be required for tomorrow, when the hunt would truly begin.

James awoke at around noon; the alcohol that he had consumed the previous night had most certainly delayed him from rising early. Not that this was really an issue, he had never intended in rising early to head over to Ironbridge. Night would be his ally in the final part of his quest for vengeance. All he had to do was to find out Michael's address, something that would not prove to be difficult. Michael wasn't Special Forces and so would not have envisaged the need to go ex-directory.

James walked down to the reception of the hotel, in part to check out and also to borrow their phonebook.

'Good afternoon, sorry I know I was meant to check out by twelve. I kinda over slept.'

'Not to worry, Sir. It's only half past and luckily the cleaners haven't got to your room yet. I don't think there is any need to charge for the extra.'

'That's very kind. Thank you.'

'Not at all sir, we hope you have had a pleasant stay.'

'Delightful, thanks. I wonder, may I borrow your phonebook? I meant to look up an old friend whilst I was in the area. Unfortunately I don't have their number.'

'Certainly, one moment please.' The concierge replied before rummaging through one of her draws on the desk. 'Here you are, I hope you manage to find the right one.'

'Can't be that many Collins' living in Ironbridge. I know it's a common name but, it's a pretty small place so hopefully I'll be lucky.' James replied as he began to flick through the directory.

Noting down a few numbers and addresses just to appear as though there were a few different ones to try, when in fact he had already spied the one that he required. 'Thanks, found a few likely candidates, enjoy the rest of your day.' He said as he gathered up his belongings and left the hotel.

The four hyperboloid cooling towers of the Coalbrookdale power station looked like giant terracotta wine jars rising majestically out of the winter landscape along the Severn as they bathed in the dwindling evening sunlight. James had intentionally waited until the light had begun to fade before making a move over to the birthplace of industry. He knew that Michael would be meticulous in ensuring that nobody would be able to come near the house without him knowing about it. So James' only option was to go in under the cover of dark. Driving through the narrow high street of Ironbridge past the most famous of Darby's engineering works. A bridge that was beautiful not just because of the way it seemed to settle comfortably into its surrounding but also because of its imperfectness, the asymmetry of the arches either side of its centre was Darby's way of mirroring nature, and demonstrating that just because something isn't perfect doesn't mean that it is not awe inspiring. If anything the engineer was making the statement that it was beautiful because it was imperfect.

James crossed the river further down stream and parked in the car park on the banks directly opposite the small industrious town. He sat in the car for a few moments to draw on all the emotions that had been battering him over the last few days, focusing his mind on the task that lay ahead of him, a task that he knew there was no coming back from.

As the night began to draw in and the moonless sky chased the last remnants of the sun away James slipped silently from his car, stealthily making his way over the uneven gravel track up towards the small cottage where he was convinced Michael was hiding.

The inside of the house looked as dark and empty as the night, all the doors and windows were firmly locked. There was no easy way in without making a noise, so James took the direct approach, smashing the front door aside with his shoulder. He heard a loud bang as if another door had slammed shut and immediately realised that Michael must have gone out the back. James ran as quickly as he could through the unfamiliar layout of the property, soon locating the back door, slightly ajar, in the compact utility room.

Following the earthy path from the cottage he entered the dense undergrowth of the forest in pursuit of the man who had caused him so much anguish. The forest path was wet, and James could clearly make out the hasty tracks of his prey from the ones that had been made earlier in the day by visitors strolling along the footpath. He couldn't see the man but he could hear his movements up ahead, as the man crashed through bushes, and low branches in his desperate attempt to escape his impending doom.

James soon realised as he crossed yet another fork in the path that Michael may have a chance to evade him. He had not realised that the network of intertwining tracks on the hillside were quite so vast and intricate. No sooner had he taken one fork at a crossroads than he would be faced with another four choices of where to go. It was just enough to cause even James to question his bearings. He was in danger of losing his prey, in the end he gave up on following the paths; stopped and waited, pricking his ears up in vain for even the slightest noise that would help him to relocate the turncoat.

Suddenly he heard it, a distant rustling in the vegetation maybe 300 meters away, over his left shoulder. Spinning on his heels in a flash he covered the ground as if he was in a hundred metre dash, and crashed full force into the dishonourable wretch of a man. Over and over they tumbled and tussled down the steep hillside, down and down they rolled until they both plummeted over the high banks and into the deep dark ice cold surging currents of the swollen river and were instantly swept away.

The rushing torrents encircled them; strong rip currents ensnared and tore them away from the safety of the river's banks, as they continued to wrestle with each other. The writhing mass of water sucked them deep down into its depths, smashing the pair into the debris of broken trees, ancient bedrock and other rubbish entrapped in its powerful flows only to thrust them back up once more towards the darkness above allowing a brief moment to gasp for life, before plunging them down yet again into the convulsive death rolls of the rabid river. The freezing cold water bit deep, relentlessly sapping the strength from their battered bodies. With the last of his energy James finally managed to wrench Michael's neck until it snapped, releasing the limp wretch to the mercy of the surging currents. With nothing left to prevent the great serpent from slamming his body into yet another half submerged boulder James finally gave himself up to the will of the river. The darkness had won, and as he slipped from consciousness his final thought was one of contentment. Vengeance was his, whatever the future held he had ultimately managed to find some sort of peace.

TO BE CONTINUED…

References:

[1] Robert Burns, 1784, The First Commonplace Book, Kilmarnock Edition

[2] Cannon Henry Scott Holland, 1910, Sermon at Westminster Abbey.

About The Author:

Richard JM Brook was born on the 20th May 1984 at St David's Hospital in Bangor, N. Wales and lived at Plas Llanedwen on The Plas Newydd Estate with his parents David and Ruth, until they divorced when he was so young that Rich has no memory of his father and mother together.

He moved with his mother to live in a stable flat on his cousin's estate Cefn Park, Wrexham (Wrecsam), Clwyd. 'I have many fond memories of Cefn and still have a sense of it being like a second home when I visit,' he has said.

At the age of four Rich underwent open heart surgery, having been born with Aortic Stenosis. Nevertheless this would not prevent him from searching for the next challenging adventure. His mother, Ruth, would frequently return from work to find that, already back from school (Bangor-Is-Y-Coed, Primary School), Rich was 40ft up one of a number of pine trees near the flat. 'I always wanted to find out just how close to the top I could get. I'm still searching for the answer.' He recently told a friend.

However, Rich recently discovered that this was not the first time that he'd found something high to climb. According to his mother when he was about three, he'd got bored of helping his cousin in the kitchen and went exploring, only to be found a few hours later on top of Cefn's roof. Apparently he'd found the white wrought iron fire escape ladders bolted to the side of the main house and wondered where they went.

Just as Rich was beginning to learn Welsh his mother remarried, to

Peter, and they moved to Croughton, Chester. Accompanied by a not so magical trunk Richard arrived at Packwood Haugh School, Ruyton-XI-Towns, Shropshire, where he would spend the next five years, making some great friends and continuing to cultivate a passion for adventure sports along with a new found love of Ancient History and Music. 'Although I loved music, it didn't come easily. I probably went through a whole orchestra of instruments without finding one I really loved. Plus the notes on the page kept moving.' He has said.

Richard was about ten when he was diagnosed with a mild form of dyslexia, which explained why the notes kept moving around. They weren't the only thing to move, as Peter retired and the family moved to the lush green countryside near Shrewsbury, Shropshire, where Peter and Ruth still live.

Now equipped with a set of green tinted glasses, that could have easily come out of the swinging sixties, Rich sat The Common Entrance exams, won the Latin Prize and followed in his father and half-brother's footsteps to Sherborne School, Dorset. 'I'm going to skip the detailed family tree, even I find it complicated. So for simplicity's sake let's just say that between Half and Step siblings there are a lot of us.'

Sherborne offered Rich the opportunity to expand into new sports and he became a keen sailor, something that would stand him in good stead for later life. It was on his thirteenth birthday that Rich finally discovered an instrument that he would fall in love with and continues to play to this day, much to his parents initial dismay. When asked what he would like, he replied, 'A set of Bongos would be fantastic.'

'I think a look of sheer terror briefly crossed my mother's face at the thought of drums in the house; hence why I was quickly pointed in the direction of one of the outbuildings whenever I returned home for a weekend or holiday,' he recently told a fellow musician.

Music, boats and sport continued to be major themes during the rest of Rich's time at Sherborne, regardless of what the Cardiologists recommended. Achieving the necessary A-Level grades, Rich gained a scholarship to study Naval Architecture at Newcastle University. Ever the adventurer Rich left Sherborne in the summer of 2002, taking a summer job on a local chicken farm. He saved enough money to cross the pond, 'Bongos in tow' and spend a month out in California, with his Uncle, Aunt and their two daughters, before beginning Uni life.

'The one and so far only time I have been to The States left a lasting impression. From the vast metropolises of both San Francisco and Los Angeles to the vast epic wilderness of Yosemite, and the challenges of the Half Dome and El Capitan, I really was in my element. Unfortunately so was my spontaneity, so all hell did kind of break loose when I decided to stay in LA for a few extra days but forgot to mention this to my Aunt and Uncle. They were less than pleased when I got back to San Fransisco; apparently even the Police had been searching for me. Sorry, 18 years old with a whole new country to explore, well part of it at least, I kind of just got caught up in the moment. Probably won't be the last time that happens,' he said reminiscing about his late teens.

Returning safely from the States, Rich set off for the bright northern lights of Newcastle 'Toon', but it didn't quite go to plan. 'I didn't really enjoy Uni life and found that I kept getting itchy feet and wanted to head off into the hills to climb. There were also parts of the course I struggled with. In the end I switched to a combined studies course of History, Politics and Economics in the hope that the variety might help. It didn't.'

Having been at Newcastle for two years Rich spent the summer working at an Outdoor Activity Centre, discovering a passion for instructing and passing on his experience to the future generations. 'I'd had the benefit of growing up with all these sports easily accessible and I decided that I wanted to give some of my experience back. I never finished my degree,' he said.

Rich spent the next eight years working in some amazing places, teaching a variety of Outdoor Sports to people from all walks of life and working with the most incredible group of people. 'I have always felt it was my absolute privilege to work alongside some of the most talented coaches and sports personalities in the world. And yes, every now and again I'm tempted to go back,' he replied, when recently asked about his time as an instructor.

Unfortunately, the cardiologists were not quite so happy about the extreme sports and when Rich developed cataracts at the age of twenty-eight, even he had to look in the mirror and ask how long he could continue to instruct. At some point the valve would need some attention too.

So after two eye operations, Rich called time on the coaching. Nevertheless it did kick start something that he had always wanted to do but had been procrastinating about for years; writing a novel. 'I may never have even started 'The Middleton Saga', let alone finished the first part had it not been for the cataracts. The best way I can describe having cataracts is that everything looks like a very grainy 1960s TV picture and then after the surgery suddenly having HD. At my first consultation, the surgeon was actually surprised I could see anything, that's how thick the cataracts were. I felt I'd been given a second chance and that life was too short for perpetual indecision, so I picked up a pen,' he replied when asked why he had started writing.

Rich spent the next five years writing his first book and making a huge amount of notes for the rest of the series. Along the way he worked for a solar construction company and a home removal business to finance his new found love of the written word, not to mention making a whole host of new friends, from musicians to baristas.

'That pretty much brings us up to date. I self-published my first novel Hellfire Rising: The Middleton Saga Part One, a few days before my 33rd birthday. I regularly play with Synergy Live Band. Meeting Juan, Glen and Juan has been one of my personal highlights of the last five years. They have been such an inspiration and at times my rocks. I still sail, rock climb and windsurf; and despite my best efforts the valve is still going strong. Life is full of expectations and yet it is often the unexpected that makes life. It will be interesting to see what adventure the next bend has in store.'

Follow Rich

Website: www.rjmbrook.com
Facebook: @Richard JM Brook
Instagram: richard_jm_brook
Twitter: @RichardJMBrook